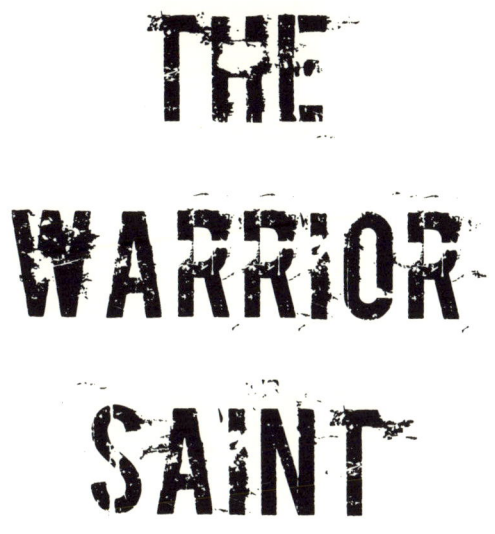

A   T. J. Leukemeyer   Thriller

Edouard A. Daunas

Copyright © 2016 Edouard A. Daunas

All rights reserved.

The Warrior Saint is a work of fiction. All characters in this novel are fictitious and arise from the author's imagination. Any resemblance to actual events or locales or persons, living or ad, is entirely coincidental.

Maps by Edouard A. Daunas

Cover design by Caitlin Alexander & Edouard A. Daunas

Edited & formatted by Caitlin Alexander

Also available in e-book

thewarriorsaint.net

For Gregg Lempp, my husband and soul mate, for being my sounding board and co-conspirator in this journey. I dedicate this adventure to you.

With thee I conquer.

Rio de Janeiro Downtown and South Zone

Tijuca National Rain Forest

Vista Chinesa

Two Brothers Mountain

Favela Roçinha

Botanical Gardens

Favela Vidigal

Alto Leblon

Fashion Leblon

Lagoon

Leblon

Ipanema

PORTO MARAVILHA
FISCAL ISLAND
SAMBA CITY
DOWNTOWN
ALBAMAR
CORCOVADO
SANTOS DUMONT AIRPORT
SANTA TERESA
BOTAFOGO BAY
MILITARY POLICE HEADQURTERS
SÃO JOÃO BATISTA CEMETERY
VILA PARAISO
URCA
FAVELA CANTAGALO
SUGAR LOAF MOUNTAIN
Y BEACH
LEME
COPACABANA
ARPOADOR

OLYMPIC PARK AND VILLAGE

FAVELA
DO
AUTODROMO

LAKE JACAREPAGUÁ

ITANHANGÁ
GOLF CLUB

BARRA

RIO DE JANEIRO WEST ZONE

TIJUCA NATIONAL RAIN FOREST

FAVELA ROCINHA

EDRA DA GÁVEA
OUNTAIN

SÃO CONRADO

TWO BROTHERS MOUNTAIN

FAVELA VIDIGAL

PEPINO BEACH

CHOEIRA

JOÁ

PROLOGUE

Any undercover agent knows a drug dealer would rather make a deal than waste a customer. Vicente and I were counting on that as El Gordo's filmy eyes watched me set the cash-stuffed duffle on the table. Distant marimba filtered through the boarded window, and the air in the warehouse was wet and mildewed. We were into our third deal with this guy and our credibility seemed established. The burly guard standing by the door was proof of that, more interested in chewing on a toothpick than keeping his gun hand at the ready.

Several years back, the DEA had singled out for eradication a high-volume Mexican cartel that they considered a major engine of the drug trade plaguing our southern border. I—Special Agent T. J. Leukemeyer—had been brought in following a long-term post in New York City to finish the job. Being Texan helped me fit the part.

The bust would make headlines. My involvement wouldn't. There are some things the public needn't know, like the way American agents had allied with one unsavory cartel in order to siphon valuable information on El Gordo's. A common enough tactic in our business. The alliance gave us access to a network of peripheral individuals who serviced all sides of the trade—money launderers, gun smugglers and the like. We courted them until the chain led us to the top.

That's where Vicente and I came in, introductions made possible by our good buddy the arms supplier. We'd worked him over for quite some time to get our first audience with El Gordo. Tonight's op would take him down. And it was going to be one of the most satisfying of our careers.

A young Mexican kid with an assault rifle had driven us to an anonymous alley just past dusk. Same kid each time—always a different dump. Hastily hung Christmas lights decorated the windows above where he parked his dilapidated sedan. We got out and followed him through backstreets strewn with rotting refuse from a meatpacking warehouse. Mutts snorted for scraps. The stench jabbed my nose as I navigated the uneven, sticky pavement.

Vicente snickered at my occasional stumble. "Losing your touch, ol' man?" I'd (somewhat) recently passed forty and Vicente was still in his thirties. I'll tell y'all, we'd been working together for what—four years now?—and he never let me forget the age difference. At my age, a promotion often pointed toward a desk job. Vicente could soon replace me as field team lead. Jacked up the stakes for both of us that much more.

"This *ol' man* saved your ass on more than one occasion."

"Hey, you're my mentor, man. I aspire to be you." He rubbed his stubbly cleft chin, mimicking my look of deep thought.

"Quiet, you'll set a bad example for the Greens." I was half joking. Greens—that's Special Ops, fresh out of the factory, two of whom were trailing behind us—could give you away with a clenched jaw or tapping foot, a nervous look; stuff experience would assuage.

The boy ahead stopped suddenly and rapped a secret knock on a door. It opened and we were greeted by El Gordo's men, a beastly duo. The older one with the toothpick handed the kid some cash and signaled for him to wait back at the car.

"Y'all stay out here and keep an eye on this guy while we close the deal," I told the Greens. It's better to let 'em hang back as security than interact with suspects. But these guys were good; their faces didn't betray them. Both were of local persuasion and looked the part of hired goons. I was the only Caucasian among us, the distributor from north of the border.

The younger thug patted all four of us down as we handed over our guns. He had a hard face, but couldn't have been older than sixteen. We knew the routine. He took our weapons to a corner cubby. We kept our phones, but he watched as we powered them off. The NSA might be on most Americans' shit list, but they'd pioneered a nifty little hypersensitive recording device designed to kick into gear exactly when a cell phone was powered off. Times like these, I was glad the DEA played friendly with our fellow government agencies.

Toothpick opened the door to a dimly lit room with a plywood tabletop and three rickety chairs. Much of the wall and ceiling plaster had fallen to the floor. One of the chairs strained to support a thickset man. His scarred face and strange features fell just short of being, well, not right. He reminded me of Jabba the Hutt. Creepy as the first time I saw him.

El Gordo grunted. "Amigos, you are becoming our best customer." He reached for the satchel I'd placed on the table and pulled it firmly to his side with plump fingers. He smiled at Vicente, leaned forward and pulled back a chair for him, inviting us to sit.

I'd handpicked Vicente based on his exceptional record of undercover work in the region. I looked over at him now as we got ready to make our move. He was a natural, bantering with ease and familiarity to El Gordo in Spanish. Back in Arlington, the guys had tagged him "the Ferret"—he was the one who'd connected the dots and figured El Gordo as the cartel's head.

Our target gazed at me without blinking; his short stubby tongue licked at his chafed lips. It was hard not to stare and just as difficult to turn away. "I am grateful to my friends who show loyalty," he said. "It's a shame that our business with you, my gringo friend, won't continue."

I heard two quick pops in the anteroom and the double thud of our Greens falling to the floor. Jumping from my seat, I knocked over the flimsy table, but Toothpick was already behind me; he cuffed my hands in front of me—an amateur move.

I glanced at Vicente—still seated—for help, but he looked away.

What the fuck?

El Gordo seemed amused. "Vicente and I have some common interests, don't we?"

My eyes fused onto Vicente, daring him to look my way. Finally he did. "It had to be this way," he said, cool as a shark, his eyes concealed by shadow.

"This makes no sense! We have him."

"Eventually it will."

"Time to go." El Gordo got up from his seat. He nodded at Toothpick, who had just tightened his hold, then picked up the cash and scuttled out of the place in a clipped waddle.

Vicente followed. At the door he turned back. "I'm figuring you can handle this." He winked and left.

Toothpick raised his gun to my face.

Punch it, Leukemeyer!

I dodged the shot, ducking to the right, and swung my cuffed hands up and over his head before he had a second chance. His shove helped me spin around with my handcuffs clutched tightly around his throat. One powerful yank sent him to the ground. He writhed, gasping, and I grabbed his gun off the floor and shot him dead. I yanked at his pockets for the keys and fumbled as I tried to unlock my cuffs. Just when I'd gripped the gun again, the door kicked open and ammunition punched my protective vest.

I retaliated as I fell backward. The second thug hit the floor—just a kid. I heard a car ignition roar outside as El Gordo prepared to flee. I checked myself for wounds: The vest had done its job but my side ached from the impacts. As I ran across the room, I reached for my gun in the cubby and looked down at Quinn and Boone—those had been their names. A bullet hole in each forehead. Fuck! How could this happen on my watch? This was a disaster, and there would be consequences.

I heard tires pealing and darted out into the alley, retracing our steps back to the boy sitting in his car, the engine idling. With my gun pointed at him, I pulled him out and got in. I raced for a couple blocks in the direction I'd heard El Gordo and Vicente take off in, catching sight of their taillights as I skidded around a corner. Even as I pushed the old Buick to its limits, I knew El Gordo owned these back roads.

A few more turns and I had no choice but to admit I'd lost him. The dusty air of this lonely desert pueblo went quiet and I realized I had no other move but to follow procedure for a botched mission. I pulled out my phone and punched in the code for assistance with a shaking finger. The empty feeling of failure washed over me.

"Two men down, one defected," I said. I couldn't get over Vicente's betrayal. What could El Gordo have had on him to compromise him this way? And when had he gotten to him? Why hadn't they shot me first?

Later, as the helicopter took me to safety, I searched my mind for clues I might have missed. None of it made sense. What I did know was that El Gordo needn't fear the DEA anymore. Four wasted years, our cover in the region blown. Two Greens dead and a seasoned Special Ops agent turned under my command.

I dreaded the interrogation that awaited me. I'd never failed a mission before, let alone one as disastrously as this. Forget about a promotion or a desk job—my head was going to roll.

CHAPTER ONE

Two days later

Fireworks illuminated the Manhattan sky as the New Year rang in. I watched from the window of our Tribeca penthouse. The percussion of pops and bangs were supposed to elicit joy and cheer, the arrival of something new and hopeful. I glanced back at Sean, passed out on the couch: hope*less* was more like it. I loved him, but I needed to get out of this relationship before it drowned us both.

"Sean, you're missing the fireworks, look." I nudged him.

Sean's head fell back with a loud snort. He spastically knocked the champagne bucket off the table.

"You fuck," I whispered.

Sean Gottlieb knew I was DEA Special Ops, of course. He was complicit in my cover as the financial director of an international nonprofit aid organization. The only thing Google would pull up with my name'd be a picture of Mayor Bloomberg and me at a charity fundraiser a few years ago. The agency made sure of that.

The secrecy of my work had added some tension to our relationship, sure, especially during my more recent and longer absences. I thought about my failure in Mexico. Vicente and those poor Greens lost in the fracas. After the helo dropped me off at the base, I'd been debriefed and put on the first flight back to the States with no further updates or instructions. Not a good sign.

Thing was, this operation had been about more than damming the drug stream. The cartels were using kids to do their dirty work, like the kid who'd taken us to El Gordo. Like the one I killed. Their numbers were greater than before; adolescents were running the show at levels that used to only be handled by adults. Boys forced into a Darwinian world of survival, missing out on any kind of decent childhood. Heck, the Greens had barely been more than kids themselves.

So it might be understandable that I blew up at Sean when I got home. Depressed and tired, a bottle of Veuve in my hand, I'd stepped off the elevator to find him standing in our apartment doorway, swaying and completely blitzed. A semblance of a hug, then I pushed past him with my bags. He followed me and collapsed on the couch.

In years past, my steady rise at the agency had been like a bee taking to honey. Sean understood my deep commitment, and he had his career in finance to focus on. When I was home in NYC, life could be pretty grand. You see, Sean was a yuppie, but he was also a Jew. Go figure. He'd grown up in Greenwich with a privileged education. His father was a leading surgeon at Sloan-Kettering, and his mother was a socialite housewife. Sean had been a Wall Street superstar by the time he was thirty. Fast cars, exotic vacations, top notch city living. We'd hobnobbed with the rich and famous because of him. Until '08 that was—mid-September. Seems somewhat surreal in retrospect, I suppose.

We'd been spending an extra-long weekend at the beach house when we heard the news. I'd just returned from a particularly difficult bust in Los Angeles and was enjoying hanging out in our brand new kitchen with our guests, Milena and Ferdi. Milena Van Gilden and I had known each other since our college days. She was now a successful fashion designer. Sean and I used to hop over to Europe to see her shows from time to time—these were not vacations I bragged about with the guys. The old don't-ask-don't-tell still lingered.

Ferdinand Gastinaro, a former world-recognized ballet dancer, had reincarnated himself as a gemologist for Cartier. He and Milena met in Paris when he was still dancing and have been inseparable ever since. It was an unconventional marriage from the start: Milena only married Ferdi to get him US papers. There was no question where his sexual orientation lay. To everyone's surprise, they'd ended up staying married and living a conjugal life in every way but one.

We'd been laughing in the kitchen, still in our sleepwear. Ferdi had just revealed the pride and joy of his latest collection: a rare square-cut aquamarine set in a contemporary platinum base and surrounded by little diamond baguettes.

"This piece could fund one of your African food-aid programs for a year," Milena said, reaching for a mug with one hand and the coffee pot with the other.

Ferdi held it up to my face. "It matches your handsome baby blues."

Sean walked in with the newspaper and a bag of muffins. His face was ashen. "It's all over, folks," he said.

"Sean?" Milena's eyes widened.

"Lehman Brothers just filed for bankruptcy. Their exposure around the world is tremendous. This is unthinkable; I mean worldwide panic."

Milena gasped, "Oh no! My clients."

Ferdi sat speechless, mouth agape.

Y'all've heard it before, the bubble burst and we were in it. Sean lost everything. Aside from millions of his clients' dollars that he'd funneled into Madoff investments through elaborate schemes, he'd also structured several debt deals that had folded with the crash. The results were disastrous to both his reputation and his firm's. He'd been lucky dodging lawsuits these last few years, armed with a team of heavy-hitting defense lawyers, but the financial toll had been severe, and his most important court date loomed just ahead. To make matters worse, Sean had had a hobby dabbling in real-estate development in the Hamptons. When the economy was flying, any bit of land out there was desirable. But in the aftermath, only billionaires were buying. Guess what? Billionaires don't want to develop former potato fields, recession or not; it's oceanfront or nothing.

So here we were, New Year's Eve, with several years of crisis between us, still in the same rut and both of us credit-maxed to Mars and back. My DEA salary was good, but it couldn't sustain our lifestyle. If I even had a salary anymore.

"I'm so fucked," Sean proclaimed while I hung my coat.

I ducked into the family room, held my finger to a hidden scanner under a bookshelf, and a metal-backed panel retracted, revealing a large nook. I pulled my gun out of my bag's secret compartment along with my official phone, placed them inside and pressed the lock button. The panel fell back into place with a pleasing mechanical sound.

"You hear me, T. J.?"

You see, Sean had not only lost his clients' money, he'd lost most of our money too. And worst of all, he'd lost his parents' fortune, just about all of it. You'd think a star Wall Street investor would know a sour grape when he saw one, but here's a prime example of how history can blind you. Going back to his Greenwich days, Sean had strong connections to a guy named William Chaffrey, having dated one of his lovely Brazilian daughters for a summer or two in high school. Chaffrey and Sean had hit it off even after the dating went by the wayside. As Sean began to succeed, he'd steadily increased his dealings with Chaffrey's investment firm, funneling vast sums of his clients' money into Chaffrey's holdings. And all that money was poured into Bernie Madoff's coffers. Sean had turned out to be a greedier fuck than I'd realized. By this point, he'd done all the song-and-dancing his lawyers could muster. Without a miracle, he was looking at heavy fines and, very possibly, jail time.

Sean's got a nervous little habit. He drums his fingers in succession up and down like he's practicing on a piano, especially when he's been drinking. He was doing it now on the glass of vodka he was holding. There was no vodka left in it, but he took a tentative swig anyway.

"Fucked," he said again, bringing the glass down hard on the coffee table.

"Easy there, tiger."

I put the champagne in an ice bucket to cool and sat next to him on the couch. I could see in his pretty heavy-lidded green eyes that velvety unconsciousness was soon to follow.

"Well, welcome home to me, right?" I said, more to myself than to him.

I looked around our apartment, lined with half-filled boxes. By the time I turned back, Sean's head had slumped against the couch.

"Hello, Sean?" I leaned over him. Nothing. I got up and poured myself a scotch, trying to control my anger.

"Fuck this crap, you're not the only one suffering here. Fucked? *I'm* fucked."

Sean lifted his droopy eyes. I'd gathered his swaying attention.

"People died. Kids, if you care to know." I clenched my fists in frustration. "I've failed in the worst possible way."

Sean stared at me blankly.

"My career is trashed, it's fuckin' New Year's and I can barely afford to buy this bottle of champagne." I looked down at his empty glass on the table. "But I see you've managed to buy gallons of vodka!" In a rare moment of uncontrolled temper, I grabbed the glass and threw it hard into the fireplace, smashing it to bits. I have to tell ya, it felt good. "What are you doing, huh? Begging for change on the corner?"

"Fuck you," he mumbled. "All this time I've been in hell, where were you?" he slurred. "Gone. It goes from bad to worse and my support is MIA."

"Whatever. Happy New Year."

Sean passed out.

Which brings me back to the fireworks. They finished with a crescendo of loud pops, the residual smoke wafting in the night breeze. I picked up the champagne bucket, then changed my mind and dropped into a chair. The family room was mostly packed up, waiting for our inevitable departure from this place, from this life. The plan was to move into Ferdi and Milena's guest room until we could get our feet back on the ground. I wasn't so sure I wanted to try.

I looked out the tall windows toward Wall Street, across to Jersey and Lady Liberty. It *had* been fun while it lasted. Sure, the last few years with Sean going through hell and back had taken a toll on our once-sparkling relationship—my saving grace'd been not being around several weeks at a time. But we'd been each other's best buddy and lover for almost half our lives.

I'd been supportive of him at first, until I began to learn about the details behind his financial dealings. Sean was not quite as honest as I'd thought. Still, I didn't relish the idea of abandoning him. I'd seen *Oz*. The Big House would not be an ideal residence for a pretty boy like Sean.

I'd been looking through the accumulated pile of mail on my desk for the last hour, mostly past-due notices. But my thoughts returned to Vicente's deception. I was picking apart every memory of him, searching for clues I'd missed, when I heard a knock at the door.

The doorman would have called if a guest were coming up. I tensed with suspicion. Another firm knock. I retrieved my gun from the locked compartment, then eased toward the front door. When I checked the peephole and saw my doorman, I relaxed.

"Carlos." I cracked the door.

"Happy New Year, Mr. Leukemeyer, your telecom isn't working. I rang you a few times. But I knew you were here, so I just came up with the gentleman, sir."

Next to him stood my boss, DEA Director Thomas Bradley.

"Come in, Tom. Thanks, Carlos. Happy New Year to you too."

Tom stepped out of the elevator, handing me his overcoat. I looked into the apartment and saw that Sean had indeed left the telecom dangling off the hook.

Tom was in black tie, a style that accentuated his Ted Turneresque looks. He appeared to be the quintessential bureaucrat, a guise that played well in D.C. But I knew he'd risen up the ranks from Special Ops like me. The time he'd busted a FARC general embroiled with the Cali cartel was still taught as a case study. I'd hoped that this past Mexican mission would've done the same for me. No chance of that now.

I motioned him toward my office, past Sean, and slid the pocket doors shut. I put my gun away again. A personal visit on New Year's Eve. How could this be good? "What are you doing in New York? Here, at this hour?"

"Rosie wanted to have a New York New Year's Eve, so I indulged her." His warm, gravelly voice was usually comforting, but tonight he sounded aloof. "I told her she could have it if I could escape on business for a while after midnight. Obviously, I have Mexico on my mind, but I also have an important project that I can only discuss with you in person, and I have to be back in D.C. in the morning. So here I am." He readjusted his jacket and bow tie as he sat down.

"Can I offer you a drink? Champagne? I'm on my second scotch."

"Same, on the rocks."

I handed him the beverage and sat, dreading the ensuing conversation.

"I don't have to tell you that we have always considered you one of our best agents, T. J." He sighed. "But Mexico was unspeakable. Two dead agents. Vicente missing. We're back to square one on what was meant to be a very important political triumph for the DEA and the president. I don't know how to defend you to the committee on this one. Your specialty is reading people, for God's sake." His voice had transitioned to a low growl.

"What do you mean, *missing*? Vicente defected... the motherfucker was working with El Gordo! That's what happened."

"Vicente is off the map. Disappeared for now, but we are still actively searching." He hesitated. "The cover you were using there is blown. Your real name? We don't know yet."

"Jesus."

"You're absolutely off any Mexico assignments for good. We've analyzed the recordings of your meeting and there's nothing conclusive. We don't know how they communicated or what exactly Vicente's role was, but El Gordo won't fall into another trap again so soon. I think perhaps you might want to take some time for yourself. Figure out what you want out of the next phase of your career." Tom sat back. His gaze made me feel like a scolded schoolboy.

"I don't understand, Tom, are you firing me?"

Tom held up his hands. "This fuckup cost a couple of lives and years of planning, all in one punch. One of our key operatives, and a contender for promotion, has flipped sides and left us with our pants down under your watch. I've got lots of pressure coming down on me from the higher-ups. Retirement and witness protection were tossed around by more than one person. I'm telling you, a desk job might be a lucky turnout."

I cringed. Here it was, the culmination of all my successes thwarted by a gaping failure. I braced myself for the dismissal.

"But I like you. I've watched you rise up over the years—this is just a stroke of bad luck. So I have an unofficial proposition for you. It's top-secret stuff; completely off the record. I'm willing to give you unpaid leave for as long as it takes, and you'd have to take the job as a free agent. I'd give you access to all of the DEA's investigative resources, however you won't be DEA, you'll be on your own." Tom leaned forward. "I'm feeding you an opportunity to take a sabbatical and prove you're still valuable as a covert agent. If not that, at least pointing you toward a profitable new career."

All I heard was that my career was over. Tom was being kind, putting me out to pasture instead of shooting me like a lame horse.

I nodded toward his glass. He handed it to me and I stood, pouring us both more scotch while he continued. "The Brazilians are cleaning house for the Olympics. They want to put on a pretty face for the world, but the shanties that dot Rio host a thriving drug trade. Corrupt local officials, increased crime. Same story, different setting. The World Cup only exacerbated the problem. The local head of the Military Police is leading the war on drugs in the shantytowns—*favelas*, they call them down there. He's reached out to us for help, but politically it's complicated."

I handed Tom his scotch. "The drug trade there is run like a mafia," he continued. "The guys at the top are very powerful people in Brazilian politics and industry. Major Pereira is looking for somebody to come in, pose as a foreign investor interested in one of their businesses, strike an underhanded deal so they know you play ball, and find some hard proof that can be used against them."

"Brazil?" I took a sip. "Tom, look, put me on the task force to find Vicente. I can be an asset to you there—I knew the operation inside and out. Let me prove myself by putting this situation right."

He shook his head. "This is not a choice if you wish to be considered for a future at the agency down the line. Eyes are on this. Now pay attention. Officially, the DEA can only work for other countries under intergovernmental agreements. But there are concerns in Washington about the potential for disrupting certain lucrative trade agreements, not to speak of the NSA's fuckup listening in on their president's cell phone. Plus, Pereira wants this off the books so as to not tip off any of the politicians they're investigating. Unofficially, we'll be providing support and resources, but any agent would have to be independently subcontracted by the Military Police."

"I speak Spanish, Tom, not Portuguese."

He raised a well-groomed eyebrow. "Something tells me you can figure it out. A leave of absence from the DEA and very generous pay from the Brazilians. In style. In the tropics. You can't beat that kind of assignment. Plus, your current alias is perfect for the job. T. J. Leukemeyer, the former not-for-profit financial director gone international investor. Mexico won't matter there. Not a lot of cross-trade between the Mexicans and the Brazilians." He reached into the inside pocket of his tux and handed me a flash drive. "You're going to say yes. This has everything the Brazilians need you to know."

"Do you know this guy? Pereira. Trust him?"

"Shortly after my dealings with the FARC, Major Pereira was involved in halting the violence in the shanties prior to the Rio Earth Summit in '92. He invited me to come down and work with his troops. He's of the utmost integrity. We've had a few of their MPs up for joint training sessions at Quantico."

"What about Vicente? He's out there. I can't just forget about him."

"All the more reason for you to disappear while we try to find him." He stood. "Look, every agent has a bad day. You're just lucky that you haven't really had one until now. Best thing is to keep moving until we get a better grasp on that situation. You've been one of our very best, I know that. But this time you've got to prove you still are. Tough work, vital mission." His fist double-tapped his chest as he proclaimed our motto.

After walking Tom to the door, I felt wiped out. The way he pitched that whole deal, he really wanted me out of here. I sensed something else was up. Something behind the scenes, beyond my clearance. I wandered absently through our half-disassembled apartment, thoughts ricocheting through my head. In the office, I gathered my diplomas, certifications and medals into a box—my past accomplishments, from ROTC during college to the Army during Desert Storm, where I discovered my talent for surveillance. Turns out I'd failed at that.

I grabbed a brightly painted chunk of concrete off the shelf and my Euro rail pass fell to the floor. I'd traveled with Milena one summer, studying art history along the way—at the time I thought I might go on to teach it, one of my secret interests. That trip led to my first experience with another man, a guy I met chipping this souvenir bit off the Berlin Wall, and the first time I knew for certain I was born this way. But that, I'll save for an entirely different story.

After Iraq, my platoon leader suggested the DEA could be a good career for me. So with Spanish and finance degrees under my belt (I never really brought up my art history degree), I applied. That was the beginning, and tonight, I felt like I was sitting at its end.

I opened another drawer and found Sean's stash of weed. Really? Damn it, I'd asked him to at least keep drugs out of the house. One more sign that neither of us had enough respect for the other anymore.

Rio de Janeiro. Hell, I'd always wanted to go. And on

the bright side, it was summer there. I could always work on my tan.

It was close to four a.m. I turned on my computer and typed *rio de janeiro* into Google and clicked Images. Looking over those pictures, I'll tell y'all, I could do time on those beaches for a while.

I glanced across the room at Sean, passed out on the couch with his left hand still hanging at an awkward angle. Then I slipped in Tom's flash drive and clicked open the top-secret folder. The screen lit up with the elaborate wreath-wrapped star of Brazil's coat of arms. I took a sip of scotch and began to read.

CHAPTER TWO

The sliding glass doors of the Aeroporto Internacional Galeão/Tom Jobim opened and the cool air conditioning vanished in a vortex of blistering summer heat. Moisture instantly condensed all over me and sweat dripped from under my chin and slid down my chest.

"It's just a few steps to the car, *Seu* Leukemeyer," the driver said, noting my discomfort. He led me to a black BMW 7 Series with tinted, bulletproof windows.

"Welcome to Rio. My name is Edson Moreira de Souza Rodrigues." The driver took my bags. Once inside the car, he reached back to give me a cool, damp hand towel from the air-conditioned compartment between the front seats. "I am your chauffeur here in Rio de Janeiro and have been instructed by Major Pereira to take you to your lodgings so that you might relax and decompress, yes? Then at three p.m. I will bring you to the major's headquarters for your debriefing and introduction to your team. Would that be all right, sir?"

"Of course, *obrigado*," I thanked him in my very rusty Rosetta Stone Portuguese.

"*O prazer é todo meu, senhor,*" Rodrigues responded, delighted by my linguistic attempt. "Is this your first time in Rio?" His bushy eyebrows jumped so high, it was like watching a cartoon character.

"Yes, it is."

"How wonderful for you."

Rodrigues started the ignition with a soft rumble. We drove in silence as I clicked through the dossiers I'd downloaded to my tablet. They told of different drug lords in the various *favelas* of Rio. In a video debriefing, Major Pereira explained in educated English that bonds of entanglement between the drug trade and the local communities' economies made the cartels' extraction all the more prohibitive. I listened through my earbuds while he gently smoothed his mustache as he spoke, looking something like a modern-day Inspector Poirot. Then I clicked open an article he'd listed.

RIO DE JANEIRO—The New Year festivities ended with the murder of Vinícius Maria Saveiro de Alcântara, the finance minister. His corpse was recovered from the Shalimar, a local love motel in Rio's South Zone. According to police, the cause of death was a bullet wound to the head and a second to the heart. The only witness was an apprehended local call boy.

Major Pereira had highlighted what mattered within the salacious read: the insinuation that the minister's murder had resulted from high-powered political gain and corruption with ties to the drug trade.

Through occasional glances out the window, I glimpsed an ugly, battered part of Rio made up of old buildings in crumbling decay overshadowed by rusting mid-century industry along the bay.

"No need to look now, *Seu* Leukemeyer. But when I tell you, you must see. Rio's beauty will demand your attention!" Rodrigues smiled proudly in the rearview mirror.

"To tell you the truth, I'd rather hear what you know about the *favelas* we are passing."

"We are up on the Red Line; it's supposed to be an elevated speedway into town from the airport." Traffic crawled. "To the right you see the northern part of the city, and *favelas* are the slums that climb the hills around it."

There were many shanties edging the outer ring of buildings; sometimes they looked like anthills, dwarfed by the city surrounding them.

"Are they very dangerous?"

I tapped Play on a video clip that showed heavily armored vehicles with gear-clad MPs entering a wire-tangled, graffiti-covered slum, its inhabitants peering cautiously from their cinderblock shacks.

"I would not recommend you visit them alone, sir. They seem calm but you never know when there will be a gang war or police raid. Both happen frequently. But it depends, each one is different."

"Are you from Rio?"

"Oh yes, I am *Carioca*. I am married to Major Pereira's niece."

All in the family.

I tapped another video file and listened to the DEA's chief of intelligence testify before the Senate Caucus on International Narcotics Control: "Brazil is currently the second largest cocaine consumer in the world, exceeded only by the US—"

The outside daylight went dark. We had entered a long tunnel—two in succession, actually.

"Now, *Seu* Leukemeyer, look!" exclaimed Rodrigues.

I put down the tablet and he was right. Exiting the tunnel was like being transported to a tropical Shangri-La. Everything was crisp and Technicolor, nature and man in paradise. No Google image search could do this place justice. Fashionable high-rise apartments circled the lagoon ahead, soaking in the surrounding lush, parabola-shaped mountains. Behind us, as we rounded the lagoon, Rodrigues pointed out the towering Corcovado Mountain with the statue of *Christ the Redeemer* welcoming me with outstretched arms. I'll tell ya, it was enough to take even a tough guy's breath away.

We drove onto the isthmus of Ipanema, leaving the lagoon behind, and crossed several intersections till we came to Ipanema Beach.

"This is the famous Avenida Vieira Souto, where the Girl from Ipanema used to walk," Rodrigues declared proudly. I guessed that's what most tourists would want to know.

The palm tree-lined beach bordered the avenue and its glamorous '50s architecture. We pulled into a gated driveway.

"Sir, it is easy to remember where you live, next door to the Rio de Janeiro Country Club. Wellington will take you to the penthouse where you will be staying. Enjoy the morning, and I will come for you at two thirty p.m. Once again, *Bem Vindo ao Rio, senhor.*"

And with a tip of his cap and his broad Brazilian smile, he handed me off to a white-gloved doorman— Wellington, quite a good-lookin' guy—and up we went.

Wellington rang the bell, and a short little lady opened the door. She had a charming gap-toothed grin and wore a perfectly starched black uniform with white lace trim. Her gray hair was pulled tightly into a bun.

"*Boa Tarde, Seu* Leukemeyer, I am Maria Jovelina Aparecida da Silva, your housekeeper. Welcome!" She curtseyed and pointed inward in a theatrical way. "The *senhor* can just call me Jovi for short." She smiled.

Good thing.

Wellington put my bags down in the cavernous hall and threw open the glass doors to the terrace, complete with a blue-tiled infinity pool. Colorful hummingbirds danced from one hanging feeder to another along the balcony's edge. He graciously accepted a tip and left.

"Allow me to show you around," offered Jovelina. She whisked me through a tour, gesticulating right and left as we marched through the luminous penthouse, not once slowing her pace. "I arrive at seven a.m. every day, but will stay in the servants' quarters and kitchen if I am not cleaning until you call for me. I work through the day but must leave at six sharp every evening." She came to a stop and punctuated the statement by tapping her watch. "So, if you wish for me to prepare your dinner, I ask only that you let me know by two thirty—three o'clock at the latest."

"Why six sharp?"

"I live in Três Rios, *senhor*, two hours and three bus rides away. And I cannot miss the *novela das oito*."

"*Novela das* what?"

"It is the eight o'clock soap opera. All of Brazil stops to watch. Of course, there are soaps at six, or seven," she said, waving her hands in either direction. "But the one at eight o'clock is *the* soap opera that everyone has to watch. And this one is the best one so far!" She swayed as if trying to catch her breath. "Tonight," she confided with fierce intensity, "tonight we find out if Tatiana, Lygia's character, has been lying to the police in order to protect her son." She clapped her hands together. "I know she did! She would risk everything to save him! Oh, she is so beautiful and we all have to watch her. What will Lygia do tonight, everyone talks about."

OK, peculiar customs. Jovelina marched on.

"This is where the laundry is, but you just leave that to me." She knocked on the door. "The refrigerator is full, and if you would like me to buy anything in particular, just ask. Remember, only drink the filtered water. All the fruit and vegetables have been properly washed and disinfected. I will be in back should you need anything." She then nodded at me, possibly with a wink? Or perhaps a look of pride. "I worked as the head housekeeper at the Brazilian Embassy in Washington for years. Discretion is my business. It is why Major Pereira hires me." She exited the living room at a purposeful pace and headed down the long corridor to the kitchen.

I stepped out onto the balcony, beckoned by the famous beach. The ocean was dotted with islands, and the long beach was anchored by the Two Brothers Mountain, an enormous green hillside capped by two oblong granite behemoths reaching for the sky on one end, and a rocky outcrop on the other that separated Ipanema from Copacabana. Golden boys and girls walked along the beach on the black and white mosaic sidewalks. Dark athletes in Speedos played an impossible hybrid of soccer and volleyball on the white sand. I had a sudden yearning to try that. Young kids hung out by the vendor huts selling coconut water and other beverages. Wasn't today Thursday? Didn't these folks work? For a moment my problems felt far away, and dang it if that ain't the truth.

I thought about Sean—he would have loved this place. But the way we'd left things . . . He'd been furious, accusing me of abandoning him. I knew he had a hard time looking beyond his current circumstances, the upcoming move, the recent plea bargain. But I'd been cutting him slack for years, and where was he when *I* needed *his* support, when *my* career was fracturing around me? I thought of him drinking away his woes. He'd already given up on himself, and I had my own problems to deal with.

I unpacked, jumped in the shower and then lay in the bedroom easy chair with my tablet. After an hour of reading, I got into one of my swimsuits and took a morning walk along the beach to acclimate. I passed a group of guys playing *futevôlei*, that soccer-volleyball thing, and was invited in to play. I'll tell y'all, I got the hang of it quicker than a jackrabbit on a date.

From that point, let's just say that I made friends quickly, possibly too quickly. But I felt free for the first time in so long, and this place was intoxicating and a bit unreal. Plus, if there's one thing I've learned, it's that knowing the locals is always key.

As it turned out, *Cariocas* love tall, blond, brawny

Americans. Back at the apartment a few hours later, I finished drying off from a joint shower and walked Marcos to the door with a towel-flick at his chestnut-colored thigh and a light bump on his shoulder. His big white teeth smiled at me.

"Will I see you again?" I asked him as he dressed.

Marcos hugged me with his intoxicating charm. His curly black hair bounced in front of his disarming brown eyes.

"You will know how to find me," he replied, and walked out the door.

His departure reminded me that I had to get moving, Rodrigues would be here in a few minutes. I buttoned up my short-sleeve shirt and was slipping on my belt when my cell phone rang.

Sean.

Couldn't even go there just then. He'd have to wait. But before I headed out, I did one more thing: I slipped my commitment ring off my left hand and put it on my right.

CHAPTER THREE

The elevator had deep mahogany panels and European-style polished brass grates. Downstairs, the doorman walked me to the car. I assure y'all, I could get used to this kind of service again. Seemed like ol' times.

We left the South Zone for downtown. In the back seat was a package addressed to me. Inside was a smartphone, my own Brazilian Military Police badge—how 'bout that—a Titanium American Express card in my name, and a Walther PPK with a couple of extra magazines. Classic! I felt its weight, recalling the first time I'd held one during training at Quantico. "Remember, fellers, this was James Bond's favorite," our instructor had chuckled. The PPK was among the world's first successful double-action semiautomatic pistols and had been widely copied. Its contemporary version still concealed well, carried lightly, but packed a lethal punch. This one had a pressure-point lock system that guaranteed only my hand would be able to fire the gun once it was programmed. Technology fresh off the press.

Rodrigues narrated the landmarks while I held the gun in my hand and punched in the accompanying code.

A small vibration confirmed that it had registered my palm's pressure points on the pistol grip. I unfolded the gun holster and flipped it over in my hands, admiring the leather's workmanship. I checked the phone out, too: same DEA-issued voice recording app and ultraviolet fingerprint scanner that'd come in real handy in the past. Just like being at home.

We crossed most of Copacabana Beach and then drove through a tunnel that exited on Botafogo Bay with the famous Sugar Loaf Mountain on the right, the Corcovado on the left and yachts dotting the bay in between.

There was a tiny clear plastic node in the envelope as well. It was affixed to an instruction card I flipped over in my hand. It said *Smart Bug*. Tom had gone all out here. It was an NSA-issued bugging device that clicked into place at the end of an Ethernet cable. It was completely invisible once installed and would transmit any conversations in its auditory radius as well as all data passing through it. State-of-the-art, light-years beyond the stuff I'd used for surveillance back in Desert Storm. Getting new gadgets always felt like Christmas.

We made our way north into the downtown area and came to a halt at the side of a pink and white-trimmed colonial edifice of grand proportions.

"*This* is the Military Police headquarters," Rodrigues said theatrically. This guy was a hoot.

I walked past the armed guards posted at the entrance. Inside the lobby, a large fan swayed precariously from the tall cupola. Pigeons clapped their wings and darted between the supporting beams.

Brazilians tend to be of average height. I was noticing that I easily towered over most of them, but not the commandeering gentleman approaching from across the room. His clipped footsteps echoed through the space. He reached for my hand.

"Mr. Leukemeyer, I presume! Welcome to Rio. I am Major Ronaldo Francisco Xavier Pereira." He greeted me with an enthusiastic handshake and another welcoming smile beneath the bristly mustache. I wondered how they all kept track of each other's names.

He led me down a long corridor. "Please, right this way. How was your trip?" he asked, opening the door to his office. An attractive young lady walked out. *"Boa tarde, Fernanda,"* said the major as she passed. "Our new intern. Can I offer you a *cafezinho*?" He motioned for me to have a seat. "Please join me, it is a national tradition."

"Thank you, Major, I will."

"Call me Ronaldo."

The tall ceiling and large windows gave the room an old-world feel. Ronaldo sat in a well-worn swivel chair. Stacks of papers and folders covered his desk. Through his window was the lovely Sugar Loaf Mountain from a completely different perspective than I'd seen before, its shape unexpectedly transformed.

"How is my good friend Tom?"

"He sends his regards."

"He and I had some good times here in the nineties. He's the . . . real deal like you say." Ronaldo leaned forward from behind his desk and rang a buzzer, an intercom, actually, the old box type with big rectangular push buttons made in the '70s. Isn't that something.

"Adriana, dois cafezinhos, por favor," he said into the box.

Within seconds, in came Adriana with the coffee and gracefully poured, filling the two tiny cups.

"Bemvindo, Seu Leukemeyer." She smiled and turned to go.

"Does everyone always smile here?" I asked.

"Indeed, a good observation—may I call you T. J.?" It really wasn't a question. "But remember, a smile can mean many things." Ronaldo confided.

Numerous maps of Rio lined his walls, with clear markings around what I assumed to be the most dangerous *favelas* in the city. Pictures of people were tacked to the maps, and their names were highlighted in multiple colors, denoting their drug trafficking hierarchy and role. Ronaldo followed my stare.

"Yes, T. J., my research is my wallpaper!" He chuckled. "As you have read in your dossiers, the *favelas* are enslaved by the many drug lords of this city. Knowing who the players are, now that is the key." He nodded. "That is our mission here at the BOPE, an acronym that loosely translates to Police Special Operations Battalion, our version of the DEA. We know a lot already, T. J."—he repeated my name, seeming to enjoy the familiarity it offered. "We understand who is who in each shanty of this city. Informants are whores for money. Whoever has the most money wins the game. The problem is that change is the only constant here." He paused, eyebrows arched. "I hope you are finding your lodgings to be satisfactory?"

Two cable cars passed each other on the Sugar Loaf behind Ronaldo's head. I turned my gaze back to him.

"What's not to like? It's spectacular. Thank you."

"I trust you find it in line with your cover."

"I'd think so, yes." I grinned. "My profile, as I understand it, is that of a venture capitalist representing an elite group of US investors interested in opportunities surrounding the Olympics. Am I to deduce that I'm after a political connection?"

Ronaldo smiled and raised his *cafezinho* in a toast.

"We need you, T. J., not to find out who is at the top, but to *prove* who is at the top."

My large fingers fumbled clumsily with the mini coffee cup.

"The key to making our fair city, our Cidade Maravilhosa, just that for the world to see, is to cut the financing, distribution, and arms behind the drug rings and militias. The source of the drugs will always be there. It is, quite frankly, beyond our control. But without proper financing and management, there are no weapons. There is no distribution chain."

Ronaldo went on to explain that the MERCOSUR trade agreement, akin to our NAFTA up north, allowed for free trade between its member countries. Coca-growing countries were transporting cocaine with other contraband through Bolivia into Paraguay, and lax MERCOSUR rules allowed for cargo with counterfeited documentation to go unchecked at the Brazilian border.

"But even with proper vigilance and checks, the vast border lands between Brazil and these countries are often unpatrolled, so the drug trade is virtually impossible to stop," Ronaldo said with a look of exasperation. "On the flip side, the *favelas* have their own extremely rigid infrastructure that entwines the residents with drug traffickers. The drug militias provide a semblance of safety and protection to the residents. In return, residents are forced to provide the drug militias cover from rival militias, the police and military."

I took a last swig of the remarkably dark coffee, and before I could put my cup on its saucer, Ronaldo punched the little intercom button again.

"*Adriana, por favor, vem com mais um cafezinho.*" Turning my way, he said, "It helps to focus and will get your mind racing."

Adriana came in once again and poured the coffee. But this time, she poured herself a cup and sat down next to me.

"Adriana is not my secretary, by the way!" Ronaldo shook his head. "No, no. Please, let me introduce you to my most important asset. Captain Adriana Meireles Pessoa de Castro. She is my special covert operations officer here at the force." Adriana nodded, flipping her gleaming black hair to the opposite shoulder. "She is the head of our Shock Battalion Task Force. She leads reconnaissance missions and strategically plans the Military Police raids in the *favelas*. Nobody knows more about the intricacies of *favela* existence. She is just serving the coffee because our intern had to leave early this afternoon, a cousin's wedding." He nodded apologetically to Adriana, who once again flashed those perfect teeth. I was beginning to think that cosmetic dentistry was a birthright in Brazil.

"It's a pleasure to meet you. Your appearance by no means reveals your profession."

"The transformation is astonishing. You would shake in your boots if she were in uniform. Adriana, please tell T. J. a little about the *favela*–drug-trafficking symbiosis, yes?" Ronaldo nudged.

"Of course." In a fluid and graceful movement, Adriana positioned herself to face me, her honey-brown eyes holding mine in full attention. "It is indeed a symbiosis," she began with her charming accent. "One cannot survive or exist without the other." She rotated her cupped hands for emphasis. "You see, in the *favelas*, there is a very clearly defined hierarchy. There are two main cartels that drive the drug trade in most of Rio. The Red Commandos and the Dragon Militia. They rival each other constantly and territories change hands frequently. In each *favela*'s various neighborhoods, there are sector generals that rule with their militias. This figurehead is often in direct contact with the *dono*, who is the orchestrator of the drug trade for that *favela*, answering to either of the two dominating cartels. The sector generals are usually in their late twenties or early thirties and their militias are composed of young men and children between the ages of eight and twenty, armed with semiautomatic weapons provided by the *donos*."

"Yes, life expectancy is considerably low in the *favelas*," Ronaldo added. "My wife actually runs a charity that helps former militia children rehabilitate to society. It is a very sad social reality here in Rio."

"These militias are in charge of policing the streets and keeping the peace between factions. Neighborhoods follow strict laws that are enforced by their sector general and that function with surprising efficiency."

"It is true, and most impressive," Ronaldo interjected. "Their laws are simple." He counted them off on his fingers. "No theft in the community, no physical fighting between residents, no rape of women, no sexual abuse of children, no wife beating, no speaking to the police, no owning a gun without the sector general's permission."

"The sector general is the judge and passes sentence on the accused," Adriana continued. "The offender may be tortured, shot in the hand or foot, leg or arm as a warning to others, or even killed in extreme situations. The purpose of such a system is to keep the police out of the *favelas* and thus away from traffickers. But you can be certain that terror rules and the worst imaginable atrocities happen when enemy factions attack." Adriana's hands clenched tightly.

"But what about all these programs I've read about in which the police force goes in and works on improving the communities and pacifying the militias?" I asked.

"Yes, there are many such efforts but they all seem to have a temporary effect. We just can't get a toehold in most of the slums to allow for social programs to take root in the community. Roçinha and Vidigal are great examples of recent success. Today, signs for the UPP— Police Pacification Unit—are prominently displayed, and surveillance forces regularly cruise the streets of several shanties. Since 2008, they have occupied some twenty *favelas*, to drive out the dealers who controlled the areas. In a short time we have seen the benefits of the UPP's presence for local businesses. The UPP makes the *favelas* of Vidigal and Roçinha, the two largest in Rio's South Zone, safer. Roçinha alone is home to some seventy thousand people, although that's only the official count."

"Might as well be its own city." The population factoid surprised me.

Adriana nodded. "These days, tourists go up there more frequently for some of the most beautiful views of Rio and for cheap restaurants with typical Brazilian food.

But it is still too premature to declare the UPP's role a resounding success."

Ronaldo took over. "Back in November we had a successful raid in Vidigal, a hotbed of the Dragon Militia. Hundreds of Special Forces agents, police and navy commandos, backed by armored military vehicles and helicopters, moved into the slum before dawn. The raid was able to target specific drug-ring members prior to the attack by monitoring their mobile phones at the time of an announced new ruling affecting the transportation of drugs across MERCOSUR borders. The ruling would have directly affected the scheduled arrival of a large cache of cocaine planned for the following day."

Clearly the Brazilians took no issue with eavesdropping either.

"We arrested the alleged drug *dono* Miguel Francisco Lopes Bonfim, widely known as Nem, as he tried to escape in the trunk of a car. Would you believe the driver tried to claim diplomatic immunity, saying he was the Honorary Consul of the Democratic Republic of Congo? He offered a bribe worth five hundred seventy thousand dollars! Of course we refused and opened the trunk to discover the hidden suspect."

I had to laugh.

Adriana said, "Nem was one of Rio's most wanted drug traffickers. After our raid and his capture, police were able to establish a permanent base in the *favela* with officers trained in community policing. City officials also moved in to provide services such as healthcare and education."

Ronaldo and Adriana both took final sips of their *cafezinhos*.

"That was just a couple of months ago," Adriana said. "Already, drug factions have retaken sections of the community and are back in business. Nem has been replaced, and a neighboring area's *dono* has taken charge, but we haven't figured out who yet."

"The *donos* parcel out the drug money that runs the *favelas* and arm their militias. They operate things from the *favelas*, from within society, even from prison." Ronaldo seemed to like punctuating his sentences with an upward-spiraling finger. "Many are actually well known to the police and society at large. *Carioca* personalities. But they are largely untouchable with their elaborate cover-up schemes. And the police are in their pockets, often selling official uniforms and equipment to the militias to further confuse matters."

"The *donos*, however, are not the top of the chain," Adriana cut in. "Those who finance and manage distribution and arm the factions with weapons are in the highest reaches of power in this country. They run the cartels. They are the untouchable ones!"

Ronaldo glanced around dramatically. "Some of them may even pay our salaries. It is why your mission is privately funded. No other government official is aware of our operation. It is the only way to avoid deception."

I tensed. This was new information to me. "Who is the private donor? How did you consider his objectivity?"

"A benign source is all I can say, but I do have carte blanche to get this job done."

"I am certain you heard about the death of our finance minister a couple of weeks ago on New Year's Eve?" Adriana asked me.

"Yes, I read about it in the dossier."

"Indeed, a troubling and sordid affair in so many ways. As you know, the minister was found dead in a love motel at the foothills of the *favela* Vidigal. Just before the murder, Minister Alcântara was hosting a New Year's Eve party. Witnesses said that he disappeared around eleven thirty, and that his wife had desperately been looking for him to bring in the New Year with their guests. Some heard loud motorcycle engines roaring in the vicinity around the time of the disappearance. A local hustler found with him was the only witness to the murder."

"The boy said he was only doing his job!" chortled Ronaldo. "We questioned him at length and he claims he did not know the attacker, an armed man he said burst into the room and shot the minister."

"But didn't kill the boy?"

"No, he left him unharmed. The minister was recently in the news because of his vocal opposition to the president's attempt to fight high-ranking corruption. The president proposed restricting transportation of agricultural products from neighboring MERCOSUR member nations, for the reasons I mentioned earlier."

Adriana explained, "The president claimed these regulations would help fight against the incoming volume of narcotics that fuel the corruption of Brazil's cities and government. Minister Alcântara had voiced concerns over the restraint such regulations would impose on economic growth. His criticism of the president's judgment turned into a national scandal."

"Yes, I read about that too," I said.

Ronaldo looked at me intently. "Their contest came to a close when the president declared to the nation in a live telecast speech that anyone who opposed the regulations could only do so because they were the bearers of guilt." His spiraling finger reached for the ceiling.

"Minister Alcântara finally sidestepped, conceding in support of the new regulation, and gave his congressional party members the cue to vote in favor. The ruling was unanimously passed into law shortly thereafter," Adriana finished off.

"The timing of the unexpected turnaround in his support of our president's anti-corruption and drug-trafficking initiatives, our successful raid this past November, and his death are too much for coincidence," Ronaldo said.

"I don't quite follow the connection."

"It's a question of interests," Adriana explained. "The minister rose to power as mayor of Rio for two terms, followed by his gubernatorial victory—all were results of elections backed by powerful supporters. His victory was almost certainly assured by promises of favors to protect his supporters' interests, especially once he was appointed to be a minister. We have a prime suspect behind his death, an extremely powerful and reputable person. We cannot charge anyone until we are absolutely certain, with proof in hand. And at this point we have extremely compelling circumstantial suspicions but not much else." Adriana's expression was bleak.

"Your job," said Ronaldo, "is to meet with this suspect as an investor interested in one of his ventures, and dig for information we can use. We believe this person to be Antonio Carlos de Melo Brasão, a major developer in Rio celebrated for his upscale shopping malls and residential towers. Any politician he's ever endorsed has always won in a landslide, even, occasionally, when the odds were against it. Most recently, he has been awarded the public contracts for the construction and concessions of the future Olympic Park and Olympic Village."

"That's a big deal." I sat forward with renewed interest. "So you think that this Brasão guy finances one of the cartels and he had the minister killed for siding with the president on that regulatory ruling?"

"And for the damage it caused the Dragon Militia. Approach from the top, we think he calls the shots. At least for the Dragon Militia. We have not yet discovered who runs the Red Commandos, but bringing in Brasão might help uncover that too. This is the only way for us to win. Only once the network falls to pieces can we secure the *favelas* and free them from the drug militias."

Ronaldo's impassioned rhetoric was compelling. "Is the mission's sponsor part of the reason you suspect Brasão?"

"No bearing; you can read about the correlations to Brasão in your files. Your job is to focus on proving the connection between him and the Dragon Militia, perhaps via the minister's murder. Adriana will now review some basics associated to your identity as a foreign investor. All of the necessary credentials have been prepared for you in conjunction with the DEA. So if anyone were to make any background checks, your cover would hold true."

"And trust me, they will check you out." Adriana warned, pointing at me. I noticed a modest wedding ring on her other finger.

"There's no danger of that, the DEA has seen to it."

As we reviewed my assignment, the afternoon faded to evening and the room was washed in amber light.

Adriana finally said, "All right, gentlemen, domestic responsibilities are calling, so T. J., why don't we continue this tomorrow morning at your apartment? I can be there around nine o'clock?"

Rodrigues dropped me off at my new home. I looked down at my coffee table and saw a Post-It from my afternoon hook-up. *Marcos—21-9954-6643 :).* I put the Post-It in a drawer by the window. The residue of guilt instantly brought to mind Sean's call earlier. I dialed in for messages and there were two. I listened while I padded through the apartment. Mama, always worrying, wanted to be sure I'd arrived OK. I was overdue for a visit, but life was in the way lately. I texted her that all was good, and added a photo of my view to cheer her up. The other message was from Sean—needed to speak with me, missed me already. I sighed.

Let me tell y'all, I'm not completely heartless and cruel; at least, I don't see myself that way. I didn't just pack my bags New Year's Day and slip out the back. Sean and I'd had it out through the haze of his hangover. I'd be only half honest if I didn't say I was hung over too. He was terrified about the upcoming court dates. He asked me to stay with him a couple more weeks, at least until the end of the trial.

I did stay. I helped finish with the packing while I filed my dismal report on Mexico and Tom made all the arrangements for my "unofficial" mission. On the day of the deliberation, I sat beside Sean's parents. His father's lips were so pursed they were hardly visible. His mother, always elegant and stylish, clasped her once-bejeweled hands tightly in her lap. Sean looked back at me from the table where he sat alongside his codefendants. His expression reminded me of the time we'd taken our first bungee jump in New Zealand.

To everyone's astonishment, Sean was spared a prison sentence. He was fined a couple million dollars for his unethical activities and was assigned 300 hours of community service. The bulk of the blame fell on his investment firm's CEO, and Sean was free to go and figure out how to pay his fine and rebuild his life. I was relieved for him. Sean had lost peoples' fortunes, but he had also made many people very rich. He had a multitude of millionaire clients who'd profited heavily from his investments before the fall, and if anything, Sean was a resourceful person. They wouldn't touch him while he was under indictment, but now that he was free, I was sure some of them would come flocking back. Yet what really rang in my mind was that it was no longer my problem.

Back at the apartment, Sean looked at my packed bags. "You're leaving me."

How the hell did he already have a drink in his hand?

"I'm sure that with all that's transpired, you've been in denial this past week, Sean, but I've been clear with you since New Year's about taking this assignment. It's a great opportunity and we can certainly use the money."

He snorted. "What gay man goes to Rio on assignment?" He held onto the door frame with his free hand, his fingers playing Rachmaninoff on the trim. "The only assignment in Rio is to get some Brazilian ass. Give me a break."

He started to say more but stopped, as though it occurred to him that a break was precisely what I was giving him. It was the soberest he'd looked all week. For a flash I saw the Sean I'd loved. "I'm taking a break from us. We'll have to play it by ear when I get back."

I hadn't been able to look at him straight on, so I'd given him a hug and that was that. And here I was.

The apartment had an insane state-of-the-art sound system. The flowing bossa nova gently stirred with the mist kicked up by the surf below. I poured myself a scotch, neat, and lay back into the outdoor lounger. I opened the folder that Ronaldo and Adriana had given me at the end of the meeting, containing a brief précis on Antonio Brasão and the politicians Ronaldo considered suspect.

Each had a more formidable pedigree than the last. Ronaldo was certain that several of these men managed the arms purchases and distribution of the Dragon Militia. It mattered to these men if new, more rigorous regulatory laws were passed—their breadwinning underground businesses would suffer the consequences.

There was also information on a man named Jucelino Neves de Castello-Branco, owner of the largest media conglomerate in Brazil. GlobeNet's vast holdings included empires in TV, publishing, and the Internet. His money was behind any successful media-related startup in the country, and he wielded enormous political influence.

The other men had equally Olympian CVs. They were major players in domestic and international business circles in an array of Brazil's most robust industries—oligarchs of irreproachable power. There was a guy named Danilo Adolfo Camargo de Lemos who owned a consultancy firm linked with many of Brasão's operations. According to Ronaldo, Brasão was suspected of financing more than 65% of the *donos* in Rio's shantytowns.

I digested the information, graphs and statistics, all documented from hundreds of interviews with *favela* dwellers, converted gang members, imprisoned *donos*, and others. Some of these studies, I noted, had been funded by reputable organizations such as the United Nations and the World Bank. The facts depicted a web of *favela* lives under fierce control by their sector generals, and they by their *donos*, and the *donos* by the men like Brasão who armed and managed the *Carioca* drug trade.

There were enough correlations between Rio's most powerful *donos* and Brasão to rule out coincidence. But there was no hard evidence to substantiate the suspicion that he also counted swaths of military and police personnel on his payrolls. Ronaldo and Adriana needed me to prove Brasão was the kingpin behind the Dragon Militia because they couldn't trust that most of their own weren't taking bribes.

I thought I'd just filled my glass. How the hell was it empty already? I got up and poured myself another. Settling back down, I continued reading. Brasão was married to a beautiful Brazilian soap opera star, Lygia de Castello-Branco. *What will Lygia do tonight?* I recalled Jovelina saying earlier. How perfect! Castello-Branco. Daddy's little starlet had been married off to Brasão—as a way to unite the families' empires? Now, that's too much for TV, I thought. I pulled Lygia's picture from the paper clip and took a closer look. Pretty lady.

I checked the time—8:15 p.m.—and turned on the tube. The news flashed on a building collapse downtown. The screen showed a pile of steaming rubble behind the Municipal Theater. I flipped the channel until I found the eight o'clock soap and suddenly, there Lygia was, enrapturing Rio—all of Brazil, rather—with her engrossing melodramatic performance.

I couldn't tell y'all what she was saying on the screen, but her range of expression certainly commanded attention. With a cut to commercial, don't you know it—slinky little vixen!—there was Lygia clutching her gold and sapphire H-Stern jewels around her neck. Lygia was a true Brazilian superstar.

After the soap opera was over, the sun set over the

ocean just beyond the Two Brothers. Silhouetted against the fading horizon, the twinkling lights of Vidigal and Roçinha crept up either side of the obfuscated mountain. I could see faint fireworks go off over one *favela*, and then as if in response, over the other. Rio was enveloped by the summery star-lit night and the crimson sky faded to black.

CHAPTER FOUR

Morning light slipped through my blinds and brought me to my feet. My watch read six a.m.—up 'n' at 'em. I slipped on my running shoes, packed my piece in my concealed holster, and went out for a jog along the beach. The rhythmic thwack of tennis balls volleyed by some early morning players matched my pace as I ran past the country club's stone walls and terra-cotta-tiled rooftops. I crossed a canal that divided Ipanema and Leblon, two of Rio's more upscale neighborhoods. At the very end of the beach, a busy avenue wove its way up and away from the coast, squeezing between the steep slopes of the Two Brothers and the pounding surf below. I began jogging uphill. Rounding a corner, I passed some impressive walled-in homes. Then the character of the neighborhood began to change. Buses careened around curves, passing each other on the narrow road. Each breath felt as though my lips were sealed to a tailpipe. Across the avenue, several men fished from the occasional poured-cement lookouts that hung over the rocky edge.

I came upon one of the few right-hand turns along the avenue. Mind you, a left turn would catapult you down the smooth granite cliffs to the boulders beneath. I crossed the street and passed a row of motels along the mountainside. Love motels, as they were more aptly called by locals. They rented by the hour.

This was where the minister had been murdered. Wouldn't you know it, the Shalimar, the motel where the crime had taken place, looked out past the avenue at the twinkling blue sea right in front of me, but all the drapes were pulled. The ocean view was not the primary interest here. I retraced my steps and turned up the hill. The road slalomed steeply upward. Uniformed officers stood on the corners chatting with each other, their machine guns slung over their shoulders and *UPP* emblazoned on their vests.

When I reached the back gate of the hotel, a *mulato* woman suddenly appeared running up the steps toward me, adjusting her short denim skirt with one hand and wiping her eye, or a tear, with the other. She reached for the gate and I noticed a nasty scar on the fleshy palm of her hand. She gave a startled intake of air when she saw me and clicked open the gate.

"Da licença por favor!" she commanded, avoiding eye contact and pressing past me.

Yes, it was a tear, many, actually, and a big ol' mascara mess. She then slipped around the corner of a wall I'd not noticed.

To the right of the gate, through an elusive entrance, a wide path led uphill to a flight of concrete steps. My gaze followed it, coursing up into a vast, vertiginous collage of concrete, cinderblock and corrugated rooftops dotted with thousands of satellite dishes. Long, colorful laundry lines swayed in the breeze and wild graffiti covered every vividly painted surface. I'd found one of the lower entrances into Vidigal. Its complexity was mesmerizing. Relatively easy access to the Shalimar, I noted. I thought about how that might have tied into the minister's last moments.

I followed the long flights up into the shanty. Along the way, the houses varied in stages of disrepair and seemed to be hanging precariously on top of each other. I checked my watch: 6:45 a.m. As I advanced, I saw another police officer flirting with a young lady smoking in her doorway, curlers in her hair and flip-flops on her feet. I noted the surprised faces of a passing group of teenagers, probably wondering what kinda Caucasian idiot would dare come up here. The path split every hundred yards or so at jaunty angles, testing my sense of direction. I caught sight of the woman from the hotel again, way up ahead as she squeezed past several young ladies walking my way. She disappeared around another bend. The girls chirped like birdsong on their way to work. I imagined they were employed as domestics in the wealthy metropolis below. They checked me out and smiled, giggling to each other. I even got a wink or two.

"*Aí Gostosão!*" one sang out. I'd have to ask Adriana what that meant exactly.

I continued to climb the daunting steps, gaining altitude. No sign of police around here. This particular long flight was carved right out of the huge slab of granite I was on. Dense tropical vegetation grew wherever it found anchor on the vertical slope. I realized nobody could arrive up here unseen. I looked behind and beneath me: the ocean stretched to the horizon as pterodactyl-like sea birds swirled over the jungle. I eventually reached a second tier of the *favela* that stank of raw sewage. It trickled down the side of the trail where half-naked children with knotted hair ran barefoot, chasing chickens. A cacophony of radios throughout the neighborhood blended hip-hop with samba and pop, even at this early hour. Barking dogs and crying children punctuated the soundtrack. The *favela* was wide-awake long before the rest of the city.

I stopped to catch my breath. I'd really broken a

sweat. The messy tangle of electric wires was everywhere. I came upon the same road winding its way up from the Shalimar. A ways down was a UPP sign, and some officers were having a smoke by the corner. To the left another path disappeared deeper into the shanty. I was starting to gather that the police only patrolled the asphalted areas. The dirt paths were beyond their scope.

I ventured up the narrow trail for several minutes more until I came upon two shirtless kids who were kicking a soccer ball between them. They had AK-47s strapped over their shoulders. When they saw me, they came running forward with angry shouts I couldn't understand. They both wore red bandanas tied 'round their arms. Upon closer inspection, a tiny bit of white powder clung to their nostrils. I gave them my best impression of a terrified, lost tourist and they laughed at me. The *mulato* boy with wild curly hair pointed his gun aggressively and yelled, "Ta-ta-ta-ta-ta-ta-ta," while his buddy laughed harder. Buddy, light skinned with dreadlocked dirty-blond hair, slashed his throat back and forth with his finger.

I got the picture and turned back down the hill against the backdrop of their jeering laughter. They yelled out some obscenities that I was certain I'd soon learn. These boys were territorial gatekeepers, probably guarding the entrance to the drug market. I felt that familiar pang inside. It was like in Mexico—kids doing the dirty work.

Back at the bottom of the hill, I stepped inside the Shalimar. A man and a woman were just leaving the reception area for their room, hand in hand. Their feisty chortles filled the little lobby in anticipation of their early morning activities. A corpulent man in a Hawaiian shirt sat behind the front desk with an unlit chewed cigar dangling from his lip.

"*Fala Inglês?*" I asked.

"You want room?" the man grunted, his pockmarked

face questioning. His hair was so slick, particles of dust clung to it.

"I'd like to look at a room, please. I may be stopping by later," I said slowly.

The man sighed heavily. His chair scraped the floor with an egregious screech when he pulled back from the counter.

"Isn't this the place where Minister Alcântara was killed? May I see that room?" I asked. He looked at me curiously as he led me to the hallway. "My girlfriend would get off on that," I added. His forehead creased curiously and he stopped to open a door.

"This was room," he stated flatly. It still smelled like fresh paint. "It was big mess. We paint, walls very bloody, no come out."

His chubby hands scrubbed at the air and his bored tone became animated as he recounted the event. It provided him a rare opportunity to be an expert on something of significance. "He was here with pay-boy. They come lots time, many month, same time every Wednesday before *jantar*, dinner. Always get same room."

We both looked around. There was a red circular bed over top of a shag carpet, mirrors above and on all sides. There was even a champagne bucket permanently fixed to the night table. He flicked a switch and the bed started turning around. He flicked another and it vibrated. I could think of a few entertaining ways to enjoy these accoutrements.

"You want later today?" he asked.

"Possibly. What can you tell me about the boy?"

I slipped a $100 bill into his plump, sweaty palm.

He took a step back and looked me over. "You want pay for boy?"

"I'd like you to tell me what you know about the boy that was with the minister," I repeated with slow enunciation.

"I no want trouble with no one," he said, flipping his

hands up, palms facing the hill behind the hotel. I had a hunch who "no one" meant.

"Hey, buddy, I'm just a curious tourist from Texas looking for a great story to tell back home," I reassured him. He looked at me skeptically for a moment and I smiled.

"You of Texas?" he asked, finally taking the cigar off his lip and flashing his few stained teeth at me. I officially retract my earlier observation regarding the Brazilian cosmetic dentistry–birthright thing.

"Hell, yeah!"

"Johnee Waynee!" He guffawed suddenly, clapping me hard on the back. "Bunggee-bunggee!"

"Bunggee-bunggee?" I repeated, at a loss.

"Yes! Bunggee-bunggee!" he exclaimed, shooting imaginary pistols with his thumb and index fingers.

Bang-bang. I caught on. "Ah, bunggee-bunggee! I'm Ted." I smiled and extended my hand.

"I Sergio," the man said, stuffing the bill in his pocket and courteously wiping his hand on his shirt before shaking mine.

"So tell me about the boy," I prodded.

"Nobody say nothing. Especially to police, but I think boy know what happen." Sergio wagged his finger. "I think he working *ministro* into trick all time." He stepped back into the hall and I followed. "They come together many time, but boy strange night of *assassinato*. He nervous, bleeding from cut and *ministro* too much drink, but it no my business. Just give key. I make happy with wife, yes?" He nudged my side.

"Did you know the boy?"

"He Zezé, he trick on Ipanema Beach. Bring many rich men here. Nice, *discreto*, no problem until *assassinato*. He and friends here with tricks long time."

I jogged the three miles back to the apartment. Once upstairs, I yanked off my drenched clothing and tossed them in the middle of the floor, a habit Sean had always deplored. It must have been about 8:00 a.m. or so when I jumped into the shower. I rinsed off and reviewed my first solo outing in Rio, feeling the excitement of a new mission. Maybe Tom was right—Mexico didn't have to be the end of the line for me.

I stepped out of the shower. The bathroom was all glass, facing the azure water outside. I stood on the balcony with outstretched arms to dry au naturel in the warm summer breeze. I felt energized by my run and this million-dollar view.

"Ai Meu Deus!" came a short, high-pitched scream.

I spun around. Jovelina, tray in hand, stared dumbfounded at my nudity. She repeatedly made the sign of the cross while hiding her face. I jumped back into the bathroom, laughing.

"Seu Leukemeyer, I'm so sorry," she cried. "I thought you were in your room!"

"Sorry, Jovi! Good morning."

"Breakfast is on the terrace. I'll be in the kitchen," she called as her urgent little footsteps faded.

Still chuckling, I dressed and walked back out onto the balcony. I sat down at the breakfast table Jovelina had so carefully laid out. Freshly squeezed orange juice in a cold, sweating silver pitcher, all sorts of tropical fruit peeled, chopped and ready to eat, and the scent of that wonderfully aromatic Brazilian coffee wafted over the table. The *New York Times, Wall Street Journal, Financial Times* and *Jornal do Brasil* were all folded neatly side by side on the white ottoman. I was glancing through the headlines when Jovelina came back, still blushing mildly, with a soft-boiled egg and warm croissants. I read my papers until the house phone rang and she picked it up. "Mr. Leukemeyer, the doorman says your morning appointment is here."

"Have him send her up, Jovi, and please bring another place setting in case she has not yet eaten."

"Yes, *Seu* Leukemeyer, right away."

Jovelina brought Adriana outside, and I rose to greet her. She gave me the requisite kiss on both cheeks and sat down.

I reached for a warm croissant and offered one.

"No, no, I'm on a diet," she said, wagging a finger.

I took notice of her wedding ring again.

"What does your husband think of you working on the force as a covert operations officer, dealing with such dangerous matters?"

"Bernardo works for the CORE, our equivalent of your SWAT. He is part of the Civil Police of Rio, so he understands my work quite well. Although lately, our adjacent careers have put a bit of a strain on our relationship."

"I'm sorry to hear that. How long have you two been married?"

"Going on five years. We met working on a few assignments together when the military and civil police paired up for certain raids. That was exciting." Adriana sat back with a sigh and looked out to the horizon. "But people are not always who they seem to be." The waves broke with a deep thunder. "That is fodder for another day." She smiled, clearly exercising her English vocabulary. "We have much to discuss and not much time."

Adriana pulled a tablet out of her bag, ending any further line of questioning. With quick motions and taps of her finger, she pulled up the folder for the Brasão family. The screen displayed pictures of its three members, with their ridiculously long names beneath. "OK, please tell me, what is it with Brazilians and these impossibly long names everyone has?"

She laughed musically. "Yes, they are lengthy, but they serve as a form of pedigree to let others know who you are. Generally, most Brazilians have a first and second name to honor parents or grandparents before them. This is followed by the mother's family name, often already hyphenated, and finally the father's family name. It is not uncommon for some to have up to six official names. The more names you have, the more important you are—or at least you think you are." She grinned. "It is really just a throwback to colonial days. We are still a very colonial-minded society, even in the twenty-first century."

"Charmingly confusing."

"Here we have Antonio Brasão." She pointed to an elegant man in his early 60s, with salt-and-pepper hair, well dressed and groomed. He would have passed for someone Sean and I might have socialized with back in New York. "He is married to one of our most famous actresses and, ironically, she's a very powerful advocate for the poor. Her father is Jucelino Neves de Castello-Branco. We know that Castello-Branco has relinquished the day-to-day management of his media businesses to Brasão's care. Brasão and Lygia have an eleven-year-old son named Paulo André de Castello-Branco Brasão."

"I watched Lygia on TV last night; she is quite beautiful and very engaging," I offered.

Adriana's wide eyes met mine. "Yes, Brazilians have an extreme love affair with her. She is without a doubt a remarkable woman. I watch her almost every night," she confessed. "I would be very surprised if Lygia were aware of her husband's alleged crimes. In fact, Ronaldo believes the couple is estranged and puts on a show for the public. We might be able to use her discontent with him to our advantage. You will likely encounter her at the country club tomorrow. Might I suggest that you not mention that you will be meeting Brasão? A staged coincidence may be critical to establishing where Lygia's loyalties lie."

Adriana tapped Lygia's picture and a list of links appeared. "She is a driven woman and uses her star power to make things happen. She makes a real difference in the *favelas* by implementing educational and outreach programs that have resulted in tangible changes for many communities."

She tapped again and a video opened showing Lygia

on a street in the *favelas*, crowded by women and children, promoting a program to assist local women's entrepreneurial efforts. From the view behind them I could tell it was Vidigal. Big smiles, warm hugs, flowers and autographs culminated in great applause. Lygia was a hero to these people; like a Princess Di.

"Roçinha is next. Soon she will have centers in all the major *favelas* of Rio. All the residents of Vidigal venerate her; they would do anything for her."

"I was there this morning," I told Adriana.

"Where?" Her eyes snapped up to mine.

"In Vidigal. I went for a run and saw the motel where the minister was killed and then checked out the *favela*. I climbed a good long way. And let me tell ya, the UPP only has eyes on public areas around the paved streets. Once you go deep inside, they're nowhere to be seen. I think I found the entrance to the drug market."

"You went to the *boca*?"

"Ran into some kids with AK-47s and red bandanas."

"The Dragon Militia! Why did you go there alone?" She looked deeply troubled. "They were probably guarding the *boca*. The *donos* and sector generals move the market regularly to keep us in the dark about where they are operating. You could have been in danger up there."

"It really was not difficult to find, to tell you the truth. I needed to scope out the *favela* and see it for myself. Get a feel for the place, the people. It helps my mind make associations. Plus"—I raised a brow and smiled—"I'm very good at taking care of myself."

"I wouldn't recommend doing that too often. Actually, I'd like you to promise me you won't go there again. You could get hurt, or worse, compromise your identity. Leave the *favela* monitoring to me. That is my specialty."

Adriana sat back and her tone shifted from alarm to weariness. "There is trouble brewing once again in that area. Since November's raid and the installment of the UPP, and even before, really, through a variety of privately funded initiatives, like Lygia's, Vidigal was showing signs of improvement. But now, the greater police presence has the local arm of the Dragon Militia feeling constrained. Tension within the community has been on the rise, but we don't know who is now in control."

Her fingers fiddled with the edge of her tablet, reminding me for a moment of Sean. "You see, T. J., the assessment of the *favelas* we gave you yesterday is somewhat simplistic and digestible. The reality is terrible. People living there are on constant alert, never knowing quite who to trust. The drug dealers are just as violent and threatening as the militias. Residents must walk a fine line between the police, militias, drug dealers and their neighbors. All residents live under constant threat." She frowned. "And so were you for going in there. It's dangerous. Stay out of there. I hope that is perfectly clear."

"Understood. After your briefing about the murder I also read the article in the dossier, where Ronaldo mentioned his suspicions of foul play in the minister's death. I got curious."

"That's another thing. Ronaldo is in the papers too often. I worry about his safety."

She put down the tablet. "Winning Lygia over will be extremely important for you in Ronaldo's estimation. She will be a fundamental key to understanding how to best ingratiate yourself to Brasão." She swiped her fingers on the screen a couple of times and pulled up Antonio Brasão's profile again.

"Brasão is Rio's largest developer, hands down. He always manages to be awarded the most important projects. The construction sector in Rio has grown thirty-five percent in recent years, and property values have just about tripled."

I whistled softly. "That is certainly a significant return on investment."

"Until recently, Brazil had been booming, and foreign investors were coming to Rio in droves." Adriana suddenly beamed with pride and sat back. "You know, I always remember people saying that Brazil was the country of the future. We always want to believe it is finally here, and the World Cup and the Olympics are very proud national symbols of that, yet that goal has never seemed further away. The truth is everything here is tainted by corruption that stalls our progress. That is why people are going to the streets, demanding better education, security and healthcare. That is why what we are doing here is so important."

Her passion had my attention.

She reached for an envelope in her bag and pulled out a letter printed on fine company stationery. The header read *International Venture Capital, LLC. The footer on the bottom, 14 Wall Street, New York, NY 10011.*

"This is a copy of your letter of introduction to Mr. Brasão that was sent by courier from a New York address prior to your departure. With the assistance of your DEA, we have created this company as a front. IVC's primary business is to scout out international investment opportunities in developing countries for a small, tight-knit group of extremely wealthy investors."

The breeze blew a long strand of Adriana's hair loose and it waved about. She reached over to hand me the document. "You are here to research the feasibility of a variety of projects for your firm, particularly those surrounding the upcoming Olympic Games."

I nodded. "I read about the construction projects in detail last night. I'll tell ya, Rio's taking on quite a task to gussy up for the games."

"It is. And Brazilians know that if anyone can make it happen, it is Brasão. He is one of the few powerful people in this town who can bring politicians, investors, and construction companies together to make mega-projects happen. You will be showing interest in two current projects being spearheaded by the state and city governments in preparation for the upcoming games. Both have been awarded to Brasão Corporações, SA in the form of a public-private partnership. The federal and state governments provide funding and plan approval, but they share the financial risk with the private contractor who is awarded the project. Brasão in turn offers the financing arm of the partnership to the most efficient bidder. The bidding must be conducted under the oversight of the Secretary of Infrastructure Projects for the State of Rio de Janeiro.

"You, however, will solicit now, several weeks before the public offering, an exclusive bid, in an attempt to secure a significant share of the returns for your investors. We need Brasão to believe that you are hip to shady dealings. In addition to favorable terms, you will offer kickbacks in return for accepting your bid."

I nodded.

Adriana tapped the tablet and a map of the city opened. She zoomed in to the area in question. "The first project regards the Olympic Park and the Olympic Village construction sites along Lake Jacarepaguá in the West Zone. The city is seeking private investment to help cover the costs of the Olympic facilities. It bought the land of the former racetrack park from two major contributors to our mayor's electoral campaign. The sale was apparently finalized without a bidding process, even though the law requires one for public land acquisitions. In addition to securing the contracts for building the two venues, Brasão is constructing new developments near the Olympic Park, and their property values are expected to soar once the Olympic Park and Village are completed."

A seagull landed on the glass rail of the balcony and flapped its wings, greedily eying the remaining croissants. I shooed it away with one hand and took the letter from Adriana with the other. Attached were supporting documents attesting to IVC's legitimacy and listing a variety of international projects they had helped finance. I glanced at the address for Brasão Corporações, SA. It seemed familiar for some reason.

"The address of his office . . . that building collapse downtown. Wasn't it on the same street?"

"Yes, it was. Crazy thing!" Adriana seemed surprised that I'd picked up on such a small detail. "Somebody was doing illegal renovations and knocked out a weight-bearing column. That night, the entire building collapsed, taking down two smaller ones. Some people at an evening computer class lost their lives, right in the middle of downtown Rio! But Mr. Brasão's building was untouched."

"Unbelievable," I muttered, and turned my focus to the letter.

Corporações Brasão, SA
Av. 13 de Maio, 13—Centro,
Rio de Janeiro—RJ, 20031-007
Brazil
Re: Solicitation to Invest—Porto Maravilha Project and Olympic Park and Village

I read my letter of introduction to this Brasão guy, informing him of the dates of my visit. I couldn't have done a better job. I noted my title at the end of the letter.

T. J. Leukemeyer
President of Project Research and Development
International Venture Capital, LLC

"I placed a call as your secretary and made an appointment for Monday at ten thirty in the morning at Mr. Brasão's office," Adriana added when she saw my eyes come off the page.

"Did you write that?"

"I did."

Those pearly white teeth could blind a man.

"Well, that there's some mighty fine English. Where'd you learn it so well?"

"We had cross-training programs with several different American agencies, so if you add them all up, I've spent a couple of years in the States. Now," she continued, "once he accepts the deal with you, he will most likely tour you through the project areas to be developed, and wine and dine you. This will be your opportunity to gradually ingratiate yourself to Brasão and his team. Your entire professional CV is outlined here." She tapped the tablet. "As you already have familiarity with the not-for-profit industry, having made that your personal cover all these years, that is included in your continuing work as well; a point that might come in handy to relate with Lygia's philanthropy."

"Clever. I bet that was your idea."

"It was." She grinned and once again tucked the waving strand of hair into place.

By now the summer heat was intense despite the awning's cover, so I showed Adriana into the welcoming air-conditioned living room. She sat next to me on the sofa and took in the surroundings.

"Not bad. I've always wanted to see how the other half lives." She laughed. "This place is incredible!" She glanced at the room's modern white marble and glass surfaces warmed by several deep mahogany colonial pieces, colorful rugs, contemporary art and furniture, and most impressively, the endless view through the floor-to-ceiling windows.

She set the tablet between us on the coffee table and pointed to the information on the screen. "Here is Lygia's basic schedule. It shows when she and her son generally go to the country club on Saturdays, and when she shoots for the *novela* in the afternoons at GlobeNet Studios up in the Jardim Botanico hills. They will be at the club tomorrow morning for Paulo André's Saturday tennis lessons. Do you play?"

"I'm pretty good, actually. Worked as a tennis pro at the River Oaks Country Club back in high school." I swung my imaginary racquet.

"Perfect, an ideal segue way to meeting the boy. We feel very strongly that Minister Alcântara's death is directly related to his longstanding relationship with Brasão. Finding evidence that Brasão ordered the minister's death would help link him to the Dragon Militia. It's the best we have to go on so far. Brasão has been at this a long time—he's not easy to trip up. The only way we can capture Brasão and bring down his network of *donos* is if you truly mesh into his personal life, gain his trust and obtain some intimate information we can use."

In other words, figure out how to follow the money. The money trail always led the way through the unknown.

I looked out the window. The seagull was now feasting on the remaining croissants with a buddy. Jovelina jumped up and down frantically, waving her arms at the stubborn creatures so that she might clear the table. Adriana followed my gaze, and the serious moment was lost to the levity of our giggles.

We discussed assignment details for the next hour, at the end of which Adriana picked up her satchel and handbag, and stood to go.

"After today, we can no longer be seen together. If you need me for any reason, just dial five-five-five on the cell phone we have provided you with. Ronaldo can be reached by five-five-six, but you should only contact him in an emergency if you cannot reach me. Those numbers connect via a protected frequency and the phone is programmed not to keep them in its history. You can add other numbers to the shield feature like this." She took out her own phone and demonstrated. "A precautionary measure. Calls can be forwarded from your American phone and shielded automatically, so be sure to shut it down and put it away for the rest of your stay. With the GPS feature we will always know your whereabouts if you have our phone with you, whether it is turned on or off." She nodded toward the tablet she'd stowed in her satchel. "These files have been uploaded for your viewing. Sign in with your MP badge number; the password is 1500, the year of Brazil's discovery."

I'll tell y'all, these folks are proud nationalists.

"A question before you go, Adriana. When I was in

the *favela*, a group of ladies walking downhill said something to me, but I can't figure out what it meant."

"What did they say?"

"*Aí Gostosão!*" I repeated.

Adriana laughed, her hand rising to cover her mouth. "It literally means 'tasty,' but I guess in slang it would translate as 'Hey, stud.'" She shook her head, regaining her composure.

"One last thing, do you have a picture of the hustler that was questioned in the minister's death, Zezé? I think I can get some information out of him. The manager at the motel said he thought he was in on the murder, even though he may have kept that from the police. The boy brought him regular business."

"You stay away from the *favela*! We questioned the guy extensively. Give me the information and I can handle that end of it." Her forehead creased with annoyance.

"I can get close to him, I think. You can't. I think he has more information to give."

"I see. How do you plan to build a rapport with him?"

"Just leave that part to me. We need to know whatever he knows. He hangs out on the beach in the afternoons."

"Yes, we have a mug shot from when he was brought in for questioning."

"I'd like to see that, could you send it to me, please?"

"I will." She looked at me solemnly. "Be careful, T. J., never let your guard down. These people are extremely dangerous."

After I'd walked her to the elevator and closed the door, I went into the kitchen for a glass of juice, but Jovi insisted with much fanfare that she'd bring it to me. I wandered across the open apartment. In the study, leather-bound books lined the shelves, an occasional artifact displayed amongst them: some Brazilian string instrument, a pair of colonial brass saddle shoes, pre-Columbian pottery. I sat down at the desk by the window and looked out at the Two Brothers. The tasteful Rio de Janeiro Country Club spread out twenty floors below, walled in from the world. The exclusive high-society playground boasted two pools, twelve clay tennis courts, three gardens and playgrounds, and an imposing clubhouse in the middle of Ipanema. Palm and almond tree-lined paths led members from one point to another. As I gazed, a text came in from Adriana. It was Zezé's picture. Handsome guy.

On my personal phone, I listened to Sean's message again. I set up call forwarding, powered down, and put it away in the drawer. I recognized that taking this assignment was a way to delay my future with—or without—him. Yesterday's fun with Marcos seemed to move me in the latter direction. I thought about Vicente and wondered what had compelled him to flip. What clues had I missed and why? Here I was diving into another covert mission with my past unresolved. All these doubts had put me off my game. Perhaps I'd been just as reckless in my relationship with Sean as I'd been in my career.

If you thought Adriana's prep session had sounded high-stakes, let me tell ya, leading a double life is nothing new to me. Being gay and athletic never went hand in hand; not at a Catholic all-boys prep school in Houston. I was always active in sports, mostly due to my parents' stressing equal amounts of stimulation for body and mind. At the time, I couldn't conceive that they'd be as accepting of my homosexuality as they ultimately were, so pretending became second nature. As a wide receiver, when I'd sprint for the end zone, my coach would yell out, "Punch it, Leukemeyer! Punch it!" to release that extra adrenaline. Power and invincibility—the ultimate feeling. That's what walking the edge during undercover work conjured. That is who I was. Had to get that back.

Jovi knocked at the door and entered carrying a silver tray with a tall glass of cold, magenta-colored juice.

"*Obrigado*, Jovi." I took the glass from her hand. "What is this?"

She reached over and placed an embroidered lace doily and silver coaster on the desktop to protect it.

"It's a very healthy and tasty fruit called açaí. You will like it," she said, and took her leave.

It was noon. In New York it would be nine a.m. I took a gulp—not too bad—then dialed the familiar number into my shield app.

Although I did not have to hide my sexual orientation at the DEA, only my immediate family and Sean knew the truth about my career. Even Milena, my oldest, dearest friend, was none the wiser. I've always had a front and an uncanny knack for inventing believable white lies and, more importantly, never forgetting them. To the rest of the world, I explained my long-term absences from Sean and New York as forays to set up new field offices in Kathmandu or Niger. Shorter trips were conferences followed by meetings with potential donors. Cocktail parties became exceptionally fun opportunities for creativity, often with Sean playing along and adding details of his own. He'd always been my social accomplice. We'd shared that. We'd shared so many things.

"Hello?" I heard Sean's voice.

"It's T. J."

There was silence on the other end. A sigh. "Hey," he said. "I'm not sure what to say." He was sober. "I miss you, buddy. I wish you were back. But I can't really blame you for wanting out of here."

I didn't reply. This was more difficult than I thought it would be.

"I start working my hours of community service next week. They've got me lecturing at public high schools and colleges in the tri-state area about the perils of white-collar crime. Ouch, right?"

"That's tough. How's the move? How are your parents holding up?"

"It's been delayed a couple of days. Everything is pretty much packed and in storage. I'll head over to Ferdi and Milena's tomorrow. Thanks again for staying to help me prep. I'll get by."

Another heavy sigh.

"So pathetic at this point in my life. A white-collar criminal and a DEA special agent, what a pair! No wonder you're there. How's Rio anyway?"

"I don't believe you were always like that."

"I know. I'm still trying to figure it out. Trying to stay clearheaded since you left. Can you tell me what you're doing down there? I don't want to talk about me."

"I can't go into it much, but I can say it's beautiful here."

I wondered to myself why we'd never been here together. I wanted to tell him it was a place we should spend time in, but I also didn't want to get his hopes up. I offered vague references to corrupt politicians.

He let out a low whistle. "That's a bit out of your usual repertoire. It sounds dangerous."

"I'll be fine."

"Milena and Ferdi had me over for dinner last night. We watched that video of our vacation together sailing down the Amalfi Coast. They actually still have a VCR. You were telling that sorry-ass gay plumber joke with those hokey Southern expressions of yours and we were all in stitches. It felt so good to hear your Texan twang, reminded me that it was the first thing I loved about you. They asked how we're doing, when you were coming back. I didn't know what to say. Are you planning to come back?"

"Of course I'll be back."

He hesitated. "I mean to me."

"I know what you mean. I don't know. It's been a really rough few years."

"But before those bad years, we were best friends, in every way, for a long, long time," he said softly.

"That's what makes this so difficult." I could feel my jaw clenching. I looked at our commitment ring on the wrong hand. "But you're not who you were, or at least who I thought you were." Vicente's betrayal had lanced my armor. I looked out at the clouds rolling in over the mountaintops. "You were my teammate, Sean. You were my partner. My family. You dropped the ball, but you did it willingly, with no regard for the consequences to us. I need time to get over that, if I even can."

"I understand. I'm working on fixing things. I love you, man." His voice wobbled. "Be careful down there," he repeated.

We hung up. I watched the day change as oncoming clouds engulfed the city slowly, feeling lonelier than a cactus in the desert on a starlit night.

CHAPTER FIVE

Ivy-covered chain-link fences separated the country club's tennis courts from each other. I watched from the open gate as Paulo André shook his instructor's hand and stepped back when the gentleman left. The boy began to practice against a far wall. He had a great backhand stroke; damn good spin on that ball. Not bad for an eleven-year-old. He was wearing baggy white shorts and a white polo shirt. Nice racquet too. After a couple of volleys, he hit the ball too hard and it conveniently arched my way. I held up my racquet to intercept it, bounced it straight up into the air and caught it with my other hand.

"*Obrigado,*" he called. His eyes squinted under the hand shielding them from the sun.

"*De nada.*" I tapped the ball off my racquet back to him.

"Are you American?" the boy asked in good English. His striking blue eyes and features reminded me of a Romanov prince.

"Yes, I am. Is my accent that strong?" I approached the kid.

"Yeah, it's strong, but also very American."

"I'm T. J., the American," I said, extending my hand.

"I'm Paulo André." Mature shake.

"How come you speak English?"

"My mother always speaks to me in English when she doesn't want people to understand. She studied in the US many years ago."

"Were you just having a lesson?"

"Yes, but that teacher is no good. He's boring. Never plays with me, just teaches. I liked my last one better."

"What happened to him?" I asked, twirling my racquet.

"He got fired. He was caught with one of the cleaning ladies in the bathroom." Paulo André smiled slyly and we both laughed.

"Well, I have a few minutes if you want to have a little volley. I'm not too bad."

We played a few rounds and the kid was pretty good. I gave him a few pointers on how to improve his swing. After a good twenty minutes, Paulo André checked the time on his expensive tank watch.

"I've got to go. Mother is by the pool with her friend and they'll be expecting me for lunch. I'm late and she always worries." He shrugged, as if worrying about him would be the most absurd waste of time. "Nice to meet you, T. J."

Paulo André grabbed his tennis bag leaning against the fence and turned back. "Are you here often?"

"I just got here, but I'll be in Rio for a while, so I'll probably come around for some exercise, I reckon."

"Maybe we can play next Saturday too, then?" he asked.

"Sure thing."

Paulo André ran off down the path toward the pool house. He swiped his racquet down and tossed a pile of dried leaves up into the air.

"See you later," I called. He wasn't the capricious little rich kid I'd expected. Pretty down-to-earth, actually.

After Paulo André's departure, I walked over to the pool house and changed into a Speedo. I grabbed my goggles and went for a swim. It felt exhilarating—long steady strokes, pumping blood, moving muscles—made me feel alive.

"Hey, T. J.!" a voice called after several laps. I took off my goggles and swam to the edge. Paulo André was sitting at one of the tables alongside the pool, finishing a hamburger and French fries. He sat next to two beautiful women in their late thirties—perhaps, dare I say, forties with help? One of them was unmistakably the famous Lygia de Castello-Branco. Everyone around the pool was aware of her presence and trying to keep up a dignified country club atmosphere by giving her space, yet unable to refrain from an occasional peek at the superstar. Waiters fluttered back and forth, making sure her table was well attended to.

"Hi, Paulo André, how's your lunch?" I asked.

A white-gloved waiter in a starched uniform was removing their dishes. He paused to readjust the parasol shade above the trio. I could see that Lygia and her friend had been nibbling at a hearts-of-palm salad, washed down with iced tea. Lygia lifted her large sunglasses up above her forehead to get a better look at who her son was addressing.

"Who's your friend?" she asked Paulo André, her eyes fully fixed upon me.

I pulled myself out, feeling the cool water trickle down my body. I shook my hair and grabbed a white towel from a nearby chaise to blot myself off with. The towels were plush and had the Rio de Janeiro Country Club logo printed on them, a blue shield with a red cross dissecting the white initials into quadrants. They would have looked great by the pool in the Hamptons, if Sean and I still had a pool in the Hamptons.

Lygia's friend nudged her under the table and mumbled something. I guessed it was a compliment by the way her giddy eyes peered at me from above her sunglasses.

I made my way over to the table, the towel now thrown over my shoulder, and introduced myself.

"Hello, ladies, I'm T. J. Leukemeyer. Hi, Paulo André." I tousled his hair.

"We just met on the tennis courts, Mother. T. J. is really good! He taught me some very cool tips." His dimples deepened.

"Is that right?" Lygia said, still looking me over. A few drops of water dove off my abs. Her self-assured eyes surprised me as she appraised me like an expensive piece of merchandise she'd just purchased at Louis Vuitton.

Now it was my turn to be impressed. Let me tell y'all, growing up with three Texan women in the house, I'm not unfamiliar with beauty pageants. I know a contender when I see one. Lygia was not just a superstar, she radiated beauty. Her skin was flawless and pampered. She had pretty chestnut-colored hair that cascaded down over her shoulders, the ends just brushing her collarbone above her bikini top. Her lips were pursed—maybe she was slightly bothered by the idea that her son had been talking to a stranger—but her big blue eyes betrayed her interest in me. She repositioned herself and crossed her shapely legs. Her fingers, still touching the glasses she had raised, were adorned with sophisticated gold rings. The rock on her left hand was so big she needed an arm sling to support it. The girl liked her jewels, and this was a secure place to show them off.

"I have not seen you here at the club before," Lygia stated. I somehow felt like she'd been expecting me. The actress was a fortified chameleon.

"I just arrived a couple of days ago. I'm living up there while in Rio." I pointed to the penthouse of the building at the opposite end of the club.

"I know that building. It's a very nice place to stay. I am Lygia," she said, extending her hand. "Lygia de

Castello-Branco. And this is my friend Valeria Siqueira de Mendonça."

"It's so nice to meet you, T. J.," Valeria said with a playful wink. I noticed Lygia nudge her again, a silent order to behave.

"It's a pleasure to meet y'all too, particularly because you speak such beautiful English."

Lygia seemed to relax a little. Could it be the pleasure of meeting someone she thought had no clue who she was for a change?

"Mother, we could play again next Saturday. Maybe he can instruct me instead of Kiko. He's so boring," Paulo André complained.

"I'm sure Mr. Leukemeyer has better things to do than teach you tennis on his Saturdays in Rio," she replied, still looking me over.

"Not at all. This young man certainly has promising talent."

A waiter noticed us conversing and brought a wooden chair over for me. Lygia seemed to flinch in annoyance but then relaxed.

"May I sit down?"

"Of course you can," welcomed Valeria. "It would be our pleasure."

"I'll get my shirt and bag over there and be right back then."

Valeria was giggling when I returned, pulling my shirt over my head. As I took my seat I felt all eyes watching our table, wondering who the man with Lygia de Castello-Branco was.

"So what brings you to Rio, Mr. Leukemeyer, and from where? Obviously you are from the South."

"You must be from Hollywood," Valeria teased.

"T. J., please." I smiled. "I am indeed a Southerner, but I'm here to search out investment opportunities for my New York based firm. Brazil has much to offer."

"Have you ever been here before?" asked Valeria.

"No, this is my first time."

"Oh how fun, a Rio virgin! There is so much to see!" Valeria sat back, giving her black curly hair a little jiggle. She was gorgeous too, but unlike Lygia, her beauty was more exotic. Her skin had a Mediterranean tone and her features were slightly Persian.

"Now, both you ladies must tell me, how is it you speak such flawless English?"

"We met and studied at Radcliffe, and have been great friends ever since," Lygia replied, smiling at her friend. "My husband and I also have a pied-à-terre in New York and go a couple of times a year. I think it is such important exposure for Paulo André," she added, looking adoringly at her son.

"And fun shopping and theater for us!" exclaimed Valeria.

"Speaking of shopping, ladies, I need to find out where to buy some clothing and a few suits. You two seem like you would know where to shop. Where would you recommend I go?"

Valeria said without hesitation, "Fashion Leblon."

"It has the best stores," Lygia added.

"There are several shops that are great for men's clothing—many top stores," Valeria said.

"My father built that shopping mall," the boy blurted out.

"Paulo André, that is not something you just tell people!" Lygia scolded.

"But it's true," he persisted.

"Don't be a show-off. Now go get changed."

"So can we play next Saturday?" he asked me with hopeful eyes.

"Of course we can."

Once Paulo André left the table, Lygia said, "I'm trying to teach him some humility. We are very fortunate, actually, all of us here at this club." She gazed at our coddled surroundings. I gazed at her serious bling. "We live in a place of such beauty, yet there is so much suffering and poverty. I think it is important for all of us who have been so fortunate to give back to those who have not had our luck. This is a quality many wealthy Brazilians lack."

"How long will you be in Rio, Mr. Leukemeyer?" Valeria asked, purposely changing the subject.

"I'm not certain. I may be here for several months."

"Do you have any acquaintances here?" Lygia sat back for the first time since I'd arrived. She adjusted her gold bracelet absentmindedly.

"No, just the three of you, I'm afraid."

Valeria looked down at my hands resting on the table. "What large fingers! Single, are you?"

"Single, yes," I replied with the slightest hesitation.

"I am divorced," Valeria said with another burst of giggles. "D.I.V.O.R.C.E. Like that song. I am free and will never marry ever again. *Deus e grande!* God is bountiful, as we say here in Brazil." She held up her tea and toasted, "To freedom."

Lygia nodded at me and explained, "Just yesterday. He was really quite a schmuck!"

As our laughter subsided, the waiter came by to see if anything was needed.

"Time for a cocktail!" Valeria announced, looking around the table for agreement.

Lygia looked my way and asked, "Would you have time for one?"

"I'd love a *caipirinha*."

"Now you're talking."

We talked about the upcoming elections here and in the States, and then turned to the recent changes in Brazil. Lygia again spoke about the inequality of society and the charities she was involved with.

"I think that's amazing. I used to work with nonprofit organizations that did similar things. We had several field offices around the world."

Lygia looked at me with renewed interest. "What programs were you involved with?"

I told her of fictitious projects I'd spearheaded in Zambia and Botswana. We discussed how governments needed to play leading roles in such matters, by securing the way for aid distribution and finance, and by providing much-needed publicity and incentives to help implement change. The difficult politics involved. Deep stuff.

Soon we were discussing the Brazilian president and the rampant corruption in government.

"I would say that most of our friends are against the president's protectionist policies. High society never wants regulation. It takes a strong hand to stop corruption and create the necessary infrastructure for our future." Lygia sipped her *caipirinha*. "But now even the lower classes are outraged by the government's spending on the World Cup and the upcoming Olympics when they so desperately need better health services, education, all those important basics. It doesn't seem to matter who is in power, left or right, the people get taken for a ride."

"I just read that a seventh minister is about to resign because of new criminal allegations," I said.

"Corruption is everywhere and people are finally getting fed up and tightening the reigns; they are dropping like flies." Valeria fluttered her fingers through the air.

Suddenly, Lygia turned gravely to Valeria. "Speaking of ministers, did you hear about Carla?" She remembered her manners and clarified, "Carla is a good friend and the wife of the recently murdered Minister Alcântara."

That perked my ears up.

"Hear what?" Valeria tilted her head in anticipation of juicy gossip.

"She is gone! They say she just left everything and bought a place in Miami. It was all too much for her."

"It was such a tragic scandal!" lamented Valeria. Her hands covered her mouth.

"I tried to be with her afterwards. We had her out to

the island for a weekend to console her, but she could not get over the humiliation and public nature of his death," Lygia told me.

They were close friends, I thought to myself. How twisted if her husband really was behind the murder.

Valeria leaned in, one hand holding her curls back. "I would never have guessed it. You see, T. J., Brazilian high society runs in small circles. Everyone ends up knowing everybody's business. It's terrible."

"For Carla, it is tragic. I think I would do the same thing," Lygia said. "What else could you do to begin again after something like that?"

"I heard she made out well on the life insurance settlement. At least that helps with the sorrow," Valeria said.

I chuckled. "It certainly makes sense. There should be a service that rebuilds your identity after disagreeable situations like that, kind of like a commercialized Witness Protection Program."

Lygia grinned.

"Hey, this is not a come-on," Valeria said, reaching across the table to tap my arm. "If you'd like, I'd be happy to show you the right stores tomorrow. I have an appointment at H. Stern to pick something up and we can eat at one of the restaurants there. It's quite lovely. Lygia, come too, we would have fun!"

"I can't tomorrow. We have lunch at the Itanhangá."

"Well, then it's you and me tomorrow, T. J.," Valeria said. "Eleven a.m.?"

"It's a date."

I couldn't imagine a better source.

CHAPTER SIX

I'm not much of a shopper. I do like nice things, but it's just not a way I prefer to spend my time. But let me tell ya, as I rode the escalator up through the atrium of Fashion Leblon, it felt much like an enclosed Rodeo Drive. Malls in the States could learn a thing or two here. I walked into the H. Stern showroom. The luxurious display cases twinkled with exquisite jewels. Valeria was seated in a private booth with a glass of champagne in hand. She waved me over.

"Come, come! Celebrate with me." She motioned as the sales lady poured me a flute.

I sat down next to her after the customary two-cheek peck.

"What amazing pieces," I commented, admiring a pair of spider web-like diamond necklaces, and thought of Ferdi. My gaze dropped from one upholstered shelf to the next in the glittering mirror-backed case. A pair of dark green eyes reflected back at me from the hall, giving me a start. I turned to look behind us, but there was nobody there.

"Those are from the Niemeyer collection. You see how they curve?"

Valeria raised a glass. "I'm so glad you are here. I love to share things of Brazil with people from abroad."

"It seems most Brazilians do," I replied and glanced behind me again, surveying the wide marble corridor and shoppers.

"Let's toast!"

"To what are we toasting?"

"To my divorce settlement!"

The clerk smiled and flutes chimed. On the table, in a velvet-lined burled-wood tray, lay a handcrafted gold necklace with the most delicate ruby-, sapphire- and diamond-studded flowers meandering along its twig-like links.

"It's breathtaking."

"Thank you, it is my design. A symbolic gift to myself for finally coming to my senses." She turned to the clerk and circled her index finger over the necklace. It was gently placed in a pretty box and wrapped into a little shopping bag.

"Bottoms up!" she said, finishing off her glass and standing up. "Where do we begin?"

"Suits. Definitely suits."

"Follow me." She led the way to the up escalator. Her curls bounced against the lapels of her couture suit jacket with each step, but I was set on finding the owner of those green eyes. The distinct feeling that their focus had been me and not the jewels made no sense—actually, it was impossible. I hadn't been in Rio long enough to garner any attention.

We were in and out of the first shop in ten minutes. Valeria was fun to be around, in command, and decisions, good ones in my estimation, were made on the spot with sharp wit and humor. My own personal shopper. I handed the clerk my Titanium AmEx as Valeria placed our selections on the counter. Not missing a detail, her eyebrows rose.

"Lunch?" she said, once we'd finished. My outstretched arms were laden with shopping bags.

"Let's go."

She led me into a nice restaurant that was open to the corridor and the mall's atrium, like an indoor-outdoor café. Across the atrium, large windows framed the mountain-surrounded lagoon and the Corcovado. The maître d' greeted Valeria warmly by name and led us to a table with a view.

"Please," I said, holding her chair out for her. I put the shopping bags on the floor next to me as I sat down.

"Thank you, what a gentleman you are."

I tucked her chair in and noticed a short rope noose on the back. All the chairs had them.

"What are these for?" I asked.

"Oh, that's for ladies to tie around their handbags so the *piralhos*, those little thieves, don't take them on the run." She looped her bag into place to demonstrate. Her purse slid through the noose, making a swipe impossible.

"Even in here?"

"Anywhere in Rio, dear," she said.

A waitress approached. *"Bom dia, Dona Valeria. Bemvinda."*

OK, I understood that one, I thought with pride.

"Duas caipirinhas," Valeria requested.

"It's a shame Lygia could not make it today," I said. I tried my best to decipher the menu with my Spanish. "Why is Portuguese so damn difficult?"

She laughed, "It takes time. Like everything worth anything does. I am certain Lygia would much rather be here than with Antonio at the club. I'm certain César, my ex, is there as well. How nice that sounds. My ex."

"Was he that bad?"

"He is a scumbag. A truly duplicitous crook," she snapped. "He made his fortune at Petrobras. Now he is the secretary of infrastructure projects for Rio de Janeiro state. You can only imagine the deals that trickle into his pockets. He and Lygia's husband are close friends and conduct much business together. They golf regularly at the Itanhangá Club across town. We always used to travel and do things as a group."

"Doesn't sound like much fun for Lygia now," I said.

"She is a tough lady. That girl has one busy schedule. It's not easy to carry around all that notoriety."

"How do you mean?"

"Well, between the studio, the charities and her wifely duties, and being an incredible mother . . . " She trailed off, spreading her manicured fingers on the starched white tablecloth.

"Is she famous?" I asked.

Valeria's lush lashes widened as she looked me over. "You don't know! No wonder she liked you. Oh, I don't mean that poorly." She giggled apologetically. "Just turn on the TV in the evening. She is everywhere. In commercials, star of the eight o'clock soap opera, and she's often in the news and on talk shows to promote her charities in the *favelas*. My friend is a Brazilian hero."

"I had no idea." I put on my best expression of surprise. "Her fame must affect you as well, being her close friend and all."

"No, I am fine. She somehow manages to keep some things private. But I know she has not been happy for a long time. Separating from Antonio would not be as easy as it was for me to leave César. Her father, the great Jucelino de Castello-Branco, and Brasão are very close and share many business interests. It was like an old mafia-style arranged marriage, poor thing."

There was the lead I'd been waiting for. "Did you say Brasão? Antonio Brasão? I have a meeting with him tomorrow! That's Lygia's husband?"

"Oh my!" Valeria covered her mouth in horror. "I've said too much. Please forget what I have told you," she pleaded. "I always forget how small a world this can be!" Her face contorted into an expression I was sure she'd rather avoid. I noticed the little surgical scar behind her ear as she turned away, but nothing could mask her true concern for her friend.

The drinks arrived and Valeria was visibly relieved by the distraction. She held up her drink. "Tell me about yourself, T. J." Her bracelets jingled. She was intent on changing the subject.

"Brought up in Texas, moved to New York. Studied finance, worked at a couple NGOs and then landed a partnership in a venture capital firm, and here I am."

"A secretive man." She observed me, tapping her fingers on the tablecloth impatiently.

"I've been doing what I do for a very long time, and with that comes a lot of travel and long absences." I casually rolled up my sleeves. "It's hard to keep a relationship going that way."

"I used to think that might be lonely, but now, I relish the possibility of it."

"It has its pros and cons. When you have a passion for what you do, that comes first."

She tilted her head. "There is no point in fighting destiny. Your calling always propels you. If you fight it you become lost in life, I believe that."

"Well, what is your calling? Yesterday, you two were talking about fabric choices for Lygia. Let me guess, you are an interior decorator," I said, turning the tables.

Her carefully tweezed eyebrows arched. "Very good. It is hard work but I love it. You are very perceptive." She took the menu from my hands. "Shall I help you with that?"

She handed it to the waitress and ordered the entire meal off the top of her head. It was a delicacy from beginning to end. We sampled many typically Brazilian dishes, and the desserts were a diabetic landmine. Let's just say I indulged.

As we ate, Valeria explained how her Aunt Giselle had been a famous decorator to the aristocratic European set in Rio. Following her parents' tragic death in a plane accident over their plantation in Mato Grosso, Valeria fell under Giselle's auspices. This gal's family hadn't come to town two to a mule: as the sole heiress to one of Brazil's great coffee fortunes, Valeria might never have worked at all had she not developed pride in her talent for it. After fifteen years in the business, she'd rightfully inherited her aunt's prestige.

"But in recent years, I began thinking to myself that my work was just an escape from my day-to-day imprisonment. My passion lay elsewhere. It was the reason for my divorce, really." She leaned forward. "I will tell you something, and you can do with it what you want." She paused engagingly. "I have a gift. I can see things. Things that have not yet happened, or are happening, mostly with the assistance of tarot cards." She held up her hand. "Don't worry, I'm not nuts. I have a huge following of clients who swear by me and trust me. They all run in our circles. I give readings regularly, twice a week at my studio in Leme by appointment. That's also where I office my design business."

"How does that lead to divorce?" I asked, beginning to question Valeria's sanity.

"I could not take it anymore. César couldn't get away with anything. I always knew when he lied. And everything at home and in public was a lie. Not just because a little voice told me." She imitated little Danny Torrance's finger speaking to him. I laughed. She was pretty funny.

"I have an understanding about people. I feel things. César was mixed up in bad business. I knew he was up to something when the phone calls became constant and he had to always leave the room to speak privately. How can so many secrets be for anything good?"

She rolled her eyes up as they welled with tears and she dabbed them with her napkin. "I'm so melodramatic! Do excuse this silliness." She sighed and recomposed herself. "It's all still so fresh. Oh, what a relief to be out of *that*. I cannot survive around so much negative energy. I become unwell." Valeria sat up straight, heaving a heavy sigh. "I didn't want to know what he was mixed up in. I didn't care. I couldn't stand his touch anymore. I just wanted out. And let me tell you"—she tapped her index finger rapidly on the tabletop—"it is a blessing that I never had children with that man. *Deus e grande*. Life goes on and begins again."

"Sounds like you've been through a difficult ordeal. But, OK, I need an example of your special talents. Tell me something," I challenged her.

"*Cafezinho* first!" she said, holding up her finger for the waitress.

"I suppose you read tarot for Lygia?"

"Of course!"

The *cafezinhos* were steaming in their tiny little cups when they were served. Valeria downed the black liquid in one gulp.

"It's really all about energy and recognizing different vibrations. That is what affects our interpretation of the cards. Now, put out your hands and let's see what your energy brings to mind."

I looked around to see if anyone was paying attention to us. Feeling a little silly, I reached forward and let Valeria turn my palms upward. She held her palms over mine, barely touching.

"*Ai!*" She snatched them away and jumped back in her seat. A shadow fell over her expression; that green-eyed gaze flashed in my mind.

"What is it? Are you OK?" I sat straighter, alarmed. Again I glanced around me, a bit freaked out by her reaction. I'll tell y'all, it was downright spooky.

"I sense danger all around you! Are you in danger?" she asked, her brown eyes wide ovals.

I stared at her in disbelief.

"What did you see?" I asked, forcing a controlled tone.

"T. J., what are you doing here in Rio?" Valeria tilted her head and examined me anew.

"I'm an investor looking for good opportunities for my firm. I don't see how the boring world of finance could be so dangerous, outside of a boardroom, that is."

She shook her head slowly. "There is something else. There is danger around you. I felt it."

"That's nonsense." I sat back. I felt the tingling of hairs rising on my arms. Spooky, I thought again. Valeria pointed at my tensed skin.

"Goose bumps are a sign of confirmation," she told me with a nod. "I'm not offended, I promise." She tossed her curls back. "I'd be happy to give you a reading one of these days. There is obviously much more to you than meets the eye."

I cleared my throat, trying to ignore how unnerved I still felt by this turn of the conversation. I changed the subject back to her. "You were saying that this gift of yours is the reason for your divorce?"

"Oh yes. You see, I started a center for metaphysical research and practice in Copacabana. I found this great little old colonial house with a Spanish tiled roof, inner courtyards with fountains, all this Zen energy. A small oasis of peace and light I named Vila Paraíso. I brought together several leaders of different concentrations of study, including astrology, numerology, dowsing, and tarot card reading, kabala studies, meditation, energy healing—the list is long. My idea was to combine all of these different esoteric and homeopathic disciplines that share like-minded philosophies under one roof."

Valeria paused and motioned for another *cafezinho* and this time they came with sugar-dusted butter cookies. I didn't really think she needed much more caffeine or sugar, but honestly I'll say I was becoming intrigued. Cuckoo or not, it sounded like a big undertaking.

"Today, it is one of the main centers in all of Brazil for metaphysical studies and services. People come from far and wide to find fulfillment in their lives, to learn to help themselves and understand the nature of their spirituality. There are, of course, many other mediums at the center who have different talents. Mine just happens to be tarot and reading people's energy. This may sound strange to you, but some incorporate spirits in order to relay messages to individuals from the other side. Others heal with energy. It is quite remarkable."

Once again I was speechless, and she laughed.

"No, really it is! Just last month an article was published in a local news magazine, about how our center was helping the police solve certain crimes. Anyway, my ex-husband, César, wanted nothing to do with the center. He was embarrassed by my gift, he thought I was crazy. But as the center gained notoriety, he became intolerable about how it would affect his political career, ruin his reputation. He made me choose between him and it, and that, my friend, was not a difficult choice for me." Valeria reclined against her seat back, arms folded, with a satisfactory look.

"Anyway, like I said, if you're interested I'll read for you at my studio sometime. I'll even give you a tour of the Vila. I know that to foreigners all of this is very unusual sounding, but here in Brazil these practices are common. On that note, my dear, I have a reading at two this afternoon, so I must dispatch myself. Can my chauffeur drop you anywhere?"

"Oh, thanks, I've got my own waiting downstairs." I rose and helped her out of her chair. "Seriously, thank you so much for all your help this morning. I'll look like a new man. And lunch was fun and . . . enlightening to say the least."

As Rodrigues took me back to my apartment, he drove along the lagoon instead of along the beach.

"Today is Sunday," he explained. "The east-bound lane of the avenue is closed to vehicles and open only to pedestrians. Everybody goes to the beach."

Warm sand might be just the thing to take the chill off my skin—I could still feel goose bumps. "Rodrigues, do you believe in the occult? Mysticism, that sort of thing?"

"On New Year's Eve I throw white roses into the ocean as an offering to Iemanjá, the goddess of the sea." He looked curiously at me through the rearview mirror.

"And most people believe in this here?"

"Yes, most people do. I sometimes go to spiritual centers to ask for help with something or other. But so does everyone. My wife and mother-in-law are very involved at their center. Some call it white magic, some call it Candomblé, or Macumba. Whatever it is, there is something to it."

"White magic," I mused, shaking my head. "Tell me about it."

"Well, Candomblé and Macumba are a mix of African mysticism and Christianity that the slaves developed in Salvador, Brazil's first capital in the northeast. They were forced to convert to Catholicism. Their priests, *Orixás*, are possessed by spirits through trance-inducing dances and drums. You make offerings and sacrifices to the spirits when you ask for help. In return, they offer healing and guidance."

As Rodrigues turned down the street toward the apartment, I wondered about the faceless eyes I'd seen earlier, writing it off as paranoia. I felt the chill again. How did Valeria know I faced danger? Her reaction had been so believable, the way in which she recoiled. How much more could she know?

CHAPTER SEVEN

I poured myself some more of that açaí juice Jovelina'd made for me. From my balcony, I watched the activity along Ipanema Beach on a Sunday afternoon. Cool *Cariocas* were out on bikes and skateboards. Friends and families strolled along the mosaic sidewalks and on the closed lane of the boulevard, enjoying the sunshine and the beautiful landscape. Every kiosk was filled with revelers. On the beach, volleyball and soccer matches were in play. I admired the athletes' agility and precision. They perspired under the hot summer sun, occasionally diving into the sand for a save. All ethnicities mixed on the beach, and I felt an urge to descend from my perch and join in.

I'd been glancing at Zezé's picture. I had a hunch this kid could be an important piece of the puzzle. He'd been allowed to live, and Sergio from the Shalimar thought that he might have been in on the minister's murder somehow. Not that much hope should ride on what a buffoon like that thought. But I wanted to find Zezé and see for myself.

Back inside, I leaned against the console and the

drawer-pull pendant jingled, reminding me of Marcos' phone number inside. Marcos would know where the gay beach was. I pulled the drawer open, grabbed the Post-It and dialed his number.

"*Aló?*" he answered.

"Hey, Marcos, its T. J., the American from the beach the other day."

"Hi, T. J.!" he exclaimed, as if hearing from a long lost friend. "How are you?"

"I just got in from some shopping and was thinking of going to the beach. Are you free to join me?"

"How funny you ask. I'm on my way to the gym and then go there afterwards, around two thirty. It's a nice gym and I can get you a guest pass if you want to have a workout first."

"Sure. Tell me where." I grabbed a pencil and wrote down the info.

"It's only couple of blocks from the fun part of the beach."

Cute accent. "I'll see you there in about an hour," I said.

"Great! *'Ta legal. Tchau!*"

I slipped on a pair of shorts over my bathing suit and put on a tank top, grabbed some SPF and headed out. After walking a block along the beach, I turned inland. I went into one of the street-side newsstands, seduced by the pretty postcards hanging vertically in long plastic display sleeves. I picked a couple to send to my mom and my sister's kids, a bunch of rascals. Lygia's face smiled up at me from a stack of magazines at my feet.

Arriving at the gym, I took the stairs up to the reception desk. I told the girl behind the counter I was a friend of Marcos', and she lit up with a smile.

"Yes, American, right? He say you come." She pressed the button to let me through the turnstile and pointed the way to the weight room.

I walked down the hall, peeked into the spin class

and waved at him. He was leading it—he worked here. I'd not asked what Marcos did for a living. Actually, I'd not asked Marcos anything much other than to invite him up to the apartment for a good time. He waved back with a broad grin when he saw me. Yep, he was as hot as I recalled. He was pedaling furiously to empowering music and leading the group with his headset microphone.

I had a decent workout in the weight room until Marcos finished his class and came out to greet me.

"I'm so happy you called," he said. "Honestly, I did not think you would." He leaned forward for a hug.

"That was fun the other day, so who better than you to show me around Ipanema?"

"OK, when you finish, we take a quick shower and go to the gay beach, you have to see it to believe it. Whether you are gay or straight, it is quite the scene, especially on Sunday afternoons."

I looked around the gym, a mixed environment, although I did notice plenty of studly guys pumping up. It was a clean gym, and I could work out here and not be recognized by anyone too high-society.

"Does the gym offer monthly memberships?"

"Absolutely. Do you want to sign up?"

"Yes."

"What a shame. You join now that I leaving."

"Where are you going?" I couldn't help sounding disappointed.

"To Salvador. I am helping the owner start a new health club for this chain there. I leave in a couple of days."

I signed up at the front desk, and we headed out of the gym. We turned down a cute street lined with old gnarled trees and open-air restaurants that seemed to serve a mostly gay clientele.

"It's easy to find the gay beach, it is opposite this street you see." Marcos pointed at the rainbow flags snapping in the breeze at the end of the block.

We crossed the avenue, kicked off our shoes and walked onto the sand. There were several service tents lined up along the sidewalk, each offering chairs and parasols for rent. Marcos pointed at one. The banner read BARRACA DA SONIA.

"That one is my favorite. Sonia makes the best *caipirinhas* of all. Not too sweet, not too tart."

The sand was hot under my toes but Marcos seemed unfazed by it. Sonia greeted him warmly. *"Aí Gostosão, tudo bem?"*

More greeting kisses and two chairs later, we were seated on the beach. I watched Marcos get out of his clothes. His beautiful brown skin was taut over his flexed muscles. He tucked his items under his chair.

"Always keep your stuff close to you. You would be amazed how quickly things can disappear on the beach." I took note that this was my second warning about theft. Things got snatched up fast, whether in a high-end shopping mall or on the beach.

Sonia soon came to take our order of *caipirinhas*. Marcos entertained me with stories about the characters surrounding us on the beach. Every couple of minutes, somebody would come up to greet him. He'd stand up, kiss and hug, introduce me, chatter for a minute in Portuguese, and sit down again.

After the third time, I asked, "Do you know everyone here?"

"Everyone knows everyone on the beach, above all on Sunday afternoons." He laughed.

Vendors of all sorts roamed around, selling beverages, sandwiches, suntan lotion and other wares. Groups of friends huddled in circles, laughing and gossiping. Some stood by, looking distractedly at the beach's offerings while they caressed their chests and posed under the hot sun. But like at the gym, even the gay beach was mixed. The gay guys were accompanied by their girlfriends, who brought their straight boyfriends in tow.

"Rio seems very tolerant and open," I said.

"It has been increasingly so. Ever since a recent *novela* had a story line about a family whose son was a closeted homosexual. The mother was played by our great Lygia de Castello-Branco. Her character was so supportive of her son that it began to change the way straight people think of us. That's how powerful the soaps are here in Brazil." He chuckled. "In the South Zone, we can openly walk hand in hand with little or no trouble, but only in certain areas, really. It's still a very macho culture."

He handed me the suntan lotion to rub on his shoulders and back. After lathering up, I sat back in the chair facing the ocean and the Two Brothers. Sonia approached with the sweet, citrusy drink and noted the cocktails on her chit pad.

"*Obrigado.*"

She smiled back and walked away.

A vendor selling sunglasses passed by and I waved him over—mine had developed a crack. We looked at different styles and Marcos picked one we both liked. I tried the pair on and checked them out in the hand-held mirror the vendor offered. I paid for them.

"These are cool. There's a little rearview mirror action on the corner goin' on here."

"That way you can keep an eye on who is checking you out! Very cool," Marcos approved.

I slurped air through the little straw and realized my cup was empty.

"You should go swimming. It's very nice and the ocean is calm today. I'll keep an eye on things." Marcos took my cup out of my hand and winked. "And order you another one of these."

"OK, but that's the last one. I'm not a big drinker." At least not until recently.

I handed Marcos my sunglasses and stretched, breathing in the sea air. I could feel several gazes following me as I walked to the ocean. The waves twinkled in the sunlight. I dove in and swam straight out. Several strokes, I rolled on to my back, floating just past the breaking point of the translucent teal waves. Looking back at Ipanema, the beach was a mass of parasols and brown bodies. The Corcovado Mountain with *Christ the Redeemer* towered majestically over the high-rises and all of this mayhem below. Mexico and New York were worlds away. The silence and waves felt like bliss. I'm certain the *caipirinha* had something to do with that too. I was startled by a flying fish that jumped suddenly out of the water over me, its silvery wet scales glistening. I swam for several minutes and could not help thinking of Sean. It felt odd not to be able to compare notes with him here. I swam back and walked out of the water.

Marcos greeted me with a new drink. As I sat down, he got up to take his turn.

"The water is amazing, enjoy," I said.

"I will."

Halfway to the water, another acquaintance stopped Marcos. I took a cool, tart sip and checked the scene out, hoping to find Zezé. To my left was a group of five black men in absurd shape, kicking a soccer ball back and forth. They wore colorful swim briefs that clung to their tight bodies. Bubbling curves wrapped in intricate tattoos flexed as they swayed from side to side in anticipation of the next kick.

To my right were two gay men with a lady friend having drinks and speaking rapidly to each other with much verve and gesticulation. I took another sip and my eyes locked onto Marcos' backside as he dove into the water. I was feeling the intoxication of Rio wash over me. I lay back and closed my eyes and relaxed in the hot afternoon sun, momentarily removed from the avalanche of new information I'd been under.

"Oh my God! I'd know that body anywhere! Is that you, T. J.?"

I tried to focus on the silhouetted figures before me

and to place that voice. It seemed so out of context. The *cachaça* had gone to my head. The two men squatted down, and I recognized Sean's friends from our Southampton days.

"Brent? Charles! Well, I'll be jiggered! What are y'all doing in Rio?" I sat up for a proper greeting.

"We've been here for a month," said Brent, lifting his Ray-Bans.

"We arrived just before Christmas," Charles chimed in. "We rented a lovely apartment in Copacabana, just past the Arpoador there." He pointed east. "We had a little New Year's party with some friends and watched the endless fireworks from our balcony. It was glorious. You look great, by the way."

"Thanks, so do you two." They were both pearing around the waist and Brent had lost most of his hair. "Are you guys here on vacation?"

"Actually, we are here to finalize adoption proceedings for our son, Nelson." Brent looked like he'd just played the gay trump card.

"Wow. That's a big step. Congratulations! I haven't seen you guys in ages." I realized as I said it that it was true.

"I think the last time we saw you was before the recession. You and Sean had just finished renovating your beach house."

Charles gave Brent a little kick. "Don't be so insensitive!"

Brent was a big-time realtor in the Hamptons. He and Charles lived out there full-time. They had sold us our beach house, and many years later Brent's business partner sold Sean and some other investors a large plot of land out there that was formerly a potato field. The plan had been to develop a community of plots and resell. Then the bottom fell out of the market. As Sean's financial woes compounded, the Hamptons potato field had turned into a gargantuan liability. I'll just say we never really got to enjoy our renovated kitchen much. Our beach house was one of the first things we lost, and I hadn't been back to the Hamptons since.

"What are you doing here anyway?" Brent asked, changing the subject. "Is Sean here with you?"

"Ah, no. Business trip for me, I'm afraid. Revamping one of our outreach programs here in Rio. I'll be here for several weeks at least. How about y'all? Until when are you here?"

"We finalize Nelson's papers at the American consulate early this week and then we're heading back to New York on Wednesday."

Brent and Charles gave each other a congratulatory smile and kissed.

"That's great," I said, glancing cautiously toward the ocean, not seeing Marcos anywhere. Just as I leaned back, a shadow fell over me from behind and cool water dripped on my chest. I looked up and Marcos pecked me on the lips from above and then sat in his chair. Droplets streamed down his glistening body. Brent and Charles looked at each other and then at me. Can we say awkward?

"Marcos, these are my friends Charles and Brent from the US. We just ran into each other by coincidence. Isn't that something?"

"It's a pleasure to meet you both." Marcos smiled. "Join us, please. Sonia!" he called.

I cringed inside.

Sonia glanced back at him and he motioned for two more chairs and another round.

"Thank you," said Charles, unpacking some SPF from his bag. He and Brent began slathering sunscreen onto each other. "You'd be amazed how many people from the States we've run into on the beach in the past month! It's like a circuit party."

"This beach *is* a circuit party," said Brent. "We've been coming here every Sunday since we arrived and it's like clockwork! The same cliques at about the same time every week. See, over there, those really hot black dudes with the killer bods, kicking the soccer ball around? The one sitting down is a dealer. He's the one to go to if you want some good dope. His name is Castro. Big stud of a guy."

"Thanks, boys, but I don't do that."

"Nor do we," Charles insisted. "We have to be responsible now."

"Whatever," Brent scoffed. "Just giving you the lay of the land."

Charles frowned. "He also pimps out a few of those boys. As we're fathers now, we can't condone such behavior." He smiled sweetly at Brent.

I looked over at the guy they called Castro. He was a big guy, all right. Next to him, a younger man, probably still in his late teens, was bouncing from foot to foot. Bingo.

"That's Zezé, he's one of the hustlers working the beach," said Brent. "He's a sizzler, that one, and he's here just about every evening. You can often find him at dusk roaming the Arpoador. Actually a very witty guy, and surprisingly bright. We've had very interesting conversations with him."

"I bet," I murmured.

"You guys sure know who's who here," Marcos laughed. "I'm surprised I have not seen you two before."

I was still watching Zezé. Castro had stood, and he and Zezé began to dance a capoeira. Marcos explained that it was an Afro-Brazilian dance that acrobatically mimics a wrestling match between two opponents. Another guy was playing a *berimbau* for some rhythm, similar to the instrument in my apartment. Zezé limberly sprung from a crouching swipe with his leg under Castro's passing jab. Skin barely brushed skin as they rotated around each other like moving cogs that never actually touched. The crowd of sunbathers clapped along. They ended the dance and Zezé and Castro high-fived. Zezé performed some backward flips and one-armed handstands. The crowd cheered. The kid put on quite a show.

While Marcos, Brent and Charles compared notes about the different people they saw here each Sunday, I tried to keep a discreet eye on Zezé. I watched him as he pirouetted in the sand toward another group of guys, a feat unto itself, ending in an arabesque pose that reminded me of Ferdi. Astonishingly, this kid somehow actually knew his ballet moves—had to be a secret passion for him to be so good. He said something and they all burst out laughing. He worked the beach thoroughly. Everyone seemed to know and like him as he bounced from group to group like a kangaroo, exhibiting his outrageously beautiful body and charm.

"The good ol' dollar still goes a long way to help things move along," Brent was saying when I tuned back in. In order to adopt, they'd had to convince the courts that they could provide an upbringing for the child that could never be matched by the offerings of the Brazilian social services system.

"Still, the bureaucracy involved was endless," added Charles.

"Hello, my gringo friends!" Zezé skipped up to us and checked me out. "Hello! Are you American too?"

He had tightly curled black hair and golden brown skin. But his eyes were a vivid bluish green with trippy chartreuse edging his wide pupils.

"I'm T. J., and yes, American." I smiled.

He was without a doubt a handsome and desirable young man. I couldn't help but notice the package in front of me, just at eye-level. His unthreatening sweet eyes, combined with a Hellenistic physique and that milk-chocolate skin would make him uniquely appealing to the higher-end trade he serviced. I could see why high rollers would want him.

"That's great! I always need practice English." He

smiled back. "Nice to meet you, T. J. *Aí Marcos,*" he greeted with a clenched fist bump. "I speak with these guys many time." He nodded to Brent and Charles.

Zezé stretched his muscles and slowly rubbed his chest as he spoke.

"They very funny guys! But leave soon, so no more practice for Zezé. How long you stay?" he asked me.

I was guessing he was below the drinking age in the States, but the boy was confident of his act.

"For a while. You can practice your English with me anytime."

"Very nice. See you around!"

He curled in his three middle fingers and extended his thumb and pinky in the typical Brazilian surfer-dude gesture for "cool" and bounced away to the next group.

We talked for a long while, Marcos and the guys giving me tips on where to eat, drink, dance, etc. As the sun descended, the beach emptied out. We finished our drinks with Brent and Charles and cleared our tab with Sonia. Marcos and I stood up to go. Brent gave me their local number in case I "needed anything."

I curled my toes into the fine white sand with each step. It was cool now in the early evening. Marcos said something, but I missed it because I was thinking about Sean getting the low-down from Brent, of all people. So busted.

I'd have to face that music later. What was important now was that Marcos had helped lead me to Zezé. I'd have to get to know him a bit. Maybe a couple more Sundays on the beach.

But first things first. The combination of sun, alcohol and all those sexy men was irresistible. I put my arm around Marcos' muscular shoulder as we reached the sidewalk. "How about one more evening cocktail at my place?"

CHAPTER EIGHT

I grabbed my watch from the night table and tried to focus. Seven thirty a.m. Good thing I'd forgotten to pull the blackout drapes shut. I felt a little on the foggy side as I sat up and looked around the bedroom. I guzzled down some water. Yesterday's clothing was strewn all about. A smile crossed my lips as I recalled the previous night.

But today was critical and I had to be focused. I put on shorts and running shoes and went out for my morning jog, hoping to sweat out the alcohol and step it up. I ran east this time, along the beach all the way to the far side of Copacabana, a neighborhood called Leme. I wondered which of the apartment buildings Valeria's office might be located in. I reached the hill at the end of the beach. A gigantic Brazilian flag snapped high upon its top. I turned around and headed back, suddenly feeling reinvigorated.

I was certain that Valeria would have called Lygia immediately after our lunch to let her know I'd be meeting with her husband today. This morning would be a test to see if Lygia was a potential ally or not. I figured that if Brasão mentioned that he'd heard we'd met at the club, Lygia might not be of use to me. But if he didn't, she must be keeping our meeting from him for some reason of her own.

I showered and pulled out a couple of my new suits and chose one. They had been tailored yesterday with Valeria, and delivered to the building by the end of the day. I folded my pocket square and tucked it in. Once I slid my tie knot into place, I had to admit I looked like a million bucks. I pulled out my briefcase and loaded it with a prospectus on IVC, a few brochures and a client list. I packed in literature about Brasão's projects that I'd be soliciting and called downstairs to have Rodrigues bring the car around. No gun today.

I got in the BMW, said good morning to Rodrigues, and we rode off. Once downtown, we drove past the Municipal Theater, a spectacular structure blending Classicism and Beaux-Arts. We pulled up to Brasão's imposing building, towering adjacent to the Municipal, as the theater was locally referred. I noticed the pile of rubble from the collapsed buildings covering the side street, and the heavy machinery being used to clear it.

Past security, I took the elevator up to the top floor. The polished steel plaque read *Corporações Brasão, SA* in bold laser-cut Copperplate font. A coat of arms was neatly branded in the thick olivewood double doors; the embossed design was the outline of a dragon. How appropriate. I took a deep breath and steadied myself before entering.

The reception area was contemporary and minimalist, appointed with Barcelona chairs and ottomans, a sleek glass coffee table and vintage mid-century accessories. On the wall hung a fantastic Fernand Léger painting depicting an abstracted construction site with muscular workmen in colorful hard hats working on crisscrossing cranes and girders. I approached the pretty receptionist and speculated that Valeria had designed the offices. If so, she was very good.

"*Bom dia*, I'm T. J. Leukemeyer here to see Mr. Antonio Brasão." I smiled and handed her a business card.

"*Bom dia*. Mr. Brasão is expecting you. Please have a seat while I announce your arrival."

She smiled and gestured gracefully toward the seating area.

"What may I call you? I suspect this will be the first of many visits."

"Christina, *Seu* Leukemeyer. You may call me Christina." Her cute little dimples reddened.

She walked to the end of the corridor to knock on Mr. Brasão's door. While she stepped away, I went over to the window behind her desk. The reception area looked out over the beautiful downtown punctuated by the coppergreen and gilded rooftop of the Municipal below. The sea of tall buildings extended to the edge of the bay, where planes took off and landed consistently at the airport in the foreground. Opaque mountain ranges far across the water added to the striking view. I made sure the recorder app on my phone was on and placed it in my pocket. I breathed steadily and focused on my mission.

"Despite what Americans care to believe, it was not the Wright Brothers who first took to the air," said a baritone voice behind me. I turned.

"It was actually our dear Brazilian pilot Alberto Santos-Dumont who took flight on October 19, 1901, flying around the Eiffel Tower in Paris." He twirled his finger in the air as he approached. "He is the namesake of our domestic airport down there. I am Antonio Brasão, welcome to my office and welcome to Rio, Mr. Leukemeyer." Brasão extended his well-manicured hand with a firm, encompassing shake; one that meant business. "We are so honored that you have come all this way to meet with us."

He carefully observed my suit, my shoes, hands and face.

"Thank you, Mr. Brasão. I'll tell ya, I've been looking forward to our meeting with great expectations."

"I am delighted to hear that."

He had a slight Brazilian accent overlaying his British-educated English. The man was impeccably dressed. Aristocratic nobility was what came to mind. He wore a grey suit that complemented his receded salt-and-pepper hair. He had the belly of a man who enjoyed good living, yet he was not in poor shape. His face was tan and handsome. And he had a most engaging smile. His eyes, I noted, were steel grey and undecipherable; pleasing from afar, somewhat unnerving up close.

I looked down at the roof of the Municipal. "Well, isn't that something special."

Our gaze moved to the rubble slowly being cleared away alongside of it.

"That there, however's, just a big ol' mess," I said.

"It is. I was here that night, working late in the office, when the entire building shook. We thought it was collapsing. We looked outside in time to see the plume of dust and smoke surround the neighborhood. Just terrible." He shook his head. "Some imbecile cuts out a weight-bearing column where he shouldn't and now the entire Rio de Janeiro building code will have more stringent regulations! But life goes on." Brasão led me down the corridor and motioned to Christina with his pinched thumb and forefinger raised to his lips as we passed. She nodded.

"Allow me to present you to our gang." We walked into his boardroom. A long, finely polished table made of some rare tropical wood was backed by large windows overlooking the airport and the bay. An impressive and ethereal Cy Twombly painting hung on the back wall. The man was a collector. I wondered if my art history might come in handy. Three gentlemen rose to greet me as Brasão made the introductions.

"T. J. Leukemeyer, this is my strategic consultant,

Danilo Adolfo Camargo de Lemos. I don't make a move without his opinion." Danilo extended his hand.

"Mr. Roberto Barroso Simões-Filho is our corporate lawyer."

"A pleasure to meet you, Mr. Leukemeyer."

"And last but not least, my dear friend, the Secretary of Infrastructure Projects for the State of Rio de Janeiro, César Siqueira de Mendonça."

"A pleasure." César nodded.

What was it Valeria had said? *He is a scumbag, a truly duplicitous crook.*

"Please all, do sit down," said Brasão. "As with all our meetings, I ask that all present power down their phones in order to avoid interruptions." He laid his own phone on the table. The others did as well.

I turned off my phone with the secret recording app still running and placed it on the table too.

"I wish to welcome you, Mr. Leukemeyer, and thank you for coming all this way to discuss investing in some of our projects. As I am sure you have a busy schedule, please allow me to give you the floor so you can present your purpose and intentions."

"Thank you. And thank you for receiving me so readily. Let me begin by congratulating you and your firm for securing the bids for these prestigious projects. As you gentlemen know, I'm here representing my company, International Venture Capital."

I pulled out a few brochures and handed one to each of them.

"We represent a twenty-five-billion-dollar venture capital fund of elite investors. I'm here to search for long-term lucrative investment opportunities. Gentlemen, we look to invest big money in mega-projects for big returns. I've thoroughly read the publicly disclosed information regarding your developments and I'm curious to learn more."

"Surely, Mr. Leukemeyer, you understand that as a

public-private partnership, all financing bids are to be tendered in the coming weeks and the opportunity to compete with standard terms is open to all those interested," tested César. "For us to arrange preferential terms with your firm at this stage, before the bidding process, would not be quite, how do you say in English? Above board."

There was an uncomfortable silence. I looked at each of these men steadily, sizing them up. César's squint held an unpious glint. Danilo's bore directly at me—no-nonsense with this guy. Brasão leaned forward, awaiting the next jab.

"Gentlemen, let me tell y'all something about myself. I'm Texan by upbringing, and one thing we Texans don't do is beat around the bush. I wrote to Mr. Brasão to meet with him privately. To learn more about these projects and to negotiate terms that were mutually beneficial. Let's not play games, fellows. If *above board* is how you play, then why am I here with all y'all as well?"

César held my gaze.

"Mr. Mendonça, why else would a man of your public standing and position be at this meeting other than to be included in a mutually beneficial arrangement?" I shrugged. "Your mere presence here tells me what I need to know. You boys play ball. It may be soccer instead of football or baseball, but it's still a game. And we all want to be on the winning side, now don't we?" I smiled across at them. They studied me skeptically.

César and Danilo had an exchange in Portuguese and looked to Brasão.

Brasão looked at both disapprovingly. "Now you are both being rude to our guest." He turned to me. "As sound businessmen, we are always open to developing new opportunities. Mr. Leukemeyer, tell us what you have in mind." Brasão leafed through the IVC brochure. "And believe me, Mr. Leukemeyer, we have studied your background carefully prior to accepting this meeting. Interestingly, you manage to keep much off the Internet."

"Yes, Mr. Leukemeyer, please proceed and tell us of your proposal," said Danilo.

The tension in the room dissipated. César sat back, nodding for me to speak.

"Thank you, gentlemen. Yes, Mr. Brasão, that is true. I value my privacy and go to great lengths to keep it, as I imagine you value yours. I've reviewed your plans for the Olympic Park and Village developments on Lake Jacarepaguá. Our firm feels there is great potential for returns in those construction projects. We also feel there is a gold mine to be had with the Porto Maravilha project. We're prepared to offer you excellent terms that won't be matched by competing bidders." I looked at César. "Once we complete negotiations, individual monetary donations will be made to the necessary parties' accounts of your choosing. In exchange we ask that in addition to interest revenue on our terms, you provide a five percent return on all future revenues earned by the sites' concessions. We are ready to invest a half billion in each project."

Brasão clasped both hands in front of him and nodded. "That seems most generous, Mr. Leukemeyer. I'm eager to hear about your unbeatable terms."

I merely nodded.

"Well, the Porto Maravilha project you speak of encompasses the view just outside these windows." Brasão pointed. "Do you see the decrepit nature of urbanity stretching from the airport past the overpass, all along the waterfront north of town? All of that will be revitalized and reclaimed. We are planning residential towers, malls, parks and bayside boardwalk promenades, restaurants and cultural institutions. It will become one of the most sought-after neighborhoods in Rio, right next to downtown, on the bay, safe, clean and livable once again. We are funding the renovation of twelve colonial edifices that are part of Rio's heritage, including the Palacio Fiscal you see out in the water. It's that graceful green castle-island in front of the bridge."

"I see it. It's a beauty," I said. Looked like a pistachio-colored Disney castle.

César Mendonça chimed in. "It will make *Cariocas* proud of their downtown once again. I would not have approved the project if I did not think it was a masterfully planned approach."

I bet.

"Mr. Leukemeyer, what exactly do you require for your due diligence?" asked Simões-Filho, the lawyer.

"I'd like to tour all the sites and meet with all the bidding contractors. Review all contracts concerning ownership of the land, governing construction and consequent commercialization of concessions to support the venues. I need to see everything that affects the risk associated with our investment and the value of our returns."

Christina walked in with the *cafezinho* and poured one for each of us.

"That is quite a bit of work, Mr. Leukemeyer," said Brasão.

"It is why I'm already on first name terms with Christina." I smiled at her. She blushed and closed the door behind her.

"Yes, Christina is marvelous." He laughed. "All right, Mr. Leukemeyer, I like your style. You mean business and get straight to the point. We will review your offer. Danilo will work up a schedule to fulfill your due-diligence requirements and work closely with you on getting the information you need to finalize your decision. Would you care to join us tomorrow at the Itanhangá Golf Club for breakfast to continue this conversation? Followed perhaps by a tour of the future Olympic Park and Village?"

"That sounds like a plan, my schedule's open for you."

"Well then, gentlemen, that concludes this meeting." Brasão slapped his palm on the table and rose. "We look forward to developing this relationship." He shook my hand again, cupped it with his other and looked at me directly, nodding his head. "Yes, I think we will understand each other well, Mr. Leukemeyer."

"You bet, 'specially if you call me T. J."

"Of course, of course, please call me Antonio."

Brasão accompanied me to the reception.

"I'll give you five bucks for the Léger," I joked, gesturing toward the painting.

His guffaw was genuine. "See you at the club tomorrow, ten a.m.?"

The doors closed. I loosened my tie and let out a deep breath. I was sweating and my heart was racing. I left the building feeling simultaneously exhilarated and a bit unnerved. I texted Rodrigues that I'd meet him in ten minutes. I walked past the rubble. The bulldozers were pulling out mangled rebar and concrete chunks from the wreckage, sounding their reverse-beeping alarms. A couple of desecrated laptops poked out from the debris, a reminder of the computer programming class that had been taking place inside that evening.

I rounded a few corners, walking rapidly, looking over my shoulder to make sure I wasn't being followed. Now that we had officially met, I couldn't discount the possibility that Brasão might have me cased. From here on out, I'd need to take extra care. At the end of a tree-lined pedestrian street filled with old colonial and office buildings, I came to a small park. I sat on a shaded bench, concealed by an ornate fountain, and kept a lookout for anyone suspicious. I pulled out my phone. I turned it on, willing my pulse to slow, and dialed 555. I leaned back, smiling, and crossed my legs as if I were sharing the news of a successful meeting with a business partner.

"T. J.?" Adriana answered.

"Yes."

"Are you alone in a safe place?"

"Of course."

"How did it go?"

"I think I'm in. We're having breakfast at the Itanhangá Club tomorrow and then they're showing me the site of the Olympic Park. Intriguingly enough, César was there, which means they were expecting to conduct an underhanded deal with me this morning. There's no way he would have been at this initial meeting otherwise. There's something else."

"What is it?"

"If you aren't already monitoring Danilo, you should be. He runs a consulting firm and seems to be an important ally of Brasão's. I got a pretty strong feeling he does much of the dirty work. Perhaps we should have him under surveillance, I think he could be an important link."

"Yes, we are watching him closely."

"Ronaldo was right about Lygia. Antonio had no idea we'd met, or that I'd met his son."

"She may also be testing you."

"True." I paused. "I also learned from Lygia and Valeria that they and Carla Alcântara were close enough friends that she turned to the Brasãos for solace after her husband's death. She's supposedly fled to Miami because she couldn't get over the humiliation of her circumstances."

"I doubt she would have had much knowledge of their dealings. Brasão is a cautious man. Be on guard with him." She hesitated. "I just had a meeting with Ronaldo. He was upset about some files that have gone missing from his office. He thinks someone broke in several days ago, maybe more; he's not sure how long they've been missing. He said there could be a mole on our task force." Anxiety shadowed her voice. "Ronaldo is distraught. The confirmation that we may not be able to trust one of our own. Your identity is safe, though. There are no files of any kind about you, physically or digitally. The only people who know your identity in this operation are Ronaldo and me. And Thomas Bradley."

"I understand. What was in the files?"

"Some financial transactions regarding our operation, but like I said, nothing that could affect you."

I wasn't fully convinced.

"Hey, Adriana?"

"Yes?"

"What are the chances of me getting my own car so I can escape without Rodrigues from time to time?"

"I don't know if that is a good idea."

"I need the freedom to move as I see fit. Having a driver at all times can bring unwanted attention. And I may need to get around after hours. I'm sure you and Ronaldo understand."

"I'll bring it up to him."

I shut off the phone, walked back toward the car, and Rodrigues drove me back to Ipanema.

CHAPTER NINE

The gym was fairly empty at this late afternoon hour, the way I like it best. Marcos wasn't here. I finished a rep and moved on to the treadmill for some cardio, thinking about what I'd learned in the last couple of days. On the murder side of things, I knew that Zezé was somehow involved and could be important to finding a connection. I knew that the Brasãos had been very close with the Alcântaras and that Brasão was largely responsible for the minister's success. I had no doubt that Brasão and César were involved in corrupt dealings that tied into political power plays. I suspected this Danilo guy was a key part of Brasão's operations. I also suspected that Lygia did not like her husband; but was she aware that his business dealings extended to drug trafficking?

If Brasão wanted the minister dead for double-crossing him, the order must have followed a trail between him and the murderer. Why would the murderer have let Zezé live if he wasn't in on it? Zezé was the key.

Brasão was a sophisticated gentleman, as Valeria had said. I was sure any culpability was as far removed from him as a field mouse skirting a rattlesnake. Nothing would easily link directly to him. Danilo, however, was, as Brasão himself had said, his right-hand man. There was a bit of a rough edge to his character.

"Excuse me, towel?"

It was the girl from the front desk. I was dripping sweat on the treadmill.

"Thank you. Hey, is Marcos still around?"

"No, this morning was last class. I think he leave tomorrow for Salvador." She frowned. "Have good workout." She walked back to the front and I soon hit the showers.

Afterward, I had a fresh smoothie at a corner juice bar. As I lay a few *real* coins on the counter, the glint of sunlight off my ring reminded me of Sean and our uncertain future. I suppose Marcos' departure was for the best; he'd served his purpose, and then some. I decided I'd head on over to Arpoador and look for Zezé.

I followed the beach a couple of blocks to the rocky outcrop at its end. Many people lined the dirt paths along the edge to watch the sunset, still a couple hours away. Further in, the trails got a bit questionable, kind of like the Rambles in Central Park, but on steroids. Loitering men solicited both drugs and themselves.

"*Aí Gostosão!*" one guy called out to me. He stood by a series of exercise stations set against the rocks at the bottom of the path. I smiled but kept walking. Then I saw Zezé just ahead, but he'd seen me first.

"T. J.!" He remembered my name from our brief encounter. A good sign. "What you doing here?"

"I could ask you the same."

Zezé was wearing tight white jeans that accentuated his very well shaped muscular thighs and butt, among other assets. He wore new sneakers, a baseball cap that said *Rock 'n' Rio* and a T-shirt with a silver chain hanging over it.

"I work here my friend. You shopping?" He flashed his teeth.

He was adorable in a very bad-boy kind of way.

"Just strolling," I replied. "Hey, take a break and walk with me."

"Sure, friend. You from New York like Charlie and Brent?"

"I am, but originally from Texas."

"That for why you English sound different."

"Your English is pretty damn good."

"It help to make tourists more *confortável*, less nervous, you know?"

"Sounds like a tough life."

"It not so bad. I love sex, so it OK." He casually adjusted his crotch. "I usually only work here, so most of guys are rich or foreign. I have few regular too. It safer that way. What you do, T. J.?"

"I'm in finance. Here on business, actually."

"Big money in Brazil now. Lots foreigners lately. Business up for everybody in South Zone!" He laughed. "Including for me. New York sound like very cool place. I like see one day."

"Maybe you will. How old are you, Zezé?" I asked.

"I eighteen."

"How long have you been doing this line of work?"

"Oh I guess 'bout four or five year." Zezé shrugged as if that were no big deal.

I looked at the kid and thought of all he could be if life had dealt him a better hand.

"Do you mind me asking these questions? It's very interesting to me."

He smiled and put his hand on my shoulder. "You can ask me anything."

"How about you spend the evening with me? Take me around and show me a few sights. I don't know anybody here and would enjoy your company. I'll pay for everything, dinner, drinks, even for your time. Name your price. No sex, just for some friendly fun."

"Why no sex? You married and no cheat or something?" He seemed disappointed.

"Or something," I said. "What do you say? I'm here alone, don't know anyone really." I handed him two $100 bills.

"Sure, T. J. where you like go?" He beamed.

"Somewhere you think is special."

"That easy. Have you go Pão de Açucar, Sugar Loaf?"

"Not yet."

"It have beautiful view of Rio. We go there, for sunset, for food and drink at top."

We walked back up the hill toward the street and then strolled over to Copacabana, chatting about the different characters at the gay beach along the way. I couldn't be certain, but I felt like we were being watched. We were in a cruising area, so I suppose that was to be expected. At the avenue, we jumped into a cab. The sun was low in the horizon and lots of people were out for their evening jogs along the beach.

"Why no sex with me?" Zezé asked again as the cab moved haltingly down the seaside avenue. "It no make sense."

"I just want some company and to hear about you. I'm taking a break from sex," I said.

"Come on, friend, I rent boy. Not much tell you." He laughed.

"Are you from Rio?" I asked.

"No, I from Ceará in the northeast of Brazil. Father in jail, so my mother come Rio like everybody else for work. I four, my sister six. We come stay in family house in Vidigal. She cleaning lady in building somewhere in Leblon, and I always keep get trouble. She say go, leave house when she know I sell sex on beach."

"That's tough, buddy. You must be very lonely."

"Lonely? I have many friends, I make good money," he said, clutching at his thick silver chain. "Not so bad."

We pulled up to the Sugar Loaf base station, got out, and I bought a couple of tickets. Once in the cable car, Zezé lit up.

"I always love come here. It long time, but view is best Rio."

The cable car rose swiftly to the first hump. I studied the people around us, still feeling on edge. We walked around the tree-covered park, looking out at the views of Copacabana and the Atlantic. I bought ice-cream cones that we licked while we strolled.

"When were you last here?" I asked.

"About two year, I work for powerful man in government. I have few of them regular. He ask me entertain friend, French man. That last time. He very nice. Like you." He licked his ice cream somewhat lasciviously.

We made our way to the second cable car and began our ascent to the top of the Sugar Loaf Mountain. The cable car was full of tourists watching as Rio spread out below in the dimming evening light. Zezé casually put his arm on my shoulder and said, "This is place of God. So much beautiful. New York is pretty place too?"

"Not nearly as beautiful as here. Just a lot of very tall buildings."

"Like in movies, I see many time. Empire Stay Building, so tall, like Pão de Açucar!"

"Maybe not quite as tall as this," I said.

The doors opened at the top and we walked over to the rail at the edge of the park. The height was dizzying with the city so far below. Zezé held up his hand. "Picture! You got have this picture! Do you have phone?"

I handed my phone over to him and he took a couple shots. I took some of him too. Zezé seemed to be having a good time posing for me when a passing man who'd ridden up the cable car with us offered to take our picture together. He held my phone outstretched in front of his crooked nose and we posed and smiled.

Zezé pointed out different areas of Rio. It was a beautiful evening and the sun was just now setting beyond Ipanema. He pointed to Vidigal, beginning to twinkle in the distance. "That where I live," he said. Fireworks went off over the *favela* again. "That tell everybody new drug arrive," Zezé explained.

"What do you mean?"

"People say *favela* now safe. UPP take care of everything. But that not true. Drug still happening there."

We sat down at a little café overlooking the view. The waiter came and while Zezé ordered some Brazilian appetizers, I discreetly turned on the recording app on my smartphone and placed it in my shirt pocket. He would need to trust me in order to spill the beans about that night.

Zezé explained what he had ordered. He said his mother used to make them to sell on the beach. They were called *pasteis*, deep-fried half-shell dough pouches with ground beef or cheese fillings, and *coxinhas*, made with fried ground chicken and potatoes. Like finger foods in Mexico, but with a Brazilian twist.

He pointed at the word on the menu. I noted that the *nh* sounded like the Spanish ñ, a linguistic "aha" moment.

They were accompanied by deliciously refreshing *caipirinhas*. I was really getting hooked on these li'l devils.

"I've gotta tell ya, you sure put on a show at that beach. Some of your moves seem like you were a trained dancer. Hell, buddy, you're like a pro. At least you could be."

Zezé sat back with a barely audible sigh and looked toward the horizon. "I wish could be different. I wish I could be dancer. That my true dream." My hunch had been right. His demeanor instantly changed from cool hipster to longing. His expression relaxed and innocent wishfulness augmented his beauty.

"I used watch ballet on TV and practice what I see. I used go often to ballet studio in Leblon and watch lesson from window and practice at home by self. But then I meet man in Cantagalo *favela* who give lesson to little girls there on street. He teach me too and I help teach them. I pretty good. But reality so difficult." He looked at the ground and nodded his head. "So I just do what I love much after that." He winked at me.

"I've got some very close friends on the board at Juilliard in New York. Someone like you would have a chance at an international scholarship."

"I no understand 'Juilliard.'"

"Juilliard is one of the best ballet schools in New York, perhaps the world. Google it. If it's really your dream, I could possibly pull some strings to make it happen."

"You play with me."

"I'm very serious. I'm sure you have more than enough talent."

"You really think so?" His hopeful eyes fixed on mine.

"You never know when something can change your life forever. You've had a rough time. Maybe you deserve a break. It's important to do something you love."

"Yes, my life no so easy."

We fell silent for a moment. "I have no idea what a *favela* is like. Tell me about it."

"You want know 'bout *favela*, it's lots people living one on top other. But not so bad. More stealing out here than in there. That for sure!" He laughed. "Everyone good in *favela*, or else deal with Malandrão punish," he said, wide-eyed. "He crazy man, no trust."

Zezé had warmed up to me. He was clearly showing me his softer side. I felt a good vibe from him, but I reminded myself to be on guard. My instincts had failed me miserably recently and my trust in them had faltered.

"You very nice. *Obrigado* for food and *caipirinha*." He swallowed the last morsel hungrily and looked at me curiously. "T. J., you good guy." His smile turned melancholy, making him look more mature. "True like you say before, very lonely. My family turn away, can't trust nobody except Margarida." His pretty eyes looked at me. "And maybe sometime a stranger."

"Who's Margarida?"

"She my cousin, best friend, like sister. Very close. She always scared of Malandrão, he her pimp. He catch her make flirt with police in *favela* when the UPP start few month ago. Shoot police dead! And shoot her hand as punish for all see."

I had to wonder if it wasn't the gal I'd seen at the Shalimar. The one with the scar on her hand.

"That's terrible. Sounds like your cousin runs with some shady people. Have you ever been in danger?"

"Few time."

"What's the craziest thing that's happened to you in there?" I asked, leaning in.

"Oh, I also almost die couple time. A few month ago, Malandrão come to me. He say I have trick for big *politico* man. If not, he kick my mother and me and all family out of Vidigal. I say OK. *Politico* was nice man, a little *gordinho*, but nice. Every Wednesday we meet and have good time. He pay very good for discreet. For many month, meeting, sometime with some my other friends. He like party that one!

"Then few week ago, Margarida come screaming, crying that I have get this man to hotel New Year midnight, no matter what, or Malandrão kill her and me." He became excited, recounting his tale with dramatic gestures. "She give me money. I no like how sound. But I have no choice." He paused, his palms facing upward, shoulder height. The waiter served a few more appetizers. Zezé grabbed one, shook some hot sauce on it and took a bite. He held one up for me to try. I took a bite and sipped my drink.

"So what happened?" I prodded.

"Man big in government, a *ministro*," he said, still chewing. "He have big party New Year. Down there." He pointed toward the lagoon. "I go to his house with some friends, text him I have VD and he have too, and I need speak with him now. He come down and we drug him and take to motel on *moto*." He smiled recalling his clever ploy. "After while, *moto* slip, we fall, bad cuts." Zezé showed me the healing scars on his leg and arm. "Blood everywhere, *ministro* hurt too, but not *conciente*."

"You kidnapped a minister?" I asked, feigning disbelief.

"It was he or me." Zezé shrugged, holding a half-eaten *coxinha* in the air. He looked me over again inquisitively. "You no police, right?"

"I don't even speak the language. Do I look like one to you?" I laughed.

"Well, just checking." He seemed convinced and finished off the treat before continuing. "So he wake up in regular room and I with him. He confused. All sudden, door kick open and Malandrão shoot him two time." He punched my chest and forehead with his finger, his arresting eyes wide. He took a long sip of his drink.

"He let you live?"

"Of course. I obey. That all he want. That my most risky story, T. J."

"And he paid you?"

"He pay me, yes. Margarida bring money from Feijão, Malandrão's *dono*. He pretend be mean with her with Malandrão, but give her secret presents. She always waiting for him visit."

Feijão had to be the former *dono*'s replacement. This guy was an important link. "Fascinating," I said. "I could write a book on your life. How dangerous it seems."

"Usually not so. I meet many cool interesting people. Like you!" He smiled. "What most crazy thing happen to you?"

"Actually, bumping into Bret and Charles was pretty crazy." I leaned forward. "You see, li'l buddy, I recently separated from my boyfriend of many years when I came down here for work. We're kind of taking a break from each other."

"Is that why no sex, T. J.?" He reached over and patted my leg with his hand, then let it rest there.

"Somewhat. But Bret and Charles saw me with Marcos and I'm sure they'll tell my boyfriend I've been messing around down here."

"You and Marcos? He nice guy. Is true?"

"No!" I lied again.

"Oh T. J., come on, let's have fun! Nobody know." He gave my leg a squeeze.

"Out of the question, buddy."

He pouted.

"Yes, is crazy coincidence you see them here. Brent bad boy, you in trouble!" He wagged his finger at me mischievously.

The sky had gone black and stars were twinkling through openings in the scattered clouds. We rode the cable car to the base, got into a cab and drove back to Copacabana. It made sense if the girl I saw was Margarida. She worked her tricks at the Shalimar and Feijão was one of them. He was our guy. I'd need to find him, and Zezé would help make that happen. I dialed Zezé's cell number into my phone and hit save as we came to a stop at Arpoador.

"You sure no sex?"

"Good night, Zezé. See you on the beach."

"Don't forget what you say 'bout ballet!" He pointed his finger at me and then held up his hand in that cool surfer-dude gesture. I headed home along the sandy sidewalks, spot lit by the tall streetlights.

Money had exchanged hands the night of the murder and now I had a couple new names to look into, the name of the murderer, and more importantly, the name of the man who'd paid them all to commit it. Progress, I thought to myself with satisfaction. All in all, a very good day.

CHAPTER TEN

Rodrigues drove around the Two Brothers, past Vidigal, westward along the coast. We crossed Pepino Beach in the fashionable São Conrado district, with its expensive apartment towers and manicured golf courses. A tunnel traversed the imposing Pedra da Gàvea Mountain that separated the South Zone from the West. On the other side, endless high-rises of the upper-middle-class section of Barra extended along the coast to the horizon. To the north, Lake Jacarepauguá, a large lagoon, separated Barra from the valley and mountains.

The Itanhangá Golf Club spread languidly between the lagoon and the foothills. From the security gate to the main clubhouse, tall imperial palms and tropical trees with whitewashed bases lined the way. The golf course was offset by the green undulating peaks. Rodrigues opened the door for me and I walked through the clubhouse to the pool area in the back. The waiter led me to Brasão's table, where he sat with César and Danilo. As they stood up to greet me, I noticed Lygia.

She was seated with them, looking beautiful and disinterested.

"Please, allow me introduce you to my wife, Lygia. This is T. J. Leukemeyer."

I looked into her eyes, but Lygia's gaze held no recognition.

"A pleasure to meet you, Mr. Leukemeyer." She held her hand out to me. An actress indeed. I had to wonder why she was keeping our encounter a secret, and how Ronaldo could have been so sure that our first encounter would not pose a problem.

"T. J., please," I replied, taking my seat. The uniformed waiters bustled busily about us, pouring juice and coffee and taking our breakfast order. Everyone's cell phones were set out on the table, turned off, as they had been in yesterday's meeting. I placed mine on the table with the others and glanced at the menu, not understanding much, so I ordered a fruit salad.

"How long will you be staying in Rio?" Lygia asked. Déjà vu.

"Several weeks, I suppose. It will have a lot to do with these gentlemen here."

Antonio said, "Danilo, César and I would like to show you the Olympic sites after breakfast. It is a short ride from here—an abandoned racetrack originally built on reclaimed marshland for the Grand Prix races in the seventies. A perfect site for the Olympic parks."

"Except for the small *favela do* Autodromo," said Lygia in a more forceful pitch.

"Ah, yes," sighed Danilo through clenched teeth. "A thorn in our side."

"The *favela* sits right on the edge of the lake between the two plots designated for the Olympic Park and the Olympic Village. It is home to local fishermen. For proper security, the *favela* would have to be removed or relocated. But the residents are putting up a good fight against the city," César explained. "A nuisance."

Lygia straightened up in her seat. "It's just not right to take their land away from them without proper settlement. That is all they are asking for."

"My dear is always fighting on behalf of the less fortunate." Brasão patted her on the shoulder. "She is a true revolutionary! But in the end, it will be moved in the name of progress."

Lygia looked away.

The food arrived just then and the waiter served my fruit salad.

"Light fare," said Antonio.

"Trying to stay in shape."

César laughed, tapping his large belly. "Me too, it's easy to watch my weight!" The waiter served his omelet with toasted French bread and a side plate of pastries and jams.

Even Lygia broke a smile.

We had an animated discussion about the prestigious history of the beautiful club and its members, embellished by Antonio's various anecdotes.

"This club was founded by the Lagessa family in the thirties. This part of town was a remote escape with European-style chalets hugging the foothills. It was the elite's weekend retreat. Rubio Lagessa was a friend of my father's. After my father died, he took a particular interest in me. He introduced me to the world of real estate. One day I was golfing with him just over there." He pointed. "I must have been eighteen or so at the time. We were accompanied by a friend of his, Nicolau Mouria, a Brazilian World War II hero. He was an aviation captain who fought in Italy and had just retired from being Brazil's aeronautics minister. He had the habit of wearing his military medals in public during the dictatorship. He gave me the most valuable advice."

Brasão mimed an erect posture and serious expression. "He said, 'Young man, remember this. The only way to keep the government from meddling in your affairs is to be in control of it. That is the key to success in this land.' How right he was. Do you play golf, T. J.?"

Lygia's head turned away once more and her chest heaved a great sigh.

"From time to time. I can hold my own." I popped the last sweet berry in my mouth.

"We will have to test you out, perhaps next week sometime. This weekend, Lygia and I are throwing a small party to celebrate the city's decision to approve our bid to develop the Olympic sites."

"You should come if you are free," Lygia suggested.

"Of course you are invited. It will be a great opportunity for you to meet with all the main players involved in our projects. Many of Rio's important society will be there and I think you would enjoy yourself. I am planning a special entertainment surprise," Antonio added. "Please be our guest and feel free to bring someone if you wish."

"I'll be there, although it will most likely just be me."

"Wonderful. Tomorrow we will be tied up in a variety of meetings. But Lygia is available in the afternoon and has agreed to show you the Porto Maravilha project site in downtown, if you wish to see it then. Usually my dear celebrity wife's schedule is replete, so this is a rare opportunity! She is the project's promotional spokesperson."

"A celebrity?" I asked, looking over at Lygia.

She blushed modestly. "I am an actress on the evening soaps, but my true work is philanthropic. I have a few charities that I am very involved in. Let's say acting is a means to an end."

"You are too modest, Lygia," said César, turning to me. "She is Brazil's greatest superstar."

"I can tell y'all it would be an honor to be shown 'round town by a celebrity and hear about your projects. You know, I began in finance working for non-profit charitable organizations, so I'm sure we'll have much to talk about. Where shall we meet?"

"Where are you staying?" She knew full well, of course, but those eyes of hers never betrayed a thing.

"Right by the country club, on Viera Souto and Anibal de Mendonça," I said, fumbling the pronunciation.

"My driver and I can pick you up at your apartment, around noon?"

"I look forward to it."

We finished breakfast off with some small talk and Lygia got up to leave. We all stood for her departure, then walked around the pool to have a better look at the manicured grounds. Antonio stopped to greet people now and again, introducing me to successful businessmen and politicians as we strolled.

We made our way around to the side of the club, where to my surprise, Brasão's helicopter sat waiting on the pad. It was a black-and-red McDonnell Douglas 600N, a model with a double-fin tail in place of the standard stabilizing back propeller. The US border patrol used a similar model, and I recalled how easily it maneuvered in tight situations.

"I trust you are not afraid of heights?"

"Not a chance. I enjoy flying, actually."

"Off we go then," Antonio said.

The four of us climbed up and buckled in. Two pairs of hand-stitched leather seats faced one another behind the pilot. Within minutes the propellers were spinning and we lifted swiftly and gently into the air, affording us spectacular views of the West Zone. We flew over an endless avenue with mile after mile of strip malls and shopping centers along the back spine of Barra, and then angled to the right over the western end of Lake Jacarepaguá. The designated parklands came into view. Not long afterwards we were standing alongside the helicopter in the empty parking lot of the old racetrack and future site of the Olympic Park.

Antonio walked beside me and pointed to the sea of apartment buildings across the lake, past where we'd just flown.

"I helped build that. When it was nothing but deserted beachfront and dunes, I saw the future." He turned to look at me. "Rubio taught me well; I knew Rio would outgrow its constrained webs of land. This was naturally the next direction the city would expand to. I pulled together the first large development project in Barra and I got investors to understand my vision. We created a middle-class paradise." His face beamed with satisfaction. "Look at that! It's vast now, but it started with my vision." He thumped his debonairly suited chest.

"Your vision and track record are why we are so interested in partnering with you, Antonio. We've been following your civic projects for some time. Your expertise and dominance in the industry combined with an Olympic platform is irresistible to us." Stroke the ego.

We walked around the vast flat land as Danilo began to describe the layout of the site.

"The aquatics arena will be to the north, the gymnastics stadium, track and field, and tennis courts will be to the east, and the velodrome will be built by the water." He pointed. "As you can see to our right, the small *favela* sits just between the Olympic Park and the site of the Olympic Village. The mayor has committed to move it completely by the end of this year."

"It will be done for certain, although doing business is getting more difficult these days." César sighed. "Since this president has taken office, all sorts of regulations to monitor industries have been implemented. In the fight against corruption, business suffers by wasting time, money and opportunities in the name of what the president considers to be transparency. But it's just another way to fill corrupt government pockets."

"It's the problem with big government," said Danilo, "reaching its fingers into the private sector to make itself bigger at our expense."

"Doesn't sound very different from what we are going through politically in the US," I said.

"Let's avoid unsavory politics," said Antonio. He reached into his coat pocket and pulled out a few cigars. "Would you care to enjoy one, T. J.? We in Brazil have open access to Havana." His grey eyes sparkled.

"I don't usually, but I suspect this is a celebratory occasion."

He handed them out and ceremoniously clipped and lit each. Once we were all puffing away, he moved in, forming a huddle of sorts in the middle of the grassy field. He dramatically spread both arms, as if he were sharing his surroundings with us.

"Gentlemen, we are embarking on a historical journey. We will shine in the world's eyes with our glorious Olympic Park. And with your generous assistance in financing, we shall all be wealthier men for it." Antonio's deep, gravelly voice was all-encompassing. "But my friend," he said to me, "be cautious. The new government is squeezing our businesses, and they are on the offensive. Out here in the field we can speak plainly, but be careful of what you say and to whom about our arrangement. There are ears everywhere. I don't even trust my office without a weekly bug sweep."

He turned away from us and looked at the mountains in deep thought. His pink silk tie fluttered in the wind. After a moment he turned back to face us and clapped his hands together, rubbing his palms back and forth.

"Congratulations, my friends. Let's get busy!"

He led us back to his helicopter.

CHAPTER ELEVEN

I was reading the *New York Times* late Wednesday morning when Jovelina appeared at the door.

"*Seu* Leukemeyer, I am going to the market for a few items, will you be having dinner in this evening?"

"I'm not sure, Jovi. Why don't you prepare something just in case? Anything you like. Your food's always a treat."

"I'm so glad you enjoy it," she said, blood flowing into her puffy cheeks. "I won't be long. Is there anything you need before I go?"

"No, thanks. I'll be going out for lunch 'round noon."

I put down the *New York Times* and picked up my tablet. I looked up the *Rio Times*, a local online paper for American expats. The headlines warned of an upcoming police strike. The police and firemen of Salvador had already gone on strike, and Salvador had suddenly become crime ridden to the point of needing military intervention to keep the peace. Now they planned to do the same here in Rio. With Carnival not far off, the police had the city in a vise grip of anxiety.

The silence was broken by the buzzer. I looked at my watch: 11:45. I picked up the receiver by the front door. "Yes?" I asked.

It was Wellington at the front desk. "Mr. Leukemeyer, good day to you, sir. Mrs. Castello-Branco is here to see you, sir."

The warble in his voice betrayed his giddiness at being in a superstar's presence.

"Send 'er up, Wellington. Thank you."

I hung up, wondering why she was coming up instead of waiting with her driver. When I opened the door, Lygia stood tall, her handbag balanced on her forearm.

"Welcome, please come in."

I caught the light scent of her fresh perfume as we brushed cheeks.

She entered the apartment and paused in the foyer. Her long hair was bound into a ponytail, held back from her sensuous features by a colorful scarf. She was dressed casually in a billowy blouse, pressed linen slacks, and jewel-studded sandals. An ancient gold coin pendant hung from a chain around her neck.

"I thought we should have a little chat about yesterday before we go. Would that be all right?" She was looking around the ample living room. "What a beautiful apartment. It is quite lovely. It's been years since I've been here, though." I must have looked puzzled. "A friend of mine lived a couple of floors below," she explained.

"Please, have a seat, tell me what's on your mind."

"Thank you." She sat on the sofa and crossed her legs. Unlike yesterday, I thought I could read concern in her eyes. "I know you must think I'm completely rude for my behavior at the club yesterday. It must have been very uncomfortable for you to have to pretend that we had not yet met."

"Not a problem at all. I'm sure you've got your reasons."

"I feel I owe you an explanation for putting you in an

inexcusable position." Lygia looked down at the various objects on the coffee table as she spoke. "Antonio and I have a very public relationship. We are always in the tabloids and society magazines, emulated as an ideal couple. But the truth is often a different story."

"Lygia, it's fine, you don't have to—"

She held up her hand. "Please, allow me to finish." The corner of her mouth twitched as she composed what she would say next. "It has everything to do with my son, Paulo André. I know my husband is involved in extremely important business projects and they involve politics, big money and unspoken kickbacks. I do not get very involved in his affairs and certainly do not presume to know exactly what your arrangements with him are or will be." She looked up, locking her intense gaze with mine. "As Paulo André is getting older, he sees his father benefitting from doing things the Brazilian way, as we say, *o jeitinho brasileiro*. Loosely translated, it means getting things done by bending the rules because of who you know. It's not what I aspire to for his future. But more importantly, it has also been dangerous lately. A friend of ours—you said you had heard about the minister's death? I do not feel safe. I am terrified for Paulo André's safety. We even had a tracking chip implanted in his leg when he was younger. That is actually common practice here for people like us. That's how bad it is. I am arranging to send him to the States to boarding school after the summer break. Antonio is not really in agreement, but I feel he should be in an environment where he is safe and rules are respected."

"I see."

"When Paulo André met you at the club the other day, he would not stop talking about how much fun he had playing on the courts with you. He even mentioned it to his father, although he never mentioned you by name, just as 'the American guy.'" Those eyes of hers that could say everything or nothing turned ice cold. "I could tell that Antonio was not paying him any attention at the time. He'd just come off one of his lengthy phone calls, always locked away in his library instead of spending time with his son.

"When Valeria called me after your lunch to tell me why you were here, I suppose I felt angry at him for tainting everything that seemed good." She looked away, hiding her embarrassment in the view of endless sky. "But rather than tell you my woes, I really just wanted to come up here and apologize for putting you in that awkward situation and for you to understand my motives."

Lygia sighed and clutched her bag. "Anyway," she said, standing up, "is there a powder room I can use before I take you on our lunch and tour?"

"Of course, there, the door on the left."

"I'll be right back, then."

I was mildly surprised at the torrent of information Lygia had just shared. I wondered how far her disdain for her husband went. Or was this all an act?

A sound came from the kitchen; I got up. Jovi was back. She peeked her head out from behind the kitchen door and waved.

"Jovi, I've got a guest, would you mind bringing out a couple glasses of iced tea, please?"

"Of course, *Seu* Leukemeyer, right away."

Back in the living room, Lygia was seated again. She was holding the long rainbow-colored quill that sat in the brass inkwell on the coffee table. "How beautiful. Nature is the greatest artist of all," she confided. I sat down next to her.

"So tell me about our itinerary." I heard Jovelina's pitter-patter footsteps approaching.

"First we will go downtown to a wonderful restaurant that I love, where you will have some excellent food and a bit of history. And then—"

"Ai Meu Deus!" Jovelina's short, high-pitched scream was followed by a clattering crash as her tray hit the floor,

shattering the glasses of iced tea. Lygia and I jumped to our feet.

Jovelina had fallen to her knees and was repeatedly marking the cross over her chest. She was struggling to speak.

"Are you all right?" Lygia leaned forward and grabbed both her arms to steady her.

Jovelina let out another gasp at Lygia's touch. I thought she was having a cardiac arrest. A tear spilled from her eye as her hiccuping attempts to speak finally summoned her voice.

"Lygia!" she managed, shaking her head in disbelief. "Lygia de Castello-Branco, touching me." Jovelina grabbed Lygia's wrist with both her hands and leaned over and kissed it. "Oh Lygia, you are so marvelous," she moaned. "I can't believe it's you! Here!"

I looked at Lygia. She glanced back with a sheepish grin. You'da thought that Jovelina had just experienced the apparition of the Holy Mother. Perhaps there was no difference.

"I bet it happens all the time," I said.

Lygia broke into Portuguese and she and Jovelina exchanged short, rapid banter. Jovelina recounted her unwavering admiration. Lygia reached into her pocketbook, pulled out a pad of paper, and with a swift motion of her coral-colored pen, wrote a short dedication followed by her autograph. Jovelina held it to her chest and said she would treasure it always. She apologized repeatedly and began to pick up the spill.

"I'll be right back with fresh ones," she said. Lygia looked at her watch.

"No need, Jovi, we are actually just on our way out. Really, it's OK," I assured her.

"Oh, how marvelous it is to meet you," Jovelina said to Lygia before returning to the kitchen.

I told Lygia of Jovelina's rule about leaving in time to be home for her eight o'clock *novela*.

"She is lovely." She laughed. "And yes, it does happen all day long. On certain days it can be quite overbearing, but my fans are the ones who empower me, ultimately, so I try to be patient. Shall we, then?"

We drove into downtown, passed under an old overpass and pulled up to an abandoned park on the waterfront. Directly in front of us, a long jetty extended out to the island palace I'd looked down upon from Antonio's office. To the left was a large colonial building housing the Maritime Museum. Lygia's driver opened the door for us to step out.

"This is where Porto Maravilha will be built," she said. "That is one project I know will dramatically change downtown." We followed the water's edge, lined with colorful, bobbing fishing boats, and entered an octagonal, Belle Époque–style glass and steel tower.

"How 'bout that lovely thing," I said.

A jet roared by for a landing at the airport just beyond the tower.

"This is where we will be having lunch," she said. "But it has special significance too. The tower itself was once part of an earlier port-side revitalization plan. In the first half of the nineteenth century, a French architect, Granjean de Montigny, planned a huge covered food market here, mainly for fish and seafood.

"That revitalization included the Fiscal Palace over there, the museum, and several other structures which are no longer here. Unfortunately, politics, the encroachment of this overpass and the Santos Dumont airport did not let the revitalization of the area take hold.

"The market had four of these lovely towers with fretworked iron girders imported from Belgium, one at each corner. In 1933, a famous businessman inaugurated the restaurant Albamar, an icon of *Carioca* seafood cuisine. The notoriety of the restaurant is what saved this lonely tower from demise when the market was torn down in the sixties." We reached the tower's door. "It is also what will save the tower from the new construction."

Once inside, we squeezed into a tiny little elevator with an accordion door and slowly ascended to the second floor. The maître d' led us to the large windows framing Guanabara Bay and the mountains beyond. Another plane approached for a landing just beyond our line of sight.

"What a charming spot. You definitely know your history." I seated her and then slipped into my chair. Several other diners were murmuring and looking our way, wondering if it was really the famous soap star dining with a tall, handsome, mystery man.

"I am the spokesperson for the Porto Maravilha project, so I need to know my lines." She smiled, paying no mind to the unsolicited attention.

We ordered bottled water and two *caipirinhas* from the uniformed waiters. They brought out a few little plates with assorted appetizers.

"I love these *coxinhas* and *pasteis*," I said, recognizing the finger food Zezé had introduced me to on the Sugar Loaf.

"Impressive." Lygia laughed. "If you're at all adventurous, try a few drops of this. It's a pepper called *malagueta*. It's quite spicy, but delicious."

"Delicious," I repeated, reaching for a gulp of water.

"After lunch we can walk along the port and I can explain what kind of development plans are already in place. I do think it will be a wonderful improvement for Rio. It will provide many jobs and new commerce. But the true profits will be in the development of real-estate opportunities right next to downtown."

"They are lucky to have you as their spokesperson. Tell me, how did you get into acting?"

The cocktails arrived just then.

"To the Porto Maravilha project," I toasted. We both sipped.

"My father is a very famous and powerful man. He owns the largest media conglomerate in Brazil. With that comes much power and money. I was brought up very comfortably and I travelled a lot. I lived and studied abroad a couple of times. That anonymity and exposure taught me some valuable lessons. My father is old and no longer able to manage his affairs. Most of his businesses are now entirely managed by Antonio. But he used to rule with an iron grip and as his only heir, he considered me to be just another asset."

"What about your mother?"

"She died when I was sixteen. It's actually another thing that Valeria and I have as a common bond, losing our mothers at a young age." Thoughts of my own mother, who'd long been in remission from cancer, crossed my mind. "My father was not the warmest, nor the most understanding parent. I stayed in the States as long as I could. I even got myself a business degree. But eventually I came back." She sighed, looking out the window at the boats dotting the bay. "Brazil is a difficult place to stay away from when it's in your blood. When it's a part of who you are."

"I can understand why." I followed her gaze.

"I actually began acting for a competing network. I'm sure I took the job just to spite my father. The soap opera became a hit almost immediately. I think part of the reason for its success was the scandal that Castello-Branco's daughter was working for the competition. My father was outraged by my lack of loyalty. He threatened to cut me off completely and I let him. But then, when I was on my fourth *novela*, my father simply acquired the network I was working for, and once again I became his property, this time under contract."

"How did you get out of that prickly situation?" I asked. The waiter placed a three-tiered seafood platter in the center of our table and deftly served both our plates.

"Have some rice and beans too. They go hand in

hand as our national staple." She delicately removed a shell and legs from a shrimp with her fork and knife and popped it into her mouth. "Mm, that's good. I continued working for the network and decided to begin a charity to help the poor. If he was going to own me, he was going to pay for it," Lygia raised an eyebrow. "I now have five different charities and an endless schedule of fundraisers and benefits. Father and Antonio are the largest contributors by far. But I can honestly say that I have been able to stoke an increasingly social and philanthropic consciousness in Rio. If I were running my father's empire instead of Antonio, I can assure you it would be doing much more for the poor than it does now."

"It's admirable, what you do. Tell me about your charity." I gestured toward the crab. "This is absolutely delicious, by the way."

"I do love coming here," she said. "Well, you know how difficult it is to have a program take root in a community. It takes time to develop trust from people who have been let down so often. Hearts of Wisdom, that's its name, was set up in Vidigal to provide education and entrepreneurial assistance to local women and children. After years of starting and stopping, we are finally having a true positive effect on the community. With the safety provided by a police presence, the charity is in full swing."

Lygia's enthusiasm was palpable. "We have helped over fifty women start their own businesses in the *favela*, employing several other women in the process, making Vidigal a better place. We also have two new elementary schools that are filled with learning children. The city government matches all contributions I bring in each month." Lygia paused and took a sip of her drink. Her eyes locked onto mine and held them forcefully in a peculiar way—as if she were providing an instruction. "It is so frustrating. I can't understand why Antonio wants me to close the program. It's another reason I've been so upset lately. It just makes no sense."

It did to me. If Hearts of Wisdom was improving the lives of women and children in Vidigal, this was a symbol of newfound security and of the militias' diminishing power. Drug trafficking there would have to come to a standstill or be conducted in a very clandestine manner, and that would not bode well for Antonio. I wondered again if she knew about his involvement.

"I don't suppose I could look to your company for some level of funding?" She smiled at me.

"Well, Lygia, that's not beyond the realm of possibility. You just let me settle these deals with Antonio and we could consider a generous contribution to a good cause like yours a collateral investment."

"If we lose Antonio's ongoing support, I don't see how I can keep the charity going without further complicating our relationship. I just don't understand him; he can be so contradictory at times." I was beginning to notice that contradiction was part of the national identity here.

We finished our tasty lunch and the waiters took away our empty dishes. A teenage girl shyly approached Lygia and introduced herself. Lygia smiled graciously, asking her some questions in Portuguese. She reached into her purse once again and out came the pad and pen. I noticed this time that the pages had her name printed on it. A quick swirl of her pen and she handed the autograph to the beaming girl, who bounced back to her table swinging her prize in the air at her parents. They waved back at us in gratitude. The waiters soon brought out the *cafezinhos* and some sweet desserts.

"I had a great time with Valeria on Sunday. She really helped me pick out some great clothes. And all the store clerks seem to know her quite well."

I sampled the flan.

"She does like to shop, my friend does," she said.

"She told me about Vila Paraíso and her tarot card reading. What do you think about all that? I never have believed in such things, but she sounded pretty convincing."

"I would trust her insights with my life," Lygia declared. "I have a reading at least once a month. It is actually much like a therapy session. You ask questions and pick the cards. Valeria has insights based on the combinations the cards appear in. Call it intuition or spirituality, I don't care, but she has never led me astray."

"You believe so firmly in it?"

"I believe that there is a dimension of energy out there that we are not keenly aware of, but that we are all a part of, made of, really. If you think about it, the building blocks of nature are atoms and they are nothing more than particles of energy, right? With focus, humans can tap into that dimension for insight, whether it's through devotion to a particular religion, tarot, positive thinking, whatever the person can put faith into. It's the faith that matters."

Her gaze made sure I was following her logic. "Actually T. J., it's one of the reasons I've been able to be at ease around you and confide so much. I can assure you that I am not an open book, as I may have seemed today. Quite the contrary—privacy is something I cherish. I had a reading yesterday with Valeria after leaving the Itanhangá, and you came up when I mentioned we would be spending the day together. She said that she was certain I could be myself with you, that you could be trusted. I would never have shared so many private matters otherwise." Lygia looked me over. "Should I have any reason to doubt that advice?"

"I've got to say that I was curious about that back at the apartment. And no, I think you can trust me if you feel comfortable doing so." I finished off my coffee.

"You should try her out. See how good your investment opportunities with Antonio will be!" She smiled and her cell phone rang.

"Speaking of the devil! Her ears always ring when I

talk about her. Excuse me a moment, T. J." She picked up the call, launching into rapid-fire Portuguese. As she spoke, I watched her beautifully animated face conjure a variety of expressions, ending with pointed laughter.

"*Beijos!*" she said as she hung up.

"*Beijos?*" I repeated.

"Kisses. *Beijos* means 'kisses.' I told Valeria after lunch we would tour the Porto Maravilha area and then we would meet up with her in Santa Teresa. It's a lovely bohemian hill-neighborhood between the Corcovado and downtown, a place you must see, unless you have other plans, of course. Valeria has managed the renovation of a beautiful hotel there and she can meet with us for a quick hello. Would that suit you?"

"Sounds like fun."

"Then it's time to hit the road."

We walked along the bayside, followed a short distance by her driver in the Mercedes, never out of sight. I'd noticed that he was armed for her protection. Lygia pointed out buildings that were tagged for restoration, or demolition. She looped her arm through mine as we strolled under the overpass where demolition had already begun, across from the baroque ferry terminal. We got into the refreshing car and drove across downtown toward the hills of Santa Teresa. Rising with the increasing slope of the winding streets, we caught glimpses of the downtown architecture between palm trees and colonial balustrades.

Rabid bougainvillea climbed over rows of charming little restaurants with live music spilling into the streets. Eventually we pulled into a long drive leading up to a castle with tall poplars framing its intricate windows. A series of manicured paths and lawns were shaded by rows of imperial palms swaying in the light breeze.

Valeria sat under an arbor-covered terrace wearing a large sunhat and dark glasses, chatting rapidly into her cell phone, a cocktail in her hand. She caught sight of us and waved us over. Mist sprayed gently down from the concealment of the arbor to keep guests cool from the hot afternoon sun. Nearby, a duo was strumming a guitar and singing a sweet Brazilian love song.

We all greeted each other with a flurry of kisses and sat down. Valeria looked me over from head to toe. "Very nice, T. J., we did a good job!"

"Thank you. I don't know what I'd have done without you," I said, adjusting my new cufflinks.

"So how was the tour?"

"Very interesting, fascinating, actually. Sounds like the project will be a great success," I said.

"I'm so glad our schedules lined up for us to have a nice afternoon cocktail. What would you like, T. J.? A *caipirinha* or something different? I'm just having some vodka on the rocks today. Too much stress here. I ordered a martini but it was simply bathed in vermouth! They just don't know how to make a martini in Brazil," she said with sigh. "I long for a dose of New York!"

"Valeria just finished the interior renovation of this place. When she called, she was just ending a site meeting," explained Lygia.

"We are now just applying some final touches to a couple of the suites and the project is done. I am pleased to say it's already becoming a popular place." Valeria looked around impatiently for a waiter, finding none in sight. "They still need to improve on a few things; I mean, look at that hideous arrangement over there! The florist must go. That corner calls for a gorgeous orchid."

"You know, Val, Vera de Andrade always has the most stunning orchids. She gets them at the Roçinha flower market in São Conrado, just past the tunnel."

"Good to know." Valeria nodded thankfully at Lygia and jotted a note into her phone. "What will it be, my friends?"

"*Caipirinhas* seem to be my new poison," I said.

"Just water for me, I have to be on the set this afternoon. We have a sunset shoot at the studio."

"*Garçon,*" Valeria called out to a handsome young boy in a French waiter's uniform. He took our order. The afternoon sun was casting long shadows across the terrace and gardens.

"Tell us really, T. J., when were you last in a true relationship?" Valeria asked.

Lygia snapped something at Valeria, then in English said, "She can be so damn forward sometimes!"

"It's all right, really. I told you, Valeria, relationships are difficult for me because of the amount of travel I do. I'm on my own. And frankly, ladies, it ain't such a bad thing."

"I have to agree," said Valeria.

"So aside from decorating gorgeous first-class hotels, what have you been up to?"

"Funny you should ask. Remember that article I told you about—the police coming to Vila Paraíso? Well, they were there all morning again. They had a couple of sessions with our most powerful medium, Carlos Eduardo. Cadu can see so much detail in his visions. They are trying to solve a murder, but their trail ran dry. A foreign businessman was killed last week. They thought the Red Commandos were behind it, some arms deal gone sour. Cadu told them that the murderer was actually one of them, a policeman. He was terrified because he knows who it was but could not say anything for fear of his life, so he pretended he could not see that. After they left, he would not tell me what he had really seen. He said it was safer for me that way. I tell you, nothing is ever what it seems."

The drinks arrived and Valeria put her empty glass on the waiter's tray. "I'm not sure how to handle the situation. I don't know who is trustworthy. The police force is so corrupt, but that is no wonder; they are all paid a pittance. It's no surprise they all want to go on strike for higher wages." She looked at me, then at Lygia and raised her new glass.

"Cheers! To our wellbeing and to higher wages for the police!" she laughed.

"Are you certain that the murderer was a policeman?" I asked. Deception on the force. Reminded me of Vicente. Ronaldo's missing files. A pair of green eyes.

"Cadu is sure of it. Say, why don't you come by? I'll turn you into a believer yet." She grinned. "What are you doing Friday?"

"I have appointments with Brasão and your ex tomorrow morning and again Friday."

Valeria looked heavenward at my reference to César.

"I suppose I'll be free in the afternoon on Friday. I could come by then."

"Please do. I have a feeling that you might benefit from a session."

"That's serious business. When she feels something, it's best not to ignore her." Lygia reached over and touched Valeria's new necklace. "Is that it? Oh my, Val, it's beautiful! *Lindissimo!*" she said, turning the precious, twinkling stones in her fingers.

I was intrigued by the police story. "How 'bout around four p.m.," I said. "Would that work?"

Valeria tapped through her phone and checked her schedule. "That would be ideal. We can meet at my office in Leme for the reading first, and then I'll show you around Vila Paraíso."

Valeria handed me her elegant calling card and we finished our drinks.

"It's about time I head to the studio. T. J., my driver can take you home after dropping me off. You are welcome to watch the shoot if you are at all interested," Lygia offered.

"Well, that sounds like a must. I'll bet it's quite a sight."

We kissed Valeria good-bye and she struck up a conversation with the hotel manager. I could tell that she was imparting her sentiments toward his choice of florist as we walked back to the car. We drove down the winding streets and Lygia told me about the soap opera she was currently in.

"I play a woman named Tatiana DuVivier. Tatiana is a widowed mother of two whose second husband was murdered. But she is also the fabulously wealthy heiress to a big lumber fortune. It turns out the murderer is one of her two adored sons. The second husband was an evil man who was trying to have her killed so that he could possess her fortune and marry his mistress." Lygia chuckled. She enjoyed recounting the elaborate plot. "When she discovers her son committed the murder to protect her, she does all in her power to save him. In lieu of any viable defense, she helps him escape prosecution. Tonight we film the episode where we say good-bye at sunset before he stows away on a European bound ship under a false identity." She laughed. "I really don't know how they come up with these plots. But I guess I'm not so different from Tatiana." She gave me that slightly unsettling look I'd felt earlier at the restaurant. "I know I would battle Goliath to save my son if I had to. Anyhow, the more sensational the storyline, the more successful the *novela*. People really do admire the protagonist and emulate her."

"You mean you," I corrected. "If Jovelina is any indication of your fan base."

"That is why I love doing what I do. Why I choose only roles that matter to me; that have a positive and progressive point of view. I'm actually very proud of my *novelas*."

"You should be. You're a powerful lady here, Lygia. You're an example that people can depend on."

We'd just exited a tunnel and turned up into the hills, winding along roads until we passed through the security gates of the vast studio compound nestled in the jungle. As Lygia walked into the building, she was greeted by everyone she passed, occasionally stopping to introduce me to somebody.

We got to her dressing room and she turned to me.

"Just wait over there a couple of minutes. I'll be right out to start working. When you are ready to go at any time during the shoot, just tell my driver to take you home. So this is good-bye, T. J." She air-kissed my cheeks. "I'll see you Saturday at the club."

"Thank you for a great day."

As I walked away, I passed a cute guy in the hall. He gazed at me before knocking and opening Lygia's door. He walked in and they gave each other a quick hug. He opened his bag on the counter and pulled out some brushes, tubes and creams and Lygia shut the door.

I walked over to the set. It was a balustrade overlooking the city. The sun would soon be setting for the farewell scene. I sat down in a director's chair and waited. Lygia came out a few minutes later transformed in costume and makeup. Her "son," a fine-looking actor, joined her on the balcony and they began the first of several takes. The set was elaborate; a high-budget production. Lygia conjured up such despair for her son's imminent departure that I actually felt moved. Of course, I didn't understand a word of it. I watched as technicians and support staff hustled about between takes, adjusting the props and set, Lygia's hair and clothing. After the fourth take, when the sunset was at its most magnificent, she delivered her final line, tears a-flowin': *"Pro meu filho eu viro o mundo!"*—something to the tune of "I'd turn the world over for my son." The director signaled a wrap and there was a round of whistles and applause. I looked at Lygia laughing with another actor as the makeup artist touched her up again. He smiled at me. I guess he couldn't resist. I caught Lygia's eye and waved. She waved back.

Outside the set on the curbside, the jungle air was crisp and fresh. I signaled the driver to bring the car around. Within minutes we rounded the lagoon and drove across Ipanema to the apartment.

I headed straight for the kitchen. Jovelina had left me some beef stroganoff with white rice and a special dessert. Bless 'er heart. I popped the dinner in the microwave, fixed myself a scotch, and went out onto the kitchen veranda while the microwave did its thing. From the backside of the apartment, *Christ the Redeemer* hovered high above his invisible mountain pedestal. I thought of Lygia and how difficult her situation really was. She was a national superstar constrained by fame, unhappy in marriage, frightened for the safety of her son.

And unbeknownst to her, she was the wife of one of Brazil's most dangerous criminals. Despite her circumstances, she was adamant about what she thought was right. I admired her. Whatever happened to Brasão, I hoped I could keep her safe from the fallout.

CHAPTER TWELVE

Visions of Sean's furrowed brow, scrawled with betrayal, passed through my mind as I sipped my scotch on the balcony. Today was Wednesday. Charles and Brent were heading back tonight. What a bummer. I knew Brent would call Sean first thing. It was the kind of guy he was. I'd really never cared for him much. He'd probably tricked with Zezé and Charles was none the wiser.

Zezé. I needed more information from him about his cousin Margarida. Perhaps he was free tonight. I dialed his number and grabbed the notepaper that Brent had given me with the list of their favorite nightspots.

"Hey, buddy, this is T. J., how's it going?"

"Hello, T. J., I am good, what is new?" He sounded happy to hear from me.

"I was wondering if you wanted to hang out again tonight, same idea as last time."

"No sex, right?" he whined.

"That's right, Zezé. How about it? I need to ask you a little favor. Why don't you meet me at Le Boy Bar," I said, reading the name from Brent's slip of paper.

"OK, I can meet you there for drink, but I working later. Eleven OK?"

"Sure, I'll see you soon."

I plugged the address into my phone, then changed into something less formal and went out into the briny night. The mist rolled inland, haloing the lights. My smartphone showed the address was just a twenty-minute walk or so and it was almost eleven. The streets were quiet at this hour, but I kept thinking I heard paces not far behind me. I found Le Boy Bar and paid my cover outside, feeling the powerful vibrations of the music's bass from within. Surprisingly punctual, Zezé stood by the bar, his muscles defined under the fabric of his tight outfit.

"T. J.! Hey, baby, you look hot!" he said, rushing up to give me a hug.

The music was pounding and some men were moving on the dance floor. For a hump day, this place was beginning to hop.

"Thanks, good to see you, buddy." I slipped him a couple $100 bills.

"We was lucky. I have work later near here and hoping to see you again." He took a swig of his drink and looked me over, licking his lips. "Let's have fun. You and me later. I like you."

I smiled at him. He was so endearing at times.

"I just wanted to see your handsome face and talk for a while, that's all. What's new with you, buddy?" I asked.

"Aw, you so serious all time. So American." He grinned.

"What does 'so American' mean?"

"You need some fun time! Loose up! Let's dance."

"OK. I need one drink first to get me going. I'll show you serious."

I had a *cachaça* shot at the bar and we went out on the dance floor. Zezé showed off his acrobatic talents. The DJ worked the crowd and I was soon sweating. Back at the bar, Zezé put his arm around my waist as we looked out at the partying men having a good time.

"You hot, T. J., I never expect you so good dancer. You surprise me." He moved a damp lock of hair away from my eyes. "Why you spend time with me, T. J., if no sex?"

"I'm fascinated by you, li'l buddy."

"But why?" He rubbed his hands up and down my chest and abs. "You feel so good," he purred. I gently pulled his hands away.

"Because you live such a different life than I do, and you're beautiful to look at. Plus, I need your help—and in return, I'd like to help you with the dance thing."

"You boyfriend never know," he assured me.

"Like I told you, I'm taking some time off from it. But there is a reason I wanted to see you. I have a favor to ask. A nice friend will be in town next week, an important business colleague who's straight, interested in girls. I was hoping you might know someone who could help him out. She'd have to be somebody sweet, beautiful and discreet; a female version of you." I poked his muscular chest with my finger and smiled. "You said you had a friend the other day, a cousin, what's her name?"

"Margarida, sure, I can talk her. She'll be with me on beach Sunday if you and your friend want meet her." Zezé checked his watch. "I have to go now, T. J., but I text you when finish? Maybe you change your mind?"

He leaned over and kissed me full on the lips. He smelled so good, not like cologne. I'll admit, I let him linger a second before I pushed him away.

"No charge for you T. J." His eyes were sincere.

"I'll see you Sunday on the beach."

Zezé's hand roamed south and squeezed firmly. "Ah ha, I don't think your body agree with you. Bye, big boy," he said with a wide-eyed laugh.

I hung back. Zezé was hard to resist. Let me tell ya, if I'd not been so focused on my objective, I might have had a struggle there. Nice to be upwards of forty and—well, get over it. I took one last look at the dance floor. Shirts were coming off, and tattooed muscles were wet and shiny. My watch said it was just after midnight. Midlife-crisis reality check: time to go.

I walked toward the beach on a quiet side street. Sunday, I'd meet Margarida. She was my link to the *dono* in Vidigal, Feijão, the connection to Brasão. Things were falling into place. A few degrees of separation still needed to link up.

Suddenly the silence was broken by a skittish sound—a bottle cap skipping across the sidewalk behind me. I spun around, and though I saw nothing, I sensed someone in the dark again. I walked a few more paces, turned a corner and crouched down quickly. Sure enough, a man rounded the bend, caught sight of me, and jumped back into the shadows before I could make out his face.

"Who's there?" I yelled.

In the dim streetlights, I saw the man hightail it off the way we'd come. I ran after him with a burst of energy—that there's from years of training. Our rapid paces slapped loudly against the uneven sidewalks as we tore up the block. He turned a corner, but I wasn't far behind. Who the hell was this guy? When I caught sight of him again, he was dodging a four-lane avenue that tunneled through the mountain ahead. Cars swerved and skidded, honking wildly. He reached the other side and ran parallel along the road, the avenue now between us. I made a break across it, having to backtrack, darting around oncoming traffic. I looked to the hill for signs of my stalker. He was running up a stairway leading to the *favela* overhanging the tunnel's entrance. I took the steps two at a time, feeling my muscles warming up. I was gaining on him when we entered the *favela*'s labyrinth. Ever climbing, I focused on my breathing, not letting him out of my sight for more than a second or two. Reeling locals cursed us as we pushed them aside on the narrow paths taking us deeper into the slum. The man knocked over trash bins, crates with bottles, anything he could to litter my path.

He jumped onto a window ledge and hoisted himself over a rooftop as I came 'round a corner. I leapt onto a delivery cart and swung myself up to an adjacent roof, momentarily snagging my foot in a jumble of electrical wires.

The man jumped across the next shack, and we slalomed past satellite dishes and laundry lines, tripping over loose tiles and corrugated sheets. We bounded from one roof to the next, all the while trying to keep from falling through. He used a thick overhanging branch to spring himself onto a rocky ledge beside the last shanty in the row. This guy was a fuckin' gymnast.

I grunted and followed onto the ledge and chased him higher up the hillside. He was only a dozen or so steps ahead when he disappeared over the top. I saw him again running up a steep grassy slope toward the crest of the mountain. The distance between us diminished steadily again.

The city lights unfolded below and I heard his labored breathing and groaning. He struggled vertically upward just above me, his scrambling feet tossing bits of dirt at my face. He stumbled suddenly and I swiped at his ankle with a growl. He fell onto me and sent us both rolling through the thin trees toward the edge. Everything blurred past. I could not be certain if it was just a sudden change in slope or the cliff I reckoned it might be.

I tried to get a look at his face as we tumbled. The only glow came from the city lights far below. We were out of time. I saw a rock to my left and snatched at it with my arm. My body somersaulted over, jolting my shoulder with the jarring halt. The man's hand slid down my leg, grasping for a hold, and his feet went over the edge. He latched onto my shoe and began to scramble and claw his way up over me while I tried to secure my grip on the rock.

He thanked me with a hard punch to the jaw that almost sent me rolling again. I regained my balance and swung back at him, catching him in the eye with my free hand. I pulled on his shirt and glimpsed a fleur-de-lis tattoo on the back of his neck, but it was too dark to see any features, or his other fist, which socked me in the stomach. I doubled over and slipped, clutching for anything I could. My fingernails dug into the surface of a root and I hung on like a mountain goat to a craggily cliff. That hold would not last. My predicament was all the time the man needed to jump up onto the rock and run back up the hill. I looked down and confirmed my fears: I was clinging to a sheer drop overhanging the tops of high-rises along the lagoon far below.

Punch it, Leukemeyer!

I was well versed in rock climbing, so I knew what to do. I felt along the rock wall for a crack and found a thin crevice. I prized my fingers into it. Secure for the moment, I caught my breath and gently felt around with my toes until they found a small gap. I heaved up with all my might and managed to swing a foot up over the edge. I carefully pulled myself back up onto the rock I'd held before. My heart was pounding in my chest, adrenaline racing through my veins. I checked myself over to make sure I wasn't too badly injured. My shoulder was a bit sore. Come to think of it, so was my jaw. The city hummed silently below and the stars twinkled quietly in the sky. There were no signs of people up here.

I walked up to the trail at the mountain's crest and looked around. The man was long gone by now and there was no way to know in which direction. Dang it! Who was that? Brasão's guy? Hell, it could also just be one of the common *Carioca* thieves I'd been duly warned about. I couldn't rule that out either. I brushed off the dirt and grass on my clothes and began my long walk back down the mountain. My phone vibrated. It was a text from Zezé.

I free for you T. J. :)

CHAPTER THIRTEEN

I woke up early feeling last night's bruises. I stepped out on the terrace and stretched my limbs for a few minutes until the soreness became an afterthought. Got dressed and went downstairs for my morning run. I went to the lagoon, crossing the wide avenue to the park along the water's edge. I jogged for several minutes and stopped near the base of the hillside I'd hung off of last night. I realized just how insanely close to death I'd been. High up above the large granite face of the mountain was the little tuft of grass and rock that I'd clung to. I looked around cautiously, seeing nobody suspicious, and continued my run.

I fell into my steady pace, wondering if yesterday's stalker might have been a spy of Antonio's checking me out to be sure I was legit. If he'd seen me with Zezé, what would that mean to them? I wondered if they knew who Zezé even was. It could also have been the mole that Adriana and Ronaldo suspected, or someone working for the mole. And if so, who was behind the deception and why?

This was becoming as complicated as I had suspected it might. I had to make this mission work in my favor. Just focus on the directive—proof positive of Antonio's connection to the Dragon Militia via the minister's assassination or any other means.

Back at the apartment, Jovelina brought me breakfast on the terrace. There was an envelope on top of the tray.

"This just arrived for you, *Seu* Leukemeyer."

"Thank you, Jovi."

In the middle of the tray was a bud vase with a rose. "*Obrigado*, darlin'," I said.

"To brighten your day, *Seu* Leukemeyer. I still can't believe you brought Lygia here to meet me!" Jovelina clasped both her hands over her heart.

"Well, Jovi, that wasn't exactly . . . "

"I will be forever grateful! Have a wonderful day." She sauntered off to the kitchen.

I sipped the fresh orange juice and slathered a croissant with some cheese. I was famished. Jovelina had prepared what had become my standard breakfast: fresh fruit salad, a soft-boiled egg and some croissants. My jaw was still pretty sore as I chewed, but I ate every last bite. I jumped into the shower and fixed myself up for my day with Brasão and his men. Examining myself closely in the mirror, I touched my tender shoulder. There was a slight shade of bruise on the underside of my chin; conveniently unobtrusive. I put on my favorite of the new suits, a deep navy blue with a charcoal pinstripe. I inserted my collar stays and straightened my tie. Tailored for power, I thought as I studied myself in the mirror once again.

When I opened the envelope I'd left on the breakfast table, out fell a key and a note card. It read simply, *Drive carefully. Ronaldo.* I turned the key in my hand. It had a Jeep logo on it. I gathered my things and grabbed the rose out of the bud vase, put it in the eyelet of my lapel, and got in the elevator. For the first time, I hit the G button and twirled the key in my fingers with anticipation as I descended to the garage. My new, fully equipped, shiny black Jeep Renegade rested in the building's prime parking spot. I got in and adjusted the seat and mirrors, then texted a quick *Thank you!* to 555. After turning on the ignition, I typed Brasão's office address into my smartphone's navigation app and placed it in the holder on the dash. I pulled up next to Rodrigues in the BMW and honked.

"I won't need you today, Rodrigues. Take the day off."

"Thank you, *Seu* Leukemeyer, but wouldn't it be safer for you, sir, if I drove you around? It would save you much difficulty." He seemed genuinely concerned.

"I'm sure I can manage. I'll text you if I need you," I said, and peeled out of the driveway. I kept a constant lookout to ensure I wasn't being followed.

It felt exhilarating to be behind the wheel in the exotic landscape, but Rodrigues was right to caution. Wouldn't you know it, people drove as you might expect in Latin America, with little regard for traffic laws. I drove to Brasão's office with a good dose of attention and made it safely to the building's parking garage. I locked my gun and holster in the glove compartment. Brasão was not the type of man you could even try to approach armed, although I felt a bit all hat and no cattle without it.

"Good morning, Christina. I believe Mr. Brasão is expecting me?" I took my rose out and handed it to the pretty li'l lady as I walked in through Brasão's double doors.

She spun it between her fingers, waving it under her nose.

"Mr. Leukemeyer, you are too sweet." She giggled, touching her pearls modestly. "I'll let him know you are here."

She disappeared down the corridor while I was left to gaze at the view once more. Amazingly, most of the rubble had been cleared below. Street traffic had once again resumed.

"T. J., welcome!" Antonio said from the hall.

He shook my hand warmly with both of his, and clapped my shoulder. I winced inside.

"Hello, Antonio. It's good to see you, my friend." I walked alongside him to his office.

"Shall we begin with a *cafezinho*?" he asked, taking his seat behind his imposing antique desk.

"Your office befits you." I was intrigued by the books, art and expensive art deco furnishings. To Brasão's right hung his diploma from Oxford, explaining his British inflection. I should have guessed that the view behind his desk would be the Corcovado, smack in the center of the window, Christ's arms outstretched over Brasão's head.

"Thank you. It was decorated by César's wife, Valeria, excuse me, ex-wife, rather. I believe you met her yesterday afternoon with Lygia."

"Yes, I did. Great lady. The hotel she's refurbishing in Santa Teresa is over the top. She is obviously a talented woman."

"And a bit of a nuisance at times, but we'll keep that to ourselves."

Christina walked in and served the tiny cups of coffee.

"Christina, please make a reservation for four at my regular place, one p.m. *Obrigado, Querida*."

She nodded and closed the door.

"Is that a de Chirico?" I asked, pointing to a melancholy oil painting on the wall.

"Are you certain you are not a museum curator? Your knowledge of art is quite professional. Yes, Lygia and I bought that de Chirico and the Léger in the reception at the Saint Laurent–Bergé Christie's auction in 2009. Those two dandies definitely had a good eye." Antonio chuckled.

As I admired the art, his eyes caught the bruise on my chin, subtle as it was. "Looks like you've been in a brawl, my friend."

"I box at the gym and I guess I got distracted." I met his mute gaze, unable to gauge if he knew more about me than he was letting on.

"What a balanced man you seem to be. A sportsman, a successful businessman, a connoisseur of the finer things. I am surprised we have not crossed paths before."

"We are fortunate to have our paths cross now."

"Indeed we are. Let's get down to the tedious specifics of your terms so we can move on to more entertaining matters, shall we?"

I detailed the terms that IVC was offering, and Antonio's voracity took the bait and we sealed our deal.

"Tell me of your afternoon with Lygia. What did you think of the Porto Maravilha project?"

"I'm excited about it. As for your wife, she is a remarkable spokesperson. She really knows her facts. We had an entertaining lunch at Albamar and then we walked the waterfront. She described the location of the planned structures and renovations. I think it has enormous potential. I look forward to learning more today with Danilo."

"Yes, good, all in due time. First I wanted to be sure you will be joining us Saturday evening for our celebration. There are many people I'd like you to meet. The favored construction bidder on the Porto Maravilha project is a good friend and someone you should know. More importantly, the mayor will be coming, along with César, of course. It should be a sumptuous affair, as are all of Lygia's parties. She has orchestrated the entire event already."

"I wouldn't miss it. Just say when and where."

"At our home. We have a beautiful property high in the Joá, a ledge on the edge of the Pedra da Gàvea Mountain. It is a very unique piece of property that I was fortunate to buy a few years back, in great part due to the crisis in the US." He handed me an invitation. The envelope was personalized with my name in calligraphy.

"Nothin' like a juicy real-estate tale. Please do tell." I took a sip of my *cafezinho*.

"We were very close friends with the Tiesenhalers, an

aristocratic *Carioca* family with German roots. I went to school with one of the daughters, Antoinetta. Her family owned the land my house is on. Antoinetta married an American investor back in the early seventies. The Tiesenhaler family invested most of their fortune with her husband—the returns were unheard of. I jumped on board with them and made a fortune. But several years ago, certain business obligations required a large influx of money, so I disinvested most of what I had with him and diversified what remained with another firm in the US, a stroke of good fortune for me. It turned out that the family's investments had all been funneled by this American investor to the infamous Bernie Madoff. The Tiesenhalers lost everything."

An alert sounded inside my brain —there was something here, but whatever it was escaped me, quick as a hiccup.

"I had always coveted the property. I bought it for a reasonable amount, wanting to help the family out in any way I could. It was the right thing to do." He shrugged. "You will see it on Saturday and understand why I am so fond of it.

"Actually, I would like to show you another investment opportunity for your firm to consider," he said, changing gears. "There is an archipelago off the northeastern coast of Brazil, about an hour's flight from Natal, called Fernando de Noronha. It is one of the last remaining undiscovered secrets of the natural world. It is fantastic, like a Tahiti on a tiny scale."

"Wasn't there an American naval base there during the Second World War?"

Brasão once again seemed surprised by my breadth of knowledge. "Yes, precisely. It's far out in the Atlantic. Nothing else is near it. The wildlife preservation is funded by the government and only two thousand people or so are allowed to visit the island at one time. Construction is extremely restricted and must follow the most stringent ecological codes. It is also a UNESCO World Heritage Site."

"That sounds like a tough place to develop."

Antonio held up his finger. "I never back away from a challenge. The place, simply put, is a paradise. Its location, by its very nature, makes it exclusive to the well heeled. Through my connections with the Ministry of Finance, which sets parameters for the island's use, we were able to get the necessary permits to create a luxury development called Paraíso Tartaruga, Turtle Paradise—overlooking the sea turtle hatching grounds. The plans call for restaurants, shops, and a yacht club. Of course, ecologists are up in arms about it, but I guarantee you it will go through in the end, albeit with stringent parameters. I think once you visit, you will agree it is a potential gold mine."

"I'm intrigued."

"Lygia and I will be going with Danilo and his wife, Sylvia, on Monday for a couple of days to check on its progress. We would love to have you as our guest. It's a three-and-a-half-hour flight on our jet from here to the island. What do you say?"

"I'll clear my schedule. Sounds like fun."

The buzzer on Antonio's phone rang and he pressed a button. Christina said something.

"Danilo has come to assist with your due diligence and is ready for you now in the conference room. Shall we?"

Danilo stood up to greet me, and Antonio filled him in that I'd be joining them on the island. "Lygia, Paulo André and I will be going in the morning to set things up. I was thinking T. J. could fly in with you and Sylvia in the afternoon."

Danilo's dark good looks held a certain provocation when he looked my way, assessing my worthiness. "Of course. That would be fine."

"See you at lunch."

"You will love Fernando de Noronha," said Danilo after Antonio shut the door—his tone gracious but his dark eyes squinting with caution. "It's a paradise where you can scuba dive, sail, and even go shooting. It will become a playground for the rich and famous when we are through with it."

"Shooting?"

"Yes, do you hunt?"

"Sure, hunt all the time at our family ranch in Texas."

"We'll have to go on a hunt together, then." Danilo smiled, perhaps warming to me.

"You and Antonio are quite the power team. How long have you known each other?"

Once again he observed me for a moment before replying. "We go back a long way. I must have been in my early twenties when we met. I provide consulting for all of his business ventures these days. We work well together."

"So it seems." I needed to find out more about this guy. If he disseminated Antonio's instructions, I needed to know how he did it.

He pointed to the folders that lined the conference table. "Now, in this pile here are the financial business plans for the Olympic Park. Next to it are the feasibility studies for the site and the city, state, and federal requirements for the project. In the following stack are the construction plans for each area and the corresponding bid packages by various subcontractors interested in the project and under consideration."

Danilo's eyes connected to mine. "Of course we know who we will choose. That is all decided and secured; this is for, as you say, the dog-and-horse show."

"Pony. Yes, of course."

"Finally, these are the concessions that are planned, and revenue forecasts that we expect them to generate. The same stacks are repeated for the Olympic Village, and those over there are for the Porto Maravilha project. Each folder has a summary page if you wish to bypass the minutiae. Your choice. Just let me know if you need anything. Ah, speaking of . . . "

Christina had walked in, carrying a tray with bottled water and a glass. Danilo continued, "The folders can remain here until you finish. You understand nothing is to be taken, no copies are to be made. You will give Christina your cell phone to hold until lunch, yes?"

Once they'd left, I began to scan the summary sheets. While I might find something here that pointed to the ways in which Brasão greased the wheels of government approval for his projects, I was certain nothing would tie his company to the Dragon Militia—they were too smart for that.

Drug trafficking aside, the financial stakes for investors on a project of this size were enormous. As I moved from pile to pile, I thought back to the Madoff scandal and what Antonio had said about the Tiesenhalers' misfortune. Something about that story was tugging at me.

Lunch seemed to drag on eternally as we discussed Fernando de Noronha and the various projects IVC might invest in. These gentlemen had underhanded business down to a science. Brasão was so crooked, if he spit up a nail it'd be a corkscrew. His financial muscle had everyone in his pocket. They openly discussed who to pay off and when as a natural course of business. I knew I'd been accepted into their party with what came next.

"Now, T. J., I believe you will be in need of this shortly. It must be destroyed when you are done with it." He reached into his jacket pocket and handed me a folded slip of paper. His nod indicated I should open it. It listed an account number in the US. Eureka!

"That's mighty nice of y'all, saves us all those international transaction fees. Cheers, gentlemen." I raised my glass and we toasted. I looked at all of them feeling their newfound camaraderie and lowered my voice. "Actually, this brings about a delicate topic I would like your counsel on."

Danilo looked up.

"I need some advice on transferring funds back and forth in a more, let's say, efficient manner. How do y'all handle that down here?"

César leaned in. "Ah yes, an art form in its creative simplicity. You see, people need such favors all over the world. The key is having well-placed, trusted friends that one can use to one's advantage. No trace, just an honorable pact between colleagues. The US is ideal because it doesn't have any tax reciprocity laws with Brazil."

"I see. How convenient. I could use a local friend like that."

César looked at the others. Antonio replied, "Of course that could be arranged when the need arises. Just let me know." He was keeping tight-lipped on that one.

I was beginning to understand what Lygia had meant by the *jeitinho brasileiro*. She was trying to protect her son from being apprenticed by the mob.

After lunch, I drove back to the apartment and went into the study. I asked Jovelina for some iced tea and dialed 555.

Adriana answered promptly. "How did it go today?"

Jovelina had come in with the tea and left it on the desk. Common sense dictated it was time to be careful what I said in any enclosed location. I felt pretty secure here but hell, you never know. I walked out on to the balcony.

"They gave me an account in the States to pay their cut to. I'm transferring you the recording of how they move money back and forth internationally without a trace.

"Antonio invited me to Fernando de Noronha to see a development he is working on that he wishes IVC to invest in. At lunch they spoke of all three projects and who needed to be paid off and when. I suppose I've made them comfortable enough with me that they could trust me with their accounts."

"That is excellent, T. J. Anything I can do to help?"

"I'll get the DEA to subpoena the investment bank listed, monitor the account and access its history of transactions. I'll need your team to analyze the data in conjunction with dates you have on file for major drug transactions, murder hits, arms sales, other criteria."

"We can do that. Any luck with Zezé?"

"Yes, I saw him last night. I'm hoping to meet his friend Margarida on the beach. She's our gal, a prostitute, and the sector general is her pimp. The new *dono*'s her trick. If we can establish that connection and match the money trail back to Brasão, we'll be halfway there. You download my recording with Zezé?" Selectively edited.

"Yes, amazing information! We've been trying to find out who the new *dono* was ever since our last raid."

"Feijão is his name and a guy named Malandrão's the sector general."

"Feijão is well known, but in Roçinha, not Vidigal. Good work!"

"Can you tell me about him?"

"His name is really Wanderlei Luis Telles, he was the president of the Roçinha association of residents. He was under investigation for alleged corruption. Feijão was actually scheduled to appear in court for money laundering and gang forming, but he disappeared and was believed to have fled Rio. But this information proves us wrong. He must have stepped in and taken over when we caught Nem, last November. Feijão would be a natural progression. When one *dono* is caught, the position is often up for grabs by the strongest neighboring *dono*. T. J., how on earth did you get all of this out of him?"

"I have a way with people. By the way, last night I was followed. Chased a guy way up into the Cantagalo slums. Almost rolled off a cliff and killed myself."

"Are you hurt? Do you know who it was?"

"Just a bit bruised. I'm fine. I can't be certain that it wasn't one of Brasão's men, but it sure didn't seem like Brasão had anything on me today. It could be just a *piralho*," I said, recalling Valeria's term for a young thief.

"Get a fix on the girl, but stay away from Feijão and the *favelas*," she warned again. "I have that covered."

"Who could know about me on the force?"

I could picture her frowning, those brilliant white teeth biting the corner of her bottom lip. "Only Ronaldo and I know who you are. All your expenses are managed only by Ronaldo. He doesn't have to report how funds are spent on this mission."

"Unless somebody found out somehow. You mentioned that Ronaldo was worried about disappearing files. What officials would be aware of our mission, other than Ronaldo? I need to be certain I'm not being followed by someone within our own team."

"T. J., I really can't think of anyone."

"Could Danilo be greasing any palms at MP headquarters? I don't think he's as convinced as Brasão."

"It is not anyone on my team. I'm confident of that."

I wasn't so sure I could trust anyone so wholeheartedly again.

"But I meant to update you on Danilo. We are monitoring his phones and Internet communications. Nothing unusual as of yet."

"Well, keep on that. I'm sure he is complicit in all of Brasão's businesses, both legitimate and shady. What can you tell me about him?"

"Danilo comes from the *favelas*. He was arrested as a teenager for peddling marijuana and for gang warfare in the slums. He served some time and was released on probation. He was arrested again in his early twenties, but by a twist of fate, through one of Brasão's charities, he ended up with an apprenticeship working for Brasão himself."

"Now that part there wasn't in his file."

"He must have made a good impression. Brasão put him through business school and set him up on his own as a business strategy consultant. He seems to partake in most of Brasão's deals. Ronaldo has become convinced that Danilo was Antonio's entry into the drug world."

It suddenly made sense to me. To buy politics you need lots of money. Danilo gave Antonio access to a vast clandestine source of income he could use to buy his controlling political power. With drug money and his successful businesses, along with GlobeNet as his megaphone, there was no end to how he could shape and control political reputations. I thought back to his anecdote at the Itanhangá about controlling government.

"You know, T. J., if we could actually hear some private conversations between Antonio and Danilo, we could find out when the next big transactions will be taking place. Can you do something about that?" Laying on the pressure. Adriana was a tough chick.

"I'm working on it. There's a party at Brasão's home to commemorate their role in the Olympics this Saturday. A grand affair from what he's told me."

"OK, good. Be careful with these people."

I hung up and stepped inside to let my thoughts percolate over a glass of iced tea. Something about Danilo tugged at me, honed my attention—something threatening.

CHAPTER FOURTEEN

I spent all of Friday morning uselessly reviewing documents at Brasão's office. At lunch, Danilo introduced me to the gentleman who would be the winning construction bidder of the Porto Maravilha project. We discussed his role and past projects, and ate another sumptuous lunch. Danilo and I walked back to the office, where Christina served us coffee. I rose to leave for the day with the excuse that I had other business to attend to. I didn't want to be late for Valeria's appointment. I blew Christina a kiss on my way out. She blew one back, bless 'er heart.

I was enjoying driving in Rio. It required quick reflexes and attentiveness. Valeria had said to think of several important questions I wished to ask about, but this visit had me on edge. I didn't believe in tarot cards, or anything of that nature, but I had to be careful what I put out there. The police visit to her center intrigued me and I wanted to learn more about that. I took off my tie and unbuttoned my collar while I drove toward Copacabana, and then Leme Beach. I rolled the tie up and slipped it into my jacket pocket before coming to the address on

Valeria's card. Upscale restaurants neighbored her building's entrance, their parasoled tables lining the wide sidewalk. A street boy with a flannel in his hand waved me into a parking spot and waited expectantly for a few coins. In return, I'm told, they keep your car from harm. I'll tell ya, somehow I find that unlikely.

I walked into the building's sophisticated lobby. A contemporary sculpture hung on the wall. I was beginning to recognize Valeria's style. Up on the top floor, Valeria welcomed me into her studio. A little Yorkshire terrier barked excitedly at her feet.

"Welcome, T. J.! I'm so happy you have come. Please come in. This is Lady. Lady, please stop barking! Shh!"

Lady had an expensive zircon-studded collar and was perfectly coiffed, just like her master. Both of them had navy blue bows on; Lady's to keep the hair out of her eyes, and Valeria's to tame her wild black curls.

Several workstations lined the windows overlooking the sea, and the tabletops were piled with fabrics, wallpaper samples, stone and other decorative materials. Stylish young ladies worked diligently at their desks.

"This is a busy operation." I was impressed.

"You seem surprised, my dear." She laughed. "Follow me to my office."

She had me sit opposite her at a small conference table. A lit candle and a glass of water sat on a pedestal; between them was a laminated holy card depicting a saint. There was a shot glass with what smelled to me like vodka. Directly in front of Valeria were two stacks of cards, one large, one small.

Lady ran a couple rounds under the table and came to rest between our feet with a sigh. She pawed at her bow until it slid off and her bangs fell over her eyes. She sighed again and settled down.

"Tell me about all of this," I said, feeling a tad bit unnerved.

Valeria pulled another shot glass over to the center

of the table. "These are for us. Cheers!" She took a swig of her shot and slapped it down, bracelets jingling.

I followed suit.

"What am I looking at here?"

"Well, let's see. The candle is to provide light to guide me with its infinite wisdom. The water neutralizes energies, providing protection, as does St. George, of course. He's known as the warrior saint because he slayed the dragon." She looked over to make sure I was following.

"Yes, of course, that makes logical sense." It all seemed a bit loony. Valeria said a prayer and then handed me the large deck of tarot cards.

"Shuffle this deck. Good. Now cut it. By shuffling, you impart your energy and destiny into the cards."

Valeria took them from me and recombined the halves.

"Don't worry, it doesn't matter if you believe in it. You just have to want to know what you seek. Are you ready to ask your first question?"

I felt silly that I was nervous. I just didn't believe in hocus-pocus.

With a nimble gesture, she splayed the cards evenly out for me like a fan. "Let's start with those that matter most." She held up her hand and instructed, "Think your question and pick three cards. Visualize the person or situation."

Valeria watched my selections with interest, then placed the cards face-up on the table, taking in the symbols of each in turn. "You are concerned about health, someone dear, a woman. Ask your question."

Wow. "My mother's health. Tell me about that."

"There are difficulties here."

She pulled the smaller cards out of a box labeled *Gypsy Oracle Cards*, counted and set aside a few, then placed the next face up over one of the tarot cards. She repeated this until each of the tarot cards had been paired.

"These provide greater detail and clarity to the message we are receiving." She scanned the cards, seeming to process their correlations. "I see challenges and successes reoccurring, but always fighting the same thing—see here, this symbolizes her illness."

I ran my hands over my forearms, warding off chills.

"Time is nebulous, rarely an exact science with tarot. But messages are clear. An end of cycle with passage to another plane. She may survive a few more—how do you say?"

"Remissions," I whispered, almost to myself.

"Yes, remissions." Valeria's finger moved from one card to the next. "I don't think you need to worry today."

"You're freaking me out. She's been fighting cancer for years now."

She smiled sympathetically and nodded. "OK, be a man," she ordered with a laugh to lighten the moment. "Shuffle the cards and ask your next question."

I shuffled the deck, she split it and gave me the cue to pick the cards.

I thought about my assignment here—let's really put her to the test. Pictured everyone involved, all that I knew so far. I imagined my goals.

Valeria analyzed the cards and once again displayed the startled wincing rigors I'd witnessed in the mall.

"My goodness! What is your question?"

"Will my investments here be profitable?"

"You are in danger, T. J.!" she said again.

She counted out several more Gypsy cards over top of the tarot cards, searching for deeper meaning.

"It seems you have been through a recent trauma. Doors have closed unexpectedly, forcing you into the unknown. Fortune in the negative. But look, you *know* you are in danger, you have just survived some form of it. Death with the Devil, and the Fool confirms it! Have you been attacked?" She reached out and touched the shadow of a bruise on my chin. "T. J.!" Her gaze was wide.

"I'm fine. Really. Can you tell me who's behind this danger you sense?"

Valeria huffed, but her hands trembled as she had me pick three more cards, then played her Gypsy cards.

"These are people with great power. But they are not who they seem to be. The Moon here brings ambiguity, or deception. Is it possible they are with the law?"

I instinctually felt she was referring to whoever was behind the stolen files, and then felt slightly silly that I was trying to draw real conclusions from a tarot game. "Will I be able to stop them?" I asked. Valeria had me pick more cards.

She looked from the new cards to my eyes, intently. "T. J., who are you? What are you doing in Rio? This card indicates you are an armed man on a mission."

She sat back and looked at me in a different light, trying to figure me out.

"My mission is to make a good deal, Valeria, and if someone is trying to stop me I need to know who and nip that in the bud."

She crossed her arms. "You've obviously not been in therapy, dear. One of the first things you learn is that it is pointless to lie to the therapist. You may as well be lying to yourself. Think of me as a shrink. Let me help you. The cards tell me death is lurking around you. This is very serious. Look, my skin is crawling with goose bumps!"

She theatrically shook out the negative energy, jingling her many gold bracelets.

"There are enemies amongst your allies, or at least close to them." She counted out a few more cards and looked at me soberly. Her eyes widened with sudden realization. "You are with the law too. I see justice entwined with your presence here."

Her jaw dropped. She was connecting the dots. "Is César in trouble?"

"C'mon now, you're jumping to irrational conclusions. Who's keeping me from fulfilling my objectives?" I took a few more cards.

She dealt a few more Gypsies on top of those. She did not seem to have an answer. She counted out several more cards, flipping the last one over. She looked up at me uncertainly.

"It's just not clear. There seems to be more than one person. And whoever they are, they have real power and deceitful intentions. The message seems to be that you have many dangers in your current path, with many choices. Trust no one. Your gut will always know the right decision, *if* you are balanced. You have the power within you to know that. But look." She tapped fervently at a particular card. "The Empress is watching over you. Whoever this woman is, she is the key to your survival and your success here. But there is deception with the Empress as well."

Adriana? Certainly she had a role in protecting me here. Was she as certain as she'd insisted that her team was clean?

"You are here for something much larger than what you are letting on. I understand now that you may not be able to share your objective with me. Your enemies are amongst your friends. Follow your instincts and be careful who you trust. That is the message coming through the cards."

Valeria closed the game with a prayer of thanks to the powers that protected her, or something like that. I was still feeling dizzy, unnerved by her revelations. How could she have seen all that? She rang a buzzer and one of her assistants brought us some coffee.

"Well, that was interesting, I've got to say. You have some strong intuition." I took a sip of the coffee. I really loved these little espresso jolts every few hours.

"Intuition has nothing to do with it, my dear. I have a large following because I see what the cards reveal, plain and simple." With that, she seemed to acknowledge that the session was over. "I'd love to show you Vila Paraíso on your way home if you are still interested."

I wouldn't mind learning more about the police's interest in the place. "All right, I have some free time. Let's go. You've made me curious about all this metaphysical stuff."

I followed Valeria's driver in my Jeep to Vila Paraíso, somewhere in the middle of Copacabana. The buildings towered over the pretty colonial villa. We parked and walked inside and Valeria introduced me to the people we passed. There was a light atmosphere to the place—soft, piped-in new age music, gurgling fountains and soothing colors on the walls. She took me upstairs to the book-filled library covering every metaphysical and homeopathic philosophy under the sun. There were people studying at tables, including a couple of Buddhist monks. "The library is actually one of my proudest achievements. It is the largest of its kind anywhere," she said, chin held high. "Now we are making it digital."

She showed me the meditation rooms, all occupied, with bamboo floors and rice paper screens. She took me into another large room with the shades drawn.

"This is Carlos Eduardo's room. He incorporates a variety of spirits in here. It depends what the patient needs. There is a child spirit to help children, there is a doctor spirit to work with health and pain issues. There is the old black man, *o preto velho*, a slave from the eighteen hundreds famous for his wisdom. Cadu, that's Carlos Eduardo's nickname, is one of Brazil's most respected *Orixás*." I recalled Rodrigues' explanation.

There was a stool in a corner with newspaper on the floor. A glass of *cachaça* and a tobacco pipe lay on top of it. "The old black man likes his liquor and smokes," Valeria said. To the side was a shrine to the Virgin Mary and several saints. "Those provide protection from negative entities," she explained. There were a series of quartz crystals around the candles. "And those refine and concentrate the energy's vibrations. Cadu is the one I told you about the other day."

"The one the police came to question?"

"Yes, he's terrified because he thinks he is being followed."

"Now, now, Val, don't you get mixed up in this." His voice came from behind us.

Cadu had entered the room silently. Valeria skipped over and gave him a hug. Her polished outfit contrasted with his simple clothing. "This is T. J., my American friend. T. J., this is Cadu."

Cadu nodded gently. There was a softness to his presence.

"A pleasure to meet you. Valeria was just telling me about the police visit a couple days ago."

Cadu shook my hand with a firm grasp, looked me in the eye, and I felt something funny. Don't know how to describe it, other than I felt exposed to him.

"They want you too," he whispered, as if from far way. His eyes didn't seem quite right.

Out came the goose bumps. "Excuse me?"

He snapped out of the brief trance when I let go of his hand.

"Sorry, what's that? Oh yes, nice to meet you as well, Mr. T. J. Excuse me that I can't stay and visit today—it is Monica's birthday," he said to Valeria. "My daughter," he added. "I have to be going soon after I finish up some work here. *Até logo Querida.*" He kissed Valeria on the cheek and walked over to his desk.

Back at the main courtyard, we parted ways.

"I am going back to the office. Feel free to hang out here if you wish to explore the place. There are many interesting books in the library, in English too."

"Thanks. I think I need to chill. See you at the club tomorrow?"

"Yes, lunch. *Tchau!*" She blew me a kiss and got in her car.

I crossed the street and bought one of those little chicken pastries Zezé had introduced me to.

"*Uma coxinha e uma Coca Cola gelada por favor.*"

The gentleman understood, and I felt like I was finally breaking ground with my Portuguese.

The snack didn't soothe my unease. Valeria knew I was here for something other than what I appeared to be here for, and she knew I was in danger. And my enemies were amongst my allies. I was unnerved. I'd barely said anything to her for her to understand so much about me.

I saw Cadu leave the Vila and walk down the street. The curly bows of a gift-wrapped package bounced against the outside of his shopping bag. A man stepped out of a doorway as he passed. He wore a tank top and I couldn't be certain, but it sure looked like he had a fleur-de-lis tattoo on his neck. My muscles tensed. I looked around to be sure he was alone. Cadu turned right, and the man did too. I left a couple of *reais* on the counter and went after them.

We walked almost a full block apart from each other. Cadu went down a stairway into a subway station, and the man followed. I waited until he reached the bottom step before I descended after him. When I got to the next level, the man was just a few feet ahead of me, focused on Cadu. He passed through a turnstile and took the escalator down to the platform. I discreetly jumped the turnstile in pursuit. I could now unmistakably see the tattoo. I had no doubt this was the man I'd chased into the hills the other night. I got off the escalator and accelerated my pace.

Who was this man working for, and why was he following both me and Cadu? Did this have anything to do with Brasão? If Cadu felt the murderer he'd been questioned about was a member of the police, could this be the guy? Valeria had said the murder was because of an arms deal gone bad with the Red Commandos. How did that relate to me?

We made our way down the crowded platform. It was Friday rush hour and there were hordes of people scurrying about on their way home. A train pulled into the station and let out a large number of commuters. As people crowded past each other, Cadu entered one of the cars. I moved laterally and positioned myself to the side of the doorway, keeping my eye on our stalker, who was following the crowd into the car. I could not let him get away, even if it meant a public spectacle. Remembering my tie, I reached into my pocket and pulled it out, winding it around my wrist. As the man stepped toward the door, I looped him 'round the neck with the tie and drew him toward me, stuffing the rest of the tie in his mouth. With his arms pinned, I backed us into the space between two cars in one swift motion. I bore down on the guy like a vise, and waited until the doors closed. Nobody seemed to notice.

As the train began to move, I held the struggling man, our combined weight on my one foot, balanced between cars. I jumped off when we reached the end of the platform, pushing my stalker with me. We tumbled down into the tunnel at the station's end. The train screeched past us, gaining speed, and I shoved him against the sooty wall. The taillights' glow flashed over his darkened face and I saw the purple hue where my fist had landed the other night. His wide eyes relayed his confusion at my presence, and with a start, I recognized those dark green eyes from the mall. Like me, he did not comprehend the association between Cadu and myself.

I pulled my gun out of the holster on my waist and dug it into his ribs. "Tell me who you work for or I'll blow you away!"

"*Mão mflu mnglmnf,*" he whimpered.

I yanked the tie out of his mouth and pushed the gun in harder.

"*Não falo ingles!*" he screamed.

Damn! I concentrated and some words came to me.

"*Fala pra quem trabalha ou more,*" I said slowly.

Once again the man whimpered and tried to struggle free. I jabbed the gun into his ribs, hard, just as a clicking sound started on the tracks behind us.

"Who?"

The track began to vibrate lightly.

"*Brasão?*"

He seemed confused.

"*Quem?* Now!" I yelled.

"*Angelo de Andrade, Delegado da Pol—*" The later part got garbled in translation. A breeze pushed from inside the tunnel and the vibration on the track was getting stronger. The stalker's arm broke free and he thrust me back. I lost balance and grabbed at anything for a hold. My hand fell upon his back pocket as he spun away from me and it tore in my grip. Something dark fell to the floor. That's when I saw his holster: he was armed too and had reached for his weapon. Light glinted off the nose of his gun as he took aim.

Punch it, Leukemeyer!

The breeze had become a whooshing wind. I pushed off the wall and swiped the gun out of his hand with my foot. The force of my strike sent the man reeling out onto the opposite track just as a train rounded the corner into the station. He opened his mouth to scream, eyes wide open, but never got the chance. I flinched back against the wall, waiting for the train to slow to a halt, apparently unaware of the life it had just taken. My hand felt around the floor for what had fallen.

It was a wallet containing a Rio de Janeiro Polícia Civil badge. Leandro Ramalho Saldanha had been his name. Fuck! I'd killed a cop! Once the train left the station and the coast was clear, I holstered my gun and dropped the wallet, keeping only the badge. I climbed back out and adjusted my suit. I looked at the bloody mess on the tracks and made for the escalator.

I was shaking badly. I'd overreacted and now this guy

was dead. Good or bad, he'd been an officer. As I reached the top, I heard a shriek from below. Steady, Leukemeyer. I walked briskly back to the Vila to get the car. I drove for a few blocks and pulled over next to a small park. I took the badge out of my pocket. There was his face. Poor guy. He'd been casing me at least since the day at the mall. Why was the Rio de Janeiro Civil Police keeping tabs on me? Why were they following Cadu? What did we have in common? Did it have to do with my association with Brasão? Or even Valeria, for that matter?

I pulled back out onto the street, taking the back way home. I could feel my adrenaline abating as my distress rose. Once back at the apartment, I dropped onto the couch to think. I needed to calm down. I remembered Sean's Klonopin pills in my dopp kit. He'd taught me years ago, it was a must for travel. I went to the bathroom and took half a pill. Jovelina always left a glass and a small pitcher of filtered water on a silver platter by the bed. I said a silent thank you.

I tore off my clothes and went out on the deck in my underwear and T-shirt. I breathed in the sea air and forced myself to relax. The sound bite came back to me. Saldanha had screamed, "Angelo de Andrade!" just before he died, and the name resonated vaguely. I reached for a pen and pad and wrote it down while it was fresh in my mind.

I dialed Adriana.

"Hello, T. J., I'm glad you called. I just finished reviewing Bradley's report on the account you gave me. It belongs to an obscure shelter company with majority ownership by Brasão, but the account is not in his name. He's covered his tracks on that front. It is clearly a tax-evading mechanism, but aside from that, we saw nothing unusual. We need to find the account he uses to fund the Dragon Militia to really put him away for good."

Bummer of a dead end. But it was proof of corruption, in any case.

Adriana continued, "Ronaldo did not think it worth mentioning, but I think you should know that Lygia's name is also tied to another account at that bank. It is part of the evidence."

Something about that just didn't sit right with me. "I want to know who else knows about my assignment."

"What's the matter? You don't sound like yourself."

"I just killed an undercover policeman. It was an accident really, but he's dead. He was the one following me the other night, and I realized I'd seen him at the mall. I saw him following somebody else today and I cornered him. We struggled in the metro, but things got out of hand and he was hit by a train."

"I just heard about that on the police wire! That was you? Oh my God! What happened?"

"The Civil Police have been consulting with Valeria's center regarding the murder of some foreign businessman involved in an arms deal. One of her *Orixás*—is that the right word? This guy named Carlos Eduardo—seems to think that someone on the civil police force is behind the murder but feigning innocence. Cadu's afraid to tell anyone. He was followed when he left the center. The stalker turned out to be the same guy that I chased up the Cantagalo the other day. I recognized his tattoo."

"Corruption is a fact of life here, even sometimes among our cops. You did what you needed to do. You did say it was an accident. We won't be able to file a report on this now, it could jeopardize your cover. I'll consult with Ronaldo about how to handle this."

"The cop said he worked for a guy named Angelo de Andrade. Do you know who that is? Why would he be following me?"

"*Delegado da Polícia Civil*. Oh my, he *is* the police chief. That's not good."

Adriana's pause seemed a bit lengthy.

"T. J., I have to go," she said abruptly and hung up.

I paced up and down the terrace, waiting for the

Klonopin to take effect. The ocean was rough and I could hear it slamming its waves down hard. The Rio de Janeiro chief of police was having me followed, possibly wanted me dead. And Adriana had sounded panicked. She—Jesus, her husband. Bernardo. She'd said he understood her work so well because he worked for an extension of the Rio de Janeiro Civil Police, that it put a strain on their relationship. Could Bernardo be the mole working for Angelo de Andrade? The consequences of that would be devastating for Adriana.

I went to the desk in the study and pulled out the tablet, punched 1500 to log in and looked up Angelo de Andrade. It didn't take long to learn that Castello-Branco had been a major supporter and campaign donor over the years. His name popped up often in association with Andrade's career. So did a senator named Junior Belém dos Santos, Andrade's former boss. It was possible that Andrade answered to Lygia's father and Brasão, who would obviously not be in favor of a successful international DEA collaboration. But his loyalties could also lie with this Santos guy. I figured a man in his position would only risk criminal activity for those he owed his position to. I Googled *Junior Belém dos Santos*. He represented Rio de Janeiro in the Federal Congress. Were all these people under Antonio's belt? This web was expanding a little wider than what we might be able to reel in.

I poured myself a Scotch and soon felt the warm liquid spread inside. The alcohol triggered the Klonopin, and my heart finally slowed down to a normal pace. I lay in bed and eventually drifted off. But my dreams were pierced by Cadu's strange trance and images of knights and dragons. Thousands of tarot cards spun around a beautiful Empress and fell to the ground, forming an endless path through the deepest heart of the dark *favelas*.

CHAPTER FIFTEEN

The weather was unusually cool the next morning, with the sun obscured by a thin layer of clouds. I stood by the open gate of the court where Paulo André was finishing his tennis lesson with the boring instructor. It was 10:30. The instructor passed me when he exited the court.

"T. J.! Nice threads."

"Thanks, Paulo André. How was the lesson today?"

His hat was on backwards and the cord of his earbuds hung out of his back pocket.

"All right. We worked on serving. I'm getting the hang of it. Want to see?"

Paulo André went through the motions he had just learned and did a decent enough job.

"That sucked! Sorry, Mother says I shouldn't say that."

"Oh, it's OK around other guys, no worries."

"Show me how you serve."

"Sure. Is your mom here yet?"

"She's coming later. I think she and Aunt Valeria are at some yoga class. We are supposed to meet her at twelve for lunch. We can play until then." He bounced the ball up and down on his racquet.

"OK, buddy," I said, taking a ball out of my pocket and getting into stance. "This is how I serve. See how I place my feet? They're positioned to give me just enough of the bounce I need to follow through—with precision and force. Your eye focused on the end point throughout the motion."

Thwack! "An ace every time."

"Cool!" Paulo André jumped in anticipation.

"You try it with me."

Paulo André assumed the position and followed my instructions. I went through the motion, explaining each phase of the serve, and positioned his body. He practiced a couple of rounds and soon got it.

"Speed, precision and force," I repeated. "Once your body is confident in the motion, your mind takes control."

"Wow, I never served like that before!"

He came over to me and we high-fived. The gate behind us creaked open and Antonio walked onto the court. He was wearing tennis shorts and a white polo shirt, just like his son, and a white terrycloth headband around his forehead.

"Paulo André, *meu filho*," he called out cheerfully. I turned to face him and he stopped short, although his smile never wavered. "T. J., you are acquainted with my son," he observed.

His impenetrable eyes did not betray him.

"I sure am, Antonio. He's an excellent player. We actually met right here last Saturday and exchanged a few volleys. I had no idea he was your son until Lygia showed me some family pictures at Albamar," I lied. "Isn't that something?"

I did my best not to seem awkward—this could be tricky. Once again I was questioning why Ronaldo had risked having me meet Lygia first.

"Hello, Father!" called Paulo André. "T. J. is the best

teacher. He taught me some great backhand tricks last week, and watch this serve, Dad."

Paulo André went through the motions and aced another beautiful serve.

"Very impressive. Congratulations to you both. So you are the mysterious American he had mentioned." Antonio came to a stop. "You know, T. J., Paulo André and I don't get to spend much time together. I thought I'd surprise you, son." He put his arm around Paulo André. "And in turn, the one who has been delightfully surprised is me." He tossed a ball at my racquet. "Isn't it a small world? Let's all hit a few volleys together. Brasãos versus Leukemeyer, shall we? I could use the exercise."

"Cool!" cheered Paulo André as he ran to join his father on the other side of the net.

I tossed the ball back to the kid.

"You serve and show us what you've got!"

Paulo André served an ace that went right by me.

"How 'bout that, big guy?" I said.

The boy laughed with delight and he wound up to serve the next one. We volleyed back and forth for a while. Antonio was much faster on his feet than I would've expected. He played with fierce intensity and was completely focused, never missing a ball. The three of us played for several minutes until I finally forced myself to miss.

"You are a remarkable player," said Antonio.

"Thank you. As are you, and you, Paulo André. Nice game."

"Tell me, T. J., Lygia was here last Saturday as well, did you not meet her then too?"

Paulo André gave me a piercing look and slowly shook his head from side to side.

"No, I went home after we played. I live right there." I pointed. "The membership to the club was part of the deal, isn't that somethin'?" I turned to the boy. "It was a fun game, though, wasn't it?"

"Sure was," Paulo André said. He ran over to the fence to pick up a few stray balls.

I turned back to lock eyes with Antonio, gauging his doubt. "I met her when you introduced us at the Itanhangá."

"Of course you did."

"Antonio, I trust there is no misunderstanding here, is there?"

"It's quite all right. I was just thinking things through." He returned my gaze.

"Well, I assure you, there's been absolutely no untowardness on my part. Of that I can conscionably give you my word."

"No doubt, my friend, no doubt. Remarkable that it did not come up when we last met, though."

"I see how this comes across as odd, but I've had a lot on my mind, Antonio, my apologies if it escaped me." My eyes didn't waver.

He clapped me on the back like an old chum, sending a shiver down my spine.

"I have a few things to attend to today, or we would have lunch. Please forgive me. Have an enjoyable day and I look forward to seeing you later at the party. Many people for you to meet." Antonio winked and gave Paulo André a hug. As he walked away, I wondered what the connection between him and Andrade might be.

"Sorry, T. J., I didn't know Dad would be coming. Mother told me when she found out you were here to work with him, that the coincidence of us meeting before Dad met you might be complicated to explain," Paulo André said softly. "She said it was real important for me not to say anything to Dad. That's why I nodded at you." He looked down at the ground remorsefully.

"Hey, Paulo André, it's OK. I understand." It sure seemed out of character that Lygia would place such a burden on her son. There were certain peculiarities in her behavior that intrigued me.

"No, T. J., it's not so OK. Mom and Dad are not happy. They fight all the time, they live in different parts of the house for a couple of years now, and they put on this act for everyone to see how perfect they are."

"They both have very difficult, complicated lives, but they evidently love you very much and want the very best for you."

Paulo André bounced a tennis ball against his racquet. "I know that's true, but they both want different things for me. Mother is always talking about moving to the States or sending me to school there. I think that would be cool, but Dad is never going to allow it. Sometimes I just wish they would get a divorce and start over."

"Why don't they?"

"Family stuff. *Vôvo*—I mean Grandpa, Mother's father—and Dad have lots of business in common. Mom is kind of in the middle of all that, her name, I mean. At least that's what I guess from when I hear Dad in his library. He's always on private calls in there."

"Sounds really complicated. Sorry about that, buddy." Private conversations in the library—that's the room I'd need to get to later.

"It's OK. I'm pretty used to it. I just try to help them keep the peace if I can. Like here today. But sometimes it's not easy." I could see the boy didn't have anyone to talk to about it. He looked up at me, a little quiver on his lip.

I reached over and gave him a hug. "That's a tough responsibility for a kid, but hang in there, be strong and trust your instincts. You're a smart, talented young man, you'll be just fine." I pulled him an arm's length away from me and looked him in the eye. "Got that?"

"Got it, T. J."

A smile crept across his face.

"Now, that's what I'm talking about. OK then, let's try that new killer serve of yours a few more times, make sure you got that down right." I twirled my racquet and moved to the other side of the net.

After a few more aces, we walked down the path to the pool area. At the snack bar I ordered an açaí smoothie and a chocolate milkshake for Paulo André, and signed for them while we waited for Lygia and Valeria to arrive.

"So what are you and Dad doing together?" Paulo André asked.

I explained the nature of my association with him—the above-board portion anyway.

"He says I'll run everything one day. He and Danilo are always working together and sometimes I get to go along with them to different places. They want to teach me the ropes." He suddenly inflated with self-importance. Poor kid was all over the map. "Have you decided yet if you will invest with us?"

"Almost certainly. But I gotta be completely thorough in assessing our risks and gains in every deal. That's why I may be here a while."

"That's good." He grinned. "We can play tennis more often!"

"T. J.! Paulo André! There you are, you handsome men, you!" called Valeria, shuffling over to us.

She gave Paulo André a long hug, then turned to send me an air-kiss. "Lygia will be here soon. She had to speak with the caterers about some last-minute menu changes or some such calamity."

"How was yoga?" I asked.

"Not so great. I pulled something and can't move my neck. I feel like Quasimodo. Don't know how I'll make it to Angra this afternoon in this condition."

Paulo André turned to his video game.

"You won't be at the party tonight?"

"I don't need to be around César right now. Lygia understands. I'm going to my little island today, a treasure."

"Well, that sounds appealing. Monday we're all going to Fernando de Noronha to see a new deal Antonio is working on. I'll be flying up with Danilo and his wife."

"Sylvia?" She leaned forward again so the boy would not hear. "That Argentine harlot, I can't stand her."

I must have looked surprised, because she waved a hand. "We spent plenty of time together. Antonio, César, Danilo and the wives. Danilo comes from nothing, the slums. He clawed his way up with good looks, charm and deception. You keep an eye on that one. His wife is just like him, but not very bright." Valeria smiled. "Lygia and I did what we could to help her style. And with her sensational looks, she passes for what she could only dream to be."

"Such contempt, Valeria."

"Oh, what's life without a little melodrama?"

Lygia arrived with her phone to her ear, speaking rapidly. Her opposite hand gestured as she walked. Discreet looks followed. She hung up and smiled at us. "Hello, T. J. Paulo André, *meu filho*."

He gave his mother a warm hug and she kissed the top of his head.

"Did you two play?" she asked.

"T. J. played against both me and Dad! He taught me his serve and beat us both. I think he even let a few go just to make Dad feel better," Paulo André said, laughing.

"Antonio was here?" Lygia seemed concerned. "That's very unusual. How did it go?" Although she asked her son, her eyes were on me.

"Don't worry, *Mãe*, we were careful with Dad," the boy blurted out.

Lygia blushed. "This is so awkward. T. J., I'm so sorry I put you in that position again."

"Lygia, we've already discussed it. I'm honored to be considered a friend, so let's leave it at that. OK?" I smiled at her reassuringly.

"It's a deal," she said. "And who said you could have a chocolate milkshake, young man?"

"T. J. got it for me, it's really good."

"Then you'll have to share with your mother!" she

said. Her fingers pinched the straw and she took a sip. "Shall we have lunch?"

Lygia and Valeria sat down at a table next to the snack bar and we got down off the stools to sit with them.

"So how is all the party prep coming along?" I asked.

"Just a bunch of madness, but I think it's all now under control. It will be a wonderful party." She turned to Valeria. "Except the most entertaining guest of all will not be coming."

"I've been to all your parties, Ly, and they are all spectacular. But I need my distance. I'm sure you will both tell me all about it." She leaned forward as if sharing a best kept secret. "I don't know if you have yet heard, but the property is to die! Just a dream."

"Antonio told me a little bit of its history."

"Oh yes, he got it for a steal. The poor Tiesenhalers. It was just tragic for them."

"The property must be quite something. I'm really looking forward to seeing the place." Once again, the Tiesenhaler story.

"Mãe, maybe T. J. should come by early. I can show him around before everyone gets there," Paulo André offered.

"If you like, T. J., you are more than welcome to." Lygia reverted back to the poor Tiesenhalers. "It was so terrible for Heloísa's father, but a deal for Antonio." She shook her head regretfully.

"We were both very close with one of the daughters, Heloísa, but she went to live with relatives in Europe. Brazilian society can be ruthless to those who fall," Valeria said.

"Antonio was friends with Heloísa's sister, the one whose American husband brought ruin to the family," Lygia said. "Heloísa actually helped me start my first charity in the *favelas*. I'd just finished the last episode of *Traços Rebeldes*, a big soap opera at the time. Remember, Val?"

"I loved that one. It was one of my favorites!" Valeria reminisced.

"The housekeeper had a major role and the secondary plot line brought home the juxtaposition of the shanty world she lived in and the glamorous one she served. It dramatized what it was like to live in the drug-run *favelas*. It was my first intimate exposure to the real conditions there, and I became outraged," Lygia said.

Paulo André dropped a tennis ball and it rolled off onto the grass. He got up to go after it.

"I felt so blessed in life that I knew this was how I would find my purpose. Heloísa felt similarly, and one afternoon when we were shopping, we talked about doing something concrete instead of just chatting about it over *cafezinhos*. After all, we were both intelligent, educated women from very powerful, and most importantly, rich families." Lygia sat upright and looked to see if Paulo André was within earshot or not and continued, "We were not naïve. We both knew that our families' money was not made in the most puritan fashion, to put it mildly. Fortunes like ours are built with the oppression of others. That's when I created Corações de Sabedoria, Hearts of Wisdom that I told you about at Albamar. We decided we'd use that money to do some good. I'll be going to the office of the Vidigal branch on my way back after lunch, some pressing matter needs my attention. You should come sometime," she offered.

"I'd love to see it another day. I'm sure with the soirée your plate is full, and I have some business to attend to as well before the party."

"Do you have the address?"

"Yes, Christina gave it to me the other day, and it's on the invite."

"Oh that one," Valeria rolled her eyes.

"She seems like a sweet li'l thing to me."

"She seems sweet to most men, I suppose. I've watched her at work when I was designing Antonio's office. When a businessman would walk in and introduce himself, she would greet them by touching her pearls. A look of deep thought would cross her face while she registered their names, just like a contestant buying time to think of something poignant to say in a beauty pageant." Valeria demonstrated. "Touch pearls, smile."

I almost lost my smoothie.

A girl in a bathing suit stood a few feet away from our table and shyly inched forward.

Lygia chatted with her in Portuguese, pulled her pad out of her purse and the girl radiantly awaited her autograph.

"Well, that made her day. I think I better ask for one too," I said, laughing.

"Oh come on. Autographs are for strangers." Lygia gazed warmly at me. "Now, I'm famished, what are you all having? *Garçon?*" she called to the passing waiter, and we ordered.

"How was your reading with Valeria? Did you enjoy the experience?"

"Actually, I found it a bit overwhelming. Scared the pants off me!"

"Most people do the first time," Valeria said.

"But I sure do think that Vila Paraíso is a cool place. I was amazed at how many people were there using it."

"Thank you. I am very proud of it. I was just there this morning to deal with a few things before yoga. I'm sorry you and Cadu didn't have more time together. He was instrumental in making it all happen."

"I'd like to meet him again sometime. Was he there today?"

"Like clockwork. He comes every morning to meet with clients who come from the suburbs on their way to work. Mostly servants and blue-collar workers."

Valeria lifted her long curls up and held them back with a violet velveteen scrunchie.

"Here comes the heat," she sighed as the full sun radiated through dissipating clouds. "I think watching Cadu's work might send you over the edge. How do you say in English? An existential crisis. You had a hard enough time with tarot cards!" She nudged me and laughed.

"An existential crisis is what I would have if it rained this evening," said Lygia.

"Well, it looks like the weather is going to cooperate for your party after all," I said.

"Thank goodness!"

After lunch I bid the ladies and Paulo André good-bye and returned to the apartment. Let me tell ya, that lightheartedness had been difficult to muster in the wake of my worries—which now included Brasão's doubt. I stripped down and got into the dipping pool on the balcony and looked out at the ocean. The water helped calm me so I could think more clearly. I felt a need to call Ronaldo. It was a breach of regulation, but I couldn't believe it was a coincidence that Officer Saldanha had been following me from the get-go. Somebody had let Angelo de Andrade know about our mission. How much confidential information had Adriana shared with her husband, and had he, in turn, shared with his boss? I wanted to trust Adriana, but something was wrong. Why had she hung up so suddenly?

I also needed to find out why Andrade was having Cadu followed. It wasn't hard to guess that he was the man Cadu knew was behind the murder. Valeria had said the foreign businessman's murder was tied to an arms deal. Was the chief of police involved with the illegal arms trade?

And then, why had Antonio really come to the club today? Both Lygia and Valeria thought it unusual that he would have paid a surprise visit. I wondered if he suspected something, and if so, was it because of Andrade? Without knowing for certain, I had to keep playing my part.

I pondered all the facts while stretching in the water and was reminded of Zezé when I rubbed my abs. I needed to see him tomorrow at the beach and meet Margarida. She was the key to getting to Malandrão and, more importantly, Feijão, my golden link to Brasão.

I got out and wrapped a towel around me and walked into the living room, tracking water along the way; another habit that used to set Sean off at our beach house. I reached for my phone to call Ronaldo. I had to make sure he knew everything I'd learned. Maybe he might know something that could be helpful. I dialed 556 and stepped outside again.

"T. J.?" answered Ronaldo. I could hear children screaming in the background and shrieks of laughter.

"Sounds like you're at a kid's party."

"Your deductions continue to astound me," he chuckled. "It's my granddaughter's birthday party today. But T. J., are you OK?" The surrounding sounds faded as Ronaldo paced to a more private location. "Have you been unable to reach Adriana?" His voice pitched with unmasked concern.

"Not exactly, but... something's up with her. I'm sure she's briefed you on the chase I had on Cantagalo the other night."

"Yes"—a lengthy *s*—"she did."

I told him about seeing the same man again at Vila Paraíso and about the accident in the subway, and that just before he was killed, Saldanha had revealed that he answered to Angelo de Andrade.

Ronaldo sighed deeply. "Oh dear, that puts an entirely new complexion on things. Adriana knows all of this?"

"I told Adriana yesterday. Dang it, just the fact that she hasn't told you yet worries me too. She told me the other day that she and her husband are not getting on so well, but he works for Andrade, as you know. Do you think he could be the mole? How much information would Adriana have shared with him?"

"I don't think Adriana would reveal anything about you, honestly I don't. Adriana is our best agent. That is why she is working with you. And the file that vanished pertained to the program's finances. It had no description of the mission or its suspects, so whoever took it would have no way of knowing who you are."

"Then why'd she hang up that way at the mere mention of Andrade's name? And how would he know to follow me? I say we keep an eye on her husband. I also think that in the meanwhile you should get someone to watch Andrade's comings and goings. It smells like he's the rat behind your stolen file."

"If that is the case, I have no idea why. Up until now I've known him to be a man with upstanding credentials. He is adored by the police force. But this may clarify many things. I have a suspicion of who the mole might be, but I don't suspect Bernardo. I'll have to look into this at a higher level." I imagined his whirly-bird gesture.

"If not my identity, what's in those files that worries you so?"

"It could be used to trace the source of the funding and therefore put that source at risk."

"A target. I've got to ask who is financing this mission. I need to know all my parameters here, if only to protect them as well."

"Unfortunately, I cannot. In order to receive the funding I had to agree to its anonymity. I gave my word and that cannot be broken. I can only promise you it is from a most benign source with only the best interests in mind."

I didn't feel quite warm and fuzzy with that reply. Ronaldo told me to continue liaising with Adriana as if nothing were wrong. He felt certain she was clean despite her husband's association with Andrade. "Adriana has deep-seated personal reasons for the work that she does. I will never doubt or question her motives or reliability."

"How can you be sure?"

"Adriana grew up in Roçinha. One by one, her brothers become enslaved by the drug militias, much to her God-fearing mother's despair. She watched one day when her entire family was murdered in a territorial clash of sectors. She survived because she played dead. She was later adopted by a kind middle-class family that gave her the opportunities she would never have had otherwise. She vowed to dedicate her life to help those in the *favelas*. I believe she once told me that was something both she and her husband shared."

Yes, I thought, but partners can lie.

It was 1:30 in the afternoon when Ronaldo and I hung up. Time to pump some iron and get the blood flowing—always improved my insight. I walked the twenty minutes to the gym and waved as I passed the receptionist. I did my crunches first, listening to Ludacris on my playlist. After I worked up a sweat, I did some bench presses as well as a few stations on the universal. Straining through a rep, I recalled Brasão's impenetrable grey gaze and wondered again why Ronaldo would have risked that situation at the club.

I thought of Basão's home and the Tiesenhaler story again. Was it just echoes of Sean and all the clients he'd fed to Madoff? Sean had invested with William Chaffrey, who was now in prison for his dealings. I pushed through one last repetition and it clicked. The weights fell back with a slam and I bolted upright. Chaffrey's wife was Brazilian. If I recalled rightly, her name was Nanette—a nickname for Antoinetta? Brasão'd gone to school with an Antoinetta. We'd met the couple on several occasions, Sean and I. We'd even gone to one of the daughters' weddings in the Bahamas; the one Sean had dated in high school or something.

Valeria did say that Brazilian high society ran in

small circles. I knew in my gut that there was a connection here. And money secrets were part of the friends-and-family package. If the upper crust had a favorite money launderer abroad, I'm sure he was shared amongst trusted friends. I'd need to find out who was transacting the money on both the US and Brazilian sides in order to prove Brasão's role in funding and arming the Dragon Militia.

I needed Sean's help.

Shit—that might be a problem after Brent and Charles.

I reached up for the pulley bar for one more rep and followed my form in the mirror. That's when I noticed a tall, muscular guy checking me out while he lifted his weights. He grimaced with each pump and the braces on his teeth caught my attention. He seemed familiar but I couldn't place him. When I looked up for a second take, he was gone. I searched the mirror left and right and just caught sight of him before he passed through the turnstile, leaving the gym.

After finishing my workout, I walked over to the nice lady at the reception desk, leaned in over the counter and asked her if she knew who the guy was.

"The man just left? He is not regular, he just get day pass. I no see him before. He was here no very long."

"Did he register a name?"

"Register, yes, but no give information," she said.

I thanked her and left the gym wondering where I'd seen that man before. I just couldn't place him. Maybe I'd seen him at the beach with Marcos?

I felt the pump and mild soreness from my work out walking along the beach—soaking in the summer afternoon, deep in thought. I got to my apartment and Jovelina was dusting and cleaning the place. She waved to me as I passed. I left Sean a message to give me a call—that I needed his help.

I jumped into the shower and thought about what to

wear to Antonio and Lygia's party. After I finished my shave, I got into one of the outfits I'd bought with Valeria. I folded a pocket square into my navy jacket and grabbed a stack of business cards Adriana had ordered for me.

As Rodrigues pulled out onto the avenue, I took the tiny plastic Smart Bug off its card and placed it carefully in my inside pocket. It was early, but I thought I'd take Paulo André up on his offer to show me around Brasão's estate before the other guests arrived.

CHAPTER SIXTEEN

The car rumbled up the steep cobblestone street. The cooling outside air enhanced the crisp sweet scent of foliage and blooms as we gained altitude. We followed the road along the base of a very steep granite precipice that towered above the neighborhood. Dense jungle surrounded the street and privacy walls and gates were overtaken by flowering vines. We came to a stop at an elaborate colonial arch with masterfully worked wrought iron gates. *VILA CACHOEIRA* was engraved in the keystone. A fountain sculpted with the Brasão coat of arms trickled pleasantly next to the guardhouse where several paparazzi were positioning themselves for the guests' arrival. Rodrigues offered my name and the guard spoke into his walkie-talkie. He pressed a button and the gates opened for us to pass.

We drove down a long allée of mature imperial palms. Several peacocks roamed the yard with their tail feathers splayed. I thanked Rodrigues for the ride and told him I'd text him when I was ready to leave. I was welcomed by a good-looking fellow in uniform who guided me through the metal detector, gave me a polite quick frisk and pointed me toward the house.

Marble steps led to a grand structure with intersecting planes of glass, steel and concrete. It was supported by baroque stone-carved columns on massive bases. Traditional blue and white tiles lined the entrance in an unusual combination of styles. The house was nestled into the varied relief of the property's unique geology. Luminaries and lanterns lined the way to the grand front door, a medieval relic, to be sure, from some Portuguese castle.

The butler ushered me inside, where floor to ceiling windows displayed the ocean and islands with the backside of the Two Brothers in the distance. A long corridor of fantastic mid-century sculpture mounted on ancient plinths led to the three wings extending from the foyer. A guard was posted there to keep an eye on any wandering guests. I suspected Antonio's library, where his private phone calls were made, was down that way. The floors were made of large travertine slabs; there was definitely a smidgeon of Mussolini in the mix here. Sean would have loved this.

The living room's glass doors were stacked back, opening the entire south-facing side to the outdoors. Antonio swung his golf club in the middle of the garden. The ball went sailing through the air out over the edge into the ocean far below. He took another ball from his pocket and placed it on a tee, straightened up and blotted his forehead with a handkerchief before taking aim. A carefully judged, smooth swing and—*thwack!* The ball sailed infinitely once again. He turned to face me, opening both arms, golf club dangling.

"T. J.! Welcome to Vila Cachoeira! Come. Allow me to show you my place."

I walked out onto the wide, manicured lawn. There were several large Great Danes of varying shades and hues roaming the gardens with bow ties around their necks. One was nuzzling against Antonio's leg.

"And these li'l critters?"

"These are my prized Great Danes. We have twelve of them. This one here is my girl, Mathilde." He pulled a treat from his pocket and tossed it to the dog.

"They're magnificent." I fondled Mathilde's ears.

"This one is Ladrão, isn't he splendid?" He pulled out another treat. "Lygia mentioned you might come early. She said Paulo André wants to show you around some of the special corners of the place." Had I assuaged his doubts?

Two tall flagpoles framed the view. One proudly waved a giant Olympic flag and the other one an equally large Brazilian flag. Antonio watched me admire it.

"It is a unique flag. Simplicity and meaning are what make it so. Most believe the green rectangle symbolizes the vast abundance of flora and fauna in our land. The yellow diamond that overlays it represents the wealth of our gold and minerals. You know, Minas Gerais, with its resplendent Baroque vestiges of power, exported eighty percent of the world's gold in colonial times."

"That's remarkable. I had no idea."

"But the true meaning of the colors harks back to the royal lineage of our Emperor Dom Pedro Alves Cabral II, and his wife, Leopoldina. The green is for the Portuguese House of Bragança that he was descended from, and the yellow, for his wife's Hapsburg blood."

"And the blue circle?" I asked.

"Originally chosen to symbolize hope and prosperity, I imagine, but it also serves as a reference to our marvelous coasts and rivers. The twenty-seven stars represent each state of the Republic. In the center you see an arched white banner crossing the blue sphere. It says 'Ordem e Progresso.' Order and Progress." He smiled. "It seems the old saying may finally be having some resonance." He extended his arm toward the neighboring Olympic flag.

Some might beg to differ.

Busy workers hustled about putting final touches on things. Anchoring the buffet table was a gigantic ice sculpture of a dragon, the symbol of Antonio's coat of arms—and a brazen reference to his nefarious empire, it seemed to me. A band was setting up in a tent with a dance floor.

"It sure turned out to be a perfect day for a party." My attention was naturally drawn to the huge towering rock looming over the property. A thin and steadily streaming waterfall slid mistily from great heights into the jungle next to the yard. Colorful birds crisscrossed above the gardens.

"On a cloudy day, it seems the waterfall comes out of the sky." Antonio said. "It's a sight to behold. It can only be seen from this property, or from the sea. Therefore the name Vila Cachoeira, the Portuguese word for waterfall. It drops from the Gávea Rock there for twenty-five hundred feet. What you are looking at is the world's largest monolith on a coastline."

Antonio leaned his golf club against the lichen-covered stone balustrade and a staff person quickly took it away. He faced me proudly, placing both hands on my shoulders. "I'm so glad you came early. It gives us a chance to speak before I let my son whisk you away." We walked toward the sea. "Lygia explained the coincidence of how you and my son met. My apologies if I made you feel uncomfortable."

"No reason to, I assure you. Antonio, this place is surreal."

"It embodies my love for architecture, our heritage, and the nature that surrounds us. It inspires me."

Antonio motioned for me to look over the edge. I felt a vertiginous wave wash over me and grabbed hold of the rail. The encircling stone cliffs formed an idyllic sandy cove with translucent emerald waters lapping at its edge. A small funicular had been installed for the long descent.

"Tell me, T. J., how is your assessment coming along?"

"Danilo's provided everything I need. I'm almost done reviewing the material, but of course this is all just formality. I'm convinced that we have two incredibly profitable opportunities here."

"Possibly three with the island." He held up his fingers. "I only ask because the public bidding will be held next month. We would need your firm's financial commitment at least a couple of weeks before that."

"That won't be a problem."

"Of course not." He smiled. "The private funds would be most useful by that time, in order to get things moving along."

"Well, partner, I don't see any reason for delay. I think I can secure your funding in two weeks' time at the latest."

I looked up at the rock. A hang glider circled high above us and then went out over the ocean.

"Daredevils," Antonio said. "They jump off a rock a half-mile up above the ocean and glide down through the air. Every day, hundreds of them." He turned his cool gaze to me. "And then sometimes the Gods of the Winds decide to change course as a mortal takes flight. From here, they look like wounded butterflies when they bump into the rock and flutter down the face of the mountain. But for them"—he paused, slowly shaking his head—"I can only imagine it is sheer terror."

Antonio blotted the moisture off his forehead with his handkerchief, and I tried not to read too much into his words. When he lowered his hand, his voice contained nothing but charm. "If you are impressed by our setting here, you are in for a surprise when we visit Fernando de Noronha. The plans were drawn up by an award-winning architecture firm out of São Paulo. We are just about to begin phase two of construction, so your participation—if you have the venture capital for it—would be quite timely."

Before I could say anything, Paulo André came skipping around a corner to greet me. "T. J.!" he called. "Hi, Dad, can I show T. J. around?"

"Certainly, *meu filho*, I had better get ready for the party or your mother will be angry." He put on a menacing expression and tapped Paulo André on the head. "Have fun," he called out behind him.

Paulo André grabbed my hand and pulled me across the lawn toward the waterfall.

"This is really cool, T. J. Just over there, see?" Paulo André pointed to the towering waterfall sliding down the mountainside. At the base, one of its tendrils splashed into a deep stone-lined pool; a natural swimming hole in an unbelievably spectacular setting.

"I sure bet it would be fun kickin' around in there."

"You should come swimming one of these days," Paulo André replied, leading me onward. We crossed a steel cable suspension bridge over a large crevasse and entered a game room built into a cave. A ping-pong table and other games were positioned near a large fire pit. A fully stocked wet bar serviced the home theater. Vila Cachoeira was over the top, and Paulo André positively enjoyed showing it to me.

We climbed a set of spiral steps leading out of the cave onto a flat platform that served as Antonio's heliport. Brasão's copter rested next to parked golf carts, ready for a speedy ride down to the house.

"What a fun place to grow up in."

"I guess so, but it can be a bit lonely here too." Paulo André frowned, looking down at the ground. He showed me that worried face I'd seen earlier that morning. "They were fighting again this afternoon. I think Mother is very upset about something, but I don't know what."

"That's too bad." I put my hand on his shoulder.

"Come on, T. J." he said, continuing the tour.

When he pouted, he reminded me of one of my nephews in Texas. I surprised him by scooping him up to sit high on my shoulders. He laughed giddily and pointed the way through terraced gardens to a little grotto area overlooking the sea. From there you could look back at the house and lawns below. We watched the workers scurry about. The temperature dropped a few degrees and the band began to practice a tune that wafted over to us.

"This is where I like to come and hang out. I can see everything, but nobody can see me," the boy confided.

"I get it, you can just chill and be yourself."

"Yeah, that's right. I can come here without my bodyguard and pretend I'm a normal kid." Paulo André let out a profound sigh and turned around. "We better get back. See over there, cars are beginning to come through the gate. People will start arriving soon, and Dad likes to have me by his side at the receiving line."

I set him down and we turned back toward the house.

"Hey, Paulo André, you go ahead. I'm going to hang out and wander up here for a while. I'll come down in a bit."

"OK. See you later." Paulo André ran off to find his father.

A couple of clouds hovered around the top of Gávea Rock from where the waterfall fell. I felt hot and suddenly realized I was jumpy as spit on a sizzlin' grill. I walked into the cave and poured myself a scotch at the bar.

There were still so many unknown variables, and I felt vulnerable, in enemy territory. Antonio had looked at me steadily when I arrived. He did not seem unwelcoming or untrusting; however, I'd not expected him to pressure me. And what the heck was all that about falling hang gliders? A warning? A threat? Refined aggression at its best. I felt for the bug in my pocket and looked down at the sprawling estate, searching the glitzy windows for where the library might be.

The warm liquid did its job. I walked over to the pool, feeling the fine cooling mist that occasionally blew across from the falling veil. Standing on the bridge, I looked at the brightly lit house and the guests making their way out onto the lawn. How could such beauty come from such corruption? I saw it all the time, yet it never ceased to amaze me.

It was time to join the party.

CHAPTER SEVENTEEN

The receiving line moved briskly. Antonio kissed the wrists of many ladies and Lygia extended hers, dripping with gold-encrusted pearls. I paused at the edge of the hallway in awe of the breadth of Brasão's power. The city's elite were arriving in full pomp. Lygia caught my eye, excused herself, and glided over with her sapphire-blue dress billowing softly about her. Her hair was coiffed high with Grecian curls framing her face. Let me tell ya, she was a vision to behold, like classic Hollywood royalty.

"T. J., I'm so glad you're here. Paulo André said he showed you around."

"You look stunning." And she did, but as she turned her cheek for a peck, I sensed profound sadness in her eyes.

"You look most dapper yourself." She smiled, her shield reactivated.

"This place is a paradise. You've made a spectacular home here."

"With Valeria's help. We'll chat later, duty calls."

She went back to her place by Antonio's side. His eyes already upon me. I smiled.

César came up from behind and clapped me on the shoulder. "T. J., how have you been enjoying Rio?"

"Nice to see you, my friend. I'm taken with your city. How can anyone not be?"

"I can think of several reasons, but let's pretend it's perfect. Have you met any of the guests yet? There is quite a roster of who's who here tonight."

"That's clear to me just by looking at the women's jewelry."

"Ha! A wise observation. I almost went bankrupt funding Valeria's!"

"I'm sorry about that, really."

"Not at all, I am happier than I've been in years. It's like taking a noose off my neck. Come, let me introduce you to some people. There is Celio Aluizio Nazaré and his wife, Mariana Pavé. He is in charge of Brazil's Olympic committee." He led me toward them. "He is standing next to Jacques Rogge, president of the IOC, who came to town for the party and to introduce his successor around. He is stepping down before the Rio Games."

César took me through the crowd of well-heeled guests, introducing me to various *Carioca* personalities. Each introduction was accompanied by a charming shared anecdote that legitimized César's high standing amongst them. For a duplicitous weasel, the guy had a polished exterior.

There were easily well over two hundred folks here, and they mingled inside the house and out, overlapped by the lengthening shadows of early evening. Waiters wove past with delectable hors d'oeuvres and cocktails.

A small circle of excited guests had gathered around César and me. The banter soon tired of English and slipped into Portuguese. César said something witty and the group burst into laughter. Suddenly realizing I was out of the loop, another gentleman translated.

"My friend here was joking that the problem with the world today is that the intelligent people are full of doubts while the idiots are full of certainty!" The man chuckled.

"Ain't that a fact." I extended my hand and the man swiped at a lock of his red hair before shaking. He had pale, pockmarked skin and wore an ill-fitting suit.

"T. J. Leukemeyer," César said, "let me introduce you to Angelo de Andrade, Rio de Janeiro's chief of police."

I'll tell ya, I think my heart skipped a beat just then, but lickety-split, I realized he had no clue who I was.

"And just over there is his wife." César pointed and waved. She waved back and nodded to me.

I felt a burst of relief. That meant Saldanha hadn't been able to provide any visual confirmation of who I was to his boss before he'd died. I'd just met one of the men after my identity. But why would Andrade be threatened by my mission here?

"A pleasure to meet you, Chief Andrade. Thanks for the translation."

"No problem. Rio can be hard on foreigners."

He snatched at finger food from a passing platter and chewed it ravenously, smiling all the while.

"Antonio sure knows how to throw a shindig, doesn't he?"

"The most fabulous party in the world!" César laughed.

"Well, well, now. That title belongs only to Carnival, and that is still a couple of weeks away." Andrade flashed his teeth. He was definitely a bit rough around the edges.

"Are you going out of town?" asked César.

"No, staying in Rio for the first couple of days. My niece Fernanda is participating in one of the competing samba schools."

"Sounds like fun," I said.

"It is. She goes to practice over in Samba City every week."

"Samba City?"

"It's a place by the port where each of the samba

schools prepares for Carnival. They practice into the late hours for audiences," César explained.

"It is managed by my nephew. I go and watch when I can after work. It's not far from my office," added Andrade.

"That must be a sight," I said.

"It is, for sure." César nodded.

"You should come with us sometime while you are here, it's a memorable experience," said Andrade.

César switched to my other side, putting me between the two when a photographer approached us. We all smiled for the camera. He took each of our names in turn and moved on to the next group.

A hush fell amongst the guests. People made way when a well-weathered man was wheeled into the center of the open foyer. He looked to Lygia and waved her over. His silver hair accentuated his seniority. He was elegantly dressed, and it was clear he commanded respect from all those around him. Lygia went over and kissed the old man on both cheeks. He went through the motions impatiently, and Lygia stepped back. She took a glass of champagne from a passing waiter's tray and sipped. Paulo André leaned over to embrace the man as well. The old man seemed to come to life with a great yellow-toothed smile. He patted Paulo André's shoulder affectionately and the onlookers applauded. Antonio crouched and the two men shared a warm embrace. I saw Lygia look away.

"That is Jucelino de Castello-Branco. Lygia's father," César said. I'd noticed that Angelo de Andrade had already run over to pay his respects. "He is one of the most powerful men in Brazil, securing many a politician their positions, including me." He shrugged innocently. "So let's go greet the man."

César and I approached Jucelino just as Andrade and his wife walked away toward the gardens. I caught a look of disdain on his face as he passed.

Antonio leaned down toward his father-in-law once

again and introduced me. "T. J. is here to invest in the construction of the Olympic parks. We are very excited to have him on our team," he said.

I shook the old man's hand.

"Where are you from, my boy?"

"I'm from Texas, sir. Houston, originally, but now a New Yorker."

"Ah, Houston, excellent hospitals!" Jucelino exclaimed. "Had my hip replacement there."

Antonio walked side by side with Jucelino, who was being wheeled by a house servant. Rio's society mingled in the gardens as the band played gentle music. Antonio took his place on a low stage set up at the edge of the lawn between the two flagpoles. He was joined by the president of the IOC, the mayor of Rio, and César. Lygia and Paulo André stood off to the side.

People chimed their glasses to bring attention to the oncoming speech. Brasão spoke English out of respect for the IOC president and other foreign guests.

"Welcome, my friends, to my home and to join me in the celebration of this grand occasion for our city and our country."

The crowd applauded and whistled.

"Tonight we celebrate Brazil. We celebrate how far our country has come. We celebrate that we are now poised as one of the great nations of this Earth. Hosting the Olympics is a firm symbol of our Order and Progress, the motto that adorns our beloved flag. I am so humbled to have been bestowed the honor of building the venues to support these illustrious and momentous events for Brazil on the world stage. I share that honor with all of you who have supported me with your friendship through the years. I would like to extend a most warm and personal welcome to Jacques Rogge, president of the International Olympic Committee, our honored guest this evening."

Everyone cheered out a warm welcome.

"We have a wonderful night of food and music in store for all, in particular, a lovely surprise to lead our celebration. Please enjoy yourselves as I pass the microphone to our wonderful queen of bossa nova, Ms. Bebela Gibela."

A wave of surprised gasps, "ohhs" and "ahhhs" rippled through the crowd as Bebela stepped onto the stage to wild applause, kissing Antonio on either cheek as she took the microphone from his hand.

"Boa noite, pessoal!" she called out and began to sing. Lygia appeared by my side and handed her empty glass to a passing waiter in tails.

"I know that song. I've heard it playing at Starbucks or something," I said.

"Shall we dance?"

"How could I refuse a lady as lovely as you?"

Lygia took my hand and we joined the crowd already on the dance floor. Folks were having a mighty fine time. The song came to an end and the band struck up a samba beat, and I suddenly felt like a fish out of water.

"A prelude to Carnival!" Lygia laughed at my discombobulation. "Here, watch my feet"—she pointed down. Lygia held her hand up to her lips and chuckled.

"What's so funny?"

"Americans never know how to samba, even when they have rhythm—like you."

"Show me again," I challenged her.

"OK, watch my feet." She took my hand and positioned my waist with her other, leading me instead of the other way around. I stumbled awkwardly as we moved. I followed the quick steps as best I could.

"Now your upper body moves in half time, like this," she instructed.

She put her hand on my waist again to adjust my posture and clapped in delight. I soon felt the motion from within. It was really all in the abs, and let me tell y'all, mine were more than suitable to handle a little samba. As we danced I wondered how much she knew about her husband and how deep her involvement in his empire ran.

"I'm impressed. Not bad for a gringo!"

I looked around me at all the smiling, gesticulating Brazilians and marveled at how they enjoyed a good time. The samba ended and we cheered.

We strolled from the tent through the crowds. Lygia introduced me to a woman from the United Nations World Heritage Organization who was working with Brasão on designating sections of the Porto Maravilha renovations as World Heritage Sites. We were having an animated conversation, and Lygia dutifully excused herself to mingle with other guests, taking a new champagne glass from the bar.

Danilo approached with his wife on his arm. Sylvia was much as I would have expected. She had long, slender legs supported by the most spindle-like golden high heels, the tips of which were covered by those little plastic lawn heel protectors that had been provided at the door. Her purse swung from her forearm with every calculated step. A platinum belt around her tiny waist held the ballooned-up dress. The top was revealing, to put it mildly.

The lovely UN World Heritage woman looked over at the couple and politely excused herself for another hors d'oeuvre before they reached us.

"T. J.," Danilo greeted. "Let me introduce you to my wife, Sylvia."

"*Encantado,*" I said in Spanish.

"*Hablas Castellano?*"

"*Si*, quite well, actually. I understand you are from Argentina." I smiled.

Sylvia's long eyelashes hid her pupils from sight. Protruding were the bottoms of her brown irises and her artificially plumped, magenta-colored lips. Bless 'er heart.

"Actually, I am from Uruguay, but I lived mostly in

Buenos Aires. I hear you will be joining us on Monday to Fernando de Noronha." Her voice had a soft purr with an urgent breathlessness to it.

"That's right, I'm very much looking forward to it."

"It's not a terribly long flight. On Antonio's jet it takes about as long as the drive to our place in Bùzios, don't you think, darling?" she said, rolling her Rs in a thick Porteño accent.

Danilo nodded as he surveyed the guests around us.

"Antonio and Lygia have the most beautiful property in Rio. Isn't this incredible?" She leaned forward on the balustrade and looked out at the sea, kicking her shoe back to reveal its red underside.

A couple of large freighters passed each other beyond the islands.

"The coast seems to be a heavy shipping lane," I said.

"It is, actually, Rio is a busy port," Danilo said.

Fireworks shot off far in the distance in the direction of the *favelas*.

"That reminds me of a fun story. When I was sixteen, I think it was around 1987," Danilo recounted, "I had my own business at the time. A freighter just like those was caught by the Coast Guard in a chase that took it down a thousand miles of coastline, all the way past São Paulo State before they were stopped. Along the way, they dumped their contraband of marijuana from Thailand, packaged in aluminum cans. The cans, over twenty thousand of them, washed up on the beaches. It came to be known as the Summer of the Can. The most pungent, exotic, mind-bending, hallucinogenic Siamese pot anyone had ever tried. And it arrived just in time for the summer holidays like a gift from God to stoners and surfers all over southeastern Brazil. I would scour the beaches early every morning for a month, carrying armloads of cans back to my sidewalk cart, and I'd sell it during the day. I made myself a fortune."

"Sounds like you've come a long way since then."

His laugh was booming. "I made enough money that summer to pay for school, got my degree and grew my business. Unfortunately, my business had a little confrontation with the law and I was arrested. But thanks to Antonio, I got out. He hired me after I participated in one of his rehabilitation charities. He was very involved in the program and saw my potential."

"Antonio seems to be a good man."

Danilo took on a serious tone. "Antonio made me who I am today. I owe everything to him. I learned quickly, and we had similar visions of how to get things done. We have good instincts, sharp intuition." He looked at me with the slightest squint in his eye, barely perceptible and quick as a flash, but unnerving nonetheless. He seemed to be sizing me up. "We're hoping you do too.'

"Antonio's a lucky guy to have a loyal man like you on his side," I said simply.

I looked at Sylvia and she was reapplying her lipstick, having lost interest in the male conversation.

"So what's the plan for the island?"

"Antonio's jet should be back by one p.m., so let's meet at Santos Dumont Airport by the private jet gate. I look forward to shooting with a Texan on the island." He smiled flipping his L-shaped fingers at me. "Mr. Bunggee-bunggee!"

It was an eerie echo of the motel manager at the Shalimar. "What is there to hunt there?"

"Wild pigs. They were brought to the island on the early slave ships that stopped there on their way to Salvador. When Antonio and I first discussed the idea of a luxury development on the island, we thought we would start by sponsoring an ecologically beneficial program as an amicable approach. The boars were a primary nuisance, so I came up with the idea of the wild boar game park and Antonio thought it was brilliant. The government was thrilled when we suggested they be rounded up and maintained in a special hunting park. They had caused considerable damage to indigenous species. The finance minister, may he rest in peace, had a big role in helping us secure the rights to build there. The game lodge was the first step toward building Paraíso Tartaruga."

All roads led to the minister's death; his path must have crossed Brasão's in more ways than one. "I've hunted wild boar back home. Good fun."

His strong chin pointed upward. "It's turned into a healthy profit center for us on Fernando de Noronha. Many tourists going to the island aren't as interested in the eco thing as their fellow travelers, so it makes for a great activity for those who prefer to hunt over watching some stupid turtle eggs hatch. And it has cleared the island of all of the invasive pigs."

Lygia walked over, champagne in hand, with a few of her fellow actors and began introductions.

Danilo joked, "This is Johnee Waynee."

One of Lygia's friends said, "Bunggee-bunggee! Are you Texan?"

Clearly, Brazilians related Texans to John Wayne and old Western movies. How bluntly stereotypical. Of course I played along, exaggerating my drawl. "That's right." I smiled.

Danilo turned away to say hello to someone. Lygia took Sylvia's arm courteously, seeing that she had been left unattended and seemed lost. We talked about the latest *novela* episode. The friends laughed about their shared experiences working on the set together. Sylvia seemed to laugh along when the others did, as if on cue.

A handsome man pushed forward.

It was Lygia's makeup artist saying good-bye and gathering the two other actresses to go. She gave him a hug and his gaze fell upon me. He smiled, recognizing me from the studio visit.

"This is Marcelo. He works miracles on my face," said Lygia.

I noticed her words were suddenly thicker from the champagne.

"Marcelo, this is T. J., a business colleague of Antonio's."

Marcelo took my hand with a firm squeeze that lingered just a bit. "A pleasure to meet you. Lygia, your face is the miracle, I just help you glow. Oh, and *'Pro meu filho eu viro o mundo!'*" He repeated her final line from the last episode with a snap of his fingers. All of Brazil was murmuring about it; Jovelina wouldn't let up.

They laughed and tossed some kisses. Marcelo gave me a parting glance as he walked briskly away with Lygia's colleagues, bouncing to Bebela's tunes.

Antonio strolled by with the mayor of Rio and César. Lygia turned away to replace her empty champagne glass with another. Evidently, something was wrong.

"T. J., this is Eduardo Pinto Canela, our marvelous city's mayor. Mr. Leukemeyer represents a group of investors interested in Brazil's economic miracle. He feels Rio is ripe with opportunity—isn't that so, my friend?" Hearing Antonio's voice, Danilo turned around to join the group.

"I'm enchanted by your glorious city, Mayor Canela. I'm honored to make your acquaintance."

"On the contrary, Mr. Leukemeyer, the pleasure is all mine. Antonio has worked with us on so many projects that have made Rio a world-class city once again, so I am pleased to meet anybody that he feels has similar objectives." He smiled, eyebrows arched.

Danilo reached out to pat the mayor on the shoulder. "Any news on moving the *favela* Autodromo, Duda?"

I had to assume that the use of a nickname implied a certain familiarity. I noticed Lygia look away again and take another sip from her flute.

The mayor grimaced. "Unfortunately, the dwellers are putting up a fight and political correctness is taking center stage. I guarantee they will be moved. But it is beginning to look like it won't be without significant relocation costs."

Lygia turned around and scolded, "Duda, you know that is the least they deserve."

"Ah, here we go again," murmured Danilo. Sylvia gave him a mild tap on the wrist.

"Lygia, you know we do what we can to assist our needy citizens," said the mayor. "It is why we match contributions to programs like your Hearts of Wisdom in Vidigal from our city budget," he reasoned.

At the mention of her charity, Lygia's stone-cold eyes shot Antonio an accusatory glance.

"Please, Lygia, let's not be egregious with our guests," Antonio cautioned.

"I am embarrassed to be among you men." Her lips quivered as she fought to maintain her composure. "Excuse me, please." She put down her empty glass and walked briskly away from us down the path toward the pool.

"I'm so sorry that the subject upset her so," the mayor said.

"No worries, Duda. It's a wonderful evening, please enjoy yourself. She has had a difficult day," Antonio apologized.

Bebela began a tune with a nice beat.

"Let's dance!" Sylvia said to Danilo.

"Not now."

"I would love to," said the mayor, taking Sylvia's arm and leading her to the dancing tent. Sylvia carefully navigated her steps across the lawn.

Antonio, Danilo and I were left alone to walk along the cliff's edge. It wasn't long before Danilo excused himself and went off into the crowd toward Angelo de Andrade's wife, who was nowhere near her husband. I saw her smile discreetly as he approached.

Antonio leaned in and said softly, "Please excuse Lygia's behavior. I gave her some bad news today and she is not happy about it. Nothing serious."

"No need to mention it, really. Time for a refill. Can I bring you anything?" I offered, to change the subject.

"Thank you, T. J., but I see the transportation minister, who I must attend to. Please, go ahead and enjoy yourself."

I walked toward the house, passing through the crowd. Once inside, it took little effort for me to pretend to admire the art. The bartender brought me a scotch on the rocks. I looked around to be sure I was alone before strolling down the grand sculpture hall I'd passed on the way in. The guard was still there, so I asked him where the bathroom was.

"Down the hall to the right," he said.

The doorways into adjoining rooms were shut and fingerprint-reading devices barred entry to some of them.

Velvety deep-red carpet peeked out from under a door. I guessed that was Brasão's library. Inside the bathroom across the hall, I put my drink down. I swiped through my apps to find the fingerprint scanner—a nifty little program that had been developed in conjunction with the CIA.

When I opened the door the guard had moved on. I quickly stepped across the hall and held the phone's camera up to the flat, two-inch panel of the fingerprint scanner itself; the last user's prints popped into view on my screen in vibrant ultraviolet spectrum. I pressed a button and the print was converted to a flesh-colored oval resembling the pad of a finger; the lines barely visible to the eye. I turned my screen to face the scanner and held my breath while its laser swiped the image. The door's lock gave a muted click.

I snuck in with a last backward glance—no guard in sight. The lights were dim and the evening's music reverberated rowdily against the windows. I looked at Brasão's impressive seat of power. He made his decisions surrounded by backlit shelves full of literature, diplomas and trophies. I searched them and the cabinets beneath until I found the Wi-Fi router and modem. Jackpot! I gently pulled out the unit and unplugged the Ethernet cable. I pulled the little bug node out of my jacket pocket, clicked it onto the cable plug and reconnected it. Nobody could ever detect this cool little sucker. The Brazilians certainly didn't have anything like this.

"Aí Gostosinha."

I froze. Heavy breathing was coming from an alcove behind a leather screen. Shit. The loud music had obscured any low sounds. I gently put the router back and moved slowly toward the screen. With the breathing came a guttural male groan—and the sight of Danilo, his trousers on the floor, banging the lovely Mrs. Andrade long and slow, like a real Don Juan. His athletic cheeks dimpled with each thrust and shuddered with his climax. I moved swiftly past the screen and reached for the door.

"Quem 'ta aí?"

I turned. Danilo was zipping his pants as he rounded the screen, catching me as if I were just peeking in.

"What are you doing here? How did you even get in?" Any sign of shame vanished instantly at the sight of me.

"I was looking for the bathroom. The door was open, so I stepped in. So sorry to interrupt you, buddy. No worries." I nodded at Mrs. Andrade, behind him, with a sheepish grin. "I didn't see a thing," I assured them, stepping back into the hallway and shutting the door. I reached for my drink in the bathroom. That was close, I reckoned. After a believable time in the restroom, I walked toward the gardens for a breather, my heart pounding in my chest. I finished off my glass and got another before stepping outside.

Down the path Paulo André had taken me on earlier, I passed a group of boisterous guests seated around the pool. The alcohol slowed my pulse. With Adriana a question in my mind, I wasn't even sure what good the surveillance might be. But if Ronaldo had full faith in her, so be it. I needed to make this mission work—so much depended on it.

When I got to the grotto, I heard soft sniffles and hiccups. I rounded the corner to find the beautiful Lygia de Castello-Branco in tears on a bench, her face in her hands. When she heard my steps on the gravel, she scrambled to her feet. I'd startled her. I put my arm around her shoulder and sat her again, realizing in the dim light that she was crying uncontrollably.

"Lygia, what's the matter? What can I do to help? Tell me what's wrong." My words made her cry even harder. She shook her head from side to side as I unfolded my pocket square and handed it to her. She blotted her eyes.

"Hey, there, li'l lady, tell me what's the matter. I'm right here to listen." The Southern lulling came naturally—like being with my younger sisters growing up.

She sniffled and looked at me through her tears.

"Oh, T. J., none of it makes sense. Today Antonio told me that he is pulling his funding from Hearts of Wisdom for good. He claims it is in conflict with certain interests! Can you believe that? Can you even tell me what that means? What interests could justify such a thing?" She looked up to the sky with a huffed exhale. "I can tell you one thing, it isn't good."

She fixed her hair and looked out at the sea. The moonbeams reflected like raining diamonds on the streaming waterfall behind her.

"It's not just the charity; I can find more funding with some effort. It's that I am a trapped woman. I am trapped by my marriage, my family, my fame. All I want is to take Paulo André to the States where he can be safe and escape all of this madness with Antonio and my father, my fans. I know it's not safe here. I hear Antonio on his agitated phone calls that he is so secretive about. I have learned to trust my instincts," she said, clenching her fist.

"Why don't you just leave? You're an intelligent, capable person."

"Oh, if only it were so easy, but our relationship is so entangled. It's so complicated—beyond belief!"

More silent tears fell down her face.

"You're a beacon of hope to so many millions of Brazilians. They identify with your strength." I gently squeezed her shoulder. "That's who you are. You will find a way to make things right."

"I know I have to be strong, if not for me, for Paulo André. But sometimes I wonder if someone will ever be *my* beacon."

She looked into my eyes, and before I knew it, her lips were pressed against mine, her arms wrapped around my torso as tightly as they could. We embraced for a moment, and then she pulled away as suddenly as she had advanced. I'd be lying if I didn't say it felt real nice.

"Lygia—"

"Please forgive me. I've had too much champagne . . . " She looked away, hiding her embarrassment.

"I understand, Lygia, we're friends, you needed some kindness and got confused. I'm here if you want to talk."

She burst into laughter. "My gosh, I barely even know you!" She put a hand over her mouth and laughed harder. Her tears were now of unbridled amusement. As if it were contagious, I started laughing too, but was perplexed.

"Oh, it sure feels good to laugh," she said. "If you could just forget that happened." Lygia dabbed at her mascara. "There are moments when I just don't know who I am anymore. Just too many roles. I get lost sometimes." She sighed, catching her breath. "All that champagne doesn't help matters. But I feel much better now. Thank you for listening." She reached for both my hands. "Truly, T. J., thank you."

"I'm not sure for what, but you're welcome. I'm the one who got to kiss the most famous Brazilian star on the planet. I should be thanking you!"

"I mean for being such a gentleman." She smiled. "Can you forgive me?"

"Don't give it another thought."

"I think I am ready to rejoin the world."

I helped Lygia up and she leaned on the balustrade and laughed again. We strolled back down to the party. As we entered the garden, solitary Sylvia's eyes fell upon us. She was noticeably relieved to have Lygia once again by her side. Not long thereafter, a show of fireworks brought the mega-soirée to a ceremonious end.

CHAPTER EIGHTEEN

The sun was high up in the sky and the Sunday crowds were beginning to descend upon the beachside promenade below my balcony. I was getting ready for a quick jaunt to the gym, followed by an afternoon at the beach to see Zezé and hopefully get a look at his friend Margarida. He had texted me earlier to make sure I was coming.

But first, I needed to touch base with Adriana. I hadn't spoken to her since Friday, and I was still concerned about Bernardo's potential role in all of this, despite Ronaldo's assurances.

It went to voicemail. "Call me."

Something Ronaldo had said yesterday struck me—he thought he knew who the mole might be. How could Andrade's man know what I looked like if Andrade did not? I thought about our few exchanges at the party. If he didn't recognize my face, who had pointed me out to Saldanha in the first place? And if Saldanha was already following me at the mall, he could only have done so with help from someone close to Ronaldo's team.

Andrade's involvement seemed a surprise to Ronaldo

and Adriana both. Maybe her husband was not the mole, but Adriana had something more she was keeping from me, perhaps from Ronaldo as well. I'd felt it when she hung up.

I changed for the gym and packed my bag for the beach. I reached for the door when my phone rang.

"Is everything OK?"

"Hello, Adriana, I got worried, you didn't answer."

"Sorry, I'm out in the field. We have informants talking about a big deal going down in several *favelas* sometime this week. We think it must be a major shipment arriving. Several rival militia gangs seem to be positioning themselves for business. I was prepping my colleagues who will be leading the next BOPE raid."

"Is this a bad time?"

"No, actually, it's good. I have a few minutes to talk."

"Great. Listen, I gotta ask you about our last chat. What happened?"

"It's a long story, it is classified, and it has no bearing on our mission," she said crisply.

"The hell it doesn't!" I was too exasperated to keep my voice calm. "I killed a man because of Andrade. Bernardo works for him."

"Don't be unreasonable. Bernardo works for a division under Andrade, yes, but he is in an unrelated covert situation. He cannot discuss the details of it with me, but it has nothing to do with you."

"For Christ's sake, don't be cryptic. Right now your husband is really the only way I can think of that Andrade would know enough about me to have me followed. What does he know? Tell me, or this op ain't gonna work."

"T. J.!" Her voice was shaken. "It is true that my problems with him relate to work, but I know he is not the mole you think he is. That is all I can tell you and you have to believe me. We often have to keep secrets from each other, and that is difficult, but he is a good person and this coincidence is simply that."

"Why doesn't Ronaldo know about Bernardo's secret missions?" I asked.

"You talked with him? You're only supposed to call him if I can't be found. We have protocols for a reason. You—it's like when you went into Vidigal! You can jeopardize your cover with these foolish decisions."

"You are changing the subject. Why doesn't Ronaldo know about Bernardo's missions?"

"For the same reasons that Bernardo does not know about you," she snapped. "Secrets must be kept in order to be successful. The way things are here, the fewer people that know about you and what you are doing the better."

She wasn't budging. And I had no choice but to trust her. It did help to know that Ronaldo trusted her too. Time was ticking. "Regardless of who the mole is, I need to know why Andrade is having me followed. If your husband is so innocent, perhaps he can help us with that. Now I need to fill you in on a couple of important developments."

I heard her sigh. "I'm listening."

"Firstly, are you getting a signal from the bug in Brasão's library? I caught Danilo misbehaving in there. I had to pretend I'd walked into the wrong room."

"I take it he was not with Mrs. Lemos?"

"No, here's one for you to tinker with: it was Mrs. Andrade. Now you tell me what that's all about."

"Actually, I can. After you left the room and the monitoring had gone live, Mrs. Andrade told Danilo that she would meet up with him after the island. It seems like they were planning against Andrade, like she's planning to leave him or something—records show a lot of communication between the two, on a daily basis prior to our surveillance. We've followed a bit of computer usage, a couple conversations in the library, but nothing pertinent yet."

"Stay on that and let me know if anything interesting

comes up before I leave tomorrow. OK then, back to Andrade. What do you know about his relationship with Brasão other than Danilo having an affair with his wife? I've got to know why this guy's snooping on me and who he's reporting to. If it's Brasão, tomorrow's trip may be a trap."

"Nothing outside of political support."

"What about this senator Andrade used to work for, Junior Belém dos Santos? I don't recall seeing him on the suspect lists."

"Santos is a Rio state senator. I know that they belong to the same political party and that Santos has also always backed Andrade's career. I will consult with Ronaldo."

"I reckon we should look into that relationship too. I'm betting whoever pointed me out to Saldanha is the same person behind Ronaldo's missing files. Which could mean Ronaldo's funding source is in danger too."

I blew out a breath. "I'll be gone until Wednesday. I'll check in with you when I can. I'm travelling with Danilo and Sylvia. That guy makes me nervous—I can't tell if he's measuring me up or if he has something on me."

"We feel Danilo must communicate with Feijão in person somehow or through another layer of people."

"I'm starting to wonder if Mrs. Andrade might be directly involved."

Adriana's team was at work around her. Radio static from their communication sounded in the background.

"OK, another question: Will I have to pass through security to get on a private jet at Santos Dumont? I'd prefer to take my gun with me, but if they stop me at the airport, I can't exactly flash my badge with Danilo by my side."

"No, people like Brasão and their guests have full clearance. Have a safe trip and be very careful."

I went to the gym and thought about Lygia and our kiss. The attraction had never occurred to me until that moment. She came across as an independent lady, but deep down I could tell she wanted and needed a good, supportive companion by her side. Don't we all. The precarious nature of her situation was alarming; the poor darlin' had no idea how dangerous it really was. Or did she? I could not gauge how deep her knowledge into Antonio's affairs ran, but she was hell-bent on shielding her son from it. I felt a responsibility to protect her. If her entanglement with Brasão was as complex as she said, I had to assume that meant money and assets in her name were used for his business needs. A divorce would surly wreak havoc on his financial mechanics.

After my workout, I stopped at the corner for a quick bite, then walked to the beach, marveling once again at all the people out and about. I found Sonia's concession tent and rented a chair more or less in the same spot as last week.

Sonia came by and asked, "Where Marcos?"

"Salvador."

"Uma caipirinha?" she asked.

"Por favor."

I looked around to see if Castro and his group of Nubian studs were here, but I didn't see them. Maybe I was too early. I waited for my drink. The sun was high in the sky, with a few passing clouds to offer temporary relief from its roasting rays; I put on some sunscreen and lay back for a few moments of silence and rest. My skin had already taken on a deeply tan color and my hair was as blond as I'd seen it in years, bleached by the *Carioca* sun.

My thoughts were broken by my vibrating phone.

"Sean?" I was actually looking forward to hearing his voice.

"You've got a lot of nerve asking me for help!"

He was enraged—not good. "Whoa, buddy, what's going on?" I braced for the answer I knew all too well.

"How do you think it makes me feel to hear from *Brent* and *Charles* about your shameless philandering in

Rio, while I'm going through the worst time of my life? One of their first calls back home. Said you weren't even wearing your ring!"

"That's not true, it never left my hands." I turned it on my right hand with my thumb.

"How can I even speak to you? I'm flipping out here. Are we over?"

I could tell that Sean was coming undone, angrier than a rabid coyote.

"Sean, calm down, I'm not seeing anybody."

"Who's Marcos?"

"A person of interest in the case. He's not even here in Rio anymore."

"Fuck you, T. J., after more than fifteen years you up and leave me at the worst time of my life. Are you even on assignment down there or are you just partying?"

I put some more SPF on my nose and sipped my *caipirinha*.

"Hey Sean, take it easy. We agreed to take a break from each other, remember? Marcos was nothing, just a means to an end, he was a big help to my assignment." I let out a frustrated groan. "Besides, this isn't about us. I—"

"Did you seriously call me for help to toss me a line like that? Really? I'm hanging up."

"No, wait. Wait! This is really important. Lives depend on it. Please hear me out."

He didn't hang up, but he was silent on the other end. Finally, "Make it quick."

"Your old friend William Chaffrey—"

"He's in prison, you know that."

"Yes, I do. You worked with an employee of his who handled all of your international investments with his firm, right?"

"Earl Cunningham?"

"Yeah, Earl. Can you trust him? I need you to ask him if he knew the money handler for a guy named Antonio Carlos de Melo Brasão. Now write this down, please. The accounts could also be under the names Lygia de Castello-Branco, Jucelino Neves Castello-Branco, or Danilo Camargo de Lemos."

"Seriously?"

"Please, Sean, just write it down." I painfully spelled out each endless name as Sean's patience ebbed. "Did you get that? They disinvested with Madoff just before the economy went south and moved their money elsewhere, and I need to know who managed their money in the States."

"Well, weren't they lucky."

"Please, I need to get Bradley to subpoena any accounts existing in those names. I have a strong hunch this will be a key factor in solving the mystery down here. Then I can come back so we can try to make things right again. I miss you, Sean."

"I hate you, T. J."

The line went dead. Perhaps my words had come across a bit manipulatively? Goddamn Brent. I realized I did miss Sean: his friendship, his humor, his understanding. I had to wonder if maybe my absence for extended periods of time had contributed to his loss of direction. Maybe if I'd been more present I could have swayed him away from some of his graver mistakes. Maybe I was being too hard and unforgiving of him at a time when he needed my support. I knew Sean would do the favor for me regardless. I felt like I was on to something big.

I bookmarked the thought with the arrival of Castro and his entourage. They planted themselves several feet away on the beach; a herd of rippling, shiny black musculature in scanty Speedos, dark sunglasses, and thick chain necklaces. High-fives and clapping hugs were plentiful as they greeted each other in the afternoon sun. Zezé was not among them. I watched all the cliques congregate on the beach. The endless eye candy—too many sexy people here. How could anybody be faithful in this town?

Just then, Zezé arrived, skipping over to Castro for a

fist bump. He stretched his sinuous body as he spoke rapidly to his posse, making outsized gestures. He began his ritual rounds from group to group, raising laughter as he went. He showed off his trademark acrobatic flips, followed by a grand jeté, legs split wide apart and arms up in graceful extension—a beautiful performance greeted with great applause from onlookers—then made his way over to a neighboring group of guys. Soon they were all in stitches, laughing about something or other. Then he caught sight of me and skipped my way.

"T. J.! You are here! Is so nice see you, my friend!"

Zezé threw himself down on his knees next to my chair and reached over to give me a voluptuous kiss.

"Oh my God, you look so hot!" he exclaimed dramatically. "You so dark now! You no look same person! Mm."

He reached over and ran his hands over my chest.

"Easy, buddy, don't get me too excited now, you just got here. How are you, Zezé? Do you want to have a *caipirinha* with me?"

I ordered another from Sonia, and Zezé made himself comfortable by my side.

"That was quite a jump you just did back there," I said. "Very impressive. You've got talent."

"Then help me that school in New York. You no forget will you?" he asked.

"I promise."

"Good, because nobody here going hire a *michê*, a hustler, to dance ballet," he said, waving the thought away. "How you doing? Tell me what new?" His finger traced circles in the sand while he looked at me intently.

"I've met some extraordinary people and have seen some beautiful parts of Rio. Good business opportunities. I can't complain. It's been great."

"But do you like here?" He seemed to really want to know.

I thought about what I'd experienced so far, the accepted brazen juxtapositions of *Cariocas* and their city—

how it appealed to me on so many levels. "I'd definitely come back."

"Where your friend? I ask Margarida come by later to meet him."

"Sorry, Zezé, he only arrives in a few days. But I thought I could arrange this as a favor. I know what he likes."

"Good friend, you are, T. J. You funny guy." Zezé patted my leg warmly. "She come by later. You meet. Tell me about New York. What like there?"

"It's a world away from here, li'l buddy, that's for sure. But it's a great place too. You can make things happen there if you really try. I bet you could."

That may have been the *caipirinha* talking. The boy had true talent. In an alternate universe, I might be able to pull some strings with Ferdi's contacts in the performing arts world to give him a true chance.

"I wish I could. But I live in reality. I know what I am and who my friends. I do what I need, you know? And I have OK life." Music was playing somewhere and Zezé's foot had been tapping to the beat. "But I do love dance." He fell back in the sand next to me with his arms splayed out over his head. His iridescent green eyes rolled back in delight. "That is the dream I go at night, to be a star ballet dancer." He stretched his body. "So silly, really, in compare to reality."

Zezé sighed and sat up to reach for the drink Sonia handed him. The afternoon breeze wafted over a delegation of his sweet manly scent. His hand still rested on my thigh.

"T. J.!" a male Brazilian voice called out.

I could not place it. I looked around with trepidation, attempting to locate the source.

"Hello!"

Zezé waved. *"Aí Marcelo!"*

I realized it was Lygia's makeup artist. Damn! He knew Zezé too?

"Does everybody know you here?" I whispered.

Zezé nodded. I gently moved his hand off my leg and got up to greet Marcelo. "I guess you know my friend Zezé here . . ."

"*Tudo bem, Zé?*" Marcelo greeted.

"That was an amazing party last night. Did you have a good time?" I asked.

"Yes, of course! Lygia always make best party in Rio. So chic. Very crème de la crème, you know? What you doing here?" he asked. He smiled at Zezé and then at me. "I never would think you . . ." Marcelo let the sentence pass.

"Sit down and join us," I invited.

"I am meeting some friends, but . . ." Marcelo lifted his sunglasses and looked around. "I early anyway. I visit a moment."

He put his towel and bag down and sat in the sand.

Zezé looked at me incredulously. "You know Lygia de Castello-Branco? How can be?" he laughed, looking at Marcelo.

"He is business partner of Lygia husband," offered Marcelo.

"Something like that," I said.

"Wow, that very impressive!"

"It is," agreed Marcelo. "I see my friends. Got to go. T. J., you look even better in a bathing suit!" He winked as he got up and blew us a kiss. "*Tchau!*"

Busted again. Now Lygia would surely know. I'd just have to play it up somehow. Shit.

The sun was hotter than a honeymoon hotel, and after seeing Marcelo, I felt a bit flustered. I needed to cool off. Too few degrees of separation.

"Hey, li'l buddy, you mind if I jump in the water for a second?"

"Sure, I watch you things." He flashed his charming grin.

I smiled at the irony of an American tourist asking a

hustler on the gay beach in Rio to watch his things while he went for a swim. Sean'd be laughing out loud. The water's coolness tingled as I dove into a wave and lapped my way out beyond the break. I looked again at the city's majestic chaos.

There was a sudden sharp sting on my toe and I recoiled in the water. Jellyfish floated in the waves and I swam slowly, searching out a safe direction in which to escape from them. I called out to other bathers, *"Cuidado, cuidado!"* pointing to the jellyfish masses, and made my way out of the water. The alluring ocean had deceived me. My toe was red and burning. It was beginning to blister, but I could tell it was just a tiny bit of poison that had touched my skin and all it would need was a Band-Aid—a close call. I looked back and saw other bathers scurrying out of the water, some not as lucky as me. When I got back to my seat, Zezé wrapped a towel over my shoulders.

"Thanks, Zezé, you're so nice."

"No, you are," he smiled, finishing his drink. "What happen over there?"

"There are jellyfish in the water stinging people."

"Oh, they come sometime, more before big storm."

He saw someone he knew and put his empty cup in the sand.

"Thanks, T. J., I go speak with some friends, see you soon when Margarida come. You be here for while?"

"For a while."

I reclined in my chair, crossed my leg and put a piece of ice from my drink on my toe to ease the pain and swelling. A woman's voice called out behind me: *"Sonia, cadê o Zezé?"*

My chair was pretty near horizontal, so I had to angle my head to look. I saw her colorful fingernails first, and then a deep ugly scar through her fleshy palm. I was facing the back of her dark-skinned, shapely legs. I'd been right: this was the woman I'd seen running up the back stairs of the Shalimar that morning. She was Margarida.

Zezé was several yards away, engaged with some European tourists. I grabbed my phone out of my bag and turned on the camera app. Sonia was pointing out Zezé's whereabouts to Margarida, whose face filled my screen. I snapped two shots without notice. Her phone rang just then and she launched into rapid-fire Portuguese, her face crossed in annoyance. I got a couple shots of her scarred palm too. Zezé came skipping up to her in the sand and kissed her cheek while she finished her conversation. He made the introductions and Margarida clearly recognized me from our morning encounter several days back; her nod reeked of suspicion. Adriana would consider this treading on thin ice.

"She say she see before, outside Shalimar last week. What you do there?" Zezé looked at me inquisitively.

"I have to say, I thought she looked familiar. The gentleman I'd like her to spend time with is a very important client of mine. I was searching for a place where he could have a nice time with a 'friend' while he was here. The Shalimar was recommended to me. It's very important that everything is set up for him to have a fun time while he's in town. Is she OK? She looks annoyed."

Zezé chuckled. "Her Feijão big baby. Very tough, dangerous, but underneath he a mama's boy. Always late see her because have to help his mama, every time they going meet." Margarida rolled her big eyes in irritation. They both sat down with me for a while and I ordered a couple drinks for them from Sonia. Zezé went over how much she would charge to entertain my friend and how long she could spend with him. Margarida was putting on some suntan oil, no SPF for this chick. She didn't look at me directly much, just texted furiously with Feijão or gazed disinterestedly at beach-goers as we spoke. I did peripherally catch a couple dubious glances my way though.

I offered a few $100 bills to seal the deal and Margarida noted the date on her phone. After a while, I slipped on my shorts and tank top, grabbed my backpack and said good-bye to both of them. I counted out a few bills for Sonia as I passed her by the concession tent. Margarida was watching me. I got the feeling she was unsettled about seeing me again. I'd seen Margarida, photographed her. I knew who she was. Once in my elevator, I texted the pictures to Adriana, letting her know this was Feijão's girl.

As she had often insisted, I would leave that side of the mission to her. But now we were one link closer to Brasão, closing in from all sides.

CHAPTER NINETEEN

The stewardess handed me a mimosa. I sat back in the plush leather seat and looked out the small round window at the sea below. The waves roiled over the blue depths, 230 miles out in the South Atlantic. The plane banked to the left and Danilo pointed.

"Look, we're arriving. You see all the rock formations below? They're part of an extinct volcanic archipelago. Here comes the main island now."

Sylvia leaned into her window. "Is so pretty! I love this place, is so marvelous!"

The island came into view all right, a towering rocky outcropping with cliffs forming dozens of paradisiacal beaches all along its coast.

"That is what we call Erection Rock," chortled Danilo, pointing to a huge oblong rock that did in fact look unmistakably like a giant erect penis, especially from this angle.

"It can be seen from almost any point on the island, obviously enhancing the appeal." He grinned mischievously.

"*Danilo, por favor!* It is called Morro do Pico! The Peak's Hill," she corrected.

The seatbelt sign came on and the pilot prepared to land.

Zezé had been right about the storm. It had been a dark and rainy morning. Rodrigues and I'd gotten stuck in traffic on the way to Santos Dumont Airport just after noon. The window wipers could barely keep up with the hard summer downpour—a real gully washer, and the mountain tops of Rio were shrouded by low-lying clouds, giving the city an altogether different feel. Traffic was at a standstill and I'd passed the time getting the low-down from Adriana.

She'd been able to eavesdrop and record Antonio's conversation with Danilo, thanks to my bug. Tensions with the Red Commandos were high, and Danilo confirmed Brasão's order for new weapons so the Dragon Militia could fight back.

"Although they speak in code, we get the gist. They mentioned the money guy you tipped me off about. He was instructed to prepare the ink to print the books and to pay the writers. We are guessing it's an order to prepare transfers for the purchase of weapons and bribes. Wednesday is when we suspect guns will be delivered to the Dragon Militia. It's critical we catch all the links in their financial transactions."

"So you're prepping for a sting on Wednesday."

"Yes, I am coordinating with my BOPE colleagues." She sounded excited at the prospect of success.

I scurried out of the car into the airport to meet up with Danilo and Sylvia at the VIP private jet lounge. We lost no time getting into Brasão's Gulfstream. Once seated, Sylvia immediately pulled out a popular weekly gossip rag and began to flip through the pages. Danilo excused himself to make a phone call. A stewardess came by and took our drink orders. Sylvia leaned forward and called to Danilo. He continued his conversation, paying her no mind.

"I think I'll have some of that." I pointed to the mimosas on the server's tray. I was getting used to libations during the day down here.

Sylvia took one as well. "Danilo, she is waiting," said Sylvia. She smiled fiercely and adjusted her sleeves nervously. Danilo lifted his hand, signaling for silence.

"He is impossible today," she huffed, and picked up her magazine.

Soon after, the jet sped down the runway and lifted effortlessly. The city disappeared under the gloomy cloud cover as the embracing g-force pressed us back against our seats. Seconds later we punched through the cloud cover to the brilliance of the deep blue sky and the reflective ocean of clouds below. Danilo hung up the phone and dialed another number. Sylvia came across someone she knew in the magazine with surprised delight and pointed to the picture. Her heavy mascara fluttered.

"Danilo, look!"

Danilo snubbed her again, waiting for the call to be answered. He spoke rapidly and authoritatively into his phone, hung up, and swiveled in his seat to face us.

"Insolent employees!" he said, and smacked his palm to his fist. "I have no time for their nonsense."

"Look, Danilo, it's Angelo de Andrade at his daughter's wedding in Angra. She looks so beautiful." Sylvia exhibited the two-page spread. The bride was surrounded by her beautiful tan Brazilian bridesmaids. One of them looked vaguely familiar.

I took a sip of my drink. Danilo was not just busy, he was avoiding Sylvia on purpose. They seemed to be playing a habitual game.

He turned his back to her and elaborated, "We have a very large business deal that we are closing later this week and certain preparatory things must be completed first. Just a few glitches. It falls to me to bark and make things go smoothly." He swiped back his jet-black hair and dialed yet another number.

"Here's a picture of Vera de Andrade, I'm sure you will want to look at that!" Sylvia snapped.

Danilo and I locked eyes for half a moment.

"Please, Sylvia, I don't like Angelo de Andrade or anyone in his family anyway."

"Since when?" Sylvia's tone was sly.

"I don't trust him. Now be quiet!"

"You don't trust anyone!" she spat. "Not even you! Imagine that." She jabbed me with her blood-red fingernails.

Danilo shot her a warning glance. She sat back and folded her arms with satisfaction.

"Well, I suppose distrusting a foreign stranger who wants to make a deal is not unheard of. We all have to do our due diligence, don't we?" I looked at Danilo and he smiled.

"That's right," he said, sitting back in his chair. I'd broken the icy moment. "Excuse me for being rude," he said, his large forehead deeply creased. "I have to finish attending to this matter and then we can talk."

If Andrade wasn't an ally of theirs, what role was he playing in all this? Danilo went back to his phone calls and Sylvia buried herself in her magazine. I wondered about the familiar-looking girl in the picture and pulled out a copy of *Vanity Fair* from the seat pocket. I leafed through while trying to understand some of Danilo's conversation. It seemed to be about setting the proper date and time for a rendezvous. I wished my grasp of Portuguese were a bit further along.

About an hour into the flight, Sylvia pulled out a brand-new magazine—hot off the press with Lygia's face on the cover—and was leafing through it when she let out another gasp of surprise and motioned for me to look.

"T. J., you are already a star! See, here you are with Angelo and César at the most talked-about party of the year!"

I looked over and there I was, looking quite dapper,

I'll tell ya—although not my most pleasing angle. Sylvia and I began to chat and she told me how she and Danilo had met a few years ago. She'd been modeling for an Argentine ad campaign shot in Rio and Danilo was jogging along the beach when he saw her posing.

"He was so exotic and handsome and he asked me if I would like to have dinner with him. I said yes immediately, and that was that." She sighed and frowned. "If I had known then that he would never have a second for me, things might have been different." She turned to gaze out the window and lightly scratched at the back of her neck with those fingernails.

Danilo finally joined us, and he told me with growing enthusiasm about the eco-friendly infrastructure they had devised in order to make the development fly on the federal nature preserve.

"The latest green technologies in water, waste management and energy production are being utilized."

He pulled a blueprint of the project out of a folder in the black leather briefcase at his feet and pointed with his circling index finger. "Entire fruit and vegetable gardens will be grown hydroponically in green houses lining the development's perimeter. Alongside them are rows of solar energy farms and a windmill."

I was impressed at the efforts they took to conform to the island's restrictive codes.

"When Antonio and I first began to pursue this project, we decided that due to the amount of time we would be spending here, it only made sense to build a corporate house to stay in during our visits."

"It is beautiful!" chided Sylvia.

"We picked that spot," corrected Danilo, "because it overlooks the project area."

"I guess all of Antonio's properties are magnificent. I don't see him settling for less."

Danilo actually cracked a smile. "That is for sure."

As we landed, I noted the low flat center of the island

didn't seem like much to write home about, and unlike Rio, it was drier than the heart of a haystack. I imagined all the beauty of the place must hug the coastline. We passed a small GOL Airlines plane unloading fresh tourists as we taxied into our spot. Inside, we paid our "environmental preservation" fee ahead of the queue, and then were guided into our waiting vehicle.

As I ducked my head into the car, I saw a man exit the airport and I recognized his eyes just before they were covered by his aviator shades. The glasses sat catawampus on his misaligned nose. A feeling of unease settled upon me as we rolled away. It was the man I'd seen watching me at the gym. This was no coincidence.

We drove along the only paved roadway on the island for a few minutes until we veered onto a dirt road that wove through a couple of hills and scrubland. Danilo and Sylvia were talking, and I was trying to focus on what they were saying, but my mind had become obsessed by my sighting. Here I was on a completely remote island, entirely exposed to Antonio's will. Valeria's words echoed in my head. *There is danger around you, I felt it.*

We rounded a gigantic boulder that marked the entrance to the home. A glass and steel house was perched between it and the cliffside. Paulo André was standing with a remote control in his hands. Lygia stood near him with her hand shielding her eyes as she looked up at the toy plane he was guiding in for a landing. It touched down just as we rolled up to the house on the gravel drive. Lygia waved and walked forward to greet us in a gauzy outfit. Paulo André put down his remote control and came running up beside her.

"T. J.!" he exclaimed.

Danilo looked mildly surprised by our familiarity.

"Hello, Danilo, *Tia* Sylvia," Paulo André said, reaching up to kiss *"Tia"* Sylvia on the cheeks.

He came up to me and gave me a hug. "Let's go swimming, T. J., the pool is great!"

"Paulo André, please let our guests relax!" Lygia smiled patiently and welcomed us all in.

"How was the flight? I hope the weather didn't cause too many problems."

"I'm surprised we left as quickly as we did."

Lygia motioned for the butler to take the bags and kissed Sylvia hello.

"It seems the rain in Rio has been terrible today. I heard there were several landslides in some of the *favelas*. It's just awful. We are fortunate, here everything is beautiful. Welcome to Fernando de Noronha. Antonio is out on the patio expecting all of you. Danilo and Sylvia, you know the routine. Please show T. J. to his guest room and I'll meet you all on the patio when you're ready."

Danilo led the way down a corridor and pointed. "That's your suite."

I nodded and opened the door. The room was cantilevered off the cliff, and a corner of the floor was made of thick, transparent glass slabs so you could see the waves crashing on the boulders underneath. A hammock hung over that corner. The windows all had jalousie shutters in case of inclement weather, and the bed had a large mosquito mesh canopy drawn to one side of its mahogany carved frame.

It didn't take long to fill the little drawers of the antique chest with the contents of my overnight bag, perhaps not as neatly as Sean would have. Two lateral depressions along the bags' underside clicked to reveal the lock of its secret compartment. I took off my gun and holster, put them inside the molded foam casing, and locked it shut. I put the bag on the closet shelf on my way to the window for a peek. The sea crashing beneath my feet felt a bit dizzying at first, but somehow exhilarating. I stepped outside. On the opposite side of the bay atop a small hill lay the ruins of a colonial fort with ramparts and turrets intact. Palm trees in front of it swayed in the lazy afternoon. I could see the ancient iron cannons gleaming in the sun.

Back in the room I grabbed my sunglasses and ran my fingers through my hair, looking myself over in the mirror before heading on out to meet the others. I was unsettled by the implications of my sighting, but I had to keep my cool. Continue as planned.

The patio was in back of the main house. Behind us was Morro do Pico, casting its phallic shadow across paradise. Antonio, Lygia and Sylvia sat near the pool and Paulo André was floating in the shallow end. Danilo was off in the corner on the phone once again. He seemed tense.

Antonio rose to greet me. "Welcome to the island, my friend. Today you relax and unwind. Tonight we have a wonderful fresh seafood dinner planned and tomorrow we go hunting wild boar with Danilo at my own hunting park. It's great sport!" he said, clapping my shoulder.

"But that's in the afternoon," said Paulo André from the pool. "In the morning we are going scuba diving. It's one of the best places to do it in the world."

Lygia laughed. "That is *if* T. J. is certified and *if* he is inclined to scuba dive with us."

"I was certified in Malta, actually, in the early nineties," I said.

Danilo ended his call and joined us. "We are going in the morning. Lygia and I will be diving, Paulo André will snorkel above us, and Sylvia . . ." He looked up at her with vague disdain. "She will sleep, most likely. We like to dive at the far point of the island at five in the morning."

"One of the reasons I won't participate," said Brasão.

"It is very early, but it is also when the dolphins come in to feed at sunrise. It's one of the most beautiful sights in the world," Lygia said.

"And the sea turtles are everywhere to feed on the schools of fish the dolphins are chasing. It's so cool!" Paulo André's lips and wide eyes looked like a fish's.

"I suppose I can't miss it, then," I said, committing to the next morning's escapade.

"Come, T. J., have a look at my little paradise." Antonio gestured me over to the rail. Down below, pylons marked the location of each future structure. Pipes had already been laid and the cement skeleton of the elevated boardwalks had been poured.

"The infrastructure you see will complete phase one. Tomorrow after your dive, we can explore it up close. Please make yourself at home. Lygia and Sylvia can show you around. Danilo and I must attend to some meetings down there this afternoon. We will rejoin you here later for sundown drinks and dinner. It's important that you have a good feel for the island. Enjoy." Antonio nodded and he and Danilo walked into the house.

"I think we should take T. J. on a tour of the island in one of our beach buggies," Lygia suggested.

"OK," I agreed.

The four of us went out to the side of the house and hopped into the buggy. Lygia got into the driver's seat and put on her large sunglasses. She turned on the ignition with a press of a button, gave it some gas, and off we drove down the winding dirt road.

We came to an intersection in the tiny village of the island. There was a cute whitewashed church with baroque yellow trim adjacent to the veranda-encircled eighteenth-century buildings that surrounded the little square. Lygia drove us up a long cobblestone ramp to the fort that I'd seen earlier from my room. She stopped at the Manuelian gates of the imposing ruin. The rusted old cannons harked back to a bygone era of imperial defense. The Portuguese coat of arms was embossed in the age-old metal. We got out and walked in through the tall, carved wood doors.

As we passed into the fort's courtyard, Lygia became the consummate docent and raconteuse. I watched her curiously. Where were all her concerns and woes now? She was alive when she performed.

"The island was first discovered by the Portuguese

merchant Fernando de Noronha in 1503 on an expedition with the famous Italian explorer Amerigo Vespucci, who, as you know, the Americas are named after. Noronha used the island as a distribution center for his monopoly on the Brazil-wood trade, the country's namesake. The island was given to him by the Portuguese crown and remained his until it was taken over by the English in the mid-sixteenth century."

Lygia walked toward the cliff wall overlooking the sea and motioned for us to follow.

"Then it was forcefully taken by the French, and then the Dutch, back to the Portuguese, then the Dutch again, until the Portuguese finally repossessed it in the seventeen hundreds. That's when they decided to build about ten of these fortifications you see all around the island for protection. This is the largest and best preserved one, and it is called Forte dos Remédios." The actress had my full attention.

The fort was high up on a bluff overlooking several beautiful palm-dotted beaches, with the formidable Morro do Pico towering above them. A long ramp climbed up to a second level that framed the inner courtyard where we stood, with defensive turrets on every corner. Paulo André was already exploring up top.

"T. J., come check out the view."

"Ladies?" I asked.

"I stay right here and wait," Sylvia said.

"I'll stay with her. You two go on," Lygia said.

I walked up the long ramp to meet up with Paulo André. The tropical summer sun was still hot in the late afternoon. From the top, views extended across the island. To the east was the marina with several fishing boats and expensive pleasure craft.

"That's where we will leave from to scuba dive tomorrow," Paulo André said, pointing. Beyond the marina was ocean to the horizon in all directions. I felt very, very far away, and truth be told, I was.

To the west, I could just make out the modernist house clinging to the cliff side. There really was not much construction anywhere in view, just raw nature. Dolphins arched across the water's surface. The ladies were sitting on a bench in the shade of a blooming jacaranda tree. Sylvia waved from below as she fanned herself desperately.

"Let's walk down to the water," she called. "It's cooler down there."

"Let's go," said Paulo André, running down the ramp to her side.

"You go ahead," said Lygia.

"I'll have a break too," I said, taking Sylvia's place on the bench in the tree's shade. Paulo André held Sylvia's hand and she shot a glance at the two of us sitting together before disappearing out the gate and down the winding path to the beach.

"I've been to many places, but I have to tell you, this island wins the prize. I can't get over how beautiful it is."

"There is no other place like it. I love it. And here I can usually relax. I don't have to sign any autographs everywhere I go." She closed her eyes and inhaled deeply the sweet scents that surrounded us. "Life can be so exhausting when you are forced to live duplicitous lives." Lygia swung her hair back with a flick of her wrist; her look was direct. "It requires lots of extra energy to act one way and think another. I do it all day long. With strangers, my characters, my husband, myself. The parameters of each reality become undefinable. It can be confusing. Like the other night. I think you know what that feels like, don't you, T. J.? Marcelo told me he saw you at the beach. It makes our moment so much more amusing."

What could I say? I was a deer caught in the headlights.

Lygia giggled at my expression.

"You are a better actor than me. I had no idea, nor does Antonio, of that I am certain." She laughed a full octave at the thought. "I think he worries we may be having an affair. And tomorrow you go boar hunting with him and Danilo. Danilo would die if he knew his hunting buddy was a fairy!"

"Now, wait a minute, li'l lady."

Lygia was smiling at me. "My world is full of gay men and women and I would have it no other way. Your secret is safe with me. I trust you somehow, even more so now that I know. So I am telling you"—her tone became serious—"I am taking Paulo André to our apartment in New York for a while. Possibly a long while. I bought the tickets, but I still haven't figured it all out. Things don't feel right here, and my intuition says I should take him and go. I want him schooled in the US and living in a safer environment."

Was she truly innocent or was she simulating naiveté? Her name was tied to at least one of Brasão's questionable accounts. How much did she know about how her husband made his money? "Why do you tell me these things? I'm here to make a deal or two with your husband. You've not painted a very nice picture of his character for me. Are you telling me to back away from these projects?"

"Many people have made their fortunes working with him and you'll probably make your share too. But Valeria saw you in my reading in the form of a key. The symbolism is clear to me. Something about our relationship will free me from Antonio. I don't know what or how, but I know you are the positive force behind the change. Your encouragement and support the other night was decisive for me. That is why I tell you these things." She looked at me familiarly.

"You really believe that stuff, don't you?"

"I know it works for me. And I don't really consider myself a dumb woman, either."

"I'll say not. When do you plan on telling Antonio?"

"Possibly tonight. I don't know. I have to figure that out. But I've made up my mind."

"Good for you." Couldn't have planned it better myself.

"Let's go check on Sylvia and Paulo André," Lygia said, rising from the bench. "She has been known to spread rumors in the past."

Later that evening at the house, we all congregated on the patio again for sundown cocktails. The views were picture perfect. I snapped a few shots on my phone. The evening temperature was cool. Antonio and Danilo were talking in a corner when I walked out. The ladies and Paulo André were playing some simple card game. Antonio saw me and walked over to the bar and served up a scotch, neat, and brought it over to me.

His fixed gaze was once again inscrutable. "I believe this is how you like it?"

"Thank you."

"How was your afternoon, T. J.?"

"Fascinating. Lygia took us to the old Remédios fort to have a look around."

"Ah yes. You know, it was built in 1736 by the Portuguese after they conquered it back from the French."

"Yes, Lygia gave me the entire convoluted history."

"But she may not have mentioned that the original fort on that site was built by the Dutch in the early sixteen hundreds."

Antonio popped a calamari into his mouth and held up his finger, indicating he had more to say. He chewed appreciatively.

"Its construction was led by the Dutch naval captain whose fleet won over the island. All Portuguese subjects fled and he was able to hold the island for several decades. The few remaining locals came to support and trust him. He provided security and order for them with his vast Euro-Brazilian trade revenues." Antonio wiped the corner of his mouth with a napkin and sipped his drink. "He entrusted the guardianship of the island to a local young man whom he had helped mold for advancement. But during the captain's absence, the young officer betrayed his master to the French for a modicum of recompense." Antonio swished his drink around in his glass. "Trust is a difficult belief to calibrate. It seems to fluctuate with information and time. People can be unpredictably double-sided." His gaze was unfaltering.

"What happened to the young officer?" Steady does it.

"The captain's crew beheaded him in the dark of night. Have some hors d'oeuvres, the calamari is delicious."

I looked over at Danilo and he looked away. Something was up. The vibe had changed definitively. They knew something, but what? I grabbed a fried calamari and sauce and took a sip of my scotch.

"I won again!" Paulo André exclaimed. The ladies laughed. Lygia reshuffled the cards and dealt them out once more.

"Tell me, how is it your firm developed an interest in our projects specifically?"

I never went undercover with anything less than total immersion. It was an easy question to answer, so why did I feel like I was back in Mexico, about to find that I'd been checkmated when I wasn't looking? "It began with the Beijing Olympics, actually. Up until then we'd focused on rustlin' up business at the annual meetings of the World Bank and regional development banks. What better place for big business to mingle with the ministers of finance than in a series of intimate red-carpet gala settings? I can tell you, it was a natural business bonanza for mega-project deals. Negotiations were handled on the spot, deals were made, account numbers exchanged," I explained.

Danilo had come closer to listen in.

"But protesters and press began disrupting the meetings, and accessibility to politicians became more restrictive. However, the Olympics, we found, were an excellent and viable alternative for investment in foreign infrastructure growth. As you know, we helped finance several venues of the Beijing and London Olympic games. Great returns from both experiences. Rio was a natural next step. Finding your firm was not difficult with a bit of research and your prestige in the region."

Antonio lifted his brow. "That does make sense." He seemed to be in deep thought.

I noticed Lygia had been listening to the entire exchange. There was a concerned look on her face. She looked to the gesturing maid and rose from her seat.

"Dinner is served, everyone," she said.

We walked over to the table and the servers brought us each our soup plates individually, European-like. The rustic room was lit by candles and soft music filled the air. A colonnade of arches spied upon the bay. Sylvia began to daintily sip her chilled cucumber soup.

"The cucumbers, along with all the vegetables used here, were grown hydroponically in the greenhouses outside," Lygia said.

"It's delicious," I replied.

"Yes," Sylvia agreed. "There is such a nice fresh flavor to it. And that spice is very savory." Her spoon never slowed as she spoke and slurped, further thickening her Rs.

"That must be the dill and peppers." Lygia pointed at her bowl. Her hands seemed jumpy, searching for something to do.

She passed around a basket of warm, toasty bread to dip in the cool, creamy soup. Paulo André was sponging up his bowl with a piece.

"Paulo André!" Lygia said firmly. "Where are your manners? Please use your fork or spoon if you are going to do that. Eat properly."

Lygia finished her soup and laid her spoon across the bowl. The server came and took our dishes away. They brought out clean china and the main course was served: fresh grilled snapper on a silver platter beautifully garnished with giant capers and lemon wedges. Steamed potatoes and sautéed collard greens with garlic rounded off the meal.

I forced myself to eat, nerves conquering hunger, as we talked about tomorrow's events. Antonio was notably silent. Lygia recounted how she had been certified in her teenage years and had dived in the most incredible spots, from Belize to Australia.

"But I still think the place we are going to tomorrow is one of the most beautiful dive spots around. We will dive along the cliff face, and as you descend every few feet, you notice the colors and wildlife changing. There are a couple of caves to go into if you are feeling adventurous."

"Are you certified?" I asked Paulo André.

"No, I have to wait until I am sixteen." He frowned.

Danilo tapped the boy's head a bit forcefully. "Soon enough." The boy winced at his touch. Danilo took a large bite of his fish and chewed. "I usually go spear fishing there, but the island has outlawed it this year. Rules, rules, rules!" he grumbled.

"I hope the weather will cooperate," said Sylvia. "Maybe while you dive, I can relax." She sighed lullingly.

Throughout dinner I noticed Antonio and Danilo watching my every move. I couldn't figure what they had on me—it could be anything or nothing. I felt sure it was related to the man at the airport. Paulo André was telling his father how he had come upon turtle eggs on the beach that afternoon after our walk in the fort.

"He was digging a hole," said Lygia.

"You should have seen your face when your hands came up all gooey!" I added.

Lygia burst out laughing. Antonio eyed us smiling at each other and frowned. Perhaps Silvia had said something incriminating about Lygia and me this afternoon at the fort. Was this a show of jealousy? Dessert was served. Antonio tapped a large dollop of cream onto a piece of tart. There was no question I was under some level of scrutiny.

"Did you know Minister Alcântara, T. J.?" Antonio asked out of the blue.

"Alcântara—no, but the name sounds familiar. Wait. The man that was murdered on New Year's Eve?"

Lygia looked at Antonio. "Vinícius?"

"Yes. Did you know him?"

"No, I didn't."

"I thought I knew him. I thought I knew him well. We worked together many years," Antonio said.

He put a forkful of tart and crème fraîche in his mouth and chewed heartily, taking his time to savor it until he swallowed. "He was murdered in the company of a worthless *michê*. He ended his illustrious life and career in the arms of a call boy." His fierce gaze tested me.

Dang it, he knew I'd been talking to Zezé.

"Disgusting," muttered Danilo.

"Antonio!" Lygia hissed with a clatter of her silverware. "How can you speak of our friends that way? In front of Paulo André?" She turned to the boy. "Go to your room, please." He obeyed without question, but his gaze caught mine with unveiled concern and fear.

Antonio looked from her to me and back again, his silver eyes glistening in the candlelight. "People are often not who they seem to be," he said again, and took a final bite of his tart. "Maybe it's time for us to retire. You all have an early morning, and I have had a long day. In the current state of affairs, I'm not so certain there is a deal to be made." He tossed his napkin on the table and abruptly rose from his chair. "Good night," he said, and stormed out.

Danilo and Sylvia barely looked at me as they said goodnight too, and walked down the long hallway to their suite. Lygia glanced at me apologetically and suddenly leaned forward and said firmly, "His ego is strong, stubborn. Stay the course. He wants this deal. I don't know what's bothering him but I will find out."

She rose to go after Antonio. I got the distinct sense just then that she knew something I didn't.

I suddenly found myself alone, so I got up and fixed myself a scotch at the bar and walked over to the terrace. The moon was rising over the ocean. Adriana's warnings about blowing my cover echoed in my mind. This had to be because of the man with the crooked nose. He had to be Brasão's man, unless he was just another of Andrade's peons. But why? What did he know? Why was he also on this island?

Risk calculations whirled through my mind, just like they had facing fire during Desert Storm. Just like they had when El Gordo's men jumped me. Only, that time there'd been a key missing factor, the one thing I never would have accounted for: Vicente's turning.

Stay the course. Stay the course. That's what my gut was saying too. But what did Brasão and Danilo suspect?

I sipped the calming liquor and walked down a path around the house. I heard Lygia's voice from inside. She and Antonio were arguing in Portuguese and then a door slammed. The ensuing lull was filled with the sound of chirping frogs in the surrounding vegetation.

I turned my phone on and it vibrated in my pocket. I listened to a message from Sean.

"T. J., you really hurt me, man. I don't even know why I'm helping you other than I know it's the right thing to do, you shit. I went and saw Earl. It wasn't easy. I've got some dirt for you. Call me."

"Hey buddy," I said when he picked up.

"No, you've lost the right to call me that."

"Come on, Sean, really."

"I miss you, and I want to kill you at the same time. My therapist is ready to fire me, and it's not because I can't pay my bill."

I relaxed. I could tell he'd gotten over his anger. "It's nice to hear your voice. I've been thinking a lot about you too. How are you? Tell me what's new."

"The community service hasn't been awful, actually. Last week I gave a talk to some students at NYU Law along with an agent from the SEC. It was pretty interesting. Ironically, he thought I should work for them, fight white-collar crime. Said they could use more people who knew what sorts of clues to look for." He snorted and didn't give me a chance to tell him that I thought he'd be great at it.

"Here's what I've got. I saw Earl. The guy's a mess. He's been out of work since the scandal broke and his wife and kids left him. She didn't want any part of it. He lost most of her family's fortune, and a very large number of their close friends had invested with him too. Obviously I can relate. I suggested that he could do what I was doing—teach—but for a fee. I had some connections for him and in return I asked him if he recalled any clients with the names you gave me."

I looked around to make sure I was alone and out of sight. I moved a bit farther from the house.

"And?"

"He did. He got back to me with the name of the person who moved funds for your Brasão guy and a few other names you gave me. The guy made transactions in and out of the accounts, usually as cash. They were closed in 2006 and the balances were transferred out."

"You know who handled his transactions?" Was such a coincidence even possible?

"He thinks it's a guy named Giancarlo Russo out of Delaware. Owns a firm called GGF Investments. I think this is where you let your DEA friends come in and do their thing."

"You sleuth! That's excellent news!" I jotted down the name in my phone.

"He handled lots of money for the Swiss/Italian set in the States, and acquired a number of Brazilian heavy hitters as well. The guy had a completely elaborate network of international players and moved money without a trace. Makes my crimes look simplistic, like a real novice."

I chuckled. "That's a great help. I'll get in touch with

Bradley and get him to do some digging. I can't thank you enough. This could be a big break."

"Great, I'm glad to help." There was a pause, and when he spoke again his voice had lost its businesslike tone. "I'm sorry for being so incensed the other day. It makes me crazy thinking of you down there with all those hot Latin men throwing themselves at you."

This irked me more than it should have, perhaps because it was true. "Yeah, Sean, I've got plenty of free time for that."

"Well, you know it wouldn't bother me as much if you hadn't left the way you did."

"I understand. Hell, Sean, my career is dangling by a thread too. This has got to succeed or I'll need to take up teaching art history."

"Fuck, man, how did we get here?"

"We'll work our way out of it. Just got to focus and give it time. I do miss you, buddy."

"I miss you too. Be careful down there."

"I will. That was really an important thing you did for me. I won't forget it. Hey Sean, tell Brent and Charles to go fuck themselves."

He laughed and hung up. I looked through the trees back at the house and dialed Tom at Arlington, another number I'd entered into the shield app, and asked him to get with Sean for the names. It was a long shot, but he said he would see what he could do. For the first time, it really hit home how much I wanted my job back, with all the resources of the DEA behind me.

Lygia and Antonio's argument continued, although at a more muffled tone. I dialed 555 and walked over to another large tree in the garden, keeping hidden, waiting for Adriana to answer.

"I could be in trouble here," I whispered when she did. "I've got good news and bad news. I think I've been able to locate a few more bank accounts in the United States belonging to Brasão and Danilo. Bradley will get the records for these accounts and will send the files for your team to analyze, like last time. Here's the big part, I think we found the money man—he launders the money across borders in Europe and Latin America. If he is really our man, he must work with whomever their money exchanger is here, the way César described. He must connect to Feijão somehow."

"T. J., I'm very impressed with your work. That's amazing! How?"

"I'm well connected."

"Indeed you are. By the way, with your photo, we found Margarida. I have operatives watching her closely."

I thought about Feijão and the money chain, something Margarida had said on the beach about him being a mama's boy. "I've got a hunch that Feijão's mother could be involved somehow. Can you keep an eye on her? I think she must be part of the money chain. After all, who can you trust more than your own mother?"

"How would you know something like that?"

"Margarida said he stopped everything for her, a constant interruption, always on the phone together about money and business. And he always meets up with Margarida in Vidigal after visiting his mama, and he only visits Margarida when he has business with Malandrão. Check it out."

"I'll get my undercover agents on it right away. Good thinking. What's going on there?"

I let her know about my stalker and the suspicion that he'd met with Antonio and Danilo. "They seemed completely distrusting of me this evening. Antonio also brought up the minister's murder and Zezé out of the blue, no rhyme or reason. He and Lygia are arguing as we speak. I assume because he may also think we are having an affair."

"You aren't, are you? That would not be very wise." I could imagine one hand on her hip, and the other swiftly flipping her long hair from one side to the other.

"Of course not."

"Be careful, there is not much I can do to help you on that island. On our end, all indicators are still pointing to a lot going down on Wednesday afternoon. We're working hard to figure out what, where and when." Just before signing off, she added, "You really are on your own way out there."

CHAPTER TWENTY

The sound of straining rope intermingled with the gently lapping waves as the boat rocked against the dock's buoys. Pelicans sat pompously upon the pylon tops, motionless like statuary under the cawing seagulls in the early morning mist. As I stepped in, I noticed Brasão's coat of arms gracing the wood-paneled stern. A fishing boat headed out to sea on our starboard side. The workmen rapidly checked the netting for damage. I held my hand out to Sylvia and helped her onto the deck. She grabbed a support bar and seated herself. I reached for Lygia and Paulo André too. Danilo brought up the rear. The captain wished us a good morning and Danilo reiterated our destination.

Lygia introduced me to the guide, Gilson. He returned to the back of the boat to dismiss the guy who'd been helping him load the supplies. The guy looked my way—it was the thug from the gym and the airport. Paulo André was sitting next to me swinging his feet, his toes just shy of the floor.

"Do you know who that man Gilson's talking to is?" I whispered.

"That's Thiago. He is Danilo's errand guy. He does whatever Danilo and Father need."

The captain gave a tip of his cap, and we were soon on our way, moving through the marina's green waves toward the open water. The rocking motion was not helping me fight the sinking feeling that I was at a grave disadvantage at this moment. The sun was just rising over the surface of the ocean and we hugged the shore. After a ways, we approached the far side of the island, where rocky arches and cliffs fell into the deep blue sea.

"Look!" cried Sylvia, pointing. "The dolphins!"

Lygia clasped both hands up to her heart and smiled broadly. Hundreds of dolphins were swimming toward the island in an army of jumping arches. The ocean surface frothed off their soaring bodies, which shimmered in the rising sun—truly a marvel of nature, but my mind was on Thiago.

"We are almost there," said Paulo André, leaning out over the edge to get a good look.

Danilo had been in the back with the guide, preparing the equipment. He came out as the captain cut the boat engines and we glided to a stop. I still had my eyes on him when Lygia nudged me.

"This is where we are diving."

We were drifting next to a cliff and the water was swelling up and down its sides when the captain dropped anchor. The chains rattled continuously for a long while.

"When was the last time you dove?" asked Lygia.

"I'll tell ya, it's been a few years. Let's see, I dove in Belize when I was there on a business trip I extended for a few days."

"With a friend perhaps?" Lygia smiled. "You are familiar with how everything works? The sign language below?"

"I could give lessons if I had to."

"OK then, let's go get ready. Paulo André," she said, turning to her son. "Here is your snorkel equipment."

Lygia helped him put it on along with his flippers and life jacket.

I stripped down to my Speedos and stepped into my wetsuit. As I stretched the material over my shoulder, I caught Sylvia eyeing me with her lips slightly parted. She blushed and turned away, nervously twirling her hair around her finger. I looked over to find Danilo glaring at me. He stood the oxygen tanks up against the wall without removing his gaze. He'd barely spoken all morning. And after Antonio's tirade the night before, I was troubled by my precarious presence on this island, to say the least.

"OK," Lygia said. "I'm ready. Would you help me with my vest and tank?" she asked. We went over to them. "That one there, with the pink nozzle." She pointed.

I lifted the tank and vest onto her back while she strapped it on.

"This vest isn't fitting me well. It seems too big," she complained.

"I can adjust the straps."

"No need, my vest is all pre-set for me. Over there, maybe?" she pointed. I looked at the remaining tank and vest on the floor and noted the vest was indeed smaller.

Lygia looked at it and rolled her eyes. "Yes, that's it. Gilson must have confused them."

I lifted it up for her to get into and we suited up, buddy-checking each other to make sure everything was in good working order. I tested her straps and weight belt and verified the oxygen flow and gauge both worked. Then I double-checked all of my equipment—habit, mostly, but I couldn't deny the sense of uneasiness I felt. Goose bumps, as Valeria would say.

We got into the water one at a time, following Gilson's direction. Once we were all floating in the sea, we let the air out of our buoyancy vests and gradually began our descent. I looked up and Paulo André was floating above us with his snorkel and goggles, giving us a thumbs-up sign.

We swam toward the cliff. It seemed to disappear into the deep blue depths. Lygia pointed at two sea turtles swimming past, and below, where a school of nurse sharks circled. We descended farther and the color of the coral growing on the rocky surface changed from red to violet. Danilo let out a gasp of bubbles when an eel darted out of a crevice. He gave us the OK signal and continued on.

I stopped to equalize my pressure and clear my goggles. I looked ahead and Danilo was rounding a bend in the rock. Lygia went on and I followed, the water cooler the deeper we dove. A school of parrotfish swam sluggishly by several stingrays stirring up sand on a ledge. They disappeared beneath their camouflage. Danilo and Lygia waited for me at the mouth of a small cave with hundreds of pink sea horses bobbing up and down around them. Lygia pointed to the cave and made the OK sign. I responded with the same and followed them in cautiously.

Danilo went first with a flashlight in hand. The passageway got increasingly narrower. We swam upward in the shaft and I noticed that the current's pull was magnified in the tunnel. It opened up into a large, cavernous space. Danilo pointed above us at a shaft of morning sunlight that punched through the rock down into this underwater cave. We turned into another passage and Lygia stopped to pick up a large conch from the sandy floor. She was about to hand it to me when I noticed her eyes go wide. Bubbles suddenly stopped coming out of her mouthpiece. She dropped the conch and made the sign for "no air." I took a breath and handed her my mouthpiece. Danilo was gone. I could not see him or his light. He must have moved on without noticing we were not behind him. If the first tunnel was any indication of the second, he would not have room to turn back, only to move forward.

It was very dark; the sunlight that reached us barely allowed for more than a silhouette. I pointed up and Lygia nodded. I filled my vest with a little air and we began to rise. Lygia's diving experience was evident. She remained calm as we gradually ascended, taking turns on my mouthpiece. When we finally broke the surface, she pulled up her gauge and we both had a look. It still read three quarters full. I turned it over in my hands, examining it, oscillating my flippers to keep us above water. I knocked it around, but the needle did not move. It was broken—or worse, tampered with.

"How can that be? I don't understand," Lygia said. "Our staff is so thorough usually."

She swiped the hair from her face, straining to stay afloat without the help of her buoyancy vest. Her hand took support from my shoulder.

I pulled up my gauge.

"I only have a quarter tank left. The only way out of here is going back down through the passage and out the opening. And we don't have a flashlight." My voice echoed eerily in the enclosed chamber.

"Oh yes we do," she said, unclipping a small flashlight from her diving belt. She clicked it and the light came on.

"We will have to move quickly and breathe as efficiently as possible. I'm just not so sure that we have enough air for the two of us."

I looked up at the ceiling of the cave. The sunlight was coming in through a small crack in the rock.

"Don't even think about it. You won't fit through that, even if you could climb up there," Lygia said. "Where is Danilo? He should have come back looking for us by now," she added with irritation.

Danilo would not be coming; this was intentional. That tank had been meant for me, not Lygia—that's what Thiago must have been doing earlier on the boat. But he'd attached the faulty tank to the wrong vest. I imagined that Danilo had simply expected Lygia to follow him into the passage just as my air would have run out, leaving her unaware of my absence until they exited. By that time, I would have been dead.

When he got to the end of the cave and discovered we were both missing, he'd have to surface because he'd be low on air. He wouldn't have a chance to turn back in order to save face. To make matters more urgent, the tide was rising and navigating the passages would be more difficult.

"I don't think we should wait for Danilo. I think he will not turn back for us. He will be low on air too," I said.

"OK, I think you are right. I don't think there is any alternative. We can do this. Let me go first, I know this cave pretty well."

"When we get to the passage at the bottom, take a deep breath. I won't be able to give you another until we are on the other side."

"There is a nook about halfway through where we can be parallel and I can take another breath. That, I think I can do," she said.

I nodded. "OK, you better ditch the tank and vest. It'll be easier for you to move."

"You're right. Of course."

She wiggled her arms out of the vest and let it drop with the tank, keeping only her weight belt. "Let's go."

She took a deep breath and went under. We dropped swiftly, decompressing as we went. The darkness enveloped us and she turned on her flashlight and illuminated the bottom of the cave. An octopus scurried out of the light's beam, leaving an inky cloud in its wake. When it dissipated, Lygia spotted the passage and took the mouthpiece from me and inhaled deeply. She gave me a thumbs-up and disappeared into the passage. I followed closely behind, straining to see the faint light of her beam pointing ahead. The tide pushed against us, and moving forward required more effort. We rounded the corner and there was a larger space we both fit into, just as she had said. I pulled up next to her and Lygia took my mouthpiece for more air and continued.

The current swiped us against the sharp edges of the

passage and suddenly the flashlight's beam died. It was darker than midnight under a skillet, and I could feel the cave's rocky sides all around me as I inched forward, trying to keep my fingers near Lygia's flippers. She moved on somehow, blindly turning a corner. I could sense the time passing and knew she would need to gasp for air any second. Then the daylight trickled in. Lygia had successfully guided us to the opening of the cave.

I handed her the mouthpiece and she inhaled deeply again. Her hair floated freely as I undid her weight belt and she began to rise as it dropped into the depthless abyss. I looked at my gauge: it read empty. I inhaled and the oxygen stopped mid-breath. Without the help of our buoyancy vests, every few feet required greater exertion. Our lungs soon revolted for air. I fought to control myself from gasping. I looked from Lygia up to the surface. It still seemed so far. I began to ache inside. I realized the spread to the surface might be more than our starved lungs could handle.

I felt a sense of loss as the pain of resisting the reflex to breathe expanded. A flash of Sean and his heartache. My family. I could see Lygia was in trouble, too. Her mouth was erupting open, her eyes disturbingly wide.

Punch it, Leukemeyer! Punch it!

I grabbed her by the shoulder and pulled her the last few feet up to the surface, straining beyond my preconceived limits because there was no alternative. We both broke the surface, taking in water and sputtering. Lygia was drowning in it and I knew I had to get her out fast. I kicked fiercely to keep us both afloat while coughing water out of my lungs. Lygia had stopped moving.

"*Olha lá!*" screamed Sylvia's voice. I turned and saw the boat in the distance. Sylvia was pointing and yelling. Paulo André began waving frantically. It felt like an eternal wait for them to raise anchor and throttle toward us. Within a couple of minutes the boat pulled up alongside us and Gilson threw out a lifesaver and I hooked Lygia's arms around it. Danilo, having just climbed aboard, was still in his wetsuit. He reached over and pulled Lygia in. Then he gave me a hand.

Lygia lay on the deck with water pooling all around her. She had stopped breathing. The captain came running over as I threw off my vest and tank.

"*Mamãe! Mamãe!*" cried Paulo André, jumping in front of the captain.

"Move aside," I commanded, just now catching my breath.

Sylvia hugged Paulo André and held him back. I knelt down over Lygia and pumped on her stomach. Her wet hair lay splayed across her forehead. We all listened for her breath, but the only sound was the boat quietly creaking as the waves slapped at its hull.

I began CPR and alternately pumped on her stomach until she suddenly threw up a torrent of seawater. Her blue eyes fluttered open and I dabbed her face with a towel. She coughed violently, and began to roll around with loud, wheezing gasps.

I held her and stroked her hair. "You're fine, everything's OK, you're safe now."

"What happened . . . down . . . there?" she sputtered between coughs. One deep raucous breath followed another. She tried to point upward at Danilo, but her arm failed her. She used her chin. "Where were you?" She sat up slowly.

His brow was deeply furrowed. "I was leading the way and thought you were right behind me. I had no way of knowing you were not there until I came out the other end. By then, I was almost out of air. I came up for a new tank and was about to go back looking for you two. What happened?"

"What happened . . . is I . . . ran out of *air!*" Tears ran down her face as Lygia struggled to breathe evenly.

"You?" he asked, and looked at me. His eyes were wide in an untamed moment of surprise.

If any doubts had lingered, y'all, they were gone. But Lygia missed it. Paulo André fell into her arms and cried. They were both shivering and Lygia was still working on catching her breath. Sylvia put a towel over her shoulders and I rubbed her back. The captain started the engine and we began our way back to shore. I looked over at Danilo and he gave me an openly hostile stare. I wondered if it was because of my level of intimacy with Lygia or because of whatever else Thiago had uncovered about me. Probably both. I looked back at Danilo innocently. I had to keep up appearances no matter what.

Valeria's warnings of danger rang ever more loudly in my mind.

CHAPTER TWENTY-ONE

Antonio stood at the dock in front of his beach buggy as we pulled in, wearing a mostly unbuttoned dress shirt hanging over his shorts and loafers. He ended a call, put the phone in his pocket and bounded over to the boat. Gilson tossed him the rope to wrap around the post and he came on board, pushing the captain aside.

"Lygia! Paulo André!" Antonio's hard silver eyes threw me a fierce warning.

"Come, my dear, I will help you from here." He took Lygia's arm and Paulo André's hand. *"Meu filho,"* he said, pulling the boy close. They walked off the boat and into the buggy.

Antonio looked back at us and said, "Please follow us back to the house. Breakfast will be waiting." He turned to Gilson and barked something authoritatively in Portuguese, then held up his hand to stave off any reply. It was clear from Gilson's expression that he had just been fired.

A second buggy took Danilo, Sylvia and me back to the house. I sat with the driver in front and the two sat silently in back. We went to our respective suites to change for breakfast.

I still felt a bit shaken as I sat down on the bed. I was in big trouble here. The plan later today was to go hunting. That now sounded like an entirely bad idea. I took a shower and let the warm water fall on my face. I had to keep up my composure. I could not swerve from my role.

Antonio was seated with Sylvia and Danilo. The three were speaking in rapid Portuguese. Sylvia enunciated certain words languidly, with lengthy gestures, insinuating something salacious. I imagined, most likely, she was speaking of Lygia and me.

Antonio took note of my arrival and stood up to greet me.

"I am so sorry for the fright this morning. Lygia is lying down for a while to rest. She is very shaken by the accident, but said she would not have survived had you not been there. For that I am eternally grateful. How are you feeling? Please forgive me if in my immediate concern for my family, I forgot my manners as your host." Everyone suddenly seemed friendly again. My instincts were on high alert. The server brought fresh orange juice from the kitchen and hot coffee. I served some fruit salad onto my plate.

"This afternoon, I was going to take you around Paraíso Tartaruga and cap the tour with a visit to the wild boar hunting lodge, but I think I had better stay with Lygia and my son today," Antonio said.

Thiago walked through the door. He made his way over to the table and stood against the wall behind Danilo. He casually held my stare. I looked from him to Antonio, fighting my anxiety and trying to remain calm.

"Danilo will take you after lunch with Thiago. I don't believe you have met. Thiago is Danilo's assistant, so to speak."

I decided it would be wise to remain mute. I nodded. Danilo looked amicably at me across the table.

Antonio continued, "Danilo will fill you in on the particulars of Paraíso Tartaruga, and we will tour it together tomorrow morning before returning to Rio."

"Really, it's no bother if we just do this another time," I said.

"Unless you are unwell, I think there is no time like the present," Danilo replied. "Sylvia will stay by the pool if Lygia needs company. Let's go on our hunt and discuss some business. The distraction will settle our nerves from this morning's accident. It will be fun. How about we leave around noon? Some time to rest and relax first?"

"Noon." I finished my plate. "I think I will go relax and read for a while."

I excused myself and went back to my room and locked the door. I was going to take a doomed ride with the mob's henchman, never to be seen again. I grabbed my bag from the closet and opened the secret compartment and put on my holster, making sure it contained an extra clip. I checked the gun to verify it was loaded. I needed to think about my next step. There was nothing good about spending a few hours with Danilo and Thiago alone. I got into the hammock and considered what was to come. Then I took my phone out of my pocket and dialed for messages.

First message, forwarded from my American phone: "Hi, darlin', it's your mama. Everything is fine, don't worry about a thing. I don't mean to bother, but I'm calling because there's just this little procedure Dr. Caldwell wants to perform. I feel fine, really I do. It's scheduled for Wednesday, if you can reach me before then. I hope you are safe, son, and taking good care. I love you, baby." I heard her voice trailing off as she hung up the phone saying, "I left a message, he wasn't there."

My soft side ached, and it only got worse when I heard Sean's voice:

"T. J., I'm calling about your mom. Lucille called, she said she tried calling you but couldn't get through. Nothing urgent, she said, but when you get a chance give her a buzz. It was great to hear your voice last night."

I tried calling him back, but it went to voicemail. I

knew that if I went hunting with Danilo and Thiago, there was a good chance either they or I might not return. I was counting on it being them, but where would that leave me in terms of getting off this island? Or completing this assignment for that matter?

I opened the French doors to a small patio on the side of my suite. A steel cable fence lined the cliff-side walkway. I needed some air to think, so I walked up a grassy hill that overlooked the compound. It was in fact quite an extraordinary feat of well-engineered architecture and the gardens were cleverly landscaped. For all his evil doing, Brasão's madness had a certain sophistication I had to admire.

It was imperative I learn as much as possible from Danilo before I killed him. I thought of what might loosen him up. I came to a large boulder and sat on the shaded side and looked at the archipelago spread out in front of me. Danilo enjoyed talking about himself. I remembered the night of the party, how he'd talked about Antonio as his savior. He was proud of where he came from and continued to apply his street smarts in his business dealings. I could understand what Antonio valued in him. Danilo was a survivor, with ambition, loyalty, and above all else, cunning cleverness—he was a master manipulator and schemer, but there was also an unbridled base aggression. Even manipulators could be manipulated.

We met at the front of the house at noon for our outing. The feeling of my handgun gave me some sense of security. Danilo was on his phone as he got in the driver's side of the buggy and started the engine. He put on his sunglasses and placed his cell on the dash when he hung up. I got in next to him and noticed a scar running down his neck I'd not seen before. Thiago jumped into the back seat with an easy flex of his powerful arms.

"How did you get that scar?" I asked.

"Back in my early days, I was in a gang. It's a knife wound, but I was able to flip the guy over and plug him with his own knife before he could do any more damage." He rubbed at the scar. "Those were younger, more unruly days."

The road went inland and I noticed the dry, scrubby terrain.

"I'm surprised there are hardly any trees on the island. I'd think the middle would be more jungle-like," I said, trying to fill the silence.

Danilo laughed, yelling above the wind whipping through the open-air vehicle. "The island served as a prison for the state of Pernambuco for over a century. The first prisoners were forced to cut down all tall trees that might be used for escape rafts. That is why there are no trees. The island has never recovered except in areas where they have tried reforestation. But really, who cares? It allowed for the construction of the airport and these main roads, and the shooting lodge we are going to. The coast is what everyone comes for, and the circumference of the island is an ecological paradise."

In the sideview mirror, I could see Thiago looking uninterestedly at the sea. I noticed how the Pico do Morro monolith looked completely different from this angle; not nearly as phallic. A group of rock climbers were taking it on. The road became bumpy as we bounced down one hill and up another. Danilo began to speak of the development.

"Paraíso Tartaruga will be the first completely green self-sustaining luxury destination. Every structure will be supported by the cliff and steel pylons secured deep into the rock beneath the beach. There will be winding boardwalks with electric golf carts and paths looking out over the terrific view." He downshifted suddenly when the rocky road steepened.

"Every structure and system will be raised above the ground so the precious turtle breading grounds remain undisturbed. The residents get a prime view of the entire breeding cycle. From their homes they can watch the turtles struggle ashore, spotlit by night, burying their eggs. They'll watch in horror too as the seagulls attack dozens of the nests." Danilo smirked. "And of course, they will see the little baby turtles make their way to the sea when they hatch."

Somehow reminded me of Antonio's hang gliders.

I wanted to hear more about his relationship with Brasão. "How is it you speak such excellent English?"

"When I began working with Antonio, he sent me to school for a business degree. We worked through many deals together and he taught me many things. And I taught him many things as well." Danilo hit the clutch and shifted gears again. "Along with my degree, I learned English. We often go to the US on business." He looked at me with a resolute expression. "Antonio is like a father to me. I would do anything for him, and I do. I can get things done for him like nobody else can. Like nobody else would."

He made a sharp turn onto a dirt road, his gaze ahead of us to mind the large potholes. The phone on the dash lit up momentarily. A quick glance revealed a text that read only: *pronto*. I knew that meant 'ready,' but ready for what? The cell went dark again before Danilo could notice I'd seen the message.

"I'm sorry I bumped into you and Mrs. Andrade at the party the other night. No hard feelings." Perhaps that might provoke a reaction.

But Danilo didn't skip a beat, eyes forward and focused on his driving. "She's a good-looking lady and Angelo's not taking care of her needs, you know?"

"Isn't banging the chief of police's wife kind of dangerous?"

"I'm not too worried, he is well taken care of—the blind opportunist." There was that cold grin. Andrade was on their payroll too. So had his man been following me because of his association with Brasão? That didn't make sense if they had Thiago here following me too. Perhaps

Andrade had his own agenda. There was something more going on here and Mrs. Andrade was definitely involved.

I felt Thiago's silent presence behind me as Danilo took a hard unexpected right turn and skidded to a halt in front of a wire and wood-post gate. The sign above it read: *Reserva Caça Brasão*. There was a big running boar below the words.

"Here we are. You will love this." He smiled. "Welcome to the Brasão Hunting Reservation."

The guard at the gate looked out the window and raised the entrance bar so we could roll down the trail to the main lodge. There were no other buggies or cars parked in the area. We walked to the colonial building while Thiago waited outside. Danilo took a key from his pocket and opened his locker, pulling out two rifles, hunting vests, ammunition and binoculars. He handed me the equipment one at a time and we hopped into one of the available golf carts provided to roam the park. Thiago got behind the wheel this time. I noticed he had a rifle at his feet as well.

"This is where we walk," Danilo said when Thiago stopped the vehicle after a brief, winding drive through the woods.

We each grabbed our rifles. I checked to see if mine was loaded and that my vest had extra ammunition.

We walked through the woods and climbed a small hill to look around. Danilo checked for tracks and recently disturbed underbrush or droppings.

"How many boars would you say are in the park?" I asked.

"Recent estimates say about fifteen hundred or so."

Given the small size of this place, hunting them couldn't be much of a challenge.

Sure enough, a wild pig darted from our left, rustling the brush and grunting as it passed. Danilo spun and fired in one expert motion, but missed by the slightest delay.

"When there is one there is usually another," he predicted. "Let's split up. I'll go to the right, you two go that way."

Before I could reply, Danilo disappeared into the woods, leaving me alone with Thiago. I suddenly saw motion in one of the bushes and fired. The boar barely squealed.

"*Muito bem!*" exclaimed Thiago.

"Thank you."

"*Vai ver.*" He gestured for me to go look at my prize. I had no choice but to show him my back. I was in their trap. I held my rifle up in my left hand and unfastened my Walther PPK with my right, away from Thiago's gaze. A staccato glint of sunlight flashed off of Thiago's braces and reminded me that I could see his reflection on the inside corner of my sunglass lens if I adjusted my focus. I moved forward, keeping him in my sights. One step—Thiago swung the rifle from one hand to another. Two steps—the rifle butt rose up to his shoulder and the tip swung my way. I gripped my gun. Three steps.

"*Seu* Lemos! *Seu* Leukemeyer!" called the running gatekeeper, fortuitously approaching from the wooded path. I spun around to face Thiago, who dropped his rifle, looking away from my gaze innocently. The gatekeeper reached us and bent over for air.

"*Seu* Brasão needs you and *Seu* Lemos," he panted, "back at the house at once. He said to find you as quickly as possible."

Danilo appeared suddenly around the bend and seemed as irritated by the turn of events as I was puzzled by them. He barked an order to the gatekeeper, who ran into the woods for our prize.

"We must return to the house. We can come back later perhaps, and pick up where we left off," Danilo said.

Or not. We walked briskly back to where we had left the golf cart, approximately a quarter mile away. My pulse was still racing when I put the rifle in the back of the cart next to Danilo's and Thiago's. We drove back to the lodge, left the gear in the cart, and drove back to the house, mostly in uncomfortable silence. When we arrived, Thiago stayed behind and the butler walked us into the library. Antonio sat at his desk overlooking the pool and the twin peaks off the coast. He was in mid-sip of his tea when we paused at the door. He seemed perfectly content and motioned for us to enter.

Ancient nautical maps hung on the wall in large gilded frames. They were carefully positioned around one remarkably large map of the island. It was dated 1504. Other paraphernalia, including a ship's wheel on the front of his desk and the antique model caravels amongst his books, added to the maritime theme.

Danilo asked anxiously, "What's happened, Antonio. Is everything OK here?"

"Absolutely fine, Danilo, nothing to worry about. T. J., would you care for some tea or other beverage?"

"Sure, Antonio, tea'd be nice." I felt anything but pleasant.

I took my seat next to Danilo and a servant soon appeared with a cup and saucer for me, poured the tea and left the room, closing the wooden double doors firmly. I looked up at the map again and saw that the island's name was misspelled.

"What a peculiar map."

"Indeed. How good of you to observe. I like that about you. The island's namesake was actually Fernando de Loronha, with an L. But once it was misspelled on an official map as Noronha, history, and the island, opted to retain the populist misnomer. A man's legacy can easily be lost to a simple misunderstanding." He waved his hand at the map. "Probably the last bit of evidence left of the man's true identity."

Antonio got up from his seat. He had a manila envelope in his hand and tapped it against his palm as he came around the desk. "It seems that you have not been entirely forthcoming with us about who you are."

I fought my sinking feeling, focusing on portraying an innocent reaction to anything he might say, despite my perspiration.

"When we first met, I mentioned how important loyalty was from those with whom I conduct business. Loyalty by definition involves disclosure—and truthfulness."

He came to a stop in front of me, opened the envelope and pulled out a series of photographs.

"I was clear with you that just as you must do your due diligence, I would do mine."

He dropped the stack of pictures onto the glass table in front of us with a slap. I braced myself, expecting to see images of me and Adriana or Ronaldo. Instead, the very first shot was of Zezé and me on top of Sugar Loaf. I looked from the picture to Antonio, astonished.

"How did you get that picture? It was taken with my phone."

But I noticed something odd. Our eyes were looking at a focal point slightly to the right. With sudden revelation, I recalled where I'd first recognized Thiago from. He was the man who'd taken our picture on Sugar Loaf with my phone! He'd handed his camera to a friend to hold, and that guy must have snapped this picture.

I realized Antonio must have a lot on me. Let me just say I did not see this as a positive turn of events. It certainly didn't explain why he'd put a sudden stop to Thiago's attempt to kill me this afternoon.

I flipped through the snapshots. Zezé and me on Arpoador, at the beach. I suppose it could be argued that we were lying somewhat intimately side by side. Thiago must have followed me from the gym.

"Please explain to us how it is you know this young man?"

"This is really a very strange way to court my business. I don't have to explain how or with whom I spend my time to anyone, certainly not you." I stood up and faced him.

"I see I have upset you." He raised his hand gently in assurance.

Surely he must be toying with me. "Yes, you have." I tossed the pictures down on the table.

"Please, I mean no insult, do sit down. Thiago, who you met this morning, was assigned to check you out. He delivered the photographs yesterday, just after your arrival. Danilo and I have been so preoccupied with other matters that we had not had a chance to review Thiago's findings until we arrived here. Up until this afternoon when you left with Danilo, these images caused us deep concern."

I sat back, looking away. "I don't see why they should. They have no bearing on our relationship."

"As a matter of fact, they do. You see, the boy with you in these photographs is the hustler who was involved in my friend Minister Alcântara's death. Danilo and I could only suspect that you and he were possibly stalking me as well. Danilo has had his doubts about you ever since he bumped into you in my library at the party. We were preparing to call in the authorities," he said. Even as I watched him fib, his steel-clad eyes revealed nothing. "There was no other explanation until after Lygia's accident this morning."

Danilo now looked as befuddled as I felt. "Antonio, I don't understand, what has changed?" His fingers stroked his two-day stubble.

"Lygia and I had an argument last night and again this morning after the accident. Since I came across you playing tennis with my son at the club, I thought you and my wife might be having an affair. Neither one of us can afford a scandal."

He walked back to his desk and leaned casually against it and took another sip of his tea. He glanced at Danilo. "And then there were Sylvia's endless innuendos after the party, and again yesterday and today. I became enraged at the brazen offensiveness of the perceived attack. I felt like you were estranging my wife and child from me as part of your plan."

"That's ridiculous," I said.

"It is indeed. When I made the adulterous accusation this morning, Lygia laughed at me. Do you know why, T. J.?"

Just slap my head and call me silly—I couldn't believe my luck.

"I don't understand," repeated Danilo.

"Our friend T. J. is a homosexual." Antonio smiled pleasantly.

"What? *Um viado?*" Danilo examined me anew.

"Yes, he is gay, but there is no need to use derogatory words. He contracted the hustler's services just like you do with your escort lady friends in New York. That is the only nature of his association with the boy." Antonio clapped me on the shoulder like a dear old friend.

Danilo recoiled. "No. I don't believe someone like you is a fag," he grunted, openly disgusted.

"Do not be rude, Danilo, you know how I feel about the matter. Rise above your prejudices!" Brasão pointed at him as he spoke.

He shuffled through the top pictures of the stack and came to one with Zezé leaning on my leg with his hand on my knee. I felt so exposed.

"This is how I know for certain," Antonio said. "Look at the top right corner. Look who is chatting with them."

We both looked more closely.

"That's Lygia's makeup guy," Danilo said.

"Yes, Marcelo. He is the one who told Lygia about T. J. and the boy just yesterday. Up until this moment, I was most fearful I would lose the opportunity of doing business with you, and IVC. But after my argument with Lygia, I reviewed the pictures anew. A remarkable coincidence is all it is. Please forgive my suspicions. Please understand. I have to be a very cautious man. I take it my assumptions are correct?" Antonio looked at me with a smile and arched brows. "Rest assured, my friend, with respect to this matter, there are no judgments here about your lifestyle. I just need to know with whom I am doing business."

He offered out his fancy Cuban cigars and we lit up and puffed. Danilo had recoiled a bit and was having a hard time looking me in the eye.

"How was the hunt?" asked Antonio, changing topics.

"I got one just before your message to return reached us." I smiled. I was off the hook.

"Fantastic, fantastic. Great excitement, isn't it? They will bring the pig butchered and ready to cook for this evening. We shall dine on it tonight! There is a storm front approaching, but tomorrow should be lovely weather. In the morning, we will tour Paraíso Tartaruga. I am certain it will impress even your highest standards."

Antonio gazed proudly out the window at the beginnings of the development.

"After the tour, you will fly back to Rio with Sylvia, Lygia and Paulo André. Danilo and I have some late morning meetings here and will return in the evening. We have a busy day tomorrow!"

I sat back, awash with relief. Who knew being a poof could be such an asset? I took a puff of the cigar, suddenly finding its flavor appealing.

CHAPTER TWENTY-TWO

The roasted boar was unforgettable. Paulo André had two large servings before his mother made him stop. Lygia seemed to have recovered completely from the morning's accident, and had no desire to discuss it. She was relatively quiet through dinner and hardly looked at Antonio the entire meal. She would often gaze away disinterestedly whenever he spoke. Danilo was also uncharacteristically quiet, though Antonio seemed practically buoyant as he toasted me and our future ventures.

My phone had vibrated during dinner, but I'd not dared look until I'd returned to my room. It was a text from Adriana. *Call me as soon as you can.* I didn't feel safe checking in with her from the room, so I stepped outside and walked. The paths were whimsically plotted along the property. This one was lined with tall, thin bamboo stalks brushing in the breeze. The temperature dropped and I looked at the sea. Clouds were obscuring the star-filled sky. I heard Antonio and Lygia's suppressed arguing again. They were speaking too quickly for me to understand and their voices were muted by the rustling leaves.

A little further along I came to a small seating area on the clifftop that was shielded from the wind and dialed Adriana.

"T. J., finally! I've been waiting for you to call. Can you speak? I have much to tell you about."

"Yes, I'm alone."

"It's all happening very fast. I just want to let you know we have received the account information from Bradley this afternoon and have been analyzing it. We never could have made this connection without your help!"

It was a snap for Bradley to access any account he liked. Getting the official subpoena took a little more time. But he wasn't one to let bureaucracy slow a mission down. Adriana's investigative team had been able to uncover an elaborate scheme of transactions that correlated to known briberies of high officials, drug distribution in the *favelas*, payrolls, weapons purchases and assassinations by the Dragon Militia. Each account randomly funded different purposes. Russo would receive cash from Brasão, and a Brazilian connection would pay out the funds here from a completely unrelated source, minus a handsome commission.

"So we just need to know who is in between the money handler here and Feijão," I said.

"I've got some good news on that front too. I've been watching Eugenia Telles, Feijão's mother. She operates a little vending stand in the flower market in Roçinha. A well-dressed gentleman came by and paid her a visit in her stall for several minutes. We have confirmation that money exchanged hands. We think he is Brasão's local money man and are watching him closely, looking into his dealings. We've uncovered a few criminal associations of his already and have enough to book him this afternoon."

"Excellent work!"

"You did most of it. We have what we need to set up

a sting operation and capture Feijão and Malandrão through Margarida. If you are right and the few missing pieces fall into place, your job here is just about done."

"What about Andrade? Any word on why he's snooping on our assignment? His wife and Danilo are definitely involved in some scheme together, and I'm guessing they are working against him, whatever it is. Can't you ask your husband about Andrade?"

"I will, but he only gets back from a debriefing in Brasilia tonight."

"Why is a civil policeman being debriefed in Brasilia?"

"It's a classified mission he's on. Like I said, he can't discuss it with me." An irksome reply.

"When do you think Feijão will make the transaction?"

"We think tomorrow afternoon. When the time is right, our agents will follow Margarida to the meeting point. Then BOPE will take over and handle the rest. How are things there?"

Rain began to splatter on the large leaves around me and thunder rumbled. The wind was picking up again and the drops got heavier as we spoke.

"I think everything is fine now. I had my suspicions for a while, but my cover is still secure. Hey, were there any unusual transactions in accounts under Lygia's name?"

"Well, one of them is unmistakably used by Brasão for his purposes. But that first account of hers we discovered seems to be legitimate. Nothing unusual, mostly deposits. Although in the last two months there were a few sizeable transfers to Brazil, but they were through proper channels and the notation states they were charitable donations, which would make sense."

I tensed. "What charity?"

"I'll have to look and get back to you. Our people will make a nice welcome committee for Brasão when he lands in Rio tomorrow. Thank you, T. J., I have a good feeling about this one. We are so close, thanks to you."

"It ain't over till the fat lady sings."
"Excuse me?"
"Just an American expression. Be careful and good luck."
"You too. Good-bye, *Gostosão*!" Adriana giggled and hung up.

I slipped the phone into my pocket and pivoted toward the path. Lightning ripped jaggedly across the sky, lighting up Lygia's wet face.

"Who are you, T. J.?"
"Jesus, Lygia, you scared the crap out of me!"

Her hair was plastered to her head by the rain. Water droplets rolled off her long eyelashes and down her aquiline nose. It wasn't just the rain; she'd been crying.

"Who are you? I must know. I can help you, whatever it is you are doing here."

"How much did you hear?"
"Enough to know you are not here to invest with Antonio."

Shit.

"We can't talk here, it's dangerous."

The rain had become a downpour.

"Then where?" She raised her voice above the storm. "Tell me what's going on!"

I led her to the side of the house and we got in the buggy. I pressed the start button and drove out into the cascading rain. The hum of the vehicle was completely muffled by the sky's rumbling. Once I was sure nobody was following, I turned downhill toward the little square and then up the ramp to the old fort. I drove through the towering gates, parked inside the courtyard and looked around to be certain there was nobody near. Lygia waited for me to come around to her side and I pointed her to an old rusted metal door I'd noticed the day before. I opened it with a jarring creak, just enough for us to enter. I lit the flashlight app on my phone and rested it on the sill. Thunder clapped loudly outside and lightning flashed eerily in the room through the bars on the window. Water dripped throughout the ancient structure.

"I don't like it in here," Lygia said. "It's a prison cell." The chamber mutely echoed her voice.

"It's safe for now."

"What has he done? Who are you? I know it's serious. I'm so scared for my son, please tell me. I have to know."

"You're gonna have to be strong now. I wasn't planning on telling you any of this until I could assure your and your son's safety. But now I have no choice. I can't protect you if things don't go as planned. And as of now, the plan's just coming together."

She was shivering. "You're frightening me."

"I'm a US Drug Enforcement Special Agent. I've been independently contracted by the Military Police to arrest your husband and Danilo and anyone else entangled in their web."

"I don't understand," she said, visibly startled. "Antonio is surely guilty of many shady deals, but I don't see how they relate to drug enforcement."

"You better sit down."

I pointed at a couple of wet crates on the floor.

She still shivered. "There are some towels under the back seat of the buggy, would you mind getting them?"

I conceded and ran back out into the rain. I scanned the vicinity to confirm we were still alone, grabbed the towels from under the seat and slipped back inside the damp, dark room. My phone vibrated and I reached for it on the sill with my free hand. The light slipped over Lygia's concerned eyes. I saw a text from Adriana.

Wires were for charity run by Ronaldo's wife. Called Ronaldo but no answer.

Now let me tell ya, that just didn't sit right with me. Lygia's eyes focused into space steadfastly—she'd been in deep thought. I put one towel over the crate and another over her shoulders when she sat down.

"Thank you. Now tell me everything." Her gaze was

steady, as if she were testing me. Perhaps she was readjusting her perspective. "What is he involved in? Valeria and I often talked about how we knew our husbands were corrupt. It's one of the reasons Valeria left César. It is the very reason I want to take Paulo André away. Oh God, please tell me."

I watched her with some level of detachment. "It's not just him, Lygia. Antonio and your father both have a network of bank accounts under various names—including yours, by the way—that they've been using to fund a variety of drug-trafficking crimes and numerous kickbacks to officials. They basically run the show."

Lygia's eyes darted as she rethought what she'd say, one of those micro-expressions I'd been trained to pick up on. What was she keeping from me? She was so perplexing at times.

"If an account in my name were involved in criminal activity, would all my accounts come into scrutiny? Would they be seized or frozen? My God, my account in New York is what I am counting on to survive with Paulo André until things get settled. What can I do? I must protect my son from this man."

I recalled that expression from the first time I'd seen her on TV and again on the set, and instantly, it all became clear as a dewdrop. Jovelina's voice rang in my head: *She would risk everything to save him!* Wasn't that pretty much her last line in that blockbuster season finale?

I pictured Lygia eyeing me that first time at the club like the piece of merchandise that I was. Describing her character's adoration for her son with such passion, all the strange looks, torrents of voluntary information. *There is deception with the Empress as well.* My skin rigored. Suddenly, what Valeria had said about the Empress card made sense. I'd thought she'd been referring to Adriana, but it was Lygia.

Her unbridled laughter the other night now made sense: She'd been playing me all along—prodding me in certain directions. Her donations to Mrs. Pereira's charity were funding Ronaldo's mission. She was using me to buy her freedom. This was her show.

I shook my head as the realization compounded in my mind; I eased the gun from my holster. "You financed this mission to get rid of Antonio. But why keep it a secret from me, Lygia, why?"

Her mask fell, and I was watching a desperate woman. "You must understand my point of view, T. J. We have no escape. My son means everything. It was too risky to let you know my intentions."

"Or you're trying to save yourself from any culpability. With Antonio out of the picture, you would stand to gain the most. All that power, GlobeNet and Antonio's empire. Didn't you say you'd run your father's business better than Antonio?"

"None of that means anything to me compared to my son." I wasn't sure I could trust her pleading face. "Please, T. J., put the gun down and I'll explain. I did not think my US account would be embroiled in this mess. I thought I would be able to get away with Paulo André while you and Ronaldo arrested Antonio. But without access to my money there, I can't leave."

I shifted on the crate again, gun still in hand. I fought to calm down, rethinking the entire operation from this new perspective. Now that I knew, it seemed obvious on exponential levels.

"Why did you come to me tonight?" I asked.

"I have not heard from Ronaldo as we had planned. I wanted to make sure things were moving as scheduled. Tomorrow will be a race for Paulo André and me to leave Rio before Antonio returns. The raid on the Dragon Militia must succeed. Antonio must be held responsible for Vinícius' death. When I didn't hear from Ronaldo tonight confirming everything was in place, I panicked." Lygia leaned forward. "Please. I need to be sure that Antonio's guilt won't incriminate me in any way."

"How can I trust you? I don't like being made a fool of, especially not when it risks lives." I realized I'd raised my voice. "Why now?"

Lygia sat upright, anguish creasing her forehead. "I went to Antonio's office one night—we had argued earlier about Paulo André and I was filming late and wanted to apologize. I—I overheard Antonio and Danilo speaking about purchasing arms and funding drug *donos*. I could not believe my ears. After all I had tried to do in the *favelas*. Then I heard them talk about how they had taken care of Vinícius." Her tears were as real as I could tell anymore. "Poor Carla didn't deserve that, it ruined her life—a completely innocent victim. And Paulo André." Her hand went up to her mouth as she thought of him.

Her next words warbled. "I could not allow my son to grow into that; with that animal as his mentor." She sighed deeply. "Ronaldo's wife was a client of Valeria's and we had met on a few occasions because we both have charities that benefit the *favelas*. Everyone in Rio knows he's the man against the drug war. I made an appointment and told him what I knew, but I had no proof. I offered him the money he needed to prove my husband's guilt. Not a soul knows, not Valeria, not even your partner Adriana. This was supposed to be a win-win for me, for Ronaldo, for the *favelas*."

The concern in her eyes seemed genuine to me. But so had Vicente's. How could I trust my gut anymore? How could I trust her? I was hoping Lygia hadn't shot herself in the foot—and me with it.

She continued. "But things went off course and I had to intervene. After Antonio's behavior last night and the scuba diving accident, I knew they were on to you somehow and Danilo would try again at the hunt. I argued with Antonio—he was jealous, accused us of having an affair. He laughed when I told him you were gay. He was delighted by the news—as if he'd had an epiphany."

Lygia turned toward the heavy rainfall outside the

open door. "I could see he was thrilled that your deal was still in play. He called the reserve and had them send for Danilo and you immediately. And he laughed some more." She picked up the towel and wrung the water from her hair with it. "I could relax then, knowing you would be OK."

"Relax?" I raised a brow. I'd barely slipped that one like a mouse through a crack.

"After that, I told him I was taking Paulo André to the States during Carnival and possibly longer. Then he got aggressive, yelling that our son's place is by his father's side. I pleaded with him to be reasonable. He slapped me hard and went into his library." I could see the shading on the side of her face emerge from the shadow.

"Well, your husband is an extremely dangerous man. He's interacting with other ruthless people in a power-grabbing game. We have him in our sights, but your involvement changes things, at least in my mind."

"This is Brazil, Ronaldo knows how to edit. I need you to make sure this finishes well and exempt my account in New York from any involvement."

"The *jeitinho brasileiro*."

She sat back, biting the corner of her lip, and seemed hurt at the reference. "That account has only *my* income in it and is legally declared in my taxes here. I never really knew about the others. I need to preserve something for Paulo André, and to use it as leverage for financing my charities. Antonio always had investments in my name and had me sign papers. I know I should have read them, but it was one of those things a young wife has no power over."

Inside, I was fuming and conflicted, but I lowered my gun and shook my head. "I get it. Everything is still moving forward. I just spoke to Adriana. Listen, it may have seemed like a brilliant idea to pay Ronaldo to hire me, but there are a few things I just don't get. Why is Andrade having me followed? Is he working for your husband or somebody else?"

"Angelo is following you?" She snapped her gaze up to mine. "Why? Ronaldo did not mention that. My father was always good to that strange man."

"Maybe Ronaldo didn't want to worry you. Is there any reason you have to fear Andrade? There's something bigger going on here. I know for sure Antonio has no clue you are behind my presence here, or today would not have ended as it did. But Andrade might. And he is on your husband's payroll. Ronaldo told you about the missing file?" She nodded. "If Andrade has the documents and they are linked to you, I'll bet ya he's wondering why you are funding the Military Police. You could be in grave danger."

Lygia looked seriously panicked. "I really don't know! What should I do? Should I leave as planned with Paulo André when we get back to Rio?"

"Get out as quickly as you can. Neither of you should be around when the MPs make the arrests. For now, just play normal and hopefully everything should be fine. Let's get through this trip. You just need to maintain the status quo like your life depends on it. Like your son's life depends on it, because it does. You'll be fine—you're Lygia de Castello-Branco, for fuck's sake."

If she noticed the snap of sarcasm in my voice, she didn't reply. "Let's get back before we are noticed missing," she said.

I took the towels. We got in the buggy and rode silently back to the house. The storm had passed and the skies were clearing, but the dirt road was still a muddy mess. I walked Lygia to her door and she turned unexpectedly and gave me a hug. Her eyes were dry, and I could see that while she was devastated, the strength that had driven her all her life was in play. How could I be certain it wasn't all still an act?

"You are a remarkable man. I am profoundly sorry

for misleading you, but as you have observed, I will do what I must to save my son. I hope you can accept that and consider my deception a form of . . . " She seemed to search for it. " . . . benevolent betrayal. I have only good intentions. If you weren't so clever, you might have never known. I didn't think you would." Her eyes conveyed such gratitude and tenderness. That's when I felt it, my undeniable gut conviction that Lygia's motives were true. It felt energizing to experience that certainty again.

It was too late when I returned to my room to call Ronaldo. I hoped Adriana had heard from him by now. I walked past my muddy shoes from the shower to the bed and lay down, listening to the surf below and praying this whole scheme didn't fall to pieces before Adriana's raid tomorrow. There was no room for fear or doubt.

Benevolent betrayal. I slept deeply and dreamt of Vicente.

CHAPTER TWENTY-THREE

The sun reflected brightly off the sleek jet's wing. Paulo André and Sylvia were sitting in the front. He was listening to his MP3 player and Sylvia snored gently, thanks to some crushed Klonopin I'd slipped into her juice before we took off. Lygia and I spoke in private. I told her to try to relax a bit, that my team had everything under control. All the proof was in place save the final sting operation, which would happen sometime today. Antonio and Danilo would be flying back in the late afternoon and the MPs would be waiting for them. Lygia planned to pack up and leave with Paulo André before then.

"Everything will be fine, as long as Antonio doesn't suspect anything," I said.

"We argued about my leaving with Paulo André, but he would never have let me leave the island with him if he even suspected I might go today." Lygia sat up in her seat and shook her head.

"To this day I can't believe this is my reality. I'm terrified and furious at the same time. My son will have this over his head for the rest of his life, an imprisoned father,

Brazil's most dangerous criminal as his legacy." She swiped away a tear. "The publicity alone . . . "

"Paulo André can take solace from the fact that his mother will always be known as Brazil's greatest hero. He has you, and with time he will understand how fortunate that is."

"It breaks my heart," she said, looking over at her son, obliviously nodding his head to his music and playing a video game. "Our entire world is about to collapse. I don't know how to tell him."

"You feel like it is, but life will go on. I know what you are going through. Sometimes these wake-up calls turn out for the best." I reflected on my own situation. I had to succeed on this assignment to have any semblance of a future with the DEA. And I was worried about Ronaldo and Adriana. They hadn't responded this morning, but I kept that to myself. Adriana must be too busy planning her BOPE mission.

Lygia stared forward. "That's why, no matter what, I must leave with Paulo André tonight. The last thing Ronaldo told me was that the raid today would allow them to capture the final links, that Antonio's case would be closed."

She had not yet been briefed about Russo and the Tiesenhaler connection, so I filled her in. She smiled radiantly. "It all comes back to Valeria's reading. We were meant to cross paths and change each other's lives. There is no coincidence."

I rubbed my arm. "Did she say that?"

"She did."

The seatbelt sign lit with a chime and I felt the plane begin its descent. It banked steeply to the left, offering a view of Rio's postcard beaches and mountains.

We dipped around Sugar Loaf and coasted over the bay onto Santo Dumont's runway. When the plane rolled to a stop, Paulo André gently shook Sylvia awake. She seemed surprised and somewhat confused that we had already landed. As we descended the stairs, I saw Rodrigues standing by the car.

I kissed Sylvia fleetingly and gave Lygia and Paulo André each a hug. Rodrigues tipped his cap and opened the door for me, but his face looked forlorn. Once seated up front, he handed me a refreshing towelette to cool my face with.

"*Boa tarde, Seu* Leukemeyer," he said, pulling away from the tarmac.

"*Boa tarde*, Rodrigues."

"Such terrible news about Major Pereira."

I looked at Rodrigues' sorrowful reflection in the rearview mirror and bile filled my stomach. "What news?"

Rodrigues handed me today's edition of *Jornal do Brasil*. Emblazoned across the top, over Ronaldo's photograph, was a long bold headline.

"What does it say?"

Rodrigues put the car in Park and translated.

"*Major Ronaldo Pereira of the Rio de Janeiro Military Police, a leader in the fight against drug trafficking in Rio de Janeiro state, was found murdered early this morning on Praia do Forte near his daughter's home in Urca. The major's downtown offices at Military Police headquarters were raided by an armed gang yesterday night and captives were taken after a shootout that left four officers dead and the building in ruins.*"

"Get me home, Rodrigues, as quickly as possible. I'm so sorry for your family's loss."

I felt clammy and broke into cold sweat. Had Brasão somehow known that Ronaldo was on to him—getting close? But how? Who else would make such a brazen attack? Andrade?

We rounded the lagoon over to Ipanema. I was upstairs in my apartment in minutes.

"*Seu* Leukemeyer, welcome home," said Jovelina with a smile. She noticed my intense disposition, grabbed my bag from Wellington's hand and closed the door. "Is there anything you need?"

"No, thank you."

I checked my phone for messages. There was one message from Sean. I listened.

"Hi, T. J. Gee, I wish you had answered. There is no easy way to say this, but Lucille is going to need immediate surgery. Apparently, she had another tumor they had not seen before and it's got to be removed urgently. My dad referred them to the best specialists in Houston and I'm on my way there now. I'll be staying with your father and will try you again when I land. Let's hope everything works out OK. Try not to worry, I'll be there. I miss you. Hope you are safe."

My anxiety jumped up a notch. I needed to finish this assignment, get out of Brazil, and now there was no way. I felt grateful Sean would be with my mother, but I suddenly felt a longing for our past, which seemed ever-more out of reach. Distressed, I thought of Ronaldo again. According to the paper, some officers had been captured. I had to make sure Adriana wasn't one of them. She'd been at the office last night when we spoke. BOPE would not move forward without her specific instructions. The MPs would not be there to welcome Brasão and Danilo. Today's operation would fall apart and I'd be fucked.

I dialed 555 and twirled a pen around my fingers, impatiently counting the rings. After the third, my hopes dwindled. I was about to hang up when I heard a sound on the other end and returned the phone to my ear.

"Adriana, where are you? Are you OK?"

"Who is this?" replied a gruff male voice with a heavy accent.

"You tell me first."

"This is Bernardo Pessoa, Adriana's husband. Who are you?"

"How do you have her phone? Where is she?"

"I was hoping you would tell me that. I was near the station when it was attacked, on my way to pick her up. I ended up being part of the investigation team at the scene and I found her phone on the floor. That's all you get until you tell me who you are and if you know where my wife may be."

Good cover; having Adriana's phone was smart too: he'd know I'd contact her at some point, particularly after hearing about Ronaldo's death. But I could hear the tension in his voice. Whatever friction there was between Adriana and her husband, it sounded like he was concerned about her.

"I'm the hired help. I've been working with her in a covert operation."

"Let's meet somewhere. Alone."

"Where?"

"Vista Chinesa, half an hour."

"I'll be in a black jeep wearing a blue shirt."

I ran to my bedroom and changed into some jeans, grabbed my holstered gun and keys, and took the elevator to the garage. Each floor took an eternity to pass, while all my hard work was falling through the cracks once again. How'd everything suddenly gone so wrong?

I called Lygia, and she answered with an alarmed voice—she'd already heard about Ronaldo and was about to call me. I told her to stay put and keep with her plan.

I entered the destination into my phone—seemed to be a tourist spot—and placed it on the dash. The engine roared to life and I peeled out of the garage onto the seaside boulevard. Within minutes I rounded the lagoon and made my way up the winding road into the Tijuca National Rainforest along the backside of Corcovado Mountain. The forest air cooled the perspiration on my face through the jeep's open window.

Arriving at the famous lookout, I pulled into a parking area in front of a giant Chinese-style pagoda. I looked at my watch—it was just 2:30—and tapped my foot nervously as I waited for Bernardo to appear. I guessed he'd picked the place because the only folks up here were tourists. I checked my gun one more time. If Bernardo was Andrade's mole, would he have kidnapped his own wife to stop this operation? Needed to look at all angles. The afternoon sun was beating down hard, and I thought of Lygia and Paulo André rapidly packing up their lives to escape. I had to find Adriana somehow, provided she was still alive.

A motorcycle pulled up next to me. The driver wore a striped racing shirt that hugged his fit upper body. He swung his thick, denim-clad thighs up and over the seat, boot heels clicking together as he finished his dismount. He removed his helmet and ran his hand through thick black hair.

"Are you the help?" Bernardo asked. His face was darkened by stubble and his brown eyes were traced with red capillaries and weighed by the worry circles beneath them.

I got out of the car and met him at the curb.

"Let's walk," he said.

"I'm T. J. Leukemeyer. I'm US DEA working on an undercover assignment with the Military Police."

"So that's what she's been up to."

"How do I know I can trust you? How do I know you are not the mole that had me followed by Andrade?"

Bernardo stopped in his tracks. "How do you know you were being followed by Andrade?"

"I was followed by one of his men. A guy named Saldanha."

"You? You killed him in the subway?" His mouth dropped.

"It was an accident."

"I can assure you, I am not your mole."

"How?"

"Let's walk," he repeated. "Please, we have very little time."

His strong legs led the way past the pagoda. I had to

give Adriana credit in the man department. He stopped in the shade and looked out at Rio.

"When I found her phone, I had to wait for someone to call. I couldn't figure out her password. She has been kidnapped and her life could be in serious danger if we don't find her quickly." He looked me over thoughtfully. "Yours as well, I imagine. I am not your mole, because I am currently leading an undercover mission that implicates my own boss in criminal behavior. I was assigned by the new Federal Law Enforcement Oversight Agency to investigate Chief Angelo de Andrade for allegations of corruption. It turns out he has been running an arms ring, bringing them in from abroad and selling them off to the Red Commandos. They are the ones who attacked the Military Police and captured Adriana."

Blindsided! "Are you saying that the attack on the Military Police headquarters was carried out by the Red Commandos at the command of the chief of police? It wasn't the Dragon Militia?"

"Who can say for sure? That's Brazil for you. I know that Adriana has been battling the Dragon Militia specifically for years. It is frustrating because we can't discuss details of our work with each other."

Just like the FBI and the CIA stumbling over each other back home. "It does seem a bit counterproductive."

"It's all so, how you say—self-defeating, but corruption everywhere forces Adriana and me to work secretly. Look at us—we are working on parallel missions!" He shook his head in frustration, and when he looked up at me, his eyes were shaded with anguish. Maybe it was a reflection of the unwavering trust for her husband that Adriana had expressed on the phone, but I could see that he loved her and I believed he was telling the truth. He was not the double agent.

"Do you have any idea who could have taken her and where? The Red Commandos have shaken us off and changed their base in Roçinha. I was hoping you might know something more."

"I'd assumed she'd been taken by the sector general of the Dragon Militia in Vidigal, but if the Red Commandos were behind the attack, I couldn't say. We have evidence that the finance minister's murder was committed by Malandrão, a Dragon Militia sector general, and ordered by Antonio Brasão. Their *dono* is an arms dealer, a guy named Feijão. We were planning to nab him in the process of their transaction. Problem is, it's happening now. Adriana was supposed to oversee that BOPE sting operation today."

"*Meu Deus!*" exclaimed Bernardo. "We are after Feijão in relation to the Red Commandos. The only problem is we have no concrete connection between him and Andrade; it's all circumstantial." Bernardo shook his head. "So the mighty Antonio Brasão is the man behind the Dragon Militia. This is a crazy world. Feijão must hedge his bets by serving both cartels." Bernardo thought out loud. "No, that man is in too deep with the Red Commandos. From what we've uncovered, we believe he is involved with all of their strategic planning. There's been chatter indicating the Red Commandos may attack the Dragon Militia. That's what he's up to."

Sweet Jesus, this was a total clusterfuck. "But Feijão is Malandrão's *dono*! He's been part of the Dragon Militia since the previous *dono* was captured last year."

Bernardo was not surprised. "These guys work every angle. I've been watching Andrade and his home. In Brasilia, my colleagues have very strong suspicions that Senator dos Santos and Andrade run the Red Commandos using Feijão. They've been monitoring his calls, but he is very careful and speaks in code. They have enough proof of corruption that they plan to arrest the senator today. My sources also tell me that a weapons deal with the Red Commandos went down yesterday before the attack, but I can't confirm that."

"So the Red Commandos attacked the MPs with

fresh new semiautomatics and plan to attack the Dragon Militia today. Yet somehow the Dragon Militia is also buying arms from the same folks this afternoon. It's nuts."

"Unless Feijão is part of the Red Commandos' attack." Bernardo's eyes twitched as he connected dots. "If the Red Commandos had the balls to attack MP headquarters, they must have thought the MP were plotting against them."

Another sinking feeling. "Somebody stole some of Ronaldo's files. They show Brasão's wife as the financial backer of our mission. We think it was Andrade because he was having me followed, but we couldn't figure out why he would be interested." Our eyes locked. "He must think that Brasão is paying the MPs to attack the Red Commandos."

I thought of Cadu and the murdered businessman—one of Andrade's deals gone bad? If the Red Commandos really had attacked MP headquarters, then Lygia's little stunt was having some serious unintended repercussions. I was doomed without Adriana.

"How can you be so sure she is alive?" Perhaps a callous question.

"They would not have taken her otherwise. They killed all the others. She is a valuable trade. That's how it works here. But when trades are not honored, the torture can be the cruelest. Do you have any clues that can help us find her?" he repeated.

I recalled the gruesome video clips Ronaldo had provided of gang torture techniques, cylinders of burning tires and the like.

"Her plan was to surveil a girl named Margarida who always meets with Feijão when he comes to see Malandrão. Malandrão pimps her out to him as a favor. But now with Adriana missing and her team dead, our plan is vaporized." I tried to figure out what to do next.

"We have to find her, quickly. Finding Feijão is our

only hope." Bernardo glanced at his watch.

I looked to the right, at the sprawling *favela* of Roçinha wrapping around the side of the Two Brothers, and remembered Adriana telling me about Lygia's projects. *Roçinha is next. Soon she will have centers in all the major favelas of Rio. All the residents of Vidigal venerate her; they would do anything for her.*

"I've got an idea. Let me make a phone call."

CHAPTER TWENTY-FOUR

I asked Lygia to meet us at her charity in Vidigal. She sounded a bit panicked and reluctant, but I made it clear that her husband's arrest and her son's safety were at risk.

"Is Ronaldo's murder related to what's happening today?"

"Perhaps. Adriana is missing. We're in trouble and I really need your help. We need to find where someone is in Vidigal. Somebody who can lead us to her captors. Without Adriana, it all falls apart, you see? I figure the beneficiaries of your charities would do anything that you might ask of them."

"But what about the airport? Paulo André?" Her words slipped past her halting breath.

"Leave him there with the nanny. I don't think you'll be away more than an hour. Please, Lygia, you must help us with this. No Adriana, no raid this afternoon."

She gave me the address. "I'll see you there in twenty minutes."

I got in the Jeep and sped behind Bernardo down into the city again, around the base of the Two Brothers, and up into the wild winding streets of the Vidigal slum on the opposite side. Crouched like a jockey racing ahead of me, Bernardo swayed with forceful agility as he rounded each bend up the steep mountainside. He made a sharp left and came to a stop in front of a building with the Hearts of Wisdom logo decaled on the windows.

A short woman with glasses met us at the door. Bernardo made introductions and let her know we were waiting for Lygia. The lady, Maria Flores, invited us in. She told Bernardo that Lygia had called and should be arriving any minute.

We were in a large room with several women taking notes as another conducted some kind of workshop. There were shelves lined with books and a table with several computer stations. Every terminal was occupied. There was also a small nursery room crowded with laughing children and a couple of young ladies singing to them. I was impressed.

The front door swung open and Lygia walked in. All the women stopped what they were doing and greeted her with applause and cheers. She waved at them and hugged and kissed a few, despite her masked anxiety, before turning her attention to me.

"Hello, T. J."

Lygia had pulled her hair back with a clip; concern creased her brow. She was restless to get back home to Paulo André.

"Hello, Lygia, we'll try to keep this brief. This is Bernardo Pessoa. He is my partner Adriana's husband. He is with the Civil Police of Rio. Adriana has gone missing in yesterday evening's raid."

"Desculpe," Lygia said, apologetically shaking Bernardo's hand.

"It's an honor to meet you, *Senhora* Castello-Branco."

"Bernardo and I believe that Adriana is being held captive as collateral should today's business go wrong. The Red Commandos are probably behind this."

Lygia's eyes widened, and a rogue tear slipped away.

"The sooner you leave, the better. But first we need you to do something to help us. We are looking for a girl named Margarida. She is a prostitute and her pimp is Malandrão, the sector general of the area. Do you think Maria Flores can speak to these people and see if anyone knows where Margarida can be found? She is a beautiful girl with a gunshot scar on her right palm. From what Adriana has told me, it's a fairly tight-knit community. We are hoping someone here may know her."

I pulled up her picture on my phone and held it out for them to see.

Lygia turned to Maria Flores and spoke in rapid Portuguese. The woman shook her head while repeatedly evoking the sign of the cross.

"She said that nobody ever knows where Malandrão is. He is always moving around in the *favela* for safety, especially since the UPP have been around. She suspects he is in the higher areas that are less patrolled."

Maria turned to the room full of women and got their attention. They all gathered around her and she asked if anyone knew of Margarida and her whereabouts. A young woman in the back raised her hand and came forward to speak with Bernardo—Margarida's cousin, Lygia explained. She wore yellow flip-flops and a simple sundress, and was shy as a mail-order bride.

Lygia translated. "Her name is Raimunda. She is saying that her cousin means well but is always in trouble. The family has turned their back on her because of the danger that often surrounds her. She knows where in the *favela* to find her and she could take you, but she is scared to go to that unpatrolled area."

"Please explain to her how important it is that we find her. That Bernardo and I are expert marksmen and undercover agents and will protect her from any danger."

Raimunda became wide-eyed and very nervous as Lygia translated. She began to cry, tugging at the colorful plastic butterfly clips that fastened her braids. She looked from Bernardo to me, and then to Lygia. But Lygia persuaded her to be strong and help us out. Nobody could refuse a request from Lygia. Bernardo put his hand reassuringly on the girl's shoulder. He said something to soothe her fears, and led her to the door.

"We will have to walk," he said to me over his shoulder.

I turned to Lygia, who was evidently satisfied that the entire ordeal had moved along quickly.

"OK, you had better head back home, get Paulo André and leave. We'll have to hope this works. Good luck. I'll look for you in New York City."

I walked her to her car. All the women were smiling at her and waving good-bye. I noticed she had come without a driver.

"Good luck, T. J. You must succeed." Her eyebrows arched in supplication.

She gave the Mercedes some gas and drove rapidly down the steep street, disappearing around the corner.

"That was a stroke of genius," said Bernardo. "Lygia de Castello-Branco. Wow!"

"Thanks. Now let's hope we can find Adriana in time."

Bernardo spoke to Raimunda and she led the way. We went into the maze of alleys winding through the shanty's upper reaches. Both of us kept our hands in close proximity to our weapons. We walked in silence, broken only by the occasional greeting from a passerby who would look at both Bernardo and me questioningly. I paid close attention to our trajectory in order to ensure our return. Spaghetti strands of electric cables formed occasional arbors above our heads. After about fifteen minutes navigating through the narrow, graffitied passageways, we came to a brick structure with a satellite dish. The window was covered by safety bars and we could hear the sounds from a TV inside. Raimunda knocked nervously at the wood-plank door while we waited out of view.

"*Quem é?*" Margarida was inside.

"Raimunda."

Her cousin opened the door and they greeted each other. Margarida quickly noticed Raimunda's unease and looked past her; our eyes locked. She let out a short scream and slammed her door. Raimunda figured her job was done. Her flip-flops clapped the ground as she fled back the way we had come. Peering in through the safety bars, I could see Margarida dialing her cell phone. She paused to slam the window's shutters closed.

Bernardo shot at the lock on the door, sparks spraying. He stood back, then rammed his large body full force against it with a loud grunt. The door gave with a splintering crack. I jumped past him through the opening and grabbed the phone out of her hand before she completed the call. Our guns were drawn and Margarida was patently terrified, scared as a cat in a dog pound. I grabbed her wrists firmly and held them down. I signaled for silence.

A soft beam of afternoon sunlight slipped through the dilapidated shutters and illuminated her quivering eyes as I held her in place. The silence was broken only by the chickens clucking outside on the dirt path, and the faint sound of laughter from the game show she'd been watching.

Bernardo spoke to her soothingly, telling her that everything would be fine if she cooperated.

I looked at her and asked, "Feijão?"

She shook her head and said something as tears began to fall.

"She is asking who you are and why you are following her and her friend."

"We need her to take us to Feijão and Malandrão."

Her eyes widened. She'd understood that.

My phone vibrated. It was Lygia. Bernardo came over and held Margarida while I answered the call.

"Lygia?"

"Help me!" she screamed. "They've taken Paulo André!" Her guttural sobbing made it hard to hear distinctly. "They killed his nanny, the guards. Oh my God!"

Lygia let out three short screams of terror in rising scale. I could only wonder what horror she had stumbled upon.

"The house has been ransacked... and they have taken... my son, oh God, oh no... my God. What should I do?" she screamed.

I looked at Bernardo. He was speaking with Margarida, who seemed calmer. I kept my gun in my hand.

I thought fast. "What about the chip you told me about—the tracking chip in his leg?"

"I'm checking now, but there is no signal!"

"Is anybody there at all?"

"No. I'm alone. This is my fault, isn't it? Oh God, help me, please help me find Paulo André!"

"Are you certain you were not followed?"

There was a pause as I heard her running. "No. I'm looking at the street camera and nobody is there." Her voice was tremulous.

"I think you've got to stay put. I mean it. You are in serious danger. If they were just there, they won't be coming back. We will find your son. Does your husband know yet?"

"I don't know. No, of course not. I'm the only one here," she cried.

"Keep it that way. When will he be arriving?"

"Around six or seven. He usually calls just before he gets here. What should I do?"

"Let me know if he does. I have a feeling that if we find Adriana, Paulo André won't be far. Stay put and don't call anyone."

Whatever his parents had done, the boy was not at fault. He deserved my help.

"I'll help you, you've got my word." I looked at Bernardo. "Somebody has kidnapped Lygia's son. Everyone at the house is dead." I stared at the wall, trying to make sense of it. "Can you send a couple of your most loyal men to protect Lygia and guard the place unofficially?" Bernardo was stunned. He nodded.

"A couple of trusted officers will be there soon to keep you safe until I can come. Call me as soon as you know when Brasão is arriving."

"I'm so scared."

"I'll be there as soon as I can. Find a room where you feel safe and stay there until help arrives." I heard her sobbing as she hung up.

I checked my watch. "What time is the encounter supposed to take place? We have to get to Feijão. Ask her."

Margarida answered unwillingly.

"Four this afternoon. She was getting ready to go meet with Feijão."

"Where?"

She turned her head in fear, refusing to speak. Bernardo shook her not so gently, and she rattled something off to him.

"Malandrão texts her where the *boca* is that week, the entrance to the drug market. She meets with a porter there who takes her wherever he is meeting with Feijão."

If we were going to the *boca*, I had a strong feeling I'd need some help.

"Where is Zezé?" I asked her.

Her eyes glazed with worry. I filled Bernardo in on the kid.

"Tell her to call him and have him come here immediately. Force her to do so if necessary." I held up my gun.

Margarida dialed the number. She spoke rapidly to Zezé.

"She says he is not far," Bernardo translated after the call ended.

"If the Red Commandos did attack the MPs yesterday, they must have been the ones who took Brasão's kid, don't you think? Attacking at all levels?"

"Feijão would know the answer."

Margarida whimpered as we waited for Zezé to arrive. The small room was hot and the air felt stale. The smell of both Bernardo's and my sweat commingled with Margarida's fruity perfume. Dust swirled weightlessly through the light beams squeezing through the door cracks. My phone vibrated and I reckoned it might be Lygia again, but it was a text from Sean.

Dr. worried, not going well. Call me when you can.

I needed some air. Bernardo had the girl under control, so I stepped outside for a moment to breathe. I was considering texting back for an update when Zezé came around the corner and paused, perplexed by my presence. "T. J., what you do here?" He frowned. "Is that gun?"

"Zezé, get inside," I ordered, as I fought back worries about my mother.

He started to back away. "You a fucking police? You lie to me?"

"Get inside and I'll explain."

"Filho da puta!" he spat. "Son of a bitch! Just make sure you understand."

"Easy, Zezé, just get inside." I waved my gun toward the door and his hands shot up.

"Come on, T. J., no need for that." His iridescent eyes slanted cynically. He stepped inside the shack and sat down next to Margarida. She grabbed his hand and sobbed. She said something that Bernardo translated.

"She is telling him that we want them to take us to Malandrão."

Zezé looked at me with alarm. "You crazy? He kill me this time for sure! I lucky to be alive."

"You must take us to him immediately, Zezé. I'm sorry things turned out this way, really."

"I don't know where he is! Who you are? What you want with danger man like Malandrão?"

"Just make Margarida take us to him. Now!"

"Agora!" growled Bernardo at both of them.

"Tell me who you are and what I get for helping you first."

Zezé sensed an opportunity. I couldn't help but soften at his smirk.

"Zezé, I'm a drug enforcement agent from the US, and you, my friend, are the key to making a much better world for the *favelas*. If you can convince Margarida to take us to Malandrão now, we will be able to arrest him and save my partner."

"You crazy?" he exclaimed again and shook his head.

Bernardo turned to me. "Enough. We have to get Feijão to find Adriana. It's our only chance." He was bordering on despair.

"We need your help, Zezé."

He crossed his arms defiantly. "You not so nice. You lie to me all time. You just use me. OK, then. How you pay?"

"How about I pay by not putting you in jail?"

"You *lie* to me, T. J.," he repeated.

"And the police have a recording of the entire story you told me."

He turned his head to the side in offense.

"Zezé, please. We have little time. Your cooperation now is your only option." I waved my gun at him again. "You don't have a choice. Get up, let's go."

Margarida said something to Zezé.

"She say we can't all go together, the *boca* guards will shoot us. She say she can't do this to Feijão. She right, they kill us all."

"She'll have our protection if she comes with us. She'll be in great danger if she doesn't."

"Your protection? That is joke!"

Bernardo dialed his phone. He spoke quickly as we stepped through the broken door into the alley. I was practically pulling Margarida along as she dragged her feet and complained incomprehensibly. Bernardo ended his call.

"I can't ask for normal backup, Andrade would be informed immediately of any such action. But I called a couple of Adriana's colleagues at BOPE."

"The guys who'd be handling the raid?"

"We can trust them, they will seal off the estate and provide protection until we arrive. Up here though, we are on our own." He looked at me gravely. "Let's go!" he ordered, picking up his pace. He pushed Zezé forward roughly.

"Hey, I help you guys, no push!"

"Just keep moving quickly," I said in his ear.

"We will have to split up," said Bernardo. "I think I can go in with her as a drug dealer, but we can't all walk in together, they would know something is up. You're so obviously foreign."

Not only did I look foreign, I was wearing a blue polo shirt. Bernardo appeared more the part—gruff with stubble, in his biker gear, sunglasses and thick silver chain.

"I can go in after the two of you as an American journalist and Zezé can be my guide. I know that's been done before."

"That's very risky, but to be honest I can't think of a better idea. Once the porter takes us to Malandrão's location, you can follow my GPS position to meet up."

"You guys nuts! I no go!" exclaimed Zezé.

"You will go, li'l buddy."

We rounded several corners, climbing the steep hillside amid the confusing jumble of shanty homes. Dark clouds were rapidly overtaking the sky and big drops began to fall when Margarida turned off the path into the dense woods and led us up a steep, muddy trail to a concealed plateau. There were a couple of guards with AK-47s at the entrance to the drug market, a tiny opening between two abandoned houses. We crouched behind a wall and reconnoitered.

"We will go in now. Margarida will introduce me as a new dealer in the *favela*. I've got plenty of practice with this, but you two have to be very convincing. I've heard of foreigners going in from time to time, it is true, but special permission is required. You'll have to say you are here under the invitation of Malandrão and act like there was some miscommunication." Bernardo looked at Zezé, but his words were directed at me. "You really trust this guy? Your life will be in his hands."

"I gotta trust him."

"You crazy, both you!" Zezé muttered under his breath.

Bernardo stood. "I just sent you my tracking link. You can see where I am in relation to you at all times." I checked my phone and accepted the link and his red dot appeared on my map. I reciprocated. "Once you get past the guards, come as fast as you can to meet up with us wherever we are."

Bernardo and Margarida went toward the *boca*. Zezé and I watched as they negotiated their way in. The guard boys recognized Margarida and let them pass. They disappeared inside on their way to meet up with Malandrão's porter. We sat and waited for several minutes.

"Are you ready for this, Zezé?" I dug for the wallet in my back pocket and handed him five $100 bills. "Tell them I'm an American journalist writing about the lives of people in the *favela*. I'm paying you well for it. That's all you know. Use that to pay our way if necessary. I will make this worth your while, Zezé."

"No, you no know how danger here. Please don't make me go in there."

"We have no choice." I grabbed his face firmly with my hands and held his gaze real close. "I need you, buddy. You'll be free after this. I'll make sure of it. I'll pull any strings I can to make your life better, because I can't do it without you. It's time, let's do this."

I stood up, pulling Zezé to his feet, and pushed him ahead of me toward the *boca* guards.

CHAPTER TWENTY-FIVE

The guards rushed toward us, yelling out warnings. Zezé held up his hands and waited for them to reach us. The taller of the two had fierce tattoos and carvings garnishing his skin. He recognized Zezé from the beach and greeted him with a fist bump but gazed at me skeptically through his gold-rimmed Ray-Bans; his rifle casually pointed my way. I resisted the impulse to reach for my gun. These kids were no more than seventeen, I guessed.

Zezé explained who we were and why we were here. They looked perplexed. I nudged him and he persisted. I heard him mention Malandrão and that snapped them to attention. They motioned for us to follow them. Their pants hung low as they swaggered, revealing brand-name underwear.

We entered through the small opening that led to the marketplace—a group of deteriorated, abandoned shanties with tarps extending over the muddy trail between them. Stray dogs wove beneath the display tables. We were drenched from the rainy walk, and in the covered alley the sticky air was hotter than a fur coat in Marfa. I could feel my adrenaline keeping me alert. Zezé was chatting with the guards, holding his own—building rapport.

The market was a hub of activity. Dealers decked in bling jostled for bargains at the various vendor tables in front of each doorway. Marijuana, cocaine, ecstasy and more exotic drugs were on display. Dragon Militia men stood sentinel every few yards. They checked us out suspiciously. I was amazed by the skill of the wild, colorful graffiti that covered every surface, demanding death to the UPP, complete with portraits of bloody effigies. The pirated jumble of electric wires added a menacing texture. Zezé stopped to greet his buddy Castro, who was filling his man-bag with several dozen ounces of drugs. They had a brief animated exchange while the guards waited.

Thunder clapped loudly and we moved on, in the direction of Bernardo's signal. We came to a stop in front of a battle tank of a man. His skin was so black it was blue. He towered over everyone around him and his eyes darted hostility. He flicked his cigarette and said something to the guards. They explained who I was and why I was here. By their expressions, Mr. Battle Tank wasn't buying it. Zezé admirably argued a few rounds and handed over the $500. The guy pocketed it with no change in demeanor. Zezé looked back at me with the same expression Sean'd had in the courtroom.

"This guy say he know nothing of visit from Malandrão."

Tank grabbed a fistful of my shirt and pulled me up close, cheek to cheek, and his other hand jammed his gun into my mouth, twisting it jarringly against my teeth. The acrid taste of gunpowder on my tongue made me gag. He screamed something at me, and folks around us stopped to watch. This was not going well.

Zezé continued to defend me, but another guard jabbed a rifle butt to his mouth and shut him up. Blood dripped from his lips. A crack against the back of my head, and the ground fell out from under me.

When I roused my eyes open, I felt the warm softness of mud against my face. A gag filled my mouth, pressing back my tongue, and my hands were tied behind me. Zezé was speaking. I think that's what woke me. He was pleading, actually. My eyes focused on the floor and I tried to sit up sideways. My head hurt something fierce, like the loudly rumbling skies outside.

Tank kicked dirt in my face. As I blinked away the particles, he righted me with one hand and pushed me back against the wall next to Zezé. No rope 'round his wrists—riding on his notoriety.

"T. J., he no believe us. I tell him you famous. If anything happen to you here, it bring bad *consequência*. Not good for business. He want proof you famous."

I looked around the decrepit room. The hut had lost most of its roof and the rain fell right on in. The brick walls were sagging and broken. Tank picked at his fingernails with a knife as he watched me. He swung his foot into my gut just for kicks and laughed. I rolled around, hunched over, and tried to catch my breath through my nose. My phone vibrated in my pocket as Bernardo's GPS location updated. I could feel that my concealed gun had been taken. My eyes searched and found the gun and holster against the wall behind my captor. Shit.

I spoke into my gag. Tank yanked it out of my mouth.

"He can Google my name."

I spelled it out for him, thinking this could go either way. Tank typed it into his phone and waited. Zezé leaned in to look at the screen too.

"He want know who Bloomberg? Say he see man in TV."

"Tell him he is the mayor of New York City and that was a picture at an award ceremony at the mayor's home for my writing." I was just relieved that had come up instead of the recent picture with Andrade at the party. The DEA was still covering my online profile.

Zezé repeated this with inflections of grandeur. I

gathered bits and pieces of his plea. He reiterated how this was a huge misunderstanding, and how bad it would be for trade if anything happened to me here. It would make international news and the military and police would have to take severe action. I'm pretty sure that's what he said.

Tank seemed to be considering this point. Sweat trickled into my eyes with a light sting and flies vied for a landing. Zezé asked him to untie me and, miraculously, he did so, but he kept his gun pointed at me. Another militiaman poked his head in the door and called Tank outside.

He came back with a red-armbanded kid from the alley; there was a trace of white powder on the boy's nostrils and a machine gun in his hands. He told Zezé that the boy'd be watching us for a minute while he got verification for our passage. If we moved an inch, he'd shoot us. I'd guess the kid was about Paulo André's age.

Tank wasn't gone a minute before the kid started shooting lazy eights up at the ceiling, bringing in more rain. He laughed with amusement as the dust settled. While he looked up, I pointed my gun out to Zezé with a nod. To my surprise, he reached for it and tossed it my way—the kid none the wiser. Zezé began working on him, buttering him up with whatever information might impress him. I adjusted my position and the kid flipped into action, his gun cocked and aimed straight at me. His nose twitched and he quickly swiped at it.

"Easy, buddy," I said.

Zezé calmed the tension down. He started up with the "famous person" story again. Then he told the boy how angry Malandrão would be when he learned his guest was treated so poorly. Those responsible would pay.

Had to give Zezé credit in the bullshit department.

The boy was confused about what to do. When he looked at me, Zezé seized the machine gun out of his hands. The boy began to cry.

Time to go.

I kicked at the back wall and the old bricks fell away. I'd grabbed Zezé's arm to step through it when Tank suddenly appeared at the doorway, looking angry as a homeless hornet, and I'll tell y'all, he knew we weren't Malandrão's guests.

I drew my gun without hesitation and fired. He fell with a heavy thud onto the mud.

Zezé looked stunned. The crying kid got up and ran out the door screaming.

"I know him since I kid."

"You still are a kid, li'l buddy. C'mon, we've got no time to spare."

I kicked a few more bricks and we crawled through the broken back wall into the storm. The steep rainforest was thick with fog. I grabbed a few creepers and we hoisted ourselves up the hillside behind the shanty. The ground leveled off and we caught our breath. I pulled out my phone and the GPS updated our location compared to Bernardo's—they were near. I heard a pop, and a bullet slashed through the leaves. The other guard was coming after us. I took aim and shot him in the leg and he went down with a yelp.

"Move, Zezé, there'll be more coming after us."

Raindrops smacked at my scalp and blinded our way. We came upon some concrete structures. I recognized the gatekeeper boys I'd seen that first day I came up Vidigal. They stood guard with their guns raised not a hundred yards away. We walked silently around the compound below their field of vision. When a clap of thunder and lightning surrounded us, we made a run for it, blanketed by the sheets of rain.

I checked my GPS again when we reached the side of a shed. Bernardo's dot was over mine—he should be right here. And he was.

He popped his head around the wall. Water slid down his face. "Thank God you made it. I was getting worried. That hut just up the hill is where they'll be meeting." He pointed about a hundred yards away. "I gagged and cuffed the porter to a tree in the forest after he pointed it out."

Margarida reached for Zezé, visibly relieved to see him, and began to cry on his shoulder, pleading for him to take her away. She was frightened out of her wits. Her phone dinged with a text from Feijão. It told her not to come.

"Something is going to go down, but it's not the deal Malandrão is expecting," I said.

"I want to make sure Feijão stays alive. Keep an eye out for the guards," said Bernardo.

"I saw them out front on our way up, I don't think they'd come around to the back. You go to the hut with Margarida and I'll stay here with Zezé and give you cover just in case. When you're safe, we'll come."

Zezé translated our plan to Margarida and she wiped her eyes and gave me a piercing look. I felt sorry for her.

Bernardo nodded to her and stood. He dodged through the driving rain, pulling Margarida along to the cabana, keeping a lookout for any of the guards. When they reached the shack, he pushed her toward the door while he stayed behind.

"Let's go!" I said to Zezé, and we darted up the hill to Bernardo. I inched up to the window and listened. Bernardo came over too and translated.

"He is pissed, asking where Margarida has been and why the porter is not with her. She said he was hanging with the guards outside."

Good one.

We both heard a loud stinging slap and I dared to look in the window in case she needed intervention.

Malandrão was a muscular thug. A mini version of the Hulk, minus the green. His face was pockmarked and he had a nasty scar on his cheek. He held Margarida by the hair and barked questions at her, making his thick silver chain beat against his broad and veiny chest repeatedly. Something was definitely not going according to plan. I saw that Malandrão's machine gun was leaning against a table. I signaled to Bernardo to circle around closer to the front door. When he was in place, I raised my gun to the window and took aim as Malandrão was about to beat Margarida again.

"*Não!*" screamed Margarida.

The door swung open just at that moment, and a heavyset man wearing a baseball cap walked in. Margarida ran to him. It had to be Feijão.

Malandrão said something in Portuguese, to the effect of "Where are the guns?" Feijão pushed the girl away from him, revealing his weapon. Margarida screamed again and he fired.

Bits of concrete chips flew off the wall against us. I turned, and lightning flashed above the compound. The gatekeeper boys were running toward us through the curtain of rain, but their guns weren't raised—they were fleeing.

"Down!" I yelled at Zezé, tackling him to the ground.

Flashes of machine gun fire came from the surrounding hillsides behind the boys. They didn't stand a chance. We crawled around to the front of the building, but the bullets seemed to come from all directions.

"It's the Red Commandos," grunted Bernardo as we joined him. "They are attacking the Dragon Militia. We are being ambushed!"

Feijão ran outside with Margarida just then and fired several rounds into the air to let his men know he was there. Margarida screamed when she saw us huddling for cover against the wall and he swung around, firing his automatic. Zezé jumped up defensively. I shot at Feijão's leg, knowing if he died Adriana would be lost. Bull's-eye—Feijão's face contorted and he screamed. Bernardo pulled him back off his feet from behind and cracked his arm with his hammering knee; the gun fell to the floor.

Malandrão lay dead just inside, a trail of blood oozing from the bullet hole in his forehead. Bernardo shouted at Feijão in Portuguese as he cuffed him. I heard Adriana's name. I reached for Zezé and realized with a gush of horror that he'd been hit and had gone limp.

Margarida dropped to her knees. "Zezé, Zezé!" she wailed over him, trying to shake him awake.

I checked for a heartbeat and felt a faint one. This was entirely my fault. Given the gunfire outside and how far we were from help, I knew he would not make it.

Bernardo was angrily questioning Feijão. "He does not know where she is, but I don't believe him." His voice was pitched with anguish.

I looked at Margarida, shaking her head over Zezé, and remembered what she had said on the beach and what Adriana had confirmed.

"Eugenia! We know your mother," I said to Feijão. That got his attention real fast. "Tell him we know she's an accomplice to his crimes. If he tells us where they are keeping Adriana and her team, we'll go easy on Mama."

Bernardo looked surprised and rattled off a few harsh phrases, but he didn't really need to translate. It worked like a charm. Feijão's demeanor changed completely as worry for his mother prompted his confession.

The Red Commandos were attacking the competition. Feijão had been given orders to kill Malandrão and take over this *boca*.

We could hear the distant sounds of the surprise attack as it moved down the hill between rolls of thunder.

"But *who's* behind it?" I asked. I cradled Zezé's head in my arms.

"He says he got his orders from Chefe, via his mother. Nobody knows his true identity."

I had a firm suspicion Chefe might be Andrade, but that didn't help us at the moment. We were burning daylight and had hit a dead end. Bernardo's hands shook as he pushed Feijão forward and holstered his gun.

THE WARRIOR SAINT

The rain outside was dissipating. It pattered steadily against the mud. Zezé's eyes suddenly fluttered open and I squeezed his hand.

"You OK, T. J.?" His voice was scratchy, his eyes full of worry. *"Que frio,"* he whispered as he shook.

I put my arm around him. "Hang in there, you're going to be OK, buddy." But those vivid irises went dull just as my words came out.

"Não, Zezinho!" screamed Margarida. She slapped at me repeatedly and spat in my face. I let her, realizing I was dropping tears too. I caressed Zezé's forehead and closed his eyes before standing. I thought of the Greens that hadn't made it back from Mexico, the boys that had been forced to die. Regret, impotence and rage roared in my chest like a freight train jumping its tracks. I'd failed him like I'd failed them.

"Tell Margarida to take us back without going through the *boca*." The girl was in hysterics over Zezé; Bernardo shook her to attention. She nodded numbly and her sobbing faltered. Her nerves had reached their limit. We pried her away from him and I lifted Zezé's limp body gently over my shoulder. Bernardo pushed Feijão forward. He cursed with each painful step.

"We have to get back to where we parked and get to Brasão's estate in time to arrest him and Danilo. He'll be learning about the attack soon enough. We'll have to figure out our next move from there."

We scuttled through the drizzle to another structure for cover, the sounds of the Red Commandos destroying the *boca* in the background. When it seemed safe, we trudged the long way down the mushy paths to my car. Feijão grumbled in agony all the way. The red earth clung heavily to my shoes, weighing them down. I was kicking the mud off against the curb when Lygia called to say Antonio's jet would land in a half hour. She'd called Valeria and Cadu over for help.

"I told you not to call anybody."

"I can't sit here and not do anything! I trust them both completely."

I hung up.

At the Hearts of Wisdom center, I unlocked the Jeep. I laid Zezé in the back seat, and Bernardo helped Feijão and Margarida in. I could see he was struggling to keep it together. He got on his motorcycle and led the way to Brasão's estate. I couldn't stop thinking about Zezé. I fought to control my anger and stay focused. Margarida cried softly in the back, and Feijão growled with every bump. The back of my head throbbed with a golf-sized lump. We almost had Antonio. But without Adriana and with MP headquarters in shambles, we had no access to the evidence we had gathered. Brasão would be arrested only as long as the Military Police could detain him.

Adriana and the boy had to be found. I shifted into gear and sped down the hill. I realized I was trembling, overwhelmed with Zezé's loss. Then there was my mother, Sean, my career—let alone my promise to Lygia.

I had a lot still left to lose.

CHAPTER TWENTY-SIX

I pulled into the Vila Cachoeira driveway behind Bernardo to a throng of reporters clamoring for information at the gate. He and I flashed our badges at the MP now guarding the entrance and we were waved inside. I noticed the bullet holes in the glass window of the guardhouse, and the blood-splattered wall behind it. We drove down the long drive and pulled up to the house. Brasão had not yet arrived.

Inside, Bernardo introduced me to Adriana's colleague, Captain Igor Luis Gonçalvo, head of the MP's BOPE division, who also happened to be a cousin of his. Ain't that a peach. He explained how the operation had to be canceled without Adriana. The only other team members that had a fix on Margarida had been killed in the attack.

"Thank you for helping us. We need you to keep the Civil Police out of here and to help with the arrest of Mr. Brasão and Mr. Lemos when they walk in this door. Bernardo will fill you in on the details." We exchanged numbers. I asked him to keep Feijão under guard and to look into his phone for clues. Margarida and Zezé's lifeless body were also left in his care. "Where is Mrs. Castello-Branco?"

He pointed to a door down the hall.

"Let me know when Brasão arrives. How come there are so many reporters?"

"They find a way to listen in to our police radio channels. Bernardo had asked that we not reveal anything about the situation to the press, so they have no details. I will do whatever I can to help find Adriana—and the boy too, of course."

Bernardo was already speaking to other colleagues of Adriana's, in search of any clues.

I stepped over the knocked-down sculptures and passed bullet-torn paintings on my way to the kitchen. The intruders had shattered every piece of glass in the place. There were pools of fresh blood on the travertine floor where people had fallen. It must have been a truly gruesome attack.

Lygia sat in the breakfast room with her head in her hands. A small TV was turned on to the local news channel. Valeria held her, tarot cards splayed on the table. Cadu sat on Lygia's other side and held her hand. They looked up when I entered, and Lygia came running to me.

"Have you found him?"

Cadu and I nodded at each other as I sat her down and filled her in. Her eyes welled with each compounding revelation. I explained the association between Andrade and the senator, Feijão and the Red Commandos.

"Any luck with the tracking chip?"

"No. There is no signal." Her lips trembled. We all knew that meant it had likely been removed. "Oh my God, what have I done? Please! You have to help me find my son." She clasped her hands together in front of me.

"Of course he will!" assured Valeria, holding Lygia tightly.

"Oh God, this is my fault!"

I knew how she felt.

"We need to figure out where Andrade would hide the boy and Adriana. But Antonio will be here any minute, and we will be ready for him and Danilo."

Valeria gestured to the cards. "That is what we were trying to do just now, look for a clue. Paulo André is safe. He may be frightened, but he is OK. I see the Sun card over the Lovers, a symbol of reunion. That is a good sign."

Valeria gave Lygia's hand a squeeze.

"Is there nothing indicating where he is?" Lygia asked.

"I can't see that, Ly, I'm sorry. It's just not coming through." A silent tear fell from her eye. "I'm worried about this one. The cards are not showing me the outcome clearly, for some reason. I think I'm too personally involved to be objective," she said.

Lygia had begun to cry again, twisting her hands together in her lap. She squeezed her fists tightly until her knuckles became white. Valeria reached over to calm her and gave her a pill.

Lygia got up for some water.

"I've always been there for her. We've always been there for each other, really. Like sisters, ever since college," Valeria said. "She kept her secret even from me."

"Come on now, you're being too hard on yourself. This is my fault," I confessed. "I dragged her into this. I asked her to leave Paulo André at the house to come help us in Vidigal."

Valeria reached out and touched my fidgeting hands. "You are the reason she is alive now."

Lygia came back looking pale and shaky. Cadu leaned forward. "I will ask one of my masters for help." He'd been quiet up until now; I'd just about forgotten he was with us. He sat up straight suddenly and began to chant. Then he rose to his feet and waved his arms up and down with his fingers snapping the air. He convulsed like a fish out of water, contorting while he deeply inhaled and exhaled. His eyes rolled upward, the way they had briefly the other day when he spoke to me. Then Cadu sat back down in his chair, seemingly in a trance.

Valeria's calming hand pressed my shoulder. I'd not realized I'd jumped to my feet, startled at the sight of Cadu's ritual. I suppose I'd overreacted to something that was a non-event for them. Cadu took Lygia's hand. His pupils were completely dilated. She looked up at him hopefully.

"I am thirsty," he said in a strange voice.

Valeria knew the routine and she ran to the bar in the next room and returned with a glass of *cachaça* for the spirit; she had all the hocus-pocus paraphernalia at the ready. Cadu spoke raspily, sounding much like an old man, as Valeria translated for me.

"The boy is frightened. He is tied down, in a large space. The wall is lined with guns, but the boy—there is blood."

"No!" moaned Lygia.

"But wait, he will be surrounded by colorful fabrics. Thousands of beads and feathers, red and yellow like a fantasy, but it's dark and closed."

Cadu shook his head from side to side and slung his arms like a cowboy lassoing his mare—a snap of his fingers at the end of the motion. None of it made sense—bunch of crazies.

His head fell down and his eyes looked up eerily at me. My skin electrified from head to toe. Can I tell y'all, that shit just freaked me out.

"It is the same man," the voice said in English now, "the one who killed the businessman. He's after you too. He will go to the boy soon."

"Andrade?" I asked.

Cadu leaned forward, his wide, dilated eyes fixed intensely on mine. "Everything will reveal itself as it should."

Just as suddenly as it had come, his entity or master or whatever you want to call it was gone. His eyes blinked and looked normal again; Cadu was back with us.

"What does that mean?" asked Lygia.

"What connection could there be between Angelo de Andrade, guns, and fabrics and feathers?" I noted that I was actually considering Cadu's visions in the wake of any alternative. Valeria drummed her manicured fingernails purposefully on the table as she thought. Lygia stood up and paced anxiously.

"Valeria, you said that Andrade's men were questioning Cadu regarding the murder of a foreign businessman selling arms, right?" I asked.

"That's right." Cadu nodded as well.

"If Andrade is dealing weapons, he has to keep them stored somewhere. I'm betting that place is secret enough to hide Adriana and the boy too."

We all looked at the TV screen. Breaking news showed shots of people in various cities across Brazil lighting candles at shrines for Lygia and her son. The press was reporting the attack with rumors that Lygia and her son were missing. Word of her absence was spreading fast over traditional and social media. She looked at her face on the TV. "This is ridiculous. I've only been missing for a few hours!"

If Antonio was hearing any of this, he would be arriving as quickly as he could. We watched GlobeNet News showing the reporters outside, with occasional close-ups of the blood-stained guardhouse. Live video showed a bird's-eye view of the ransacked estate. It felt strange to hear the helicopters outside and watch the house on TV at the same time. I was amazed to see that candles had been lit and hundreds of flowers already left outside the gates. Lygia's and her son's pictures appeared side by side, superimposed over the view of the house.

My face appeared on the screen just then, the picture from the party. Lygia gasped. "The police are claiming you are behind this!"

Andrade must have posted an APB on me. Damn if that ain't a twig in my spokes. The helicopters grew louder, and I realized Antonio's must be arriving from the airport.

"Y'all stay put right here until I tell you it's safe."

I ran down the hall to find Bernardo and Igor in Brasão's library. The door had been busted off its hinges. So much for fingerprint security. His precious leather-bound books lay scattered on the floor; any decorative objects were likewise smashed to the ground. A large bloodied hatchet stuck insultingly in the middle of the wood-carved coat of arms on the front of his desk, driving home the terror that must have engulfed the house. A guard standing next to the desk nodded at me and handed me a crumpled note.

"This was held to the desk by the ax," explained Bernardo. He translated.

"If you wish to see your son again, you will cease all of your business in the favelas, *what is left of it after today. You will order your top rank to be integrated into the Red Commandos with your blessing within twenty-four hours. Once they are indoctrinated we will contact you to arrange the release of your son."*

I stood by the window and watched Brasão's helicopter land on the pad. I imagined Antonio would think the MP cars were here to investigate the attack rather than to arrest him—he had no reason to suspect otherwise. I watched as he got out of the helicopter and jumped in one of the golf carts to rush to the house. My pulse skipped when I saw Danilo was not with him.

There was a commotion at the front door. Antonio soon charged into the library angrily, arguing with the soldier who had cuffed his arms behind him, his back turned to me.

He then met my stare and his face turned red. Well, perhaps more like purple.

"You!" he roared, the veins of his neck corded like the roots of a mangrove. He tried to lunge but one of the MPs held him back. I motioned for the soldier to sit Antonio at his desk, then I stepped toward him. He tried to stand, but the soldier pushed him back into his seat.

"Danilo was right. I should have had you killed!" Spittle flung from his lips.

"Where is Danilo?"

"What have you done with my son?" he demanded, shaking his cuffs again. He looked at Bernardo and then around his library, assessing the damage.

"I was hoping you could tell me that."

"You duplicitous weasel," he snarled. His shirt lapels were askew, his hair, disheveled in long shards.

I approached the desk, scanning the note in my hands.

"I'll have you killed for this! You think you can just arrest me? You'll live the rest of your life looking over your shoulder, you son of a bitch!"

I slapped it down in front of him. "Do you really love Paulo André? Enough to work with us to save him?"

His steely eyes moistened as he scanned the note. His lips trembled. "*Meu filho*. Where is he?"

"With whoever's running the Red Commandos. Do you know who that might be?"

Antonio scanned the note again. His mind must've been racing to try to understand what was happening. "We know you and Danilo command the Dragon Militia," I said.

"That's ridiculous!" He yanked at his cuffs.

"We've got more than enough proof to put you both away for life. We've got Russo. We've got Feijão." I left out the part that none of the evidence would hold without finding Adriana. "The question is, can you help us save your son? He was taken by the Red Commandos."

"I have no idea. It's not as if we exchange holiday greeting cards." His forehead creased with lines of irritation. He looked down at the knocked-over portrait on his desk. "Paulo André, *meu filho* . . . " he repeated. "He has a chip in his leg!" he remembered.

"I'm sorry to say there is no signal."

Antonio swallowed hard at the implication. He was rummaging through his mind, realizing there were no options. He looked out the window, where several of his dogs lay dead. "My beautiful Danes, they slaughtered them all too," he said to himself, taking in the savagery of the attack. Antonio felt his defeat wash over him and dropped his head into his hands on the desk.

With sudden realization, he snapped, "You mentioned only Paulo André. Where is Lygia?"

Like an actress on cue, she appeared at the door; she'd been listening. She beelined straight to Antonio, leaned over the desk and swung her hand hard across his face with a stinging slap. "What have you done to us? You animal!" she screamed. This was the real deal, no acting here. She was wild.

I reached over to calm her and she flung my arm away with unexpected force and dove onto the desk, knocking a large orchid to the floor. She clawed Antonio across the face. A clean cut gouged by her diamond ring began to drip blood. All he could do with his cuffed hands was lean back. I pulled Lygia off gently.

"You've destroyed our lives! Our son's! You are disgusting!" she sobbed.

Valeria came into the library with Cadu behind her. She ran over to Lygia and held her as she wept.

Antonio was profoundly confused. "Who the fuck are you and why do the Red Commandos think I'm Dragon Militia?" he yelled, devoid of his usual etiquette.

"DEA Special Ops, at your service. I'm the man your wife hired to arrest you."

His coloration changed and his face contorted in a spooky way as he realized that treachery had come from within.

"Trouble is, the Red Commandos got wind through Angelo de Andrade and demanded retaliation, thinking you'd hired the MPs to do them in."

He fixed his gaze on the sobbing starlet. "You stupid cow! Do you realize what you've done?" He glowered at me. "Andrade has my boy? That double-crossing indigent! He'll pay for this!"

I watched as he struggled again with his handcuffs. "Fuck!" The rage in his steel-grey eyes was bottomless. He jumped to his feet and I stepped back, stumbling on the overturned plant. The MP pushed Antonio back down again.

I looked at the mangled orchid on the floor and remembered the afternoon in Santa Teresa. Lygia had told Valeria that Vera de Andrade bought her orchids at the Roçinha flower market. That's why Andrade's name had sounded vaguely familiar when I'd first heard it from Saldanha. I spun round to Bernardo.

"It's Vera de Andrade. She's the connection. She collects the money from Feijão's mother and arranges the deliveries of weapons at the flower market. She also arranges arms sales with Danilo on the side. Andrade may not even know she's dealing to the Dragon Militia. She might know where the weapons are kept and where the boy and Adriana are."

"How can you be sure?" Bernardo asked.

"I'm not, but Adriana told me when I was on the island that the bug I planted in here had picked up that she and Danilo would be meeting after the island. She has to be the missing link!"

"That bitch!" spat Valeria.

"How did you bug my library?" Antonio asked.

"Where is Danilo?" I faced Brasão.

"With all due respect, go fuck yourself. I want my lawyer here, now."

Bernardo barked some orders at the MPs. "We have to go to Andrade's house, now."

"Ladies, you and Cadu stay here under the protection of the Military Police."

"Please find my son!" Lygia pleaded.

Broken glass crunched underfoot as we hustled down the hall to the front door.

"You better be cautious. My colleagues are on the lookout for you," Bernardo warned, reminding me of Andrade's APB.

"I don't really have a choice. I'll follow you—let's go."

Night had fallen upon the city. We drove across São Conrado and through the tunnel to the lagoon. The afternoon's rainstorm had introduced a cool front. I drove up the steep cobblestone streets to Andrade's home in an exclusive neighborhood. A tall white stucco wall topped by bougainvillea-entwined barbed wire secured the compound within. There was no car on the driveway inside the gate. Andrade wasn't home, but some lights were on.

We parked a little ways down the street and walked up to ring the buzzer. Up here in the hills, the symphony of insects performed with exuberance. The streetlight sputtered above us as we waited, casting flickering shadows upon the cobbles.

"Sim?" a woman's voice answered. Mrs. Andrade, I presumed.

In a whisper, I imitated Danilo's murmured endearment I'd heard during their moment of intimacy at the party. *"Aí Gostosinha."*

"Dani? É você?"

"Mhm," I replied. The gate clicked and Bernardo looked at me with a tilt of his head. I think he was impressed. We walked in.

Ms. Andrade opened the door smiling and suddenly halted, realizing I was not Danilo. I'll bet ya my disheveled and filthy appearance startled her. She was wearing a light summer cardigan, and she stuffed her hands into its pockets. I could see her trying to place me, while checking for Danilo behind my shoulder. "Where is he? You're that American from the party!"

"Mrs. Andrade, I'm sorry to call unannounced. My name is T. J. Leukemeyer." I flashed my gun, grabbed her wrist and pushed my way in through the darkened foyer. "You see, it's a matter of life and death that I find your husband. Do you know where he is?" Bernardo came in behind me.

Mrs. Andrade looked at both of us and hesitated. "I don't care where he is. I know nothing."

"I think you must know quite a bit, actually. Where is Angelo?"

We moved through the house to the back as I questioned her. A wrap-around terrace looked out over the city.

"Please, what do you want?" asked Mrs. Andrade, trying to wriggle from my grip. Danilo's taste in women must be quite diverse. She was the opposite of Sylvia. Her Roman nose added determination to her fierce, no-nonsense expression. She did not seem threatened by me in the least. I let go of her and she moved aside. She looked at Bernardo and recognized him.

"You work for Angelo, don't you?"

"We need to find your husband in order to save a boy's life. Antonio Brasão's boy, specifically."

She lifted her wavy hair from her eyes and looked directly at me. "Do what you want. I'm leaving Angelo, leaving here."

I noticed her bags by the door. She was in for a surprise. I flashed my Military Police badge.

"How soon will Danilo be here?" I asked.

"No!" She pulled a tiny pistol out of her pocket, but my trained reflexes were much quicker. I grabbed her arm and forced her to toss the gun out over the balcony. Bernardo cuffed her and Vera shot me the slit-eyed look of a serpent.

"Does Andrade approve of your fondness for Danilo?" I asked.

"I don't care what he thinks."

"So he doesn't know about your arrangements with Danilo and Feijão?"

Concern creased her brow.

"We have Feijão in custody, so the more you confess now, the better it will be for you." Bernardo began grilling her about where the arms warehouse was while I looked out for Danilo's arrival—handcuffs and gun at the ready. Vera was a practical lady; she evaluated her position and gave up the address. Bernardo made a quick call.

"I have to go find her, T. J., I can't lose a minute. Can you handle this on your own until Igor's men arrive?"

"Piece of cake. Go."

Bernardo ran out the door. Seconds later, his motorcycle revved loudly down the street. Vera sat on the floor stoically with her hands cuffed in her lap. I leaned into the kitchen, grabbed a dishtowel.

"When did Angelo leave?"

"A few minutes ago. He was crazy. I hope I never see him again. I hope he dies!"

"Well, darlin', I don't think you'll be seeing him anytime soon. I'm gonna have to put this on you now for a little while. Won't hurt a bit." She fought as I tied the towel over her mouth. "Can't be lettin' you warn our friend when he gets here."

The intercom rang soon after. I pushed Vera to the center of the foyer. The bell rang again and I pressed the buzzer to the gate and left the door ajar. I stepped behind it, gun drawn, and waited for Danilo.

"Vera?" He stepped in and stared at her gagged appearance—just the time I needed to cuff him from behind, fast as small-town gossip. Swift cuffing techniques were a basic part of training. He spun around and I raised my gun to his face.

"You! I knew it!" He turned to Vera. "Are you OK?" There seemed to be true concern. She nodded and her eyes dropped downward. With my gun, I motioned for them both to sit on the floor.

"Relax, Danilo, Antonio and you are finished. Mrs. Andrade, you as well, I reckon."

"Fuck you!" he said, swinging his foot up in an attempt to kick the gun out of my hand. I fired and he fell over with an agonized scream, rocking over the bleeding hole in his shoe. I couldn't help but wonder what plans of theirs I had destroyed.

We sat with his guttural moans until the MPs arrived. A wave of exhaustion washed over me when they came through the door. It was after eight and it had been a long, stressful day. They told me that Bernardo had called to say he and a few soldiers had converged on Andrade's warehouse.

Wasn't long before he called with an update. "We have her! She has been beaten and drugged, but she is alive." His voice trembled with emotion. "T. J., Andrade knows the MPs are on to him. When his men were refused access to the crime scene at the estate, he must have figured it out. Plus, news of Senator Santos' arrest is breaking on every channel. He took the boy as collateral and left before we got here."

My hopes sank. I was guessing that two hostages had been more than he could handle on the run.

"He only left a couple guards watching Adriana and we took them down. You gotta see this place, it's better equipped than our military."

"Where do you think Andrade went?"

"We don't know. Sorry, T. J. We tried to track his phone's GPS, but he's smarter than that. It's not live. I'll call you if we learn anything more. I'm heading to the hospital with Adriana."

It would have to be somewhere safe where he could hide to figure out his next step.

I ended the call and walked into Andrade's office. With Adriana saved and Feijão arrested, we had all the proof required for a sound conviction. But I knew I couldn't live with myself if I didn't help find Paulo André. Andrade was now a desperate man on the run. I shuffled through his bills, Carnival brochures, and miscellaneous correspondence. Nothing. I checked the drawer and found a copy of Sylvia's magazine, with the pages folded open to the photograph of Andrade, César and me at Lygia's party. My name was circled in red marker—*O Americano* scrawled beneath it and underlined. There were three red dots on my face, from his marker's stabs.

I recalled meeting him at the party. Something he'd said. I picked up the Carnival brochure again with its pictures of revelers. The costumes were made of colorful flowing fabrics, feathers and beads. My arm hairs stood erect. Wasn't that what Cadu had described?

I flipped the brochure over. Samba City. He'd said his nephew managed it—a perfect place to hide. But even if I knew where he was going, how could we keep him there? I had an idea and called Bernardo.

"I think Andrade is going to hide with the boy at Samba City until he figures out his next move. I say we give it to him."

"How do you mean?"

"Brasão's jet. The kid's Andrade's ticket, so he'll have to call Brasão to work something out, right? I suspect he'll be calling real soon. Antonio can provide a means of escape in return for the boy. Andrade doesn't know we've arrested him—he still thinks the MPs and Brasão are in bed together."

"Of course. He will have to call at some point to ransom the boy."

"Have Brasão offer cash and his jet with safe passage anywhere Andrade likes. But stall for time—to make the jet ready. And have Igor send lots of backup to Samba City. We're going to need it."

"We will be ready."

I left Danilo and Vera with the MPs, ran to my Jeep, and roared down the hill toward downtown. I knew Antonio's love for Paulo André was stronger than his self-preservation. He had no choice but to play along.

CHAPTER TWENTY-SEVEN

The late evening traffic slowed me down, and I watched folks taking their after-dinner walks under the tall streetlights of Copacabana. I wondered how I'd ended up here, stuck bumper-to-bumper in an absurd moment of crisis in this foreign land. I passed a large group of people laying flowers around a picture of Lygia on an easel in the middle of the sidewalk. Candles poked through the sea of offerings. Seriously. It would be the headline in all the Brazilian papers tomorrow morning: *Where Is Lygia?*

I could feel the second hand ticking. There was no knowing if Andrade would still be at Samba City. I called Bernardo, but there was no news.

"How is Adriana?"

"We just got to the hospital. She's better, gradually waking up. She is not making sense yet, but my lady is a fighter."

"Yes, she is."

"Thank you for helping to save her." Bernardo's deep voice was choked when he hung up.

Every passing moment made me more agitated. Andrade would be a caged animal—Arlington always taught us that despair was a dangerous, unsustainable state. My heart sank with thoughts of Zezé's death. I realized my mother's might be imminent at this very moment too, while I sat in traffic half a world away, worrying about strangers. I looked down at my hands. My thumb had been nervously spinning my ring around my finger again. It helped knowing Sean was in Houston with her and my family—our family. I knew the effort he was making was just for my peace of mind, and it dawned on me that I craved the dependability of our friendship, our love. Maybe Bernardo and Adriana had just shown me that. We deserved a second chance. Hell, Sean was one of the reasons I'd been able to nail Brasão. I moved my commitment ring back to its rightful finger on my left hand and clenched it tightly as the traffic briefly lurched forward.

With this assignment behind me, what would my career be like back in the States? I checked my bruised and battered face in the mirror and stared into my eyes, measuring myself up. My patience was spent. I leaned on the horn and swerved onto the sidewalk with a mammoth bounce and drove on it for the remaining block. The Jeep rocked wildly and folks jumped out of the way, cursing at me. I knew I had to be careful because of the APB, but sitting in traffic when a boy's life was at stake was ridiculous.

I scanned the vicinity of the intersection. The last thing I needed was to be stopped by Andrade's men. I'd just turned left toward the downtown tunnel when I noticed lights flashing red and blue in my rearview mirror. Shit! I floored the Jeep through the tunnel, but the police car was gaining on me. On the other side of the mountain, two more police cars slid to a halt across the avenue, blocking the road. These guys were loyal to Andrade to the end.

I veered hard to the left and jumped the raised median, crashing through its fence. Oncoming traffic swerved and screeched to avoid me. Just outside of the tunnel, I turned aggressively to the left at a corner marked by tall high-rises. In my rearview mirror I could see the police cars bouncing over the median too. I came to a fork and stayed left again, hoping to give them the slip. The tree-lined residential street was dark and cars were parked on either side, narrowing the two-lane road into one. I was about to pull over and check my GPS when one of the police cars came around a corner, sirens and lights blaring. We raced down the long slender street with nowhere to go but forward—until a white wall filled my headlights' beams.

I slammed on the brakes and screeched to a halt. The street had come to an end and there was nowhere to turn.

The police car was only a block behind me. I had no choice but to run. I made sure my gun and holster were secure and leapt out of the car. The wall appeared to be about fourteen feet tall. From the roof of the Jeep, I jumped onto a house's wrought iron fence, then hoisted myself onto the ledge of a second-floor window as the police car skidded to a halt. An officer got out with his gun raised.

"*Mãos pra cima!*" he yelled, taking aim.

More squad cars were coming down the constricted street. In the dim light, I could see the silhouette of jagged broken glass lining the wall's top. Crap. I yanked off my shirt and wrapped it around my left hand, took aim and leapt from the window ledge. My estimate was right on, but despite the shirt, the glass tore right through into my palm.

"*Pare!*" the officer yelled again, firing a warning shot. It hit the wall just shy of my swinging feet.

Punch it, Leukemeyer!

I held on, feeling the glass cut deeper into the flesh of my left hand while I hoisted myself up over the top of the wall with the right. Another shot just missed my leg, slapping bits of shrapnel against me. I hurled myself over, arching through the air, and felt warm blood from my palm splatter across my face as I fell. All I can tell ya is it was a long way down in the darkness. I landed hard on my side and it knocked the wind out of me. I may have actually passed out for a second, I couldn't say for sure.

The commotion on the other side of the wall brought me out of my reverie and I assessed the damage. I pulled my phone out of my pocket and turned it on for some light. My hand was cut pretty badly, so I kept the shirt wrapped tightly around it. The side I'd landed on ached and would surely bruise nicely. There was fresh bump rising, this one on my forehead. All in all, though, I guessed I was mostly unscathed.

I figured it would take the police a minute or two to get over the wall, so I held my phone out to illuminate my surroundings, jumping back at the sight of a stone cross directly in front of my face. I could have fallen on that and killed myself. As Mama would say, thank you, sweet li'l baby Jesus. The arc of light didn't need to reveal much more before I understood I was in a cemetery—how could this be a good omen?

I got up, testing my limbs, and walked quickly, using my phone to light the way. I rounded several corners in the labyrinth of tombs in order to elude my pursuers, their lights shining down on the cemetery as they reached the top of the wall. It seemed like they were passing a rope up over it with which to climb down. I picked up my step. It was dawning on me that this place was quite large. I ran uphill, thinking I might have an advantage viewing the landscape from higher ground. Walking up the gentle slope, I spotted another wall at the end of the path. The clouds parted just then and the moonlight shined through. Above the wall was a tall mountain. I turned around to face the opposite direction and gasped at the vast, endless cemetery sprawled out in front of me. *Christ the Redeemer* glowed through the wispy clouds straight ahead atop the Corcovado.

Give me a hand here, buddy. Time was ticking and I needed to get to Paulo André before Andrade got away with him. I surveyed the cemetery's perimeter wall and followed its circumference until I spotted the front gate. It had to be at least a quarter mile away. I could feel time slipping away. Now that I had a basic sense of direction, I hurried back into the alleys of tombs and graves. Sculpted angels seemed to smile eerily down upon me as the moonlight illuminated them. The skies closed again and the cemetery darkened. I checked my phone: the battery was low, so I put it into sleep mode. The only light now came from the city's own orange luminosity reflecting back down off the low cloud cover.

I could barely hear the policemen. They had definitely gone in another direction. I sprinted past the endless graves for several minutes, until I reached the front gates. There was a guard watching his TV set in the guardhouse. The gate was locked. I looked up and the top of the wall was covered in protective shards. I can assure you, I wasn't about to try that again.

I squeezed the shirt around my palm more tightly as I thought. 'Open' is *abrir* and 'door' is *porta*. I drew my weapon and marched right up to the guard, bloody and shirtless, pointed the gun at him and yelled, "*Abrir a porta!*"

Screw verb conjugation, he got the picture.

The poor guy buzzed the gate open without hesitation, and I ran out before he had a chance to react. I scurried along the avenue and turned onto a side street, and didn't stop running until the end of the block. I tried to hail a cab, but the two that did slow down took one look at me and kept going. A third taxi was coming up, so I went to the corner and waited for the light to turn red. When the cab stopped, I jumped in.

"Samba City, *rapido por favor.*"

The driver looked in the mirror wide-eyed and began to yell something in Portuguese. I held up a hundred dollar bill alongside my gun. He put the car in gear and drove off fast without another word. We turned onto an avenue that followed the bay toward downtown and soon passed the airport and the restaurant Lygia and I'd been to. My phone vibrated. It was Bernardo.

"He called Brasão, just like you thought he would. Brasão did as he was told and pretended to make the arrangements. Andrade said he will meet Brasão with the boy at the airport in forty-five minutes. I estimate that buys you about a half hour."

"I'm almost there. Are Igor's men on their way?"

"Yes, but they are not in the area and there are traffic delays. They're coming as quickly as they can." Shit. I hung up.

The taxi eased right onto the exit ramp. A bunch of aged and dilapidated warehouses lined the bayside that would have become part of the Porto Maravilha project. What would happen to any of that now?

We made a left under what remained of the old overpass and pulled up near a fenced-in compound with a series of large warehouse-like structures. A sign over the entrance read *Samba City*.

"Para aqui," I said.

The car stopped, I paid the driver and got out. I cautiously stood on the opposite side of the street and observed the guarded gate. There were several police cars staked out by the main entrance, but not an MP in sight. That wasn't gonna work. I supposed Andrade wasn't taking any chances. I had to find a way in without being noticed.

Loud music was coming from the buildings, with lots of whistle blowing, tambourines and percussion. Practice for Carnival was in session. I watched a couple leave and walk hand in hand toward the gate. They were wearing elaborate costumes and holding their decorative headdresses in their hands. The man laughed as the girl spun around three times, waving her multilayered skirts into the air. There was my ticket. I'd need a costume to get inside.

The gate rolled open to let them out. I followed them for a block or so. The girl was singing a song and they both walked with a little dance in their step, her heels clicking the pavement. I felt like a real creep, but I had no choice. I had to get in before Andrade left for the airport. I reached them just as they got to the corner. Gravel caught under my feet and they spun around, her skirts once again taking flight. I raised my finger to my lips. The girl was about to scream, but I showed her my Military Police badge. They both looked at me curiously.

"Give me your costume," I said firmly, pointing to the man.

I suppose I must have looked a bit insane with my disheveled hair, bloody face and battered bare chest. He shook his head and indicated that he didn't understand.

"*Roupa,*" I said, recalling the word for clothes. I pointed at his costume, realizing it would be a bit small for me.

"*Ai!*" exclaimed the young lady, seeing my wound. She looked at me quizzically. By now I'd learned that in a pinch, Spanish will do. I tried to explain to them that I needed to get inside and the only way was with a costume. They seemed to understand me. Then I said Lygia de Castello-Branco's son's life was at stake.

The girl's hands covered her mouth. "*Meu Deus!*"

They understood that unmistakably. Spanish seemed to work just fine, and Lygia's name was a passport of power with the people. The man stripped down to his shorts and wife-beater and handed over the props. I tried to squeeze into them, but it took quite a bit of effort.

"*Grande,*" she said, referring to the costume size. Not my kind of *grande*.

I stripped my jeans off and jammed my legs into the

sequined pants, hopping up and down to get them over my thighs to my waist. My shoulders barely made it through the armholes of the matching vest, and I struggled to close it. I heard the side seams tear around my lats. A wild Styrofoam-and-feather top hat finished off the costume. The effect was that of a shrink-wrapped, sequined circus ringleader. I grimaced when the woman let out a giggle. It would be the end of me if anyone back home ever saw me in this getup. I secured my gun beneath the tassels. She told her friend she would be right back and grabbed my hand, leading me back toward Samba City's gates.

"*Sou T. J.,*" I introduced myself.

"Maria Bonita," she replied.

I was amazed; she was going in with me. She led me right past the guard, who was watching TV and barely gave us any notice. The compound was mobilized with policemen positioned at the entrance to each building. They were mostly chatting and smoking cigarettes. We walked right on past them. I asked her why there were so many police here.

"Chief Andrade give free entry tonight to all police just little while ago."

The place was cavernous and the loud festive music reverberated throughout. An ocean of spinning people surrounded an enormous float of a fire-breathing dragon. Skirts and pants flared in hues of blue and green, while the dragon swung its head and red and orange ribbons flared from its nostrils. Up on the balcony surrounding the open floor, tourists and spectators danced and cheered, several policemen among them. We were in, but I had no time to figure out where Paulo André might be. I might be crazy as a bullbat, but the only thing I had to go on was Cadu's vision. He'd said the boy was surrounded by red and yellow fabrics with beads and feathers, so I asked Maria Bonita if she knew which samba school wore such an outfit.

She thought for a moment and then lit up. "Yes, those are the *Borboleta* colors!"

She led the way through the entranced crowd to the other end of the room, and we took a long corridor to the next samba school's arena. Now that I was past the guards, I pulled off the hat and unbuttoned the vest so I could breathe. I caught Maria Bonita's roving eye and she smiled bashfully. I thanked her.

"Save Lygia's son! You must be successful! God be with you." She kissed my cheek and ran back down the hall.

I entered a sea of humanity gyrating around yet another astounding float: a giant red and yellow butterfly gently flapping its sparkle-edged wings. The costumes fit the bill—red and yellow, beads and feathers. I stepped back into the shadows and looked around.

I had to find the place where the costumes were kept. I looked down the walls and saw a door with the word *Fantasias* above it. Hadn't Cadu said something about fantasy? I snuck in, gun in hand. Igor and his men should be here any minute.

The room was partitioned into large staging areas on either side of a collaborative assembly line. Bolts of fabric lined one wall, cubbies of beads lined another. A series of sewing tables were stacked with costumes awaiting their final touches. There was another door at the end of the hall, where a man stood guard with a machine gun, and I'll tell ya, he was definitely not an officer. How clever of Andrade to surround the place with cops, and yet nobody knew he was here.

The lights were dim and the walls shook from the pounding samba music outside. I shuffled along the edge of the hall, just past the watchful guardsman's field of vision. The door swung open and I jumped back into an alcove full of feathered strips. A tall black man stepped forward. This guy was big. I figured he must be a leader of the Red Commandos. He said something to the guard and Andrade followed him out into the hall. The two of them walked briskly out the door into the arena.

I cautiously inched closer. When I was in range, I took aim and fired at the guard. The music was so loud, the gunshot was barely audible. The man slouched forward and his weapon fell to the floor. I holstered my gun, slung his rifle up to my shoulder, and kicked open the door.

Surprisingly, the thug inside was alone. He spun around to face me but never had a chance before I took him down too. I quickly scouted the room. Stacked balls of twine, heaps of costumes, and bolts of fabrics and tassels filled the cubbies against the wall. I saw movement in one of them. There, amongst papier-mâché angel wings framed by old tennis racquets, were Paulo André's tied hands. His face emerged from the costumes, his eyes wide open in terror. Relief washed over me. I carefully removed the duct tape from his mouth and untied his hands.

"T. J.! Help me!" he cried, throwing his arms around my neck and letting his tears flow. "They hurt me." He pointed to the wound on his leg where they'd dug out his tracking chip, now half-covered by a poorly administered bandage. He was disheveled and bruised—scared as a sinner in a cyclone. "Chief Andrade was so mean. He cut me . . . Is this because of Dad's business?"

"Everything's gonna be fine, my friend. You're with me now," I said.

"But those were just the guards. Patrão, their leader, is coming back soon with Chief Andrade. Dad's giving him his plane in exchange for me. I heard everything," he warbled—his maturing vocal cords slipping. "Quick, help get me down."

I put the rifle in the cubby and reached for the boy.

"Damn you!" I heard Andrade's nasal voice from behind.

I spun around to see him standing next to Patrão, whose weapon was aimed at me. I aimed mine back. My luck was that Paulo André was just where I needed him.

Andrade looked me over with disdain.

"Don't bother, you don't have a chance. There are police all around this building who are looking for you and will kill you on sight. I suggest you drop your weapon and kick it over to me, or the boy dies."

I tossed my gun on the floor and kicked it to them. Andrade slouched down to retrieve it.

"The Military Police will have the place surrounded in minutes," I said.

He only shrugged. Then he pointed my gun at me and pressed the trigger.

Nothing happened. I love these gadgets. He tried again and again with no effect. I leaned close and whispered into Paulo André's ear, "Ace it."

As Andrade threw the gun down in disgust, I reached for a ball of twine and tossed it into the air. Paulo André had grabbed one of the angel wings, and now he used it to slam the ball at the two men, who raised their arms to shield their faces. I turned to reach for Paulo André, but before I could help him down, a third man appeared at the door. A shot fired, hitting the man's arm, and he went down screaming. Andrade and Patrão jumped for cover again. I turned back to see Paulo André still in the cubby, the rifle I'd stuck there in his hands.

The boy seemed stunned. "You did good," I reassured him. I kicked a rack of costumes over both men before they could scramble back up, then pulled the boy and rifle down. Perhaps there was a bit of Antonio in him after all.

We ran out of the room into the corridor, reaching for the arena door just as a couple of Red Commandos stepped in and blocked us from the exit. They pointed their weapons at us. Swiping aside a bunch of hanging costumes, one of them cuffed my throbbing, bloody hand to a thick bar bolted to the wall, kind of like the practice bars you'd see at a dance studio. The other, bigger guy socked me twice in the face like I was a punching bag.

One landed square in my eye, another busted my lip. So much for worrying about those dark circles. Andrade adjusted his now-broken glasses and grabbed the boy's arm roughly.

"T. J.!" Paulo André cried.

Andrade slapped him hard across the face. "You shut up!" he warned.

The Red Commandos followed Patrão out the door and into the raucous arena, except for one. The big, mean-looking guy who'd slugged me stood sentinel with a machine gun held against my stomach.

Andrade looked smug. "You Americans, always interfering in matters that are not of your concern. You think you understand how things work here? You don't have a clue."

"I found you and the boy, didn't I?"

He pulled a pack of cigarettes from his shirt pocket and hopped one up through the opening into his cracked, dry lips and lit it. His exhaled smoke filtered through his mustache straight at my face. It seemed to calm him.

"You should be wishing you never set foot here. Sorry to keep our visit short, but Antonio's jet is waiting."

"And his kid's just a bit of insurance."

"That's right. I'll decide what to do with him soon enough. Good riddance, Mr. Leukemeyer."

He tugged Paulo André by the ear, exhaled another puff, and flicked the cigarette away.

"T. J.!" Paulo André squealed in terror.

The door slammed shut. I looked over at Slugger and he was lifting his automatic to take aim.

Punch it, Leukemeyer!

Grabbing tight on to the steel bar, I swung my leg up in the air and smacked the gun out of his hands. It fired a round that singed my hair. The motion tore the inseam of my tight pants—came real close to pulling my groin muscle too. I kicked hard again and nailed his face, snapping his neck back, and that was that. His foot smacked the cigarette when he fell, and flames flared where it skidded onto a pile of costumes.

I tested the strength of the steel bar again. It was solidly fastened to the wall. The blaze had caught quickly, and black smoke was already filling the air. I looked around but could not see anything that could be useful to break free with. I flipped my body up onto the bar and began to flounder on top of it, hoping my weight would pry it free. On my third pounce, the supporting arm popped off the wall and the bar inclined a few inches, sending me and several garments to the floor. I slid my cuffed hands free and ran blindly for the door as the air grew stifled with sooty smoke.

The fire had now spread to additional stacks of costumes, and the flames were reaching high up into the rafters. I slammed through the door and into the mêlée of spinning bodies, looking in every direction for Paulo André. I spotted them off to the side, weaving through the revelers. Just then, somebody screamed, *"Fogo!"*

The music decomposed into a jumble of straggling instrumental fragments and people began to scream and run at the sight of the flames. I pushed against the crowd to get to Paulo André, jumping up and down to keep him and Andrade in my sights. To my right, the towering butterfly's wings, devoured by the inferno, became moving rings of fire. One fell on top of the crowd and forced Andrade to change direction toward me.

In the pandemonium, he had been separated from his thugs. I waited until he was upon me, then lunged for Paulo André and pushed past Andrade in the opposite direction. He cursed at me but already there were panicked dancers between us.

The flames had ascended to the roof and the beams were on fire. I pushed my way through the crowd with Paulo André in front of me. The double doors ahead were clogged with escaping people squeezing through with their cumbersome outfits.

"T. J., look!" screamed Paulo André.

Up above, the ceiling was collapsing inwards. The building was coming down. The entire crowd was heading toward the two large side doors. To our right I saw the stairwell, our only chance. I looped my cuffed arms over Paulo André and lifted him to me. With four or five running steps, we lunged toward the stairs and dove beneath them. The roof collapsed all around us with a thunderous smack.

I can't tell y'all how long I was out for, but I came to hearing Paulo André's whimper.

"Are you OK?" he asked.

"I'm not sure. Are you?"

"I think so, but my arm really hurts. I think it's broken."

I tried to adjust my eyes to the darkness, but it was pitch black. I tested my limbs to be sure everything was functional.

"Was I passed out a long time?" I asked.

"I don't know. I just woke up too."

Aside from my entire body's dull throbbing, everything seemed OK. I reached into my pocket for my phone and turned it on. It flashed for a moment, telling me it was 3:50 a.m. The red line on the battery icon predicted that my phone was about to go dead. Whatever smacked us had hit us hard and knocked us out for quite a while. In the phone's light, I could see that a large slab of concrete had fallen across the stairwell, enclosing us in the small niche we were so lucky to have found. Paulo André was scratched up and a little bloodied, but overall seemed to be OK. I tried to dial 555, but just as I pressed the green button, the phone powered off.

"Everything'll be OK, Paulo André. We just have to wait now. How do you say help in Portuguese?"

"*Socorro.*"

We both began to yell for help as loud as we could. We'd take turns or call out together. I'd guess we went on like that for about an hour or so before we heard someone replying with a megaphone.

"They found us!" cried Paulo André.

We soon heard the vibrations of heavy machinery breaking away chunks of the debris that blocked us in. Within the hour, a searchlight filled our nook and the cement slabs were soon pried away. An MP pulled us out of the rubble; first Paulo André, then me. They put blankets around us. Paulo André told them who we were. The soldiers smiled broadly and yelled something out to the crowds. Everyone cheered.

"What did he say?" I asked.

"We found Lygia's boy!" He smiled.

A bunch of rescue workers and MPs gathered around and clapped us on the back. I pointed to Paulo André's arm and somebody fashioned a temporary sling. He winced as they put it on but held back his tears stoically. This kid was gonna be just fine. Bernardo came running up to us in the glow of twilight and had an MP remove my handcuffs.

"Andrade?" I asked.

"Injured in the collapse. We got him." He looked at me quizzically. "Where are your clothes?"

"Don't ask. Just do me a favor and get me a shirt and a pair of pants, please?"

He asked one of the soldiers in Portuguese, and he soon came back with an MP uniform that I got into.

Bernardo walked us to a large elevated area in the complex that had been converted into a triage center for all the wounded. "Your phone's GPS conveyed your location, but there was too much rubble in the way. Come on. Lygia is upstairs. We brought her here to see if we could find her son among the wounded. You know, right after you left last night, she called the studio and went on TV to clear your name and point the finger at Andrade. Asked the public for their help finding her son."

We climbed up a few steps, to where blanketed victims were laid out all over, illuminated by outdoor lights and the dawning sky. Lygia was standing with a nurse, looking over the wounded.

"*Mamãe!*" Paulo André called out when he saw her.

Lygia turned around and her boy came running to her.

"*Meu filho!*" She knelt and embraced him tightly, rocking back and forth, showering him with maternal kisses. The sun peeked over the horizon just then. It washed the reunited pair and the Corcovado, towering behind them, with its warm, penumbral light, just as Valeria had predicted.

EPILOGUE

I couldn't wait to get back home to Sean. He'd called to let me know that Ma's operation had been tough, but she'd pushed through it and the surgeon was confident he'd removed all the cancer. But at stage IV, we all expected that just meant a little more time.

I wasn't sure how Sean and I would move forward from here, but we both knew we wanted to try again. Zezé's death had really jarred things into perspective for me. That crazy kid had saved my life, and I deeply regretted the thankless nature of his death. Somehow, it made me value what Sean and I had more.

I had a couple obligatory debriefings before I could head on home. The triple-play arrests of Brasão, Senator Junior Belem dos Santos and Chief Andrade were front-page news, and the stream of related anti-corruption cases that exploded in the ensuing days imploded the local drug trade, exactly as Ronaldo—may he rest in peace—had hoped. With the major factions' infrastructure of money and guns disrupted, BOPE was in the process of raiding the most troublesome *favelas* and the UPP was taking them over. It would make for good cosmetics during the Olympics, but sooner than later the void would be refilled—this was Brazil, after all.

My hunch about Vera de Andrade had been right on. She'd arranged the sales of arms to the Red Commandos via Feijão's mother. She'd taken the cash and scheduled the deliveries. When Feijão began working both sides after the BOPE raid last year, she began to get chummy with Danilo and started arranging the sales for the Dragon Militia too, without Andrade's knowledge. Danilo's plan had been to kill Andrade and take over the arms business, adding an additional lucrative layer to Brasão's empire. But in the end, Feijão's loyalty had been to Andrade and the Red Commandos.

Bernardo and Adriana became the accredited heroes for the high-profile arrests, my work having been undercover and all. Wouldn't be surprised if they were rewarded with major promotions. Turned out Ronaldo and Adriana's very own intern, Fernanda, had been the mole. She was Andrade's niece, the bridesmaid I'd recognized in the magazine, and his eyes and ears to find out what the MPs were investigating. She'd taken the files that notified him of our operation. Andrade had sent Saldanha over to identify and follow me when I came into headquarters that first day. Sealed Saldanha's fate when Fernanda pointed me out to him as I left Ronaldo's office. How 'bout that?

Lygia became international news following Brasão's arrest. Soon, she'd be at the helm of her father's media empire and her husband's conglomerates, and who knew what she might do. I'd bet on it being for the greater good. And let me tell y'all something else about that pretty lady. She taught me a thing or two.

Benevolent betrayal. That's what opened my eyes to Vicente. Bradley too, actually, and my relationship with the DEA. Since the island, I'd begun to have a hunch that for whatever reason, they'd needed me out of the Mexico operation, to disappear for a while and believe I failed—for El Gordo to think the same so Vicente could truly infiltrate until the time was right to bring down a bigger operation than just El Gordo's. In the meanwhile, Bradley had tossed me this job to keep me on my toes until they were ready for me to jump back in.

In not so many words, Bradley had confirmed all that by phone this morning on his congratulatory call. Said to prep for many briefings upon my arrival in Virginia. To be perfectly honest, I wasn't so sure my time at the agency hadn't run its course. The thought of having my own private gig was tugging at me too. I mean, it would be a win-win—like Rio.

Whatever my decision would be, I was counting on jumping back in—with Sean, with work. Just need to follow my instincts—should never have doubted them in the first place. I had a good thing going. And next time I'd play by *my* rules.

CHARACTERS BY FIRST NAME

Adriana Meireles Pessoa de Castro—captain in Rio de Janeiro Military Police and T. J.'s partner
Angelo de Andrade—Rio de Janeiro civil chief of police
Antoinetta (Nanette) Tiesenhaller-Chaffrey—William Chaffrey's Brazilian wife
Antonio Carlos de Melo Brasão—oligarch and leader of Dragon Militia cartel
Bernardo Castro—Adriana's husband; Rio de Janeiro Civil Police CORE agent
Brent—Sean Gottlieb's real-estate friend from the Hamptons
Carla de Alcântara—murdered Minister of Finance Vinícius Alcântara's wife
Carlos Eduardo (Cadu)—spirit incarnator from Valeria's Vila Paraíso spiritual center
César Siqueira de Mendonça—Secretary of Infrastructure Projects for the State of Rio de Janeiro; colleague of Antonio Brasão's
Charles—Brent's husband

CHARACTERS BY FIRST NAME

Christina—Antonio Brasão's secretary
Danilo Adolfo Camargo de Lemos—Antonio Brasão's right-hand man and business colleague
Earl Cunningham—Sean Gottlieb's and William Chaffrey's former business colleague
Edson Moreira de Souza Rodrigues—T. J.'s driver in Rio, assigned by Ronaldo
Eduardo (Duda) Pinto Canela—mayor of Rio de Janeiro
El Gordo—cartel leader in Mexico
Eugenia Telles—Feijão's mother
Feijão (pronounced *Fayjau*)—literally *bean* (nickname); Wanderlei Luis Telles; drug-trafficking kingpin (*dono*)
Ferdi (Ferdinand) Gastinaro—T. J. and Sean's friend in New York City; Milena's husband
Fernanda—Ronaldo's intern
Giancarlo Russo—money launderer
Gilson—Antonio Brasão's employee on island
Igor Luis Gonçalvo—captain in Rio de Janeiro Military Police heading the BOPE; colleague of Adriana's
Jucelino Neves Castello-Branco—Lygia's father; founder of GlobeNet
Leandro Ramalho Saldanha—Rio de Janeiro civil policeman working for Chief Angelo de Andrade
Lygia de Castello-Branco—Antonio Brasão's wife, Paulo André's mother, and TV superstar
Malandrão—literally *trickster* (nickname); Dragon Militia sector general in Vidigal shanty
Marcelo—Lygia's makeup artist
Marcos—T. J.'s local friend from the beach; physical trainer
Margarida—a prostitute of Malandrão's from Vidigal; Zezé's cousin; Feijão's girl
Maria Bonita—dancer at Samba City
Maria Flores—director of Lygia's charity in Vidigal
Maria Jovelina (Jovi) Aparecida da Silva—T. J.'s housekeeper, assigned by Ronaldo

CHARACTERS BY FIRST NAME

Miguel Francisco Lopes Bonfim (Nem)—former Dragon Militia drug-trafficking kingpin (*dono*)
Milena Van Gilden—T. J.'s longtime friend in New York City
Patrão—Red Commando thug
Paulo André de Castello-Branco Brasão—son of Antonio Brasão and Lygia de Castello-Branco
Raimunda—cousin of Margarida's in Vidigal shanty
Roberto Barroso Simões-Filho—Antonio Brasão's lawyer
Ronaldo Francisco Xavier Pereira—major in the Rio de Janeiro Military Police; head of T. J.'s mission
Sean Gottlieb—T. J.'s longtime significant other in New York City
Senator Junior Belém dos Santos—Rio de Janeiro state senator and former Rio de Janeiro chief of police
Sergio—Shalimar hotel manager
Sonia—gay-beach concession stand vendor
Sylvia de Lemos—Danilo de Lemos' Uruguayan wife
T. J. Leukemeyer—DEA special agent
Thomas Bradley—director at the DEA and T. J.'s boss
Tiago—Danilo de Lemos' henchman
Valeria Siqueira de Mendonça—Lygia's best friend and tarot card reader
Vera de Andrade—Chief Angelo de Andrade's wife
Vicente—T. J.'s DEA partner in the Mexican operation
Vinícius Maria Saveiro de Alcântara—murdered finance minister
Wellington—bellhop in T. J.'s building
William Chaffrey—Sean Gottlieb's former business colleague
Zezé (pronounced *Zehzeh*)—gay hustler from Vidigal

GLOSSARY

A—the
Abrir a porta—open the door
Aí—hey
Aló—hello
Aqui—here
Até logo—good-bye
Berimbao—an Afro-Brazilian string instrument
Boa noite—good night
Bom dia—good morning/hello
BOPE—Rio de Janeiro Military Police's Special Operations Battalion
Borboleta—butterfly
Caça—hunt
Cadê—where
Candomblé—Afro-Brazilian religion involving the occult
Carioca—a person from Rio de Janeiro
Conciente—concious
Consequência—consequence
Corações—hearts
CORE—Rio de Janeiro Civil Police equivalent of SWAT
Coxinhas—fried ground chicken and potato appetizer
Cuidado—be careful
Delegado—police chief

GLOSSARY

Desculpe—sorry
Deus é grande—God is great/bountiful
Dono—head of a drug ring
É (ser)—to be
Eu—I
Falar—speak
Garçon—waiter
Gordinho—fatso (nickname)
Gostosão—stud
Iemanjá—Afro-Brazilian goddess of the sea
Jeitinho—method
Jornal—newspaper
Ladrão—thief (dog's name)
Lindo/a—beautiful
Macumba—Brazilian form of Santeria or voodoo
Malagueta—a strong pepper
Mamãe/Mãe—mother
Mãoes pra cima—hands up
Meu filho—my son
Michê—male hustler
More (morer)—to die
Não—no
Novelas—soap operas
Ordem e Progresso—Order and Progress (Brazilian flag)
Orixá—spirit-incarnating medium
Ou—or
Para/pra—for/to
Paraiso—paradise
Pasteis—deep-fried appetizers
Pedra—rock
Pessoal—people
Piralho—young thief
Polícia Civil—Civil Police
Por favor—please
Preto velho—well-known spirit of an old black slave
Quem é?—Who is it?
Querido/a—dear

GLOSSARY

Rapido—quickly
Real/reais—Brazilian currency
Reserva—reserve
Roupa—clothes
Sabedoria—wisdom
Sim—yes
Sou—I am
'Ta legal—OK/cool
Tartaruga—turtle
Tchau—good-bye
Trabalha (trabalhar)—to work
Traços Rebeldes—*Rebel Traces*, a soap opera
Tudo bem—all good
Vai/ir—to go
Ver—to see
Viado—stag; derogatory for queer, gay
Virar o mundo—turn the world
Você—you
Vovó—grandpa

ACKNOWLEDGMENTS

Caitlin Alexander, my editor. Thank you for helping me transform my story and lift it to the next level. What a revelation working with you has been!

Dornith Doherty, your approach to life inspires me, as does your ever-transforming art of photography. Thank you for your insights on the various revisions you read, and the advice to work through each obstacle.

Douglas Mahew, for your adventurous *favela* anecdotes that helped me color my prose with brushes of reality.

Elizabeth Flock, my unique and wonderful friend, who inspired me to put pen to paper with her own literary success. Thank you, Liz, for helping me scratch my writer itch.

Jose Daunas, my father, for instilling in me a sense of curiosity, and correctness.

Leonard Seligman, my Spencertown neighbor, whose stories of his son-in-law's DEA career first triggered the story.

Myriam Malty, my friend, interior decorator, and astounding tarot card reader! OK, perhaps I made Val a bit too much like you, but how could I resist? Thank you for your help with the other side.

ACKNOWLEDGMENTS

Nicole Daunas, my mother, for her unwavering love and support and observations. I owe my lifelong fascination with Brazil and its complexity to you. *Te amo.*

Rick Livingston and Jim Brawders, with whom I had my very first reading of the book. Boy, did I realize then how much more work was required. Thank you both for your endless generosity and friendship.

Robert Pahnke, my dear friend who first read the entire manuscript upon completion. Thank you for your wonderful input and support.

The *Rio Times*, thank you for the expat point of view and for some factual fodder.

Yael Kruman, for egging me on to continue after reading an early version of the first few chapters.

And my many dear friends and family whose love and support add joy, interest, and direction to my work and life, including my sisters, Angela Meredith, Victoria Horstmann, and Patricia Daunas, and my brother, Philippe Daunas.

I love all y'all!

ABOUT THE AUTHOR

Edouard Alain Daunas spent five years at the New York headquarters of Brazil's largest publishing company, Editora Abril. He has an MBA from Fordham University and for the last decade has been the COO and Marketing Director of a high-end custom rug firm, and lectures regularly at the New York School of Interior Design.

Fluent in five languages, Edouard has family roots in various countries, including Brazil, but New York is where he and his husband call home. *The Warrior Saint* is his first novel.

thewarriorsaint.net

Printed in Great Britain
by Amazon